ORPHAN OF ANGEL STREET

Annie Murray graduated from Oxford in 1983. She has worked as a journalist and a nurse, has had short stories published in several magazines, and won the *SHE*/Granada Television Short Story Competition in 1991. She now lives in Reading with her husband and four small children, Brummies all. *Orphan of Angel Street* is her fourth novel.

Also by Annie Murray

Birmingham Rose

Birmingham Friends

Birmingham Blitz

Annie Murray

Orphan of Angel Street

PAN BOOKS

First published 1999 by Macmillan

This edition published 2001 by Pan Books
an imprint of Pan Macmillan Ltd
Pan Macmillan, 20 New Wharf Road, London N1 9RR
Basingstoke and Oxford
Associated companies throughout the world
www.panmacmillan.com

ISBN 0 330 35025 0

The author and publishers would like to thank Mr Hugh Nayes
for permission to quote from 'The Victorious Dead'
by Alfred Noyes, taken from *The Elfin Artist and Other Poems*
published by William Blackwood & Sons in 1920.

7 9 8 6

A CIP catalogue record for this book is available from
the British Library.

Typeset by SetSystems Ltd, Saffrom Walden, Essex
Printed and bound in Great Britain by
Mackays of Chatham plc, Chatham, Kent

For Rachel, in memory of a Mashhad taxi ride

ACKNOWLEDGEMENTS

With special thanks to Mike Price, Jonathan Davidson, and to Birmingham City Council Library Services for their help and support.

Prologue

The woman who called herself Lily was making terrible, high sounds of pain.

''Ere – what's all the racket about? You awright in there?'

Ethel Bartlett stood outside the attic door, her breathing laborious and asthmatic. She wore a threadbare coat wrapped round a yellowed nightshirt with a filthy hem, and handknitted socks through which poked her big toes with their black, overgrown nails.

A helpless whimper of distress came through the door. Ethel knew those cries all right. She'd heard them in slum houses where she'd lived all her life: the noise of birthing women trying not to disgrace themselves or disturb their other children, defeated by the intensity of their pain.

'You can't 'ave a babby in there – not on my mattress. Think of the mess! I'm coming in to 'ave a look at yer.'

'No!' the young woman gasped from the other side of the door. 'I'm quite all right – thank you. I shall sleep now. Please – go back to bed.'

Truth to tell, Ethel was mightily tempted to do as she said. After all, it was none of her business. She'd had more than enough troubles to last one lifetime already, ta very much. It had been as clear as day to her why this well-spoken stranger was here. But that wasn't her business either of course. Push up the rent, no questions asked.

She'd passed the woman two days ago outside the

Barton Arms, and heard her enquiring of someone else in a low voice about lodgings. Ethel butted in.

'I don't take in children, you know,' she said, giving her a sharp look as if she might have a family of six stowed up her sleeves.

The white-faced woman had been wrapped in a sea-blue cloak and was carrying only a small case. She stared steadily back at Ethel. 'No. No children.' There would be no children.

Of course, as soon as she had moved in, the pregnancy had been impossible to hide. It had all happened a bit soon for Ethel, who decided to hang on to her for a while for the rent then move her on. She'd closed her mind to the fact that this stranger calling herself Lily, who barely ever set foot out of the house, would soon have to give birth.

Ethel pulled herself up straight, coughing so that phlegm rattled in her chest. If there was one thing made her feel bad it was women having babbies and all their carrying on.

'It's no good. I can't 'ave yer going on like this in my 'ouse. I'm coming in.'

As she pushed open the rough door a groan, more of mortification than pain, came from the bed. The woman tried to sit up. She had been lying on her side on the stained mattress. Though it was the coldest of nights, she had only a thin blanket for cover, and that one so darned and patched with scraps of cloth that it was impossible to tell what its colour had once been.

The face lifted from the pillow had a sharply defined nose and jaw, white, waxy skin and a head of long white-gold hair darkened by sweat.

Except for a chamber pot, Lily's holdall and a low chair beside the bed on which rested a cup and a stub of candle, the room was completely bare. Even the drip of water which on milder days seeped through the roof of the slum attic was silenced tonight, frozen to a gleaming rind on the tiles under the cold eye of the moon.

'Please go,' Lily implored. 'Leave me . . .'

But in a second she pulled herself up on her knees in an animal posture, seized by the terrible, compressing pain.

'No . . . oh no . . .' Her teeth bit down into the rotten, sawdust filled pillow as the force of it built and built in her, breath hissing through her teeth, nostrils flaring. Her head flung back, hands gripping convulsively now at the edges of the mattress.

'Oh God . . . God . . .' Her mouth stretched open as if to scream, but she let out only a breathy croak as it reached its height, and as the pain seeped away she slumped forward, too exhausted even to sob.

Moments later she found strength to push herself up and take a sip of water from the enamel cup. The hand holding the cup's blue handle was slim and smooth, not calloused by the relentless, lifelong work of the poor. But despite her soft good looks, the pale eyes were full of fear and sorrow.

The landlady stood watching her, lungs sucking in and out loud as old bellows.

'Yer can't carry on like this,' Ethel hissed. 'I mean, I ain't no good to yer. I'll get Queenie Rolf from over the way.' She turned to go, socks catching on the rough wood.

'No – I don't want – ! No one, please . . .!'

But Ethel was off down the stairs. Finally a door slammed making the cracked windows vibrate.

Alone again, Lily listened in despair to her thumping steps. She had never imagined it was possible to sink to a state of such pain and degradation. She screwed her eyes tightly shut. It was coming on again: more and yet more, like an endless road to travel with only more pain waiting at the end.

'Our Father,' her lips moved. 'Who art in Heaven, Hallowed be thy . . .'

The rest of the prayer was taken up into gasping through the next, wrenching agony.

These first days of a new century had brought no special relief to the living conditions in the tightly packed workers' houses of Britain's – in fact the British Empire's – prime industrial city. Mayor Joseph Chamberlain may have razed a great swathe of ramshackle back-to-back dwellings in order to build the grand sweep of Corporation Street in the image of a Parisian boulevard, but there were still plenty of slums left. Their raw edges rubbed almost up against the splendour of the Council House on Victoria Square.

Into these slums were packed the worker bees to staff the great industrial hive of Birmingham which gave of its creativity to the world in metalwork, engineering, jewellery and a whole host of other trades. The children who survived the insanitary conditions were raised knowing no other options but working the factories or in service to the rich until they could hand over the burden of toil to their own children, as had generations of hard-working Brummies before them.

Into one such house on the north side of the city, on an icy night in January 1900, another child was born. Attending the birth were Ethel, yawning frequently to the full stretch of her jaws, and Queenie Rolf, who was built like an all-in wrestler, could drink many a man flat on his back and had tarnished silver hair long enough to sit on, which gave off a rancid smell.

The baby girl came into the world to her mother's silence. The woman's face was pulled into a helpless rictus of pain as she squatted in the candlelight, undergoing the seemingly impossible feat of pushing her child out into life. Then came the catlike cries of the baby, and the blood. Oh heaven, so much blood. Something she'd never known about, such was her innocence.

'It's a little lady!' Queenie cried, hoiking the child up by the legs and giving her backside a robust smack.

Lily lay back on the crinkled sheets of the *Birmingham Despatch* which Ethel had stuffed under her and, not looking at the child, let out a long moan of relief and sorrow.

'Yer awright now, bab,' Queenie said. With skilled hands she dealt with the umbilical cord and, a little later, the afterbirth. She washed the blood and pale waxy rime from the baby's body with water from a cracked pudding basin and was about to wrap her in an old rag when Lily protested in a weak voice.

'No – look! In there . . .'

She pointed to her leather bag. Queenie bent down and her capacious bloomers gave a loud rip.

'Oh Lor' – they'll be round me flamin' ankles in a minute!' She opened the small bag and she and Ethel exclaimed at the sight of a neatly folded and beautifully stitched layette.

'Don't take it all out,' Lily snapped, seeing Queenie's beefy, blood-smeared hands about to reach into the case. 'Please,' she added more politely. 'There are the things she'll need on top.'

Queenie drew out a tiny flannel vest and napkin, a strip of muslin for binding the cord and a tiny nightshirt and shawl for swaddling the child.

'She'll want all this on tonight. Proper brass monkey weather.'

Lily herself had begun shaking violently, teeth chattering.

''Ere, Ethel, fetch 'er a cuppa tea, eh? That'll be the shock of it as well as the cold, bab – takes some people that way.' She handed over the tightly wrapped baby into Lily's trembling arms, her foul breath making the young woman shrink from her. 'You'll be able to give 'er a bit o' titty now – that's what she'll be after. Then you can give yerself a good wash over and get yer 'ead down.'

'And we can all do the same,' Ethel added resentfully.

They saw though, that Lily made no attempt to suckle the child. She reached down into the case and pulled out two pound notes. Queenie's and Ethel's jaws nearly hit the floor and their hands whisked out quickly.

'Well!' Ethel's face was all gummy smiles. 'Ooh yer shouldn't really. . .' The money had already vanished into her coat. 'Ever so good of you . . .'

Queenie was stowing the money somewhere deep in the recesses of her cleavage and grinning into Lily's exhausted young face, its blonde hair matted and tumbling on her shoulders. 'You make a picture, the pair of yer. And she's as fine a babby as any I've seen into the world.'

Through chattering teeth, Lily managed to say, 'Thank you. Thank you both for your help.'

An hour later, disregarding her body's crying need for rest, Lily had washed herself as well as she could. She used two of the napkins from the layette to stem her own flow, her hands still shaking as she tried to dress herself. She could hear Ethel's snores, like those of an ancient hound, from down below.

Ethel had cleared away the newspaper from the bed and the room was as bare as it had been before. Lily sat for a few moments on the edge of the mattress in the guttering light of the candle, holding her sleeping baby, looking solemnly into the wrinkled face. The terror had gone from her eyes and now there was only an infinite sadness. She knew the child needed food, but she must resist her own instincts and deny her her mother's milk.

There was not time to sit for long and suddenly her movements were urgent again. Hanging on the back of the door was her blue cloak which she wrapped round her, pulling its velvet hood over her head. She arranged the warmly swaddled child on one arm, and taking the case with her other hand she crept as silently as she could manage down the rough stairs and let herself out into the frozen night.

As morning dawned, winter sunlight seeping through air choked with the effluents of Birmingham's hundreds of factory chimneys, the blue-brick pavements were white with frost which put an illusory shine on the city's grime. Rooftops sparkled as the sun rose, melting the frost into dark, damp patches on the tiles.

The streets gradually came to life: men in broken down boots, collars up on their coats, hurried to early morning shifts, breath swirling from them. Horses' hooves clashed over the cobbles pulling delivery carts and drays, steered by men still red-eyed with sleep as the 'lighter uppers' were extinguishing the last gas lamps street by street. Women were feeding families, sweeping out houses and calling to neighbours in their everyday work clothes: blouse, long skirt, boots, sacking apron and often a cap to top it off. Their day had long begun.

In Kent Road, Aston, the bolts were being drawn open behind the heavy doors of one of two solid, red-brick institutions which faced each other along that street. On one side of the road stood St Philip's Elementary School. Across from it, with its pointed gothic windows and wrought iron railings, Joseph Hanley's Home for Poor Girls, founded 1881, as spelt out by the brass plaque beside the front porch.

One of the heavy doors now opened and a middle-aged woman stepped out, hair caught up in a bun, clothes covered by a white apron and holding a workmanlike broom. She leant the broom against the wall and raised both hands to try and fasten some stray hanks of her hair, then stopped, catching sight of the little bundle in the narrow porch.

'Oh my Lord!' – stooping at once. 'On a night as cold as this. It'll be a miracle if . . .' She lifted the baby close to her, and was satisfied to hear her breathing. The baby woke and began to snuffle, then cry.

The woman, who was called Meg, carried the baby down the steps to the street, instinctively rocking her and saying, 'Ssssh now, will yer.' Seeing no one she could connect with an abandoned baby, in truth hardly expecting to, she turned back, shaking her head.

She didn't see from the steps of the school, a little further along, a young woman in a blue velvet cloak squatting to watch her over the low wall. One of her hands was clenched to her heart, the other pressed tight over her mouth as this stranger holding her child climbed the steps.

Meg looked round one more time and then stepped inside and closed the door. As she did so a great moan of anguish escaped from the young woman at the gates of the school.

'Looks a fine enough child,' the matron said, unwrapping the baby on a table softened only by a piece of sheet. She picked her up for a moment, carefully scrutinizing her face, and went to the window through which poured hard winter light. The baby sneezed twice. 'Doesn't seem blind, at any rate. Pale of skin though, is she not? Could almost be an albino, except the eyes look normal enough.'

'Don't we 'ave to get the doctor in?' Meg suggested nervously.

'Oh, later'll do.' Matron carried on with her inspection at the table, pulling at the naked limbs as the child yawled furiously at the cold and interference by this heavy-handed woman.

'Well, this one's got a pair of lungs and a temper to match!' she bawled over the baby's screams. 'That umbilical cord'll need some attention. You can take her up to the infants in a moment or two, Meg.'

Matron's hands felt along the top of the baby's head, fingers burrowing in the fuzz of gold hair for the fontanelles. The screaming rose higher. Meg, a softer-hearted woman, winced. This new matron, Miss O'Donnell, fresh over from the west coast of Ireland, seemed more at home with livestock of a farmyard variety than children.

'No deformities that I can see.' She started to close the white garments back over the child. 'Honest to God, leaving a child on the street on a night like the one we've just had. The ways of these people! Shouldn't be allowed to breed – someone ought to have 'em castrated, the whole feckless lot of 'em. Mind you – this one's not of bad stock, I'd say – good strong spine and limbs . . .'

Meg was waiting for Matron to say something about the quality of the child's fetlocks when the woman exclaimed, 'Well now – what's all this then?'

From where they had been tucked between the layers of soft white linen, Miss O'Donnell's thick fingers drew out a wadge of money, and folded neatly with it, a white handkerchief. The matron seized on the notes, counting them eagerly.

Meg picked up the handkerchief and held it out to Miss O'Donnell who was still taken up with the money.

'Five pound – would you believe it! Well, isn't this the fruit of genteel fornication if ever I saw it. Five pound!'

'Look – there's this too.'

Miss O'Donnell took the handkerchief. On one corner of it, embroidered in mauve silk thread, she read one word: MERCY.

'Have mercy,' Meg pondered.

'Ah well.' Miss O'Donnell tossed it back on the table, slipping the folded notes into her apron pocket. 'If she's given her nothing else at least the child has a name. Let her be called Mercy Hanley.'

Part One

Chapter One

June 1907

'Mercy – come on, 'urry up!'

The second morning bell clanged down in the hall. Even up in the dormitories they could sense Matron's impatience as she rang it. Waiting around for anything was not one of Miss O'Donnell's favoured occupations in life.

'If you're late for breakfast again there's no telling what she'll do!'

Amy, three years older, tugged the worn flannel dress which was really too small, over the younger girl's head. Mercy knew she was quite capable of dressing herself but each of them adored this game of mothering and being mothered.

Amy was kneeling, frantically trying to fasten Mercy's buttons with her bony fingers, her waif-like face puckering with frustration. Playfully, Mercy picked up the two mousey-coloured pigtails from Amy's shoulders and stuck them up above the girl's head like rabbit's ears.

'Oi – pack it in. You don't care, do yer!'

Mercy's solemn little face stared back at Amy as she tugged her plaits back into their normal position, tutting to herself. In spite of herself Amy smiled, and saw a gleam answer her in the little girl's wide grey eyes. Mercy grinned all of a sudden, an expression of complicity and mischief which she reserved for no one else but Amy, and flung her arms round her friend's shoulders, clinging tight like a baby monkey.

'Give us a love, Amy.'

'Mercy!' Amy was pushing her off, laughing. 'Yer 'opeless, yer really are. Come on.'

The last sounds of the other girls' feet were already receding down the stairs. The dormitory held fifteen girls aged between seven and fourteen. The black iron bedsteads were arranged at regimented intervals along the bare floorboards, three rows of five. There was nothing else in the room except a portrait of Queen Victoria at least twenty years before her death, a frozen expression on her face, her eyes focussed on the far distance. At the long windows hung threadbare curtains in a sun-bleached navy.

Amy seized Mercy's hand and the two of them tore along the echoing corridor, feet clattering on brown linoleum, then down the stone stairs. They managed to close the gap between themselves and the last stragglers into the dining room. Miss O'Donnell stood outside glowering.

'You two again – get along now.' She was fingering a bunch of little plaited leather strings she kept tied to her waist in case she felt the need to dole out punishment at short notice.

The dining room smelt of stale wash-cloths, disinfectant and porridge. The girls joined one of the long tables at the far end but there were not two spaces left for them to sit together. Mercy couldn't bear to be separated from Amy.

'Move up,' she hissed at another girl.

The girl shook her head.

'Move up.' Mercy gave her such a sharp ram in the ribs with her elbow that she had to stifle a squeal.

'You're a little cow, Mercy.' Rubbing her side she surrendered the space so that Mercy and Amy could sit together.

The two of them were inseparable in the orphanage, and now that Mercy had started school across the road at St Philips, Amy with her ethereal looks and Mercy, blonde and tiny, were forever together in the playground.

They'd been the closest of friends since they were tiny infants. Amy arrived at the Hanley Home aged two, the year before Mercy. As the two of them grew up they developed an almost miraculous affinity for one another. Since Amy was older she spent much of her days in a different room from the austere nursery where the babies lived out their regimented, white clad existence. But there were frequent cries of, 'Where's that child gone now?' when Amy slipped away into their territory of strained, milky foods and plump hands to find baby Mercy. Miss Eagle, with her assistants, was in charge of the babies. She came back into the nursery one day to find Amy sitting beside Mercy who was then about a year old, a heavy scrubbing brush gripped between both hands, trying to brush Mercy's mop of hair with it. Mercy was crowing with delight, hands waving. The tiny girls' eyes were fixed laughingly on each other's. Miss Eagle slapped Amy hard and sent her away.

'We thank Thee Lord for these Thy gifts . . .' Miss Rowney, the Superintendent of the Home intoned piously over the meagre breakfast. The girls stood motionless. Mercy saw a fly looping round Miss Rowney's head and hoped it would fly up her nose. The live-in staff ate together at a smaller table near the door: Miss Rowney, Miss O'Donnell, Miss Eagle and Mrs Jacobs – Meg, who had first found Mercy. Others, like Dorothy

Finch, the kindest of the staff, only worked there in the daytime.

The tin bowls clattered on the tables and one of the older girls doled out a ladle of watery porridge into Mercy's bowl. Above the fireplace hung two small Union Jacks and a portrait of King Edward's well-fed face after the Coronation in 1901.

They were expected to eat in silence, so the chief sound was the tinny rattle of spoons in the bowls. Mercy wrinkled her nose at Amy. The porridge was lukewarm and slimy on her tongue. She dripped it off her spoon mouthing, 'lumpy' and Amy grimaced back. The food left white tidemark moustaches on their top lips. Even though it was thin, lumpy and tasteless they ate every scrap, for lunch would almost invariably be watery stew and tea a thin soup.

Mercy looked round the table as she ate and Lena, the girl opposite, pulled a face at her. Mercy didn't care, and stuck her tongue out until Amy nudged her to stop although she continued to stare back defiantly. Mercy and Amy's closeness seemed to rile some of the others. Affection was very thin on the ground here, living in a house with sixty other girls with no one to provide real care or attention. Maybe the others were jealous. But Mercy didn't bother about what they thought. She'd got Amy and that was all that mattered. When they'd finished eating she pushed her hand, warm and slightly tacky with porridge, into Amy's under the table.

Miss Rowney stood up, chair scraping the floor.

'Get wiped up now and stay sitting for a few moments. I've got something to say to you all.'

The girl in charge of each table hastily smeared the pale globules away with a sour-smelling cloth. They waited.

Miss Rowney walked to the middle of the dining room and stood looking round at them. She seemed rather excited about something and was massaging the back of her left hand with her right, her expression coy with pride.

'Now girls, today I have a very special announcement.' Her voice echoed slightly. 'I'm going to read out the names of eight girls, and I'd like them to come up here to the front and stand in a neat line.' She pronounced the names rather grandly, as if they were the titles of queens.

'Lisa Maskell, Josie Flanagan, Sarah Smith . . .' The last, and youngest on the list was Amy Laski.

Amy glanced in bewilderment at Mercy, and, pulling her hand away, obediently joined the line of girls with their backs to the staff table.

'I am delighted to tell you that with the help of the John T. Middlemore Homes we have secured places for eight girls to begin a new and rewarding life. So—' She beamed round at them. 'On 9 July, Lisa, Josie, Sarah . . .' she reeled off their names again . . . 'will all be travelling on a big ship across the Atlantic Ocean to *Canada* . . .' this was spoken in fairy tale tones '. . . to a place called New Brunswick where they will all be given homes by some kind and godly Canadian people.'

She put her hands together and everyone saw they were expected to clap, which they did as mechanically as striking clocks, watching the faces of the eight girls, the emotions of wonder, pride, bewilderment, uncertainty, flitting across them like summer clouds.

You could hear her screams from one end of the orphanage to the other.

The other girls were ready, regimented in crocodiles downstairs in the long dayroom where all chairs had been pushed to one side.

'She's gunna get it good and proper now,' a snotty-nosed little girl called Dulcie whispered to to the child she was paired with. 'They'll give 'er a right belting.'

The staff, trying to keep the other children quiet and orderly, listened with tense faces. Mercy again. Today of all days. A couple of the girls started giggling and were given a sharp smack round the back of the head for their cheek. They were all scrubbed clean after last night's toiling with tin baths of tepid water, last minute rough wiping of porridge from faces after breakfast, the starching of pinafores, plaiting of hair and polishing of little boots, so that they were not just Sunday clean, but cleaner than ever the whole year round.

'Now just you remember I want to see smiles on all your faces,' Miss O'Donnell boomed at them after breakfast. 'When Mr Hanley graces us with his presence today he'll not want to see sullen faces round him, but a good example of Christian Cheerfulness. Just you remember – if it wasn't for Mr Hanley, none of youse would have a place to lay your heads or fodder in your bellies. Would you now?' Silence. 'WOULD YOU?'

'NO, MISS O'DONNELL,' they all droned, sitting in lines down the long tables.

But now, here was Mercy, splayed across her bed, clinging to the iron bedstead and screaming as if someone was trying to murder her. The white-blonde hair was slipping out from its shoulder length plaits, her face a livid pink, and she was violently kicking her legs. Miss Eagle, who had been despatched to try and force her back under control, could barely even get near her.

'Will you stop that!' Miss Eagle, a thin, flint-cheeked

woman tried to catch hold of Mercy round her waist and was rewarded by a backward sock in the face as the girl loosed one of her hands for a second and flailed it behind her.

'You miserable little bugger! You needn't think I'm going to ruin my best dress just because of you – 'ere, you can 'ave another of these!' She landed a hard slap on one of Mercy's bare legs which produced only more anguished yells and metallic screeching from the bed-springs. The child was not big for her age, but she was a red hot wire of fury and the energy in her was extraordinary.

'Miss O'Donnell'll be up here any minute,' the woman hissed in her ear, trying to prise Mercy's hands away from the bedstead. 'And then you'll be for it. I 'ope she flogs you within an inch of your life, you evil little vermin.'

She managed to yank Mercy off the bed and started slapping her, only to have the child slide through her hands like blancmange and continue raging on the floor, pummelling it with her fists.

The woman landed a violent kick in Mercy's ribs and suddenly everything went quiet. Mercy gasped, then groaned. To Miss Eagle's satisfaction she at last saw tears start to roll down that normally inscrutable little face. The child finally opened her mouth in a roar of pain.

'What in the name of God is going on?' Miss O'Donnell loomed in the doorway of the dormitory, walking stiffly as if she were attired from head to foot in cardboard. Her long black outfit was topped by a black feather-trimmed bonnet and her cheeks, already florid, were plastered with circles of rouge. She was quivering, more with nerves it seemed than anger.

'D'you not know himself will be here on the hour?

Get that child downstairs immediately and stop this horrible commotion she's making!'

Miss Eagle blushed a nasty red. 'I can't. Since Amy Laski went she's been impossible to handle.'

'In God's name she's only – what? – seven years old and a third the size of you!' Miss O'Donnell clearly had no intention of risking the pristine state of her garments either. 'If you can't sort her out go and get Dorothy Finch. She's the only one can knock any sense into that one.'

Mercy was left alone on the cold stone floor. She raised her head and looked up, surrounded by the black bedsteads with their threadbare candlewick covers from which the colours had long been washed out.

Her large grey eyes looked dazed, as if she'd returned from another existence somewhere. She could find no satisfactory way of expressing her need, her sense of being utterly lost. She longed to be held, loved, cared for, yet so alone was she in the world, had seen so little of such care that she scarcely knew for what it was she hungered. Pain speared at her ribs. She lowered her head again and started banging her forehead with a steady rhythm against the floor, muttering to herself, 'Hate you, hate you, hate you . . .' This was how Dorothy Finch found her when she arrived, flustered, upstairs.

'Mercy! Oh Mercy, you silly babby. You've got to stop this!' She swooped down and pulled the girl off the floor hearing her give a squeal of pain. 'Mr Hanley's coming today and the minister's already 'ere. They're all waiting for you. Quick, wipe your face on this.' The woman held out a hanky and brushed the dust from

Mercy's clothes. She avoided looking straight at Mercy, as if unable to face the raw pain in her eyes.

Dorothy had come to work at the Hanley Home when Mercy was still the smallest of infants, about four months old. She had watched her grow into a toddler with a solemn, appraising face and dead straight hair. Dorothy remembered how Mercy had gone everywhere with her hand thrust into Amy's, looking up at her with adoration and absolute trust, trotting along beside her to keep up.

When Amy left, for three days Mercy had spoken barely a word. At first no one noticed, not even Dorothy, for she was always a withdrawn child. But one day when the older ones had gone to school, Dorothy found her lying on Amy's old bed, absolutely silent and still, her face a blank.

'Mercy?' Dorothy had come upon her cheerfully. 'You didn't ought to be 'ere, eh, bab? You'll get it from Miss O'Donnell if she catches you!'

Mercy raised her arm back behind her head and started banging her wrist, hard on the metal bedhead until she cried out and there were tears in her eyes.

'What the 'ell d'you do that for?' Dorothy shouted at her in alarm. 'What you playing at? Go on, get off with you downstairs. I've got quite enough to get on with without you playing me up!'

The rages began and grew wilder. They could strike any time and burn through Mercy with an intensity that no one could control or penetrate. They found her throwing her body about, screaming, biting, banging her arms or legs or head on hard objects.

'She's got the devil in her,' Miss O'Donnell decreed. 'Plenty of hard work, that's what she needs.' She set out to file down Mercy's will and temper by physically exhausting her. As soon as they were big enough to manage it the girls were expected to carry out nearly all the domestic chores. Mercy spent long periods of her days mopping floors, scrubbing floors, polishing floors. But still her unhappy soul flared in outbursts of pain and frustration. Only Dorothy could soothe her, by grasping the little girl's flailing body, holding tight and talking about any old nonsense until the fight suddenly dropped out of her and she surrendered to being quiet, being held.

'Come on, stand proper now,' Dorothy urged. 'Look at the state of you!' With her deft fingers she straightened out Mercy's clothes. There wasn't time to retie Mercy's plaits and the little girl looked quite dishevelled with her rumpled hair and blotchy face. She was small for her age, and with her pale skin and large eyes, very like a delicate, china doll.

'Come on – Violet's waiting,' Dorothy fibbed. 'She wants to walk in with you.'

Silent now, one hand clenched to her burning ribs, Mercy followed her along the corridor to the main stairs. From the dayroom they heard a man's voice in the hall and the eager-to-please twittering of the women, '. . . so nice . . . such an honour . . .' before the nod was given to file into the hall under the Union Jack.

Chapter Two

A visit to the orphanage by its benefactor Joseph Hanley was a rare occasion. His Home for Poor Girls (1881) had been built shortly after the Home for Poor Boys, a mile further out of the city. Joseph Hanley had been in his forties then, and was now a rather corpulent sixty-six-year-old, who had recently passed on his brass foundry on Rea Street to his twin sons and moved to the clearer air of the Staffordshire countryside.

Every so often he made ritual visits to his 'ministries'. He was an intensely religious man, a passionate nonconformist who had incorporated in the homes a more than average number of washrooms to inculcate Cleanliness and Godliness, and established close ties with the Baptist church on the Witton Road, roughly halfway between his two institutions. On most Sundays the girls and boys – about fifty of each – were frogmarched along to morning worship, swelling the local congregation no end. Every six weeks or so the minister, Mr Ezra Vesey, held a service for them in the orphanage.

Mercy sat cross-legged on the floor which smelt of fresh polish. The staff sat on chairs at the ends of the rows of children. There were windows along one side of the hall and a longer one at the end through which could be seen young horse chestnut trees, the late summer sunlight casting the restless shadows of leaves on the parquet floor. It was on this window that Mercy kept her gaze throughout most of her time spent in the hall, on its shadowland of changing light.

Violet, who was eight, turned and peered at her to see if she was still crying, but the tears were wiped away now, and Mercy's face solemn, eyes raised to the light. Violet elbowed her in the ribs to get her attention.

Mercy's face contorted. 'Ow!' It was almost a yelp. 'Gerroff!'

Immediately Miss Eagle's head snapped round at the end of the row, her face wearing a vindictive scowl. You again, it said. I'm going to get you later on.

Mercy stared hard at the window. When I'm a princess, she thought, I'll show all of them . . . I'll have lovely clothes and a hat for every day of the year and my own carriage and Miss Eagle'll be on 'er hands and knees doing my floors all day every day and I'll have a great big horse whip to keep 'er in order. And I'll keep the people I want living there. And the only one who can do nowt is Amy 'cos she'll have her own rooms in my castle, with . . .

'Stand up!' Violet was pulling at her pinafore. Everyone else was on their feet and the almost tuneful piano started to thump out, '*What a Friend we have in Jesus . . .*'

The younger girls had been placed nearer the back of the hall, no doubt as they were expected to be less well behaved than the older ones. Standing on tiptoe Mercy could just glimpse Mr Hanley, crouched in a special chair at the front. She could see the bald, porridge-coloured circle at the back of his head and his stooped little shoulders. Every now and then he let out a wheezy cough.

Mr Vesey was a very tall man with almost no hair left on his head but lots on his face, as if it had somehow slipped down round his chin, and great big spidery hands. He sang much louder than everyone else except Miss

O'Donnell who almost seemed to be vying with him, loudly and off-key, the feathers on her hat quivering.

'This is the day that the Lord hath made!' Mr Vesey declared in a nasal Rochdale accent. 'We shall rejoice and be glad in it.' His hands traced webs in the air.

Eventually they sang 'All Things Bright and Beautiful' and the piano plinked out the tune until they ran out of verses.

'Now girls.' Miss Rowney moved as if on wheels to the front of the hall. She had a gruff voice, more like a man's. 'Before we go from here you are all going to come to the front and shake Mr Hanley by the hand to show him how ve-ery much you all appreciate all he has done for you. Come on now – from the front!' She beckoned with a beefy finger, directing the older girls to move forwards. Mercy couldn't hear what Mr Hanley was saying to them, only the high, squeaky tone of his voice. Inside she boiled and bubbled. I hate . . . I hate . . .

They filed slowly along the middle, shook hands and dispersed round the sides, some making a little bob, almost a curtsey, all trying to turn their mouths up as hard as they could. Miss Rowney and Miss O'Donnell stood by watching with steam-powered smiles as well.

Mr Hanley sat enthroned on his chair, scrawny legs placed apart to fit his well-rounded belly between, his weskit buttons laced with a gold chain which strained across his front. He had an amiable, ruddy face and, as she drew nearer, Mercy saw that one of his eyes was clear, the other rheumy, and he kept dabbing at it with a large white handkerchief.

A girl called Daisy was in front of her. Shyly she held out her hand.

'Well, my dear,' Mr Hanley said. This didn't seem to

be about to lead to anything else so Daisy gave a confused little bob and scuttled off.

'Ah,' Mr Hanley said as Mercy stood before him. 'What a pretty little lass.'

'Yes, now.' Miss Rowney suddenly swooped forward, gushing at Mr Hanley in a voice that suggested he was very sick, very foolish or possibly both. 'We wanted to tell you particularly about Mercy. She's a true foundling. Abandoned at birth – not even a full name. So in your honour, sir, we have taken the liberty of giving her the surname Hanley.' Miss Rowney smiled with great satisfaction at having conferred this extraordinary favour.

Mr Hanley saw two large, and disconcertingly cold grey eyes fix on him, fringed by pale eyelashes.

'Well, my dear,' he said again. 'So you're my kith and kin, so to speak!' He gave a snuffling laugh. 'Won't you shake hands, child?'

A gnarled hand with veins like purple rivers came towards Mercy. She stared at the hand, looked hard for a moment into Mr Hanley's eyes, then caught hold of the end of his fingers. All around the chapel every person's mouth jerked open into a horrified, gasping Oh! as Mercy leant down slowly, almost reverently, and sank her teeth into the loose, fleshy bit between Mr Hanley's finger and thumb. His skin felt stringy between her teeth. The old man let out a yelp of pain and surprise, trying to fling her off.

Mercy's next view of life was of the wooden floor rushing past her eyes, door jambs, alternating shadow and brighter light and the furious swish of black taffeta as Miss O'Donnell seized hold of her and swung her upside down over one shoulder like a newborn calf. The other girls' heads swivelled, some apprehensive, some gloating, as Miss O'Donnell speedily whisked her offensive presence from the hall.

The cellar was almost completely dark. Only the palest lines of light seeped round the upper part of the door.

Mercy sat crouched on the wide top step right next to the door, arms clenched round her knees, rocking back and forth. She was hurting so much, her ribs from Miss Eagle's kicking, her cheeks raw from Miss O'Donnell's violent slaps after she had dumped her down hard on the floor outside the cellar door with a force that jarred right up into her back.

'There – you evil little rat!' she snarled between clenched teeth, her great hands slapping her again and again. 'You don't deserve to live – you're a bloody disgrace. I've half a mind to throw you back on the streets where you came from and good riddance. Now then.' She unlocked the cellar and yanked Mercy up into her arms again, holding her with her head facing down. 'Right down at the bottom, that's where you can go, my girl.' She clumped down blue-brick steps into the dark, cavernous cellar. Inside were ghostly shapes, some long and thin, the shadowy outline of an old mangle against the far wall, then fading to a solid blackness at the back. Miss O'Donnell forced her down on the damp floor against the wall.

'And you can stay in there 'til you rot!'

With heavy tread she hurried back up the steps and slammed the door with such force that the planks reverberated. Mercy heard the bolt rattle across. And then it was dreadfully quiet. All she could hear was her own jagged breathing and a slow dripping sound from somewhere in the blackness.

She stretched her eyes wide, trying to see any speck of light, but there was none at first. After a few moments, at the far end she made out a block of grey, strained light from a grating on the street. Mercy pulled herself up while she still had the courage to move and crawled up the cellar steps where there was a crack of light from under the door. She sat on the top step, hugging herself. From here she couldn't see the ghostly light from the grating. The darkness in front of her was like a gaping well, full of invisible, whispering presences.

She felt a twinge in her belly and realized her bladder was urgently full. Pulling her legs in even closer, she sank her teeth into her forearm, rocking back and forth, making a little moaning noise to herself, needing to hear a sound from somewhere because if she stopped it was so silent and there would be nothing but the dark. She clenched her eyes shut and kept rocking, rocking . . .

'I want—' A whisper escaped from her and became part of the rhythm. 'I want I want I want . . .' as her back banged harder against the rough wall. At first it was angry, hard rocking that jarred the breath in her lungs. 'I want I want . . .' A cry she had never been able to use in her life escaped from her 'Mom!' And then, 'Amy . . . Amy . . .'

But Amy was gone to be a servant in Canada. She'd left weeks ago via Liverpool, with a tin trunk, cloth bag and a label on her coat. In the hall they'd sung 'God Be with You 'til We Meet Again', and after, Amy had hugged her tight and told her she'd always love her and be her friend.

She rocked more gently, tired, her tiny body aching, sobbing at last, so that tears fell on her cotton pinafore and she had to wipe her nose on it, having no hanky. Mixed in with her rage and grief was the thought of the spread of cold meats and salads, of pudding and cakes laid out upstairs, of all the other girls with their hair ribbons, eating plates of this out of the ordinary food, when every other day it was stew, stew, stew. Dorothy had told her there would be jellies: quivering castles of ruby red, royal purple of crushed blackcurrants, the cool sweet smoothness of it down your throat . . .

She cried herself to exhaustion, the sobs making her ribs hurt even more. Her belly was tight and uncomfortable. Putting her hands down on each side of her to shift her weight, her left hand met something long and soft, and she jerked it away, panting with revulsion, breaking out in a sweat. Her palm was coated in a slimy stickiness. She shifted quickly to the other end of the step, wiping the hand frantically on her pinner. All those things, those shapes, down there, that drip, drip, drip . . . things she couldn't see, were they getting closer, were they, were they? And the slimy thing next to her, where was it, what was it doing? Panic swelled right up into her throat until she was gasping with it, and she could hold on no longer. The warm rush of urine, so dreadfully wet, soaked through her bloomers, through the skirt of her dress, fast turning cold on her skin and splashing her ankles, nasty-smelling. She whimpered in distress, holding her knees tightly with her arms, not daring to move to the dryer part of the steps because that slimy thing was there waiting for her.

The door seemed the one solid thing of safety and she thrust her fingers in her ears, and pushed her head down on her knees making herself keep her eyes shut.

If I can't see them they're not there, she said to herself. Nothing's there. Just me, that's all. Nothing can hurt me. Nothing can ever hurt me.

She rocked herself until her arms slid down again and

circled her legs, her head lolled sideways against the door and she fell asleep.

The clatter of the bolt being drawn back came so loud after the long, long silence. Mercy jumped, still half asleep, and immediately tensed, cowering away from the door in dread as to what was out there.

'Mercy?' Dorothy Finch's scared face peered in at her. She spoke in a whisper. 'Oh, you silly, silly girl. What the 'ell did you go and have to bite Mr Hanley for? What's 'e ever done to you, eh? You're your own worst enemy, you are. 'Ere—' She held out a chipped white bowl. 'Get this down you. I'll be skinned alive if Miss O'Donnell catches me giving yer it.'

She saw that the little girl's eyes, screwed up against the light, were fixed on something at the other end of the step. A huge, pale brown slug lay oozing beside the door frame, and Mercy shuddered violently. She was shamefully aware of her wet clothes.

'Ugh!' Dorothy flicked the slug down the steps with the toe of her boot. She held out the bowl and Mercy saw two jewelled scoops of red jelly in the bottom.

Dorothy knelt down, her lithe body dressed in a high-collared white blouse tucked into an ankle-length black skirt. Her long brown hair was pinned up becomingly above an almost pretty face. She took in the little girl's sorrowful expression, her blotchy cheeks.

'Got anything to say then?'

Mercy swallowed a big gulp of jelly and without looking up said, 'Ta.'

'Thank you, you're meant to say.'

'Thank you.'

'You're a proper nib, aren't you? What d'you do it for, Mercy?'

She straightened up suddenly in alarm. Someone was coming.

'Oh my God!' Dorothy stepped inside the cellar, pulled the door closed. 'Ooh – ain't it dark in 'ere?' she whispered. 'Pongs a bit too!' She squatted down next to Mercy who continued, undeterred, to shovel jelly into her mouth.

The tread came closer and stopped outside the door. Whoever it was let out a hearty belch. Mercy snorted with laughter. Dorothy clamped a hand over the child's mouth, praying that whoever it was hadn't heard. There came the sound of metal buckets clanging together and by what seemed a miracle, whoever it was went away again.

Mercy and Dorothy exploded with giggles.

'You don't care, do yer!' Dorothy pushed the door open and ruffled Mercy's hair. 'You just don't give a monkey's you don't. Look, I've got to get out of here. Give us your bowl. You're going to have to stay put in 'ere though, Mercy, 'til Miss O'Donnell comes to get you out. And when she does you'd better start behaving yourself or she's going to have you down on your hands and knees scrubbing floors the rest of your days!'

Before she shut the door again she looked down at Mercy with solemn eyes. Suddenly she swooped forward and kissed her cheek. 'Not long now, eh? Just hold on.'

The door closed again. It was bedtime when Miss O'Donnell came. What she wanted was Mercy penitent, broken. But when Mercy looked up at her the look of brazen defiance was burning there, fuelled by a bowl of red jelly and the knowledge that there was one single person at Hanley's who cared about her.

At least I've got Dorothy, she said to herself as she lay in bed in the dormitory that night. She stroked the spot on her cheek where Dorothy kissed her. Dorothy's got time for me.

Chapter Three

November 1911

'Mercy?' Miss Eagle's voice was shrill with disbelief. 'Mercy Hanley?'

'Do we have any other girl called Mercy in our care?' Miss Rowney asked dryly. She was at the desk in her sitting room-cum-office, her thin hair pulled into a tight knot which made her already large-boned face look even heavier. Miss O'Donnell and Miss Eagle stood before her on a rug so threadbare that patches of the wooden floor could be seen through it. However much they felt obliged to fête Mr Hanley for his generosity, money was nevertheless tight in this establishment.

The sky outside was so thick with cloud that the room was almost dark and there was no fire in the grate, although it was viciously cold.

'But—' Miss Eagle tried to find a way of protesting this madness without sounding thoroughly impertinent. 'Mercy's, well – she's . . .'

'A damn nuisance, so she is,' Miss O'Donnell butted in with no hesitation, hands on her staunch hips. 'She's a flaming little wildcat and now's our chance to get shot of her.'

'We thought boarding out might be the way to settle her down,' Miss Rowney said, attempting to sound a little more professional. 'I mean, heaven knows we're hardly beseiged with requests for foster children. It ought to be a good chance for her. The lady asked for a girl of Mercy's age – well, perhaps what she meant was a little older, but no matter, Mercy's nearly twelve. And she seemed firm enough of character. She has a respectable address in, let's see—' She picked up a sheet of paper and held it at arm's length, squinting through pince-nez. 'Handsworth. Husband employed in a whip factory, I understand. No children. We'll have the place inspected of course . . .'

'We should've packed her off to Canada with the last lot.' Miss O'Donnell strode over to the window and stood looking at the murk outside. It was beginning to rain. 'Heaven knows, I shouldn't mind going to Canada. See a bit of grass and some trees for a change instead of this filth-ridden hole with its strikes and its wife murderers.'

Last year's execution of a Dr Hawley Harvey Crippen who'd deposited his slaughtered wife's body under the floorboards was still playing on Miss O'Donnell's mind as a sign of England's depravity. Even the lavish Coronation of King George V had not persuaded her she was any better off living in the heart of the Empire.

Miss Rowney ignored her. 'We can get this settled as quickly as possible. As for the inspection – I'll have to do it myself. We're not Dr Barnardo's after all – doctors for this and inspectors for that.' She tutted. 'We're short enough this week, with Dorothy Finch taking bad.' Suddenly she waved her hand at the other two women. 'All right, all right, you can go. I'll sort it out.'

The children stood with faces pressed against the railing of St Philip's playground.

'Look!' a little boy shrieked with excitement. 'It's coming – it's getting closer!'

In the road outside a horse clopped slowly past along the cobbles, pulling a dray loaded with barrels. But behind, gaining on the stately pace of the cart, was the object of their excitement.

‘’Ark at it go!’ the boy shouted.

‘Look at them wheels!’

‘Ain’t it beautiful? Oi – give us a ride, mate!’

The Austin motor car bowled past, bodywork gleaming even in the dull light. The wheels were like small cartwheels coated in rubber, and the the two behatted men sat high above the road. They kept their faces turned to the front, not heeding the children’s cheers and claps as they leant on the railings straining to get the last views of the automobile before it turned the corner.

‘Eh – who’s that shovin’? Pack it in!’

There came a jostling and a very forceful pushing from the back of the tangle of children, and one of the smallest girls, all sharp elbows and knees, forced her way to the front, supple as a fish.

‘Who d’you think you are, Mercy?’ One of the boys pulled her arm, trying to force her back. ‘Barging in – we all want to see.’

The boy found the girl’s strange, catlike eyes turned on him and a second later received a kick on the shin so hard it brought tears to his eyes and he doubled up to rub his leg. ‘Oi, ’er kicked me, ’er did!’

‘’Ere—’ The boy drummed up a group of his pals as the others started to move away. ‘That Mercy didn ’alf give me one.’

‘She’s a vicious little cow!’

‘Come on – let’s get ’er.’

She saw them coming, circling her. No one stood up for her. The other children watched apprehensively.

Mercy stood quite still, arms crossed tight over her

chest. Her hair was longer now and the bright plaits reached halfway down her back. She was neat-looking as ever, frock straight and clean and hanging below her knees, feet together in her little boots, eyes flaring defiance.

'Come on then, Mercy,' one of the boys goaded as they danced round her. They started to run at her, mocking, then retreating back. 'Gunna shout at us? Gunna scream? Go on – let's see yer, Mercy-Nursie!'

The taunting children circled, faces moving in and out of her view. 'Mercy-Nursie!' they chanted, 'Mercy-Nursie, the Hanley bastard!' Their voices meaner and meaner when they met no satisfying response, no tantrum or any sort of reaction, however much they goaded her about carrying the name of the orphan's patron.

Mercy looked up beyond them towards the red-brick school building. The freezing buffeted her raw cheeks. She felt she was watching everything from the other end of a long, long tube, like looking down through a chimney, the children's faces turned up towards her from several storeys below. She felt nothing for them. She had learned to retreat somewhere deep into herself that no one could touch; nothing they said or did could hurt her. What she could feel, most immediately, was the itch of her rough wrapover vest round the tops of her arms, how her left boot was pinching her burning chilblains, the rough ache of her sore throat. But the other children she let flit around her, distant as summer swallows.

One of the boys shoved Mercy's shoulder hard and she reeled backwards, tumbled on to the hard ground, skinning her elbow.

'Look, she's gunna blart now!' one of them cried triumphantly as tears of pain sprang into Mercy's eyes.

'Come on, let's see yer. 'Er's like a statue – can't move 'er bleedin' face!'

I'm not crying for 'em, Mercy vowed. I'm never doing anything they want – never.

She lay on the ground and curled into a ball on her side, face hidden in her hands. If she couldn't see them they weren't there. She'd killed them. They didn't exist.

The handbell to summon them all inside began ringing, growing louder as one of the teachers, Mr Paget, came out, his arm beating the bell up and down in the icy wind.

'What's all this?' He strode across to the ring of children. 'Get inside the rest of you. Go on – hurry up.' The children fled, giggling with relief at avoiding trouble.

'On your feet, child.' As he bent down Mr Paget saw a dark, creeping line of blood along the girl's wrist. With impatience he pulled her hands from her face and saw her nose was bleeding, huge, plum-coloured drops falling on her school dress. Though she had tears in her eyes she stared up at him with that blank yet insolent look of hers which seldom failed to aggravate.

'What've you done?' Mr Paget fished round irritably in his jacket pocket to find his handkerchief for Mercy to hold against her nose. 'Someone hit you?'

Mercy just looked at him.

'Well did they?'

'No.'

'No, Mr Paget.' He stared at her, tight-lipped. Who could fathom this child?

'We've all had enough of this, Mercy. You cause nothing but trouble. I'm sending you back across the road and I don't want to see you in school for the rest of this week.'

This was Wednesday. A terrible crime, the worst, being

sent home from school. It 'besmirched' the good name of the Hanley Homes if they got into any trouble outside.

Mr Paget added grimly, 'We'll let Matron deal with you as she sees fit.'

Miss O'Donnell's footsteps were coming closer.

'Come here, child!' She loomed into view along the corridor, hair wrapped in a starched white cap.

Not the cellar! Mercy's heart seemed about to leap out of her chest. She felt as if she'd fall down if she moved, but she turned and forced herself to walk towards the huge woman who was bearing down on her.

Miss O'Donnell stopped with a swish of skirts and apron and gaped at the girl. Mercy's nose had stopped bleeding, but it felt dry and caked up with blood and she was still dabbing at it with Mr Paget's hanky. She lowered her head and closed her eyes tight, waiting.

'Lord above, we can't have you looking like that – look at all those stains!' Mercy opened her eyes cautiously to find Miss O'Donnell bent over and staring right into her face. She could see the enormous bready pores in the woman's nose. 'Come on, girl, quickly now, off with that frock and we'll find something presentable to put on. It's a blessing they sent you home or we shouldn't stand a chance.'

Matron was hustling her along towards the staircase, prodding her in the back every few steps as if she were a work-shy donkey. Mercy was more astonished than she had ever been before in her life. She'd done the worst thing she could do and Miss O'Donnell not only wasn't punishing her, she was being nice!

'Skin a rabbit!' Matron's bosom veered alarmingly upwards as she pulled Mercy's blood-spattered dress over her head as if she were a five-year-old. 'Now then, let's get you cleaned up.' She looked the girl over, pulled the edge of her vest to see if there were bruises on her torso. Fortunately she seemed clear, although her elbow was scabbed.

'You, Mercy, are going to start a new life today,' she explained, kneeling in front of the child and vigorously washing her face.

'A lady is going to take you away from here to board out with her. She has no children, so she's giving you a great opportunity which you are to make the most of, d'you understand? She has a very respectable house in Handsworth.' Rather bare and sober, Miss Rowney had reported. Perhaps this was some austere religious way of living? But respectable enough, and the woman seemed very keen.

'You'd better behave yourself, Mercy,' Miss O'Donnell threatened suddenly. She was buttoning Mercy into a plain grey tunic several sizes too big for her. Mercy smelt her bitter breath as she hissed, 'If you play this Mrs Gaskin up and make her send you back here, I can promise you, I'll make sure your life isn't worth living.'

'Well, what a pretty little girl!'

After getting cleaned up Mercy had been given a thin piece of bread and butter and a cup of milk which almost made her forget the sore throat. Now she stood feeling very small and bewildered on the holey rug in Miss Rowney's office while the three of them stared at her.

Miss Rowney and Miss O'Donnell were beaming away at her as if their hearts were going to explode with love and pride. And that Mrs Gaskin was smiling for all she was worth too.

'You'll find she's an intelligent child,' Miss Rowney was saying. 'Doing so well at school. Of course, all our children attend St Philip's Elementary School across the way, and Mercy's progressed so very well – learned to read in record time, I gather.'

'Oh well, that's very good,' Mrs Gaskin said, sounding as if her mind was on other things completely. 'She must be a credit to you. Bit small though, ain't – isn't she?'

There was something funny about the way this Mrs Gaskin was talking, Mercy thought. It was like the way Dorothy and Miss Eagle talked but sort of poshified.

'Small perhaps, but very strong and wiry. Come and shake hands, Mercy,' Miss Rowney instructed her. 'Mrs Gaskin has very kindly offered to take you in and she will in effect be your new mother, so you have to be a very good girl for her.'

Mercy stepped forward and shook Mrs Gaskin's cold, fat hand. The woman had black hair which was taken up under a wide, flat hat perched on top of her head, and she was wearing a long, jade green skirt and jacket, which strained across her hips, the buttons of the jacket appearing quite desperate to release themselves. Mercy looked up into a face with dark, rather hooded eyes, round cheeks which protruded more as the woman smiled down at her, and thick lips between which Mercy could see square yellow teeth.

'Well, say something, Mercy!' Miss O'Donnell urged her.

'Where's Dorothy?' Her voice had risen high in panic.

Miss Rowney laughed nervously. 'Dorothy is one of our staff,' she explained to Mrs Gaskin. 'Mercy is rather attached to her. As you know, Mercy, Dorothy's very poorly at the moment – touch of pneumonia, I gather.

She won't be with us for some time. Never mind that dear. Is there anything you want to ask Mrs Gaskin?'

Mercy looked up again into the face of this woman whose relentless yellow smile was beating down on her. She could think of nothing to ask about another life, for until now she had known only the almost unchanging rhythm of the orphanage and school. All she wanted was Dorothy.

Eventually she said, 'Do I 'ave to take my bed?'

More tittering from the women.

'It's awright, bab,' Mrs Gaskin said, her posh accent slipping for a moment. 'I've got a bed for you at home. And you'll have some pretty clothes for yourself and some toys. We'll 'ave a lovely time together, won't we?' She turned to Miss Rowney and asked with sudden abruptness, 'Can I take 'er now then?'

''Er, yes – a few papers to sign of course. Matron, could you make sure Mercy's things are ready?'

'Oh they are,' Miss O'Donnell said fervently. 'Yes, all shipshape.'

Miss Rowney handed Mrs Gaskin her payment for Mercy's first week. 'You'll be sent the rest regularly. It's only a supplement, of course,' she said. 'But then your husband . . .'

'Oh yes.' Mrs Gaskin nodded hard. 'Albert's earning a good wage. But could you give a week or two's in advance – for a few extras for 'er like?' Miss Rowney hesitated, then handed over a ten-shilling note.

'We shall of course be calling on you to see how things are going, Mrs Gaskin,' she said. 'And if there are any problems – which I'm sure there won't be – you can always contact us.'

'Oh I'm sure we'll get on very well, won't we, Mercy? Got a coat, has she?'

Mercy found herself wrapped in an old gaberdine and Mrs Gaskin carried her bag to the door.

'Before you go, Mercy—' Miss Rowney actually had to lay her hand on Mrs Gaskin's arm to stop her rushed progress out of the door. Her tone changed to that of memorized speech. 'We'd like to present you with a little gift, as we do to all children who go forth from here. We know you'll take the good name of the Hanley Homes out into the world with you.'

Mercy found a parcel wrapped in thin brown paper laid in her hands.

'I want Dorothy!' Tears welled in her eyes. How could she go without saying goodbye to the only adult who had ever shown her any kindness?

'Don't be silly, dear, Dorothy's not here.' Miss Rowney pushed her briskly towards the door. 'We'll tell her where you've gone, don't fret.'

None of the other children were summoned to say goodbye as Miss O'Donnell and Miss Rowney saw Mercy off with no embraces, kisses or demonstrations of any kind.

'Be good now, dear!' Miss Rowney called as Mrs Gaskin took the girl's hand and led her down into the road.

'Good luck,' Miss O'Donnell shouted, hissing to Miss Rowney, 'and won't they just darn well need it.'

Still holding the parcel, Mercy turned and looked back at them as they stood, arms raised benevolently, on the very step where she had arrived as a newborn baby. She was too bewildered even to wave.

Part Two

Chapter Four

'Come on, get moving then – we've got a ways to go from 'ere.' Mrs Gaskin said as they set out along the road in the cold, grey afternoon. 'Blimey—' She rubbed one hand vigorously round her jaw. 'Got a proper face ache after all that smiling!'

Mercy looked around her, full of excitement suddenly, despite all the confusion of it. She was going out somewhere new, to a new home! She imagined homes as warm, comfortable places with soft furniture to sit on, flowers in the gardens and kind, benevolent people.

'Give us yer things,' Mrs Gaskin snapped, almost snatching Mercy's woven bag from her which contained her very few possessions. Mercy held on tight to the parcel though. 'Can't stand kids dawdlin' round me. We're going to 'ave ter get on the tram. Will yer come on – I want to get out of 'ere, smartish.' Mercy couldn't help noticing that Mrs Gaskin's smile had dropped away as quickly as had her posh accent.

One hand lifting the green skirt up out of the muck in the gutter, the other carrying Mercy's bag, Mabel Gaskin jerked her head to indicate that they should cross the road, and strode across so fast Mercy had to run to keep up and avoid being hit by a fast trotting horse and carriage.

In her entire life so far the furthest Mercy had ever been was Minister Vesey's church on the Witton Road.

Everything else had revolved round Kent Street. Now they were going to go right across Birmingham to some green and mysterious place Miss O'Donnell had called Handsworth.

' 'S'Handsworth nice?' she asked, panting a bit.

'Yer what?' They'd reached a main road and Mabel was looking up and down. 'Where's that cowing tram stop?'

'Handsworth,' Mercy persevered. 'What's it like?'

'Ah – there . . .' Mabel dashed off along the road. 'Right in front of me bleedin' nose. And there's one coming – quick!'

The tram trundled towards them. 'Ooh – can we sit on the top?' Mercy pleaded, bold in her excitement. The open top of the tram was edged by ornate iron railings and she thought it must be heaven to sit up there and see everything.

'With sparks coming down on yer, and in this weather – you off yer 'ead?'

The tram swayed to a standstill and Mabel didn't have to prod Mercy to climb up inside. They managed to find two places on the wooden seats downstairs.

'Don't trust them buses,' Mabel murmured, straightening her skirt under her. 'Least with a tram yer know it's got to stay on the tracks.'

Mercy watched, thrilled, out of the window as they lumbered along the cobbled streets past shops, churches, small workshops and dwellings. The walls were painted with signs advertising all manner of things: Birds' Custard, Hudson's Soap, Fred Smith's Ales and Stout, and Mercy tried hungrily to read them all. And it was such a big place! They seemed to have been on the tram for ages already. Mercy kept her eyes fixed on the view through the whole journey, except once when they passed a building which to her looked like a palace. The front of it was all coloured tiles with scrolls and flowers, fruit, and two rounded bay windows with bits of brightly-coloured glass making a pattern at the top.

'What's that?' she asked Mabel urgently. 'Cor – that's beautiful, that is!'

Mabel had taken her hat off and was busy trying to pin it back on top of her twisted skein of black hair. She half looked, seeming agitated. 'What – where?'

'There!'

'That's a pub. Ain't you never seen a pub before?' She stared at Mercy for a moment. What was it about this girl with her peculiar piercing eyes that got on her nerves so much already?

'Right – off 'ere,' Mabel ordered a few stops later. Mercy followed her fat behind along the tram and jumped down behind her.

'Is this Handsworth?'

'No – it's not bloody 'Andsworth!' Mabel was suddenly enraged. 'We ain't going to 'Andsworth so would you shurrup keeping on about it.'

'But I thought . . .'

'Yes, well you know what Thought did . . .' They were walking very fast, jostling passers-by, turning into a wide street with enormous buildings, their walls blackened and the tops of them only hazily visible up there in a soup of damp, gritty air.

'Where then . . .?'

'You'll see. Now shut yer trap for a bit, will yer? We gotta get 'ome quick.' She spoke with such peculiar venom that Mercy decided to do as she was told.

As they turned left out of that street with its grand shop fronts, Mercy saw a sign high in the wall, CORPORATION STREET, and then they were in another road with more huge windows full of clothes, shoes, china and glassware and cloth, the like or quantity of which she had never seen. The street was bustling with people and she gawped at some of the more smartly-dressed ladies with their beautifully fitted gowns in soft colours, after all the grey and black at the Joseph Hanley Home.

Even though she was full of the thrill of being out in all these new places, Mercy began to feel despondent. Her throat was raw in the cold air and she longed to sit down somewhere warm. Mrs Gaskin was walking faster and faster, cursing people who got in her way.

'Come on, yer wretched girl,' she nagged Mercy. 'We gotta get back!'

When they reached the Bull Ring, for a time Mercy forgot she had a sore throat. She forgot her tingling nose and her shivers and this horrible, bad-tempered woman she was with. How exciting it was! From where they came into it, walking down the slope of Spiceal Street, Mercy could see a church at the far end with a tall spire and a big clock with gold numbers marking the face. In between snaked the row of market stalls, most protected by sagging tarpaulins, and a sea of hats: bonnets with little ribbons or posies, cloth caps and Homburgs, even the odd boater here and there.

Everywhere there was movement and a great outcry of sound, with the traders trying to outdo each other shouting out the prices of their fruit and veg.

There were others selling crocks, trinkets and bags and flowers and Mercy's feet were dragging as she stopped to gape. The light was beginning to die and some of the traders were lighting flares at the side of their stalls which burned with a bluish-yellow flame, giving the place a cosy air.

'Keep with me,' Mabel shouted at her over the racket

and seized her arm. 'If I lose yer 'ere I'll never find yer again.'

There were so many smells that were new to Mercy: smoke from cigarettes, and a thick mouthful of it made her cough. But then there came the sweet smell of potatoes baking in a big green and gold handcart which made her mouth water, and other smells, discarded cabbage leaves, crushed onions, bruised apples and oranges left to rot in the street. But not for long. Mercy watched as three ragged children, their clothes caked in filth, slunk round the stalls, darting down now and then to grab some piece of refuse even though the stallholders tried shooing them away.

'Can't we just stay a bit longer?' Mercy begged as Mabel dragged her past a man selling wire toys and a knife-grinder showering sparks.

'No,' Mabel snapped. A woman approached them and tried to push a posy of lavender through Mabel's buttonhole.

'Bugger off, will yer!' She slapped the woman's hand away. They hurried past a big statue behind some railings, and the church. The clock made it well after five.

Soon after they were hurrying up a long, very steep road called Bradford Street. It was dark and the buildings felt high and close together. From every side came the most amazing din Mercy had ever heard. Banging and clanking sounds met them not only from the openings of buildings on the street but from under the ground through the gratings. In some places jets of steam unfurled through holes from down there and drifted raggedly into the air. The hammering and rattling, the sudden scream of metal and tearing crashes of noise met them all the way along.

'What's that?' Mercy yelled, her throat rasping.

Mabel gave her a look which implied the question was almost too stupid to answer. 'Factories. Brass works and that. Don't you know anything?'

'Is this still Birmingham?

'No, it's bloody Timbuctoo.'

Mercy took this to mean yes. Birmingham really was a big place then. They turned off Bradford Street and there were more factories, and then houses too. Now they'd got out of the bustle of the market Mercy's excitement was beginning to wear off. It was fast getting dark, the air felt damp and harsh and when they crossed the road the cobbles were slippery underfoot. She felt the throb of her chilblains in the pinching boots, her raw throat and empty belly, and her head was starting to hurt. She wondered again when she was going to see Dorothy, now she was in this strange, dark place. Her dream of a green paradise was dissolving fast.

'I don't like you,' she said, still clinging to her parcel as the one thing she had left of the home. 'I want you to take me back to Matron. She said you could.'

'Oh no,' Mabel Gaskin sniggered spitefully, 'you won't be seeing them again in a hurry. See, they think we're in my old 'ouse in Winson Green – near enough to 'Andsworth. Me husband's 'ouse, that is – when I had a husband. They ain't going to find you again where we're going, so yer'd better get used to the idea. Least I got that ten bob off of them while I had the chance, 'cos they won't be seeing us no more. I've got plans for you, and you ain't going anywhere without my say-so. Down 'ere—'

She elbowed Mercy down another side street even darker than the last. Soon, pausing by a drunken-looking street lamp she said, 'Up the entry,' and pushed her into one of the pitch black alleys between the houses, which quickly opened up into a court of back houses. As they walked in, the gas lamp in the middle of the court flared into life and Mercy saw a man standing under it with a long pole.

'Bit late, aren't yer?' Mabel said to him in passing.

'And a very good evening to you too,' he quipped.

A gaggle of children was playing up at the far end. There were three houses parallel with the road, and what looked like two smaller cottages to one side of the yard, but Mercy had barely had a look when Mabel swept her at high speed through the door of the house on one side of the entry.

Inside it was completely black.

'Stand still or you'll only go and break summat.'

Mercy stood just inside the door clutching her parcel. Her head throbbed and she felt very small and frightened. There was just her and this nasty woman and she didn't know where she was and it was so dark and smelly in this house. There was a nasty mouldy stench which she didn't recognize as damp, a stale odour of cabbage and onions. And yet another smell which took her with a shudder right back to the dormitory at the home: urine. She really felt like crying again now.

There came the scratch of a match and Mabel lit the gas mantle at one side of the room. She also lit a tiny stub of candle and abruptly disappeared upstairs. Mercy stared round her. The Joseph Hanley Home had been austere and unadorned, but never had she been in a place like this before.

The feeble light from the gas lamp only just reached the walls even though the room was tiny, and all the surfaces gave off a weird yellowish tinge. The ceiling seemed very low and in one corner was a big hole with rough bits of wood sticking out of it and in other parts it sagged and bulged. The room had been distempered long ago but now the paint had flaked away in large bare patches and the dirty plaster showed underneath. With a shudder she saw something scuttle along the wall.

The floor was of rough, uneven bricks, worn down in some parts where there had been the greatest passage over them, and holes where bricks were missing in others. In the middle of the room was a table and two rickety chairs, one with Mabel's coat and hat flung over it, and in one corner stood the range. A broom stood propped against one wall and beside it a couple of old tea chests with a few things sticking out. One looked like a picture frame. Apart from that the place was empty.

Mabel was soon down again. She stooped to stoke the range, saying defensively, 'I've only been in 'ere a few days,' as if sensing Mercy's horrified gaze lighting on the place.

'Oh Lor'!' she exclaimed suddenly, leaping up. To Mercy's astonishment she started unfastening her clothes and stripping them off, first the tight green jacket, then the skirt, wriggled down over her meaty hips. She made grunting sounds of relief.

'That's better. Can't go shovelling coal in this get-up – that's going to Chubb's tomorrow.'

Mrs Chubb, as Mercy would soon know well, ran the local pawnshop round the corner.

'Got 'em off a lady sells second-hand rags in Balsall Heath.' Mabel grinned in satisfaction at her own trickery. 'Got your gaffer believing you're living with a proper lady, din'it?' She laid the skirt over her chair, standing in a grey corset and torn petticoat. 'Shame 'aving to 'ock it, but there we are.'

'You got anything to eat?' Mercy dared ask. The room was so cold she hadn't even taken her coat off yet.

'Eat?' Mabel was struggling into a shapeless brown dress. I've only just got the fire going, what d'you think I am? I'm hungry as well, yer know. Just sit down and shurrup for a bit.'

Mercy sat on the spare chair. She felt overwhelmingly tired, and shivery as if she was getting a fever. All the day's changes had taken it out of her and though she was used to a meagre diet she was starving. Mabel though, did seem to be making an effort to get some dinner ready.

'You going to open that package then?' she said from by the range, giving Mercy a sly look. 'Let's see if it's anything worth 'aving.'

Mercy pulled the loose string away from the parcel and slowly tore off the paper as Mabel breathed heavily over her shoulder.

The first thing to fall out was a small white handkerchief. On the corner Mercy saw that her name had been embroidered neatly in mauve silk. A parting gift from the home? She wondered if Dorothy had sewn it for her. With it was a book with a pale brown cover, designs of black and orange flowers printed on it, the title embossed into a panel of gold. It was by a Dr J.W. Kirton. *Cheerful Homes*, the title read. *How to Get and Keep Them.*

Chapter Five

Mabel heated up a meagre amount of scrag-end. When it was ready, she fished around in the scullery at the back and came out with a new candle which she lit and fixed on a saucer. Taking a plate of stew and a spoon she said, 'Back in a tick,' and climbed the stairs.

A moment later Mercy heard her voice, apparently talking to someone. Mercy frowned. She was sure it was Mabel. But then the walls of these houses were wafer-thin. From next door she could hear plates rattling and people talking. Someone was snoring. Then a woman's voice, 'Get in there. I said get in there, will yer!' very loud and angry. Whoever it was didn't 'get in there' and this was followed up by more yells. A man's voice snapped, 'Oh leave off, yer nagging bitch . . .'

'Who's that up there?' Mercy asked when Mrs Gaskin reappeared, minus the plate and spoon.

'You'll see soon enough.'

They sat at the table together. The sight of the stew was disgusting, the grey meat nearly all fat and bone but it tasted better than it looked and Mercy ate everything she could actually chew, despite her sore throat. She had an uneasy feeling though, about this unseen person upstairs, and strained her ears to hear any sound.

Mrs Gaskin made tea and gave her a cup and she began to feel warmer.

'Where will I sleep?'

'Upstairs, where d'yer think?'

'Have you got a bed?'

'Don't you worry about it, there's beds all right.' The woman seemed a fraction mellower now she was home and fed. Mercy looked up into her blunt-featured face and felt herself shudder.

'You my mom now then?' she asked doubtfully. She had a beautiful fantasy in her mind about what real moms should be like and Mabel didn't fit the bill at all.

Mabel stared across the room and her mouth twisted suddenly, her face taking on an odd, melancholy expression. 'You don't want me as yer mom. You'd better call me Mabel. Can't stand you calling me Mrs Gaskin.' She stood up abruptly. 'Come on – up yer go.'

She picked up Mercy's bag and led the way up the creaking stairs.

'Watch that one!' Half of one of the treads was missing, broken and splintered. 'Proper 'ell 'ole this is,' Mabel muttered to herself.

'I sleep in there,' she nodded to the left when they reached the tiny divide at the top of the stairs. It was a two-up house, with no attic. Two bedrooms upstairs and only the living room and scullery downstairs. 'You'll 'ave to bunk up in there.'

As the door opened, there was already an unsteady circle of candlelight in the room but for a moment Mercy couldn't make out anything. The smell of urine though, was almost overpowering and made her stomach lurch. She saw that most of the space in the tiny room was taken up with a double bed and its dark, heavy bedstead, the footboard so high that from where she was standing she couldn't see over it.

Mabel marched over to the bed and said, 'Finished then, 'ave yer?'

There was no reply that Mercy could hear. Very slowly, even more full of dread, she moved round the end of the bed. For a moment as she looked in the poor light she could see nothing but a jumble of ragged bedding. But as Mabel moved with the candle nearer the head of the bed she saw the light reflect in two dark eyes, and heard herself give a gasp. Could there really be someone under there, in all that mess, making this awful smell?

The head turned and Mercy saw dark hair, and the eyes, set in a small, delicate face, were now fixed on her.

'This is Susan,' Mabel said harshly. 'My daughter. One of my daughters, I should say. This one's the only one I got left and she's a cripple. That's my luck with mother'ood. You'll be sleeping in 'ere with 'er. 'Er's got no feeling in 'er legs so if she needs to go—' – Mabel's gaze rested on the chamber pot down on the floor by the bed – 'you'll have to give 'er a hand. Anyroad, there's ample room for the both of you.'

She picked up the plate from which Susan had evidently managed to eat her tea and went out.

Mercy found her legs were trembling. She went round and sat numbly on the other side of the bed, elbows resting on her knees and hands cupping her cheeks. I won't start blarting in front of her, she thought, I won't! I should have run, when we were in the Bull Ring, while I had the chance! Mrs Gaskin would never have caught up with me . . .

''Ello.' She heard the girl's soft voice.

Mercy didn't answer. She didn't turn round. For a time she just sat there, but she could feel the girl watching her as if her eyes were burning into her back. Eventually she stood up and started to unbutton her frock which she left hanging over the foot of the bed. The room was perishing cold. She knew, despairingly, that she was going to have to get into that foul, stinking bed. The thought made her want to heave but what choice did she have?

The bedclothes, such as they had, were a mixture of old scraps of torn blanket and a couple of old coats. As she pulled them back the smell got worse.

'Oh my God.'

'Sorry – only she's hardly been 'ere for days to help me. Only first thing. I can't move, see.'

The bed was in a terrible state. Where Susan was lying, helpless, it was drenched. Mercy's side was not so absolutely soaked, but definitely damp. There were tears in Susan's eyes and Mercy saw they were tears of shame.

'You cold?'

Susan nodded. Mercy was shivering convulsively now, and when she touched Susan's arm she, too, was icy cold.

'You'd best come over this way a bit,' she said abruptly. 'D'you need to go now?'

'No – she lifted me when she got in.'

Susan was all skin and bone, quite easy even for Mercy to shift a little way across the bed. The two of them didn't speak any more.

Mercy blew out the candle and crawled into her little space at the edge of the bed, careful not to touch Susan who lay silently beside her. The ammonia smell of urine burned in her nostrils. Bugs scurried along the walls. She felt so ill, her head throbbed and she was shivering hard, unable to stop. Finally, in exhaustion, fear and bewilderment, she let the tears come, wretchedly sobbing and shaking. She tried to be quiet but her emotion flooded out.

It was only after she'd begun to quieten a little, snuffling now and gulping, that she felt a little touch on her shoulder and furiously shook it off. But after a few moments the hand was back, stroking her at first, and then a small, bony arm crept round her body, holding her tight. She felt Susan's face against her back and finally the two of them slept, their bodies giving each other warmth.

'Mercy – can you give us a hand?'

The room was still almost dark. A dull light was just attempting to seep through the filthy window. Mercy turned quickly on to her back, completely confused for a moment, thinking it was one of the girls in the home she could hear. Then she took in the sodden coldness of the bed and the crumbling, filthy walls. She was also scratching: there were bugs in the bed.

Susan was trying to sit up. 'You'll 'ave to cop 'olt of me . . .'

'Why should I?' She was rigid with cold and anger.

There was a pause. 'Please 'elp me,' Susan begged wretchedly. 'I'll go in the bed again else.'

Mercy climbed stiffly from the bed, teeth chattering and slid her arms under Susan's and round her chest.

'Skinny, aren't you?'

'Good job, innit?'

Though slightly smaller than her, Mercy had little difficulty in dragging Susan off the bed and positioning her on the pot.

'Ta,' Susan whispered, so humbly that Mercy felt ashamed of herself. She stared at Susan's white legs. She'd never seen such scrawny, wasted limbs before.

'So've you ever been able to walk then?'

'For a bit I could – I can remember walking. I was taken sick years ago. They call it infantile paralysis. My legs 'ave got a bit better lately but they don't think they'll ever be any good.'

Susan looked up at her, her face ghostly in the dim

light, her eyes coal-black like a snowman's and a pudding basin of black hair.

'You come to stop with us then?'

'No!' Mercy snapped, then added helplessly, 'I dunno.' She couldn't even have said at that moment just how much she didn't want to live here with Mabel and her crippled scrap of a daughter. Nothing was real. It was as if she were trapped in a dream and couldn't wake up.

'You don't 'alf bang about in your sleep,' Susan commented. After a moment she indicated that she'd finished and Mercy hoisted her back on to the bed.

'Mom wants you to 'elp look after me like, so I'm not stuck 'ere on my own. She's got to go and find a job or she says we can't pay the rent or eat.'

'Haven't you got a dad?' Mercy pulled the remnants of bed clothing up to cover Susan so just her head was visible.

''E just went. A few months back. Left us.'

She could hear the desolation in Susan's voice, but could only say, 'Oh,' unable to imagine a real dad or real mom, then added, 'Why?'

'Dunno. 'E were a good dad really. Didn't want us any more, I s'pose. And then we had no money so we come to live over 'ere. We 'ad a bit of a nicer 'ouse before but Mom couldn't keep up with the rent.'

Mercy sat down on the edge of the bed, shivering.

'D'you just lie 'ere all day then?'

'I didn't used to before we came 'ere. She'd get me up and that. Miss Pringle – one of our neighbours – she used to come and sit and do things with me. She were a teacher when 'er was younger. It was 'er taught me to sew and knit like. She said if I couldn't use my legs I might as well keep my hands busy. Mom never did nothing with me. Miss Pringle said it was a shame.'

'How old are you? Don't you go to school?'

'No, never. I'm thirteen.'

'Thirteen! Blimey I reckon you're smaller than Amy was!'

'Who's Amy?'

'My best pal. They sent her away to Canada.'

'Miss Pringle was my best pal.' Susan sounded dismal. 'Don't s'pose I'll be seeing 'er now neither.' She swallowed hard. 'How old're you?'

'Twelve – nearly.'

'What's it like in an orphanage then? And school?'

'It's awright.' Mercy couldn't think of anything to say. It was all she knew. What was there to say about it? 'We had much bigger rooms,' she brought out finally, looking round at the bleak space the bed was squeezed into.

It was growing lighter. Mercy went to the window. There was no sign of frost and the glass was running with a mixture of condensation and grime. She wiped one of the lowest panes with the back of her hand and stood wrapping her arms round herself to try to keep warm.

The lamp was still lit outside, reflecting in puddles on the uneven bricks. Mercy could just make out the long stretch of the yard, reaching along to a high building in the far corner. As she watched, a woman came out from one of the houses beside Mabel's and walked briskly across carrying a bundle with one hand and holding her long skirt up out of the wet.

I'm not stopping here, Mercy said to herself. I'll go back to the home and tell 'em. They can't leave me here.

She'd never seen a more desolate place. But she thought of the journey here the day before, and knew she didn't have the first idea where she was or how to go about getting back. She also remembered Miss O'Donnell's warning about what would happen if she did. She swallowed hard. Oh Dorothy, she cried inside. Where are you? If you were here it'd be all right.

'Mercy?'

She didn't want to turn round and let Susan see the tears on her face.

'What?'

'Could yer empty this for me? Mom hates doing it and she'll keep on. She weren't so bad before but she moans all the time since we come 'ere.'

'So she's got me 'ere to be your slave, has she?' Mercy snapped, angrily wiping her eyes on her sleeve. She pulled the rest of her clothes on quickly and went round to Susan's side of the bed to pick up the chamber pot.

'There's a suff out in the yard.'

Mercy straightened up. 'If your Mom thinks I'm staying 'ere she's made a big mistake,' she announced haughtily, and went to march out of the room. But she caught her foot in a trailing loop of blanket and tripped. The chamber pot leapt out of her hands and smashed with a great noise and splash. Mercy fell against the foot of the bed banging her head.

'What the 'ell was that?'

Mabel waddled across the landing like a bloodhound, still attired in the same corset, chemise and bloomers, that Mercy had seen last night.

'Oh yer 'aven't gone and broken the po'?' She stared accusingly at Mercy who was rubbing her cheek. 'Yer clumsy little bitch. Who's going to pay for a new one, eh? You, I suppose?'

'No— ' Susan spoke up. 'It weren't 'er fault it were me. I tipped it over – knocked it with me arm. Mercy didn't do nothing.'

Mabel stared from one to the other of them, eyes gluey with sleep, the skin under them wrinkled like rice paper.

Even she could see it was pretty unlikely Susan could create a crash like that, but she wasn't in the mood to keep on about it. She wanted her morning cuppa.

'Pick up the bits,' she ordered Mercy. 'Don't cut yourself or there'll be that to deal with as well. Take 'em down the yard. You'll 'ave to do your business in the bucket from now on, the pair of yer.'

She went off, heavily, down the stairs. They heard her cursing over the broken tread.

Still rubbing her sore head Mercy gaped at Susan in bewilderment. Susan's face broke into a broad, mischievous smile.

Chapter Six

May 1912

'Come and see, Mom – Mr Pepper's nearly finished it!'

Mabel Gaskin sat on a rickety chair outside number two, Nine Court, Angel Street, her face bullish with resentment. Susan's joyous cry as she came rattling towards her along the yard only made her scowl more and pull her arms tight across her pendulous bosom.

Susan's face was alight with hope and laughter as Mercy hurtled along with her, squeezed into the go-kart belonging to the twins, Johnny and Tom Pepper, from number one. Susan was clinging to the sides of the ancient black pram from which it was made, her wasted legs and feet flapping up and down over the end.

'I ain't shifting nowhere,' Mabel snarled.

Her eyes met Mercy's for a second over Susan's shoulder. The girl's hair was a tumbling skein of gold after last night's dunking in the tin bath, and there was so much of it it almost seemed to overwhelm her delicate face. Her prettiness was marred though, by harsh mauve bruising round her left cheekbone, and the expression of loathing in her narrowed eyes directed at Mabel could have melted lead. Mabel glowered back. Every time she looked at that kid nowadays she longed to batter her. And that was often what she did.

''Ere—' Alf Pepper called. He was a huge bloke, a

Black Countryman with a ruddy, bashed up face from boxing and the nickname 'Bummy' on account of his low slung trousers. 'I'm gunna need them wheels off o' there in a minute.'

Eyes smouldering with triumph, Mercy struggled to turn the go-kart and, leaning all her weight on it, rattled back along the blue-brick yard to where a gaggle of the neighbours was gathered round Alf who was building Susan the first wheelchair she had ever had.

Susan turned her head for a moment, eyes pleading, but Mabel stuck her nose in the air and looked away. She wasn't going to stay out here to be shamed any longer. She got up and carried the chair indoors in as stately a manner as possible and slammed the door.

'Old misery,' Elsie Pepper said, bending to pick up little Rosalie who was 'momming' at her skirts. She was a sturdy-looking woman, dressed in her usual attire: a long, rough skirt with a blouse tucked in. Her thick auburn hair was usually taken up under a man's cap when she was working, which was nearly always, but she'd left it off today. 'There's summat wrong with 'er, that there is. That child's right enough given a bit of kindness.'

Elsie was in her mid-forties, had given birth to nine children, eight surviving, and believed implicitly in hard work and family life. She was blessed with more energy than the average person, had a sound idea of how to feed a big family well on Bummy's modest but regular wages as a chippy and, to make means stretch further, took in washing. She always had a house full of it.

There were several things which made Elsie's blood boil and these were dishonesty, men with no sense of responsibility, and cruelty, especially to children.

Cruelty was what she saw in Mabel Gaskin, and Elsie had made it her business, as she did frequently for folk in need, to look out for Mercy and Susan and take them under her wing.

Inside the house Mabel climbed the rotting stairs shaking with rage and humiliation. Going to the girls' room she stood back from the window, peering out at the far end of the yard which was buttressed by the high wall of the wire factory.

They were all out there, laughing and carrying on, all against her as usual. Most of all she loathed the Pepper family with all their kids and their self-righteous ways. Elsie, who everyone seemed to regard as the yard's gaffer, handing out her opinions left, right and centre. 'Course, she'd got Mercy well under her thumb. And all her flaming kids. No one should have that many kids. There were the twins who Mercy adored, and more infuriating still, the Pepper family were so taken with her. And now thanks to that scheming, interfering Mercy, Susan was going to have a wheelchair and she'd be out, for everyone to see her as the cripple she was.

'She's mine!' Mabel's voice came out in a harsh, irrational outburst. 'My baby. I won't let you take her away. She's mine, mine, mine.'

Unable to stand watching any more of this merriment outside she went to her own room. She loathed Mercy for her energy and guile, for her devotion to Susan and for being more than she herself would ever be. Yet now she couldn't do without her. She wanted the very best money could buy for Susan, but she barely had any money and couldn't bear anyone else to be the one to help her. She was above all these slummy people yet had to live among them.

She fell on the bed in a turmoil of self-hatred provoked

by the crowd out there all bunched against her, Susan's glowing hope, the wheelchair – yet another of the things she'd failed to provide. Failed. That's what she was, in every way, and Susan, her one scrap of hope, the one who would always have to stay with her and depend on her, was pulling away now as well.

Mabel Smith was born in 1873 in the workhouse at Winson Green. Her mother, already in poor health, died of TB two years later never having left the workhouse, and Mabel and two older siblings, a boy and a girl, were orphaned. She never knew who her father had been.

At fourteen Mabel was put into service as a kitchen maid to a family in Handsworth. Over the next couple of years her thickset features, which had given her a skulking, toadlike appearance as a child, spread and thinned to an earthy sort of glamour with those gappy teeth, the hooded eyes and long black hair. Her body was generously curved and stayed lithe through housework.

Albert Gaskin – then seventeen, whirling along the streets on a baker's delivery cycle – started shilly-shallying at this particular door in Broughton Road, hoping to catch a glimpse of Mabel's broad hips and supple waist bending over a bucket, the breasts full of promise, strong arms wringing a cloth, sleeves rolled, muscles moving under the skin.

Mabel, whose head had been rammed full of the notion that as a workhouse orphan she'd never be of anything more than heavy domestic use to anyone, suddenly found a more generous slice of hope than she'd been expecting.

Albert, thin, gangly, with high cheekbones, shorn brown hair and a jauntily-angled cap, pursued her with cheerfulness, persistence and a seething eroticism that quite took her by surprise. The sounds of desire he let out even at their first kiss were something she'd never forget.

When eventually Albert said, 'Will yer marry me, Mabel, my true love?' she had long ago made up her mind.

Things started well. Albert moved into factory work and Mabel carried on in service as a 'daily'. They rented a couple of rooms. After all the anticipation the wedding night in 1893 was a sad disappointment (Albert had had several too many pints of Butler's Ale). But things improved on that front and others. Mabel fell pregnant. She bloomed. She had a home, or half a one, a sweet-natured husband in work and she was to be a mother. Workhouse-born she may have been, but look what she was making of herself now!

The baby, a girl who they named Victoria, was born dead. Albert stayed off work for a week and promptly got the sack. After, he came home with two finches in a cage who chirruped mournfully and pecked their ash-coloured breasts until Mabel screamed for him to take them away again.

By the time a second baby was on the way, Albert had long found another job, and the sad darkness haunting the rooms near the canal thinned and blazed into hope again. Dulcie was born on All Hallows Eve, a plump, fair baby. Albert wept again, this time for joy.

At three months Dulcie contracted whooping cough. Mabel rushed for a doctor, uncaring of the expense and cursing the mother with a whooping child she'd spoken to when crumbling crusts for the ducks over in Handsworth Park. In five days she was dead.

Mabel fell into mourning and depression. They didn't see Albert's scattered family, and with none of her own to mourn with her she took it all on herself. Somewhere in her nature was a dulled, lugubrious space reserved for grief and disaster, perhaps cultured in the workhouse. But this was not the case with Albert. He was sunshine and tears all at the surface, his personality as slim as cardboard, enough to accommodate only the thinnest of shadows.

He didn't start drinking heavily though, until later.

Susan was born in 1899, with Mabel's dark eyes. She smiled from the first week – Mabel was certain of this even though the few people she allowed near the child said it was wind. She was placid and sweet and thrived steadily, if delicately, into a solemn-faced yet mischievous child.

Afterwards Mabel came to think of these as the last years of her marriage. Albert, his frame already shuddering under the terrible weight of responsibility – all these lives, these deaths – was kept steady by Susan. By the light in her eyes when he came into a room, the frantic, joyful kicking of her legs as he lifted her high in the air as a baby, her running to him as she grew into a five-year-old with his own loving nature. Of all his daughters she charmed him the most, softened him as Mabel no longer could, gave him hope.

When she fell ill they thought at first the fever was influenza, unseasonably in July. When the doctor pronounced it something far more serious the first image that blazed through Albert's mind was another small white coffin.

Memories of those days, then weeks were almost impossible to recall, so strange and fragmented were they as to be discounted as a dream. Absolutely sure and certain for Mabel six months later though, was that she had a child who would never run into her father's arms again, a drunk for a husband and that her hopes for an increase in the good things in life had been sadly misplaced.

There were another seven years of something that passed outwardly for marriage. Susan stayed small and loveable. Albert stayed drunk on and off, no longer sweet, sometimes working, sometimes not. He tried to be tender with Susan, wanted to take her out and about.

'But she's a cripple!' Mabel raged. 'Look at 'er legs. She'll 'ave to stop at 'ome. I'll not 'ave 'er wheeled out like a freak show.'

She took over Susan in a perverse, compulsive way. Overprotective, smothering yet ashamed, shutting Albert out. She kept even Susan's existence as secret as possible, only letting very few people see her, like the crusading Miss Pringle with her pince-nez, her bag of coloured sewing threads and offcuts of cotton and felt.

'She has such dextrous fingers,' Miss Pringle said. 'Such a pity to waste a skill like that. She could be marvellous at the piano, you know, or the violin.'

Mabel stared at her as pigs struggled to take wing around the room.

But Miss Pringle did make it possible for Mabel to live with all the contradictions of her feelings towards her remaining daughter. Susan, whom she would have been mortified to take out in the street, Susan, her companion for life who would never leave her because she couldn't walk away and no one would marry a girl with wizened legs. Susan would always be there. Susan, in whom all her guilt, her compassion was invested. Who for so much of the time she couldn't stand to be anywhere near, embodying as she did all the loss, all the failure of a life in which Mabel had once found hope.

Their possessions – not plentiful to begin with – Mabel was pawning piece by piece. They were already poor when Albert left. He had not been getting regular work and the jobs he did get were now unskilled and insecure. He'd had two spells in Winson Green prison for drunkenness. At home he was neither raucous nor violent. Sober, he was gentle with Susan. Drunk he was silent, lost.

And then he was gone. On a beautiful summer day when birds sang in small gardens and there was a breeze to blow the city smoke away, he left and never came back. Mabel who had believed, whatever his state, however distant they grew from one another, that he would always be there, was more shocked than she'd ever thought she could be again. She knew he wasn't coming back – in the summer warmth he had taken his coat and hat.

Her time living as a respectable married woman was over. Now she and Susan were on their own. She was that workhouse nobody again, living in the slums where you had to burn the bugs off the ceiling with a candle before you could get to sleep, and surrounded by slummy people whom she hated almost as much as she hated herself.

'Mom!' Susan's voice rang up the staircase. 'It's finished – come and see.' There was a pause. 'Please?'

'I'll go up,' Mercy said, muttering 'miserable cow' under her breath.

Mabel's hands gripped the cover on her bed, her teeth grating together. She heard the clatter of two pairs of boots on the stairs, an abrupt knock at the bedroom door and to her outrage Mercy and Johnny Pepper appeared.

'Get out!' she shrieked, sitting up in fury. 'What the 'ell d'yer think yer playing at coming pushing your way in 'ere?'

'Susan wants you to come,' Mercy said in a voice of

steel, standing firm in the doorway. She looked in disgust at Mabel whose appearance had deteriorated over the past months. She'd spread and sagged and her clothes were unkempt and often dirty.

'Oh you always know what Susan wants nowadays, don't you? Well, you can tell 'er from me she's gunna 'ave a long wait, 'cos I ain't coming just to see where Mr God-Almighty Pepper's nailed a couple of wheels on to some planks.'

She lay down on the bed again feeling Mercy's piercing look of loathing through her back. Mercy and Johnny went back down again.

Susan was sitting enthroned in her ingenious, very straight-backed chair at the threshold of the house. Her face fell as Mercy reappeared.

'Never mind—' Johnny set out to cheer her up. 'Come on – 'ave a ride!'

He took hold of the metal bar at the back of the chair and careered along the yard so fast that the neighbours had to scatter. Mercy's eyes followed them. It had worked! She laughed with delight. Now she and Susan would be able to get out!

'Johnny!' Elsie bawled at him. 'Go easy!'

'She won't come,' Susan said as they skidded to a halt. 'She ain't feeling too well.'

Everyone saw this for the thin excuse it was.

'Never mind,' Elsie said. 'She'll come round to the idea.'

'Go on then,' said Bummy. 'Take it off up there again – I want to see 'ow well it's going.'

Susan managed to turn the wheels a little on her own, but being unused to any form of exertion was soon exhausted. Mercy completed this next lap of honour for her as everyone clapped, down towards the entry then back up to the factory wall, past the soot-dusted cabbages in the little garden at the front of the two cottages.

'She's evil, that Mabel Gaskin,' Mary Jones spat out in Susan's absence.

'Nah.' Her husband Stan, a taut, stocky bloke with black hair and a thin moustache was smoking, leaning against the brewhouse wall. 'She's all right really, she is.'

'And what would you know?' Mary turned on him. 'You wanna keep yer eyes to yourself, you do.'

'Eh, you two,' Bummy said, then called to Susan. 'D'yer like it then?'

The expression on her face was enough of a reply.

Mabel's fury had been building up all that Sunday, and by the evening she was an unexploded bomb.

Mercy knew she was only biding her time, waiting for an excuse. She knew the signs: the silence, Mabel's clenching of her jaw, the way she averted her eyes from both of them.

Susan was at the table (the wheelchair was to be stowed in the brewhouse at night – Mabel said she wouldn't have it in the house). Mercy was moving round her laying the tin plates and the few eating implements they had, and Mabel was at the range with her back to them, stirring a pot. The room was lit only by the last of the summer evening light.

'What's to eat then?' Susan asked cautiously.

'Wait and see,' Mabel snapped. She looked a dreadful mess from lying round on her bed half the afternoon, hair tumbling everywhere, and she knew it.

Mercy stepped round her, eyes downcast, went to put a fork on the table and dropped it with a tinny clatter on the bricks.

Mabel jumped and struck out savagely with her spare arm, knocking Mercy across the room so she crashed into the wall.

'Yer clumsy little bitch!' Mabel roared. 'You're useless, that's what you are. Dropping things all the time and breaking them!' It was true. Mercy lived in such a state of nerves around Mabel that it made her clumsy and there were frequent breakages. 'What do we want forks for any'ow, when we're 'aving broth? No bloody brains in yer 'ead, that's your trouble!'

Mercy slid down the wall, curling into a ball, head and arms pulled in tight to her knees to protect herself, a position she'd had to take up so many times in her life, it came now by instinct.

Mabel thought she would burst from rage. She grabbed one of Mercy's arms and dragged her with no difficulty to her feet, fingers pressing viciously into her flesh.

'Look at me!'

The child raised her eyes, those glittering grey eyes, which even in her fear were stony with disgust at the woman in front of her and Mabel almost flinched. She squeezed her fingers as tight as claws into the tops of Mercy's arms.

'Mom, don't, please . . .' Susan begged.

'You're nothing,' Mabel went on. 'Filth from the gutter, that's what you are. That's what your own mother thought of you, you know that, don't yer? She didn't want you so she just threw you away. Dumped you on the steps of Hanley's. That's 'ow much she thought of yer.'

Mercy stared at her, stunned. She'd never, never heard this before. As far as she'd understood she'd been spawned in some mysterious way by the Birmingham streets and taken in. In a high voice she said, 'But I never 'ad a mother. I was an orphan.'

Mabel laughed nastily. ''Ark at 'er! "I was an orphan!" Didn't they tell you nothing in that place? We all 'ave a mother, deary – ain't no way of getting into the world without one. But some babbies is wanted and some ain't and you was one of the ones that ain't. Least I never gave none of mine away like your mom did.'

Seeing the genuine shock in Mercy's eyes she loosed her arm and began slapping her face until she'd made her cry.

'Don't, Mom!' Susan was sobbing. 'Stop it, you're hurting 'er!'

Mabel pushed Mercy away in disgust. 'Get out of 'ere. Yer can go up to bed without no tea. I've had enough of yer for one day.'

Later Mabel carried Susan upstairs and plonked her on the bed saying, 'If you need any 'elp you can ask 'er Majesty there.'

Mercy lay with her eyes closed, hugging her badly bruised arms tight to herself. When Mabel had gone she felt Susan's hand tapping her shoulder.

'Brought you this – look.'

From out of her clothes she drew a chunk of bread and held it in front of Mercy's face. 'Don't you want it?'

There was a pause, then Mercy shook her head.

'I wish I could stop her treating you so bad.' Susan leant over her, talking close to her ear.

Mercy shrugged as if to say, who cares?

'Mercy go on, turn over.'

Reluctantly, obviously in pain, Mercy turned on her back. Susan saw that in one hand, close up to her face, she was holding the little handkerchief with her name embroidered on it. Her eyes though, were dry.

'What she said about your mom . . . You never knew?'

Mercy shook her head again. Her face showed her pain as she spoke. 'No one ever said. They never told us much about where we'd come from. They never said I'd had a mom. I always sort of thought that if I'd had one she must be dead, and that's why I was there . . .'

Susan stroked her hair, unable to think what else to do. Mercy caught hold of her hand and gripped it hard. She couldn't explain how Mabel's cruel revelation had made her feel. Shocked, rejected, lost. Her mother wasn't dead, she'd abandoned her, thrown her away! She felt filthy and crumpled like rubbish on the street.

After a long silence Susan said, ' I know 'ow I felt when my dad went.' There was more silence, then she said, 'You won't go away too, will yer?'

Mercy looked up at her. Susan's dark head had a halo of light round it from the candle behind her. She had quickly come to feel even more tenderness and devotion for Susan.

than she had for Amy. Even though the younger of the two, Mercy was the protector, the fighter.

'No – 'course I won't.' She squeezed Susan's hand. 'Where've I got to run away to?'

Chapter Seven

For months Mercy had stayed home with Susan and acted as Mabel's unpaid skivvy. She soon became a familiar figure in the Highgate yard, in her old dress from the home, a piece of sacking round the waistband, labouring back and forth from the tap with buckets of water, kneeling scrubbing the step, her bright hair tied back with a red rag, smudges on her face.

She'd started out determined to make Mabel's house somewhere more fit to live.

'I mean the home wasn't pretty or anything, but at least it was clean. We don't have to have it looking as bad as this.'

'I s'pose not,' Susan said doubtfully.

It was a woefully thankless task. She swept and scrubbed, washed down the windows and rubbed them with newspaper. Some of the window frames were so rotten they had to be stuffed with old rags. She brushed down the walls which sent showers of dusty, yellowed distemper on top of her and Elsie showed her how to stove the house with a sulphur candle to keep the bugs at bay. But however hard she worked she couldn't disguise the fact that they were living in a cluster of jerry-built, mouldering slums and that theirs was one of the worst of the bunch. The paint just flaked more and more, the floor was in a terrible state, and the effluents from the factories coated the windows and step as soon as she'd finished washing them.

They were living in such poverty that they never seemed to have the simplest things they needed, like scissors to cut their nails or a comb that wasn't broken – let alone any new clothes.

But she did like the freedom from Miss Rowney's regime, being able to come and go as she needed, when Mabel wasn't around. And there was Susan.

'You don't 'ave to sit there doing nothing,' she said to her, the very first day, when she'd struggled to help her downstairs, step by step, the two of them sitting squeezed in side by side.

'What can I do?' Susan said, legs dangling from the chair, not even touching the floor. Mercy was hot from her exertions, but Susan was still huddled up, cold.

Mercy caught hold of the chair and inched it over to the black iron range, glad to see it was much smaller than the one in the home. She handed Susan an old rag, and the small amount of polish Mabel had left.

'I'll do the bits you can't reach. No good you sitting there gawping at me all day, is it?'

Susan peered from under her fringe with a grin of delight. 'Mom never lets me do nothing!' She set to work, bony shoulder blades poking in and out as she exerted herself.

The two girls, thrown together, grew close in a short time. Elsie was always popping in to see them, bringing gifts of food: stew, pease pudding, soup – 'I always 'ad to cook for ten before so it won't 'urt me now, will it?' – and asking how they were getting on. The yard was forever strung across with washing, either that of the other neighbours or Elsie, who was in the brewhouse – the shared wash-house in the yard – at all hours, toiling over the copper, maiding tub and mangle.

After school finished was the best time of day, when

the boys came roaring back into the yard. ''Allo Mercy!' they called out every day, and Mercy would feel her heart lift with excitement. 'Come on!' she'd say to Susan, and drag her chair out into the yard to watch. The twins were two years older than her, Jack roughly the same age. The twins were her favourites: freckly, red-haired Johnny, mad as a hatter on boxing, and Tom – kind, brown-haired, quieter. They let Mercy play with them – football with an old pig's bladder tied at the top, tipcat with a ball and a bit of wood, marbles . . .

'Yer not bad, for a wench,' Tom told her now and again as she slammed the football along the yard.

She thought they were wonderful, the whole Pepper family.

They were all out in the yard one freezing winter afternoon, when the sun couldn't break through the clouds and smoke, Susan muffled up on a chair in as many layers as they could find. Tom had carried her out there. Mercy liked the way the twins, wild as they were, were gentle with Susan.

They'd dealt out a few marbles and begun a game when three girls marched in from Angel Street. There was something about them that made Tom and Johnny stand up, hands on waists, elbows out, before they'd even opened their mouths.

They looked like sisters, all with lanky brown hair, the eldest with plaits coiled above her ears, pale faces and narrow, squinty eyes. Mercy felt herself bristle. She didn't like the look of them at all.

'What d'you want?' Tom demanded, defending his territory, chin jutting out.

'Where's that Cathleen?' the eldest said. She wore an old grey skirt, too big, dragging on the ground.

'So who wants her?' Johnny pushed himself forward.

'We do.' The eldest one was left to do the talking again in a harsh, aggressive voice. 'Few things we need to straighten out with 'er. Who're you, any road?'

'We're 'er brothers,' Johnny said, elbows sticking out. 'She ain't 'ere, and I don't reckon she'd want to see you if she was.'

The girl looked brazenly round the yard. 'What's 'er gawping at?' She latched on to Mercy suddenly, who was standing by Susan's chair. 'Ain't you got nothing better to do? Oh my word, what's this then?'

The three girls moved nearer to Susan with jaunty, menacing walks. The second girl pulled the cover off Susan's knees and made a face on seeing her white, scaley legs.

'Urgh, look – she's a cripple. That's 'orrible, that is. Looks like fish skin!'

'Was you born like that then?'

'Can yer walk? Go on, show us, 'ave a go!'

Susan, who had been so hidden away all her life that she'd never been treated anything like this before, shrank down in the chair, eyes filling with tears.

'Ooh, look, she don't like being called a cripple, she's gonna blart now. Go on, cry, cripple – boo-hoo-hoo . . .'

The eldest girl felt her plaits being grasped like handles so her head was yanked backwards and she found herself looking into two grey eyes full of a cold, intense fury.

'That person you're talking to is Susan,' Mercy spat at the girl, tugging on the hair to give emphasis to everything she said. 'And no one talks to 'er like that. No one. Got it?'

The girl scowled, wincing in pain. 'Who d'yer think you are, eh?'

'Me? I'm Mercy. And this 'ere's for you.' She loosed the girl's hair, drew her hand back and gave her a socking great punch on the nose.

'That's from me. And if you come back talking to 'er like that, there's plenty more where that come from.'

The girl was cursing and whimpering with pain.

'Look what you done, you little bitch!' her sister cried. ''Er nose is pouring!'

'Serves 'er right,' Mercy yelled as the boys watched in amazement. 'And so will yours be too if you don't clear off out of 'ere!'

'You vicious cow . . .!' They shouted over their shoulders as they slunk out of the yard.

'Blimey,' Johnny said.

'What's been going on?' Elsie emerged from the brewhouse.

'Mercy punched that girl in the kisser!' Tom cried enthusiastically.

'She called Susan a cripple,' Mercy said, rubbing her knuckles. 'And I'm not 'aving that.'

'I don't blame you,' Elsie said, gradually getting the picture.

Susan was all blushes. 'You didn't have to hit 'er that hard, did you?'

'Oh yes I did!' Mercy was still flaming. 'What does she know – she's never had bad legs, has she?'

The days were all right until Mabel got home, always foul-tempered. At first she'd found herself a job in a button factory, cutting metal blanks for buttons of different kinds. She complained bitterly about it. 'It's a right bind with my eyesight – I 'ave to practically put me nose in the machine. My 'ead's thumping terrible.' She carried on with it for a few weeks, growing even more demoralized and bad-tempered.

One night she came home and said, 'I've found you two a job an' all.' She emptied out the cloth bag on the table. Inside was a box containing what seemed an endless number of safety pins and a heap of small cards. 'There yer go – yer can earn yer keep. They want one of each size on a card and there's nine sizes. We get tuppence a gross for 'em. Yer might as well get started now.' She pushed the box towards Susan who did as she was told with her dextrous fingers. 'Plenty more where they come from, hooks and eyes, buttons, the lot.'

Every night, in common with many kids in the poor areas of the city, they sat carding, straining their eyes by gas or candlelight until their fingers were raw, while Mabel sat groaning that her head and eyes hurt.

Eventually she got a new job at the Anchor Bedstead Works in the packing department, but her temper didn't improve much and she took all her spite out on Mercy.

'This 'ouse looks like a pigsty,' would be her complaint almost before she was through the door.

'But I've been cleaning all day,' Mercy protested at first, quite tearful after all her efforts.

One day as Mabel came in with her 'This 'ouse looks like a pigsty,' complaint on her lips, Mercy rounded on her.

'That's 'cos it is a pigsty. So what's the use in saying it ain't?'

Mabel loomed before her, breasts heaving with fury. 'You saucy little bitch!'

Mercy saw Mabel's hand coming at her, ingrained with dirt. She gave Mercy a massive slap which knocked her to the floor.

Susan was shouting too, protesting, 'Mom – stop it!'

Mercy lay on her side, rubbing her stinging cheek. There were tears of pain in her eyes but in her fierce pride she wiped them away, determined not to let Mabel see them.

'You've just got me 'ere as your skivvy, and it ain't right,' she snarled. 'Elsie's kids are at school and that's where I should be – and Susan.'

'School?' Mabel narrowed her eyes and gave Mercy such a look of overpowering loathing that many another child would have cowered. 'Oh, you needn't think you're going off anywhere, my girl. What do workhouse brats like us ever need to go to school for, eh? I 'ad a bit of schooling – 'er father 'ad more than I did and look what became of 'im! Whatever yer do you'll end up in the factory so it makes no odds. I didn't bring another mouth to feed in 'ere for you to sit about all day. Yer 'ere to work for me, and work is what you're going to do. You'll do just whatever I say and that's that.'

Chapter Eight

'Quick, she's gone!'

Mercy was peering, terrified, after Mabel who had just disappeared to another day's work. When she was certain Mabel had really gone she tore along to the Peppers'. Tom and Johnny, now in their last year of school, were looking out for her.

'Get the chair from the brew'us!' They ran over, both of them in long trousers too big for them.

It had rained in the night and the yard stank. The twins clattered across with the wheelchair and Elsie came steaming out of her door, already in a state of nerves. She was having misgivings about this school lark. It didn't seem right deceiving Mrs Gherkin or whatever the hell her name was. She was the kids' mom – sort of anyway. And what if she was to find out? But one look at Mercy's set little face and Susan's mix of nerves and excitement as the twins swung her into the wheelchair made her swallow her doubts.

'Careful!' Susan laughed, and clung to their arms as she landed on the old bit of baize padding the seat.

Mercy was so edgy she couldn't keep still.

'It'll be awright, won't it, Mrs Pepper?' Her eyes radiated hope and anxiety. 'They will let us in?'

'Oh, I s'pect so. We'll just 'ave to see.' She wasn't at all sure about Susan. Plenty of children her age had left school already, and she hadn't even started yet! But she couldn't bring herself to say this to Mercy. Give them a chance, she thought, that's all.

She prodded Cathleen who seemed thoroughly clogged up with sleep.

'She don't look too good,' Susan said kindly.

'She always looks like that,' Johnny said, going to push the chair.

'No!' Mercy ran in front. 'I'm pushing Susan.'

Johnny shrugged. 'It'll be hard work.'

Mercy could feel the sun on her face as they got out of the dank yard where the sun only ever shone, if they were lucky, in the late afternoon.

'You awright?' she asked Susan, who nodded hard, too full up with everything to speak. There was the morning street coming to life, a horse snuffing in an empty nosebag at the side of the road, people coming and going. She could smell fresh bread mingled in with the factory smells and horse manure, hear the morning cries, cartwheels on the cobbles.

It was so exciting! And Mercy said that at school she'd learn new things. Find out how to read properly, not just spell out her letters with one finger on the table. Maybe she could be a bit more like the others!

Cathleen said goodbye and went off to work. Johnny and Jack ran back and forth in front of the wheelchair urging Mercy on, Tom walked rather protectively beside Mercy and Elsie came along behind, watching Mercy push on the chair with her slender weight, leg muscles straining. The sight of her wrung Elsie's heart. Her clothes were in a pathetic state: patched and worn, grubby and obviously too small. She'd grown more and more worried about Mercy, heard the shouts coming from Mabel's house, seen Mercy's bruises and cut lips. After all, a quick cuff or a smack when necessary was one thing. No one'd argue with that, but this was different.

'Does she belt you hard?' she'd asked some time ago. Mercy had simply said yes.

She'd tried having a go at the woman and was told to 'Bugger off and keep yer nose to yerself,' and variations on this. What else could she do? She saw now that the child was limping.

'What's up with your foot – boots worrying yer?'

'They're ever so tight,' Mercy said. She'd had no new ones since she'd been with Mabel and they were falling apart. She'd got paper stuffed in the sole to keep the wet out.

Elsie made a mental note to make sure, somehow, that Mercy got new boots. Otherwise the child would be barefoot the winter through. Asking her so-called mother would be a waste of time, the hard-faced bitch.

'Let Jack push Susan for a bit now,' she cajoled. 'You'll wear yourself out.'

'No. I'm doing it.' The reply wasn't rude, just resolute.

When they reached the enormous red-brick school, the boys called out 'Ta-ra!' and vanished into the boys' entrance at the far end, Johnny punching the air as he went.

'Ain't it big?' Susan said in a small voice.

Noisy groups of girls were arriving at the school, all staring at them. Mercy glowered back. What were they gawping at, nosey cows?

'Don't you go losing your temper,' Susan pleaded. 'I don't mind 'em looking. It does no harm.'

Elsie hesitated, even more nervous herself now. 'Wait 'ere. I'll try and get you sorted out.'

After what felt an age she appeared with a flustered

young teacher, austerely dressed in a grey skirt to the floor and a high-necked white blouse. She had a round, plain face.

'Well, that one's all right,' she said sharply, pointing at Mercy. 'But we can't possibly take the other one. This is a school for normal children. We can't have the likes of her here. There are special schools for that sort.'

Susan cringed, visibly flayed by the cruelty of the words.

Mercy gripped the bar of the chair, head held up defiantly. She felt as if someone had their hands tight round her throat.

'I'm not coming in if Susan can't come too,' she managed to say, huskily.

'Well!' The teacher's cheeks flushed a mottled pink. 'What a rude and unpleasant child. You can go somewhere else if that's your attitude. This is not a school for cripples – we couldn't even get that—' – she pointed to the unorthodox-looking chair – 'up the steps. Take it away!'

Although she meant the chair, her whole manner implied that 'it' meant Susan.

Elsie was usually full of respect for authority, but now it was her turn to speak out.

'What kind of a thing's that to say to the poor girl? Call yourself a teacher? You're s'posed to be 'ere to get some learning into their 'eads, not chase 'em away when they come begging for it!'

The teacher spoke in a low, icy voice. 'The fact remains, this is not a school for cripples. Now is this other child going to come in, before you waste my time any further?'

'No,' Mercy said. 'Not without Susan.'

'You don't make decisions at your age!' The teacher seemed set to hoik Mercy bodily up the steps. 'You're supposed to attend school. It doesn't matter about her!'

'You go, Mercy,' Susan said, trying to hide her terrible feelings of hurt. 'You can come 'ome and tell me all about it.'

Elsie Pepper found a lump aching in her throat at this brave show, at the care these kids had found for each other.

'Come on, Susan – we'll go 'ome.' To Mercy she said, 'Go on, bab. She can stop with me in the daytime. We'll be all right.'

'No!' Mercy stood helpless, fists clenched tightly as Susan and Elsie disappeared down the road, Susan craning round, trying to smile.

'Right then,' the teacher prodded her shoulder. 'Hurry up and get in.'

When Mercy and the boys arrived back in Angel Street that afternoon, Mercy was still seething with rage on Susan's behalf. She found her at the table in Elsie's house, chopping onions and carrots. Jack and Johnny grabbed chunks of carrot and ran off outside, and Tom sat down next to Susan.

''Ow d'yer get on then?' she asked Mercy in a bright voice.

'Awright,' Mercy spoke glumly, for she was tired, hungry and emotional. Although she was glad to be at school it had been a miserable day. It was a harsh environment, the rows of little sloping desks, the teacher's cane always there in the corner to remind you of her authority. But it was certainly no worse than life with Mabel, and at least she'd learn a thing or two instead of just being a drudge all day long.

'What've you been doing?' she asked Susan.

'Oh, giving Mrs Pepper a hand. She's been ever so good to me.'

'She patched my other skirt and she's done it beautiful, and now she's 'elping cook our dinner. She's a good pair of extra 'ands round the place.'

Neither of them was going to tell Mercy how Susan had sobbed her heart out when they got back to Angel Street, for so long that Elsie began to wonder how she'd ever console her.

'Now I can see why Mom never wants me to go out,' Susan gulped, cheeks soaked with tears. 'People're that cruel. I can't help how I am, can I?'

Elsie had had to concede that Mabel, while keeping her hidden too much from the world, had at least protected her from the kind of verbal abuse that had so shocked her this morning.

'There's still a lot you can do without school,' she tried to comfort her. 'In any case, it's a bit late to be starting at your age. But you can sew a bit, can't you, and 'ow about I teach you a bit of cooking?'

'Oh Mrs Pepper, you're so kind to us,' Susan sobbed.

She did cheer up and began to enjoy herself with Elsie. She kept little Rosalie occupied while Elsie struggled with yet another load of washing. It was good to be in a proper family, Elsie was in and out, chatting to her, and her married son Frank popped in for a cuppa and a moan about his wife. He was brown-haired like Tom, handsome in his copper's uniform, and he cracked jokes with her. Susan liked him.

'We've been keeping our eye on the neighbours too, 'ain't we, Mrs Pepper?' Susan laughed.

Mr Jones, with his greased back hair and little moustache, had been out in the yard that afternoon in his grubby trousers and singlet, muscles on parade, peering in a not especially subtle manner through the window of number two. He'd sidled back and forth several times, until they heard Mary Jones shouting out of number three amid the bawling of children, in a shrill, end-of-her-tether voice, 'Stan? What're you doing?' And he'd nipped back into his house right quick.

'And Mrs Jones and Mrs White had a fight over the mangle,' Susan chattered on. 'Mercy're you listening?'

'It's not fair!' Mercy exploded, the pent-up emotion of her day gushing out. She burst into tears. 'It's evil and wicked to say those things about Susan. And now she can't even go to school!'

'You know, Mercy,' Elsie consoled her, 'Susan could make a living sewing, she could, she's that nimble at it.'

But another problem was gnawing at Mercy too, now the excitement of getting out was wearing off.

'But 'ow'm I ever going to get anything done when I'm out all day?'

This was a real problem. However was she going to fit all the day's chores into a couple of hours so that Mabel wouldn't notice the difference?

'We'll do it.' Tom spoke up suddenly from where he was sharpening a knife against a whetting stone.

Elsie gaped. 'What – you and Johnny?'

''S'not fair is it?' Tom said. 'Why should she 'ave to do it all?'

He called Johnny and Jack in and after a moment of baffled reluctance they agreed.

Mercy stared from one to the other of them, overcome by such kindness, and started crying all over again.

It worked a treat for a while. Mercy, now easier in her mind about Susan, set off in the mornings with the Pepper boys, laughing and joking on their way. She adored their company.

'More than time that one got to be'ave like a youngster,' Elsie remarked to Mary Jones as the four left the yard one day, with their usual split-second timing, moments after Mabel. 'Only that one' – she jerked her thumb towards Mabel's house – 'ain't s'posed to know, so don't go letting on, will yer?'

'Oh no,' Mary replied meekly. She was a pale, skinny woman, completely intimidated by the energetic competence with which Elsie greeted every task when she could barely keep her head above water with her own family. ''Course I won't.'

Mercy came home tired, but ready to make up for all the housework. With the boys mucking in, it became a laugh as well as a chore as Tom, Johnny and Mercy darted about with brooms, rags and buckets of water, Jack rubbed ochre on the front step as if in a frenzy and Susan began cooking.

'They'll all make nice little wives for someone by the time you've finished!' Elsie teased Mercy. But in truth she was warmed to see such generous spirits in her sons.

Usually, by a huge effort, they'd completed most jobs before Mabel got in and the boys melted away as if they'd never been near the place. She always found something to criticize though: the floor wasn't dry or the dinner not ready.

'No use to no one, you ain't!' she'd rant at Mercy. 'Can't you get anything right?'

On these warm nights she'd insist on locking the door and Mercy bringing her water so she could half strip off and wash. Mercy felt horribly overfamiliar with Mabel's body, the fleshy upper arms and heavy breasts, the ripe smell of her filling the room. She always tried to look the other way.

*

One evening, Stan Jones, who seemed to be in and out of jobs as fast as a rabbit its burrow, was standing out on Angel Street by the entry to Nine Court, smoking, leaning against the wall in the balmy summer air. Idly, he watched the slow progress of a water cart as it dripped its way along the street.

In fact Stan Jones, who had the body of a bantamweight wrestler and the face of a petty thief, was not loafing about completely without purpose. He had two objectives: one was keeping out of the way of his missis so that she had to deal with the stormiest part of the day with four kids – four too many in his view. The other was running into Mabel.

Stan had had his eye on Mabel Gaskin for some time now. There she was, a woman on her own, with an earthy look and a body that Stan, at least in his mind, couldn't keep his hands off. And there was Mary his wife, scrawnier with each babby she suckled and always scared stiff of catching for another. And Stan had caught a peek of Mabel a week back, stripped to the waist downstairs. Oh, the thought of it! Breasts with enough stuffing in to hang heavy, not like Mary's little pinheads. Stan had worked himself up into a great state of anticipation about the 'widow woman' (Mabel's public version of why she was alone).

Mabel soon turned into the street, scowling to herself, lost in thought, carrying a bag. She'd called into the factory on the way home to fetch a new set of pins for carding.

'Evenin'!' Stan called.

It wasn't the first time Mabel had found him hanging around when she got home. She looked appreciatively at the bulging muscles on his arms. She knew a fine specimen of a man when she saw one. His lean face was smiling appealingly at her and in his eyes – there was no mistaking what she saw in those eyes. For the first time in a very long while, Mabel's mouth curved up in a smile.

'Shall I carry that for yer?' Stan indicated the bag, taking it from her with exaggerated effort as if it contained gold ingots.

'Ta very much,' Mabel tittered.

But then Stan said, 'See you've 'ad your little team on the go again – be awright when my lot're old enough for that!'

Mabel frowned. 'Team?'

'Oh, they'll've finished now.' Stan scratched under one hairy armpit with long, lazy strokes, the bag swinging to and fro. 'You've got 'em well trained doing that, soon as school's out.'

'Mine don't go to school,' Mabel said dismissively, looking full into Stan's eyes. It wasn't kids she wanted to be talking about. She was reluctant to move, was basking in the almost forgotten sensation of being lusted after.

'They do,' Stan corrected her. 'That yeller-haired chit any'ow – gone all day with them, she is.'

Mabel stared at him, the smile wiped from her face, and strode off to her house, slamming the door, leaving Stan holding a huge bag of loose safety pins.

Within minutes Mabel was giving Mercy her most violent beating yet.

She caught them so much by surprise, whipping out with, 'What's this about you going to school?' that they hadn't been prepared for brazening it out.

'So you'd deceive me, would you, you cunning little bitch?' Mercy tried to dodge the slaps that were raining down on her. Mabel caught her hard across the eye and she yelped in pain. 'You'd better not be taking Susan anywhere she shouldn't be or I'll be taking a match to that dustcart of a chair, that I will!'

'No—' Mercy lied feverishly, trying to put the table between herself and Mabel. She had a hand clasped to her watering eye. 'I haven't – honest!'

Mabel strode round and caught hold of the back of Mercy's old cotton frock. They both heard it rip. She yanked the girl round and started punching her, hard, on the chest and face.

'No – no, Mom, no!' Susan was shrieking hysterically, and for the first time ever, Mabel turned and slapped her hard round the head.

'Shut up, you useless little cow. You're just as bloody bad as she is.'

'Don't hit her!' Mercy screamed.

Both Mercy and Susan were crying with pain as Elsie appeared at the door, horrified by the sight in front of her. Mercy's face was bleeding and she was crumpled, weeping in pain, but Mabel was still hammering into her.

Mabel let go of Mercy and shoved Elsie out with the force of her weight and slammed the door so hard that the house rattled.

'Interfering, stuck up bitch!' she yelled, shooting the bolt across. Elsie, along with Stan Jones and the twins, moved to the window. Stan, impervious to Mercy's suffering gazed at Mabel's plump arms and her wide, love-handled hips.

'Bugger off!' Mabel bawled towards the window.

'You—' – she grabbed Mercy again as Susan sat whimpering and sobbing – 'can get down 'ere—' She opened the entrance to the coal-hole and shoved Mercy down on to the filthy slack-covered floor underneath the kitchen. Bolting it shut she shouted, 'Yer can come up when I'm ready and not before!' Mercy sank down on the gritty coal dust, beginning to sob with pain.

'And you lot—' – she heard Mabel shouting out of the window – 'can all mind yer own cowing business.'

'I'll report you,' Elsie shouted. 'Yer not fit to be near children!'

'Oh yes. Report me? Who to?' Mabel bawled. 'Even if there was anyone, who'd listen to you – slummy trollop, breeding like a bloody rabbit!'

Late one afternoon a couple of weeks later a woman appeared, wearing a smart dark uniform, a coat and felt hat with a narrow brim and low-heeled, well polished shoes.

She walked uncertainly across the yard, looking at the house numbers.

Elsie came out of the brewhouse immediately, pointing.

'Who the 'eck's that then?' Mabel peered out of the window. 'Eh – you . . .' Mercy heard the panic in her voice. 'Get upstairs, quick!'

'Why? I'm doing . . .'

'Don't argue with me – get up there, now!'

As she ran upstairs Mercy heard knocking at the front door. She waited, listening, at the top.

The woman was well-spoken, her voice smooth as cream.

'Mrs Gaskell?'

'Gaskin.'

'Oh, I'm sorry. I'm from the NSPCC.' Rather uncomfortably she explained the meaning of the initials to Mabel. 'I wonder if I might see your little girl? I've had a complaint through one of our welfare officers.'

'She's 'ere, as yer can see,' Mabel said unctuously.

'Hello,' Mercy heard the woman say to Susan. 'And how are you, my dear?'

'She's lying.' Elsie was standing at the door. 'There's another girl, she's the one. 'I s'pect she's locked down the coal 'ole or summat. That's one of 'er favourite tricks. She can take 'em off of you, yer know,' she sneered at Mabel.

Hearing this, Mercy's hand went to her mouth. She was so frightened she felt as if her muscles had tied themselves in knots. Who was this woman? Was she from the home, come to take her away again?

'There is another child lodging with me,' Mabel admitted. 'But she ain't 'ere just now.'

'Oh yes she is,' Elsie raised her voice. 'She's 'ere awright.'

'Perhaps you'd like to leave us now, thank you?' The NSPCC woman said. Mercy heard the door closing, then the woman's voice, sharper in tone. 'How old is the child in question?'

'Er – twelve,' Mabel said.

'Oh – I was given to believe she was a lot younger. Still, I'm afraid I've come rather a long way, and if you can't present the girl to me I shall be obliged to search the house to make sure she's really not here.'

Mercy shrank, trembling, into the bedroom. What if this woman saw the bruises, her swollen lip, the half healed graze on her forehead where Mabel had knocked her into the wall? Would they take her to a home, or worse still, the workhouse? She might never see Susan or Elsie again!

'Mercy!' Mabel called up to her in a silken voice. 'Can you come down 'ere a minute, Mercy love?'

She wiped her face frantically on her skirt and walked down on unsteady legs, trying to pull her hair forward to hide her face. Immediately she saw the woman's shrewd eyes appraising her.

'Hello, my dear,' she said again. 'So your name's Mercy?'

Mercy nodded, mute with fear. Susan was at the table, watching her with desperate pleading in her eyes.

'So you live with Mrs Gaskin?'

'Yes.' Mercy turned wide eyes towards Mabel. 'She's my auntie.'

'My sister's child,' Mabel added quickly. 'It were tragic really – she died when Mercy was only a titty-babby so I took 'er in. She's been like me own ever since.'

The NSPCC woman looked sceptically at Mercy's skinny frame, her filthy, threadbare dress, her bare feet, the marks on her face.

'And how are you, Mercy?'

Mabel was looking daggers at her.

'I'm awright, ta – er, thank you.' Her voice was hardly more than a whisper.

'There's no need to be afraid. Are you getting enough to eat?'

'Yes.' This at least was almost true. One thing Mabel was good at was managing with food.

'Come over to the light, child.'

By the window she put her fingers under Mercy's chin and tilted her head back. 'How did you hurt your face like that?'

'I fell over and grazed me 'ead. And there was this girl at school hit me like. We got into a fight.'

The woman released her face. 'And does Mrs Gaskin ever hit you?'

Mercy shook her head. 'No – least, not much. Only, you know, like a mom. She's bin very good to me, taking me in and that.'

For the first time the officer smiled. 'Bright little thing you've got here.'

'Oh yes, she's a good 'un,' Mabel agreed, nodding like a mad horse.

'And where d'you go to school, Mercy?'

Mercy's eyes met Mabel's for a second. Mabel had strictly forbidden Mercy to go to school, out of pure spite since she got the chores done anyway.

'Down Alcester Street.'

'And do you get on well there?'

'Oh yes. It's very nice.'

'It's just a pity about some of the neighbours round 'ere,' Mabel was saying in her poshest voice. 'Where I used to live in Handsworth, you got a better class of person. But 'ere . . .' She rolled her eyes. 'Lord knows what 'er out there's been telling yer, but it's a pack of lies. We're quite 'appy us, aren't we, Mercy? We're a family, and we stick together.'

Mabel showed the woman out at last, all smiles, as if she quite believed the fairy tale she'd been spinning.

'Well, we soon got shot of 'er,' she said. Then turned and saw the granite hard expression on Mercy's face.

'I'm a good little liar, ain't I? D'you know why I lied for you? Because of Susan. I don't care what happens to you. If she took you away and put you in prison I'd be the happiest person alive. But whatever you do I'll never leave Susan. I did tell 'er one true thing though – that I go to school. And if you don't let me go, and if you don't treat us right from now on I'll get her back and tell her what sort of a mom you really are!'

Chapter Nine

November 1913

'You're vile and disgusting – the pair of yer!'

Elsie, sleeves rolled, was gathering in washing from the line slung across the yard, an expression of fury and revulsion in her blue eyes.

Stan Jones, still fastening the last of his fly buttons was swaggering along the yard from the privy at the far end on his way to his Saturday evening rendezvous with Mabel. Cocky as ever, he spat out the cigarette stub from the corner of his mouth and crushed it with his heel, smirking at Elsie.

'Just mind yer own, eh? If you was getting a bit more of it you wouldn't need to stick yer nose in everyone else's business, would yer?'

'What about that wife of yours?' But Elsie was shouting at an empty space. Mabel had left the door unlocked and ready for him.

'Where are yer then, yer great big beautiful hussy?' Stan blared up the stairs in high spirits, not caring who heard. He knew Mabel would be waiting. She always was. She'd undressed, putting on her newest pair of bloomers and a camisole which pulled tightly across her breasts, and was lying on her bed in the dreary room with her hair hanging loose and what she hoped was a seductive smile on her face.

Stan made a loud noise of appreciation on seeing her, hand going straight back to his belt buckle.

He stopped. 'You 'ave got shot of them two?'

Mabel gave a girlish giggle. 'Packed 'em off into town. What about 'er?'

This was ritual, questions they always asked.

'She won't be back from 'er mom's for a good while yet.'

Stan leant over and pulled up Mabel's camisole. She squirmed with pleasure, flexing her back as his hands moved over her breasts. Getting a bit of life for herself she was, at last. Stan's loud and urgent arousal was very gratifying, especially as he got no joy with that miserable scarecrow of a wife of his. And maybe – though she'd never mention this to Stan – maybe she'd catch for a babby. Things could get better. Maybe Albert had been her curse?

Stan ran his hands up and down her flesh, forcing her like sweet dough, eyes narrowing.

'You're a real woman, Mabel. By God you are.'

Now it suited Mabel to have the house to herself she'd relaxed her strictures about Susan going out. Every Saturday, late in the afternoon, Mercy pushed her into town.

'It's the best bit of the week!' Susan said many times. Being out of the gloomy confines of their yard in Mercy's company and going to see all the shops and market stalls – heaven! And Mercy enjoyed it too, hunting for bargains and seeing all the sights. She was canny with money and Mabel, lazy as she was, had long trusted her to do the shopping. It was hard work on the way home though, pushing the chair and the bags back. The middle of

Birmingham was like the dip in the middle of a saucer, hills all around.

'Thank heaven Mr Pepper's put some new wheels on 'ere,' Mercy said as they bowled along the backstreets. 'The other ones was on their last legs.'

'Let me ask for the meat this time,' Susan said. She loved being out, learning to shop, use money, all the things she had never been allowed to do. Mercy felt very sad for her sometimes. She demanded so little of life, Susan did, while Mercy was restless and hungry for it.

She pushed Susan to Jamaica Row first, round the back of Smithfield Market where were sold a great variety of livestock, feed, straw . . . At the meat market Susan shouted out for 'a bag of cagmag, please, and proudly held out the coins from Mabel's little pouch of hard-earned money as the red-faced butcher swung over a bag of the cheapest off-cuts of meat.

'We'll get a rabbit later.' Mercy had to yell over all the racket of the carts clattering and shouting voices of this bustling area. 'When they're selling stuff off cheap.'

The Bull Ring was also full of its usual activity.

'Ooh,' Susan called out as Mercy slowly manouevred her through the crowds and past St Martin's Church. 'Can yer smell that?'

There was a delicious aroma of meat roasting in Whiteheads' cook-shop just opposite the church. Mercy felt saliva gush into her mouth. They were used to the fact that whenever they ate they were left wanting more, but she was ravenous now after the exertion of pushing Susan along.

'Let's 'ave some,' she said. 'A penny dipper – on the way 'ome.'

'We can't – she'll kill us!'

'She won't – you know what she's like Sat'dy nights nowadays.'

Poor Susan had grown used to balancing loyalties between Mercy and her mom, but she knew Mercy was right about this. The girls were completely ignorant about what Mabel got up to with Stan Jones. All they knew was that when they got back on Saturday nights, they found Mabel sated and mellow and not in the mood for a fight.

They meandered along to the market stalls, low sunlight slanting between the tarpaulins, amid the cries of the stallholders.

They bought onions from a lad not much older than them who winked as he tipped them into their bag.

''Aving a nice stew, are yer? You'll want some swede as well – lovely swede, we got today.'

'I can't abide swede,' Mercy said. 'Give us a pound o' carrots instead, eh?'

With Susan holding the meat and veg on her lap they moved along Spiceal Street.

'Oh look!' Mercy cried, stopping outside a shop. 'I wish I could get some of them for Johnny.'

The shop, Green's, sold all sorts of leather goods. There were piles of trunks outside and hanging in the window were footballs, wallets and beautiful, sleek pairs of boxing gloves. 'Wouldn't 'e love them – and those footballs for Jack!'

Johnny and Tom were both out at work now, Tom the more studious of the two, apprenticed to Stern's, the silversmiths, Johnny a delivery boy for a bakery. And Bummy had decided that now he'd come of age he could go along to the boxing with him.

The prices in the shop were way beyond anything they could imagine.

'Someone somewhere must 'ave some money,' Susan said. 'Why do some people 'ave money, Mercy, when the likes of us 'ave hardly any?'

Mercy shrugged, walking on. 'S'pose they own the factories and shops. That's just the way it is.'

Susan was growing despondent. She eyed a shop selling bolts of cloth and sighed, wishing so hard that she could do something better. Really learn to sew properly, make things. She had been doing odd bits of mending for people under Elsie's guidance and word was beginning to spread round the street, but she still had only the most basic needles and threads. She never normally complained, but suddenly she saw their poverty for what it was for the first time.

'Blimey, what a racket!' Mercy stopped again.

This shop sold pets, and outside stood cages with African grey parrots, cockatiels, budgerigars and finches making such a noise that Mercy laughed.

But Susan remained quiet. Mercy stooped and looked into her face. 'What's up with you?'

'I'll never do anything me, will I? I'll always be just an 'opeless cripple.'

Susan hardly ever talked like this. Mercy took her hands and spoke fiercely into her ear.

'You won't, Susan. Not long now and I'll be out at work – we'll 'ave two wages coming in.' Even with Mabel's pay, the carding and the few pennies Susan received for her mending, there was barely enough to pay the rent and eat, let alone keep them even adequately clothed.

'I swear to you, Susan, soon as I get some money of my own you'll 'ave everything you need. I'll set you up so you can always earn a living no matter what happens to the rest of us.' Susan was smiling and starting to cry all at the same time.

'I'll always look after you, Susan. And you know what else? I'll get you one of these birds and you can teach it to talk to you!'

Susan wiped her eyes and, as Mercy straightened up, someone tapped her shoulder and she turned, frowning. For a moment she couldn't think who it was, then the frown melted into an overjoyed smile. 'Dorothy! Dorothy Finch!'

To Mercy's surprise, Dorothy's dark eyes were brimming with emotion. 'Mercy? It is you, isn't it?' Her hand lifted to her mouth for a moment and she stood staring, seeming overwhelmed.

Mercy introduced Susan to Dorothy, but Dorothy, wiping her eyes, barely seemed to hear her.

'Look at you – you've grown!'

Mercy saw Dorothy examining her hungrily, taking in the state of her ragged clothes, the worn-out boots of Jack's that Elsie had handed on to her and her pallid, slum-dweller's skin, and her anger spilled out.

'She 'ad no right to do it, Mercy, that woman, taking you from Hanley's like that and hiding you away so none of us knew where you'd gone. Miss Rowney was – well, she was upset like.' This was a slight exaggeration of the truth and Miss O'Donnell's reaction had been 'Good riddance. She came from the streets and now she's gone back to 'em.'

Mercy's eyes widened with fear. An awful dread seized her.

'I don't want to go back,' she gabbled. 'I can't go back there – I want to stay 'ere, with Susan. I'm never leaving 'er!'

Dorothy smiled, remembering Mercy's devotion to little Amy Laski.

'I don't work at Hanley's no more. I went back after – into service, I mean. Listen Mercy, where're you living?'

'Nine Court, Angel Street. Behind St Joseph's.'

Dorothy nodded. It was a poor, run-down area of the sort she knew well, having grown up on a back yard herself. No wonder the child looked so ragged and pasty-faced.

'And what about that woman? She treat you all right?'

Mercy's expression of utter loathing spoke more than words could have done. 'She's awright,' was all she said. At least the beatings had mostly stopped.

'Look, I've got to get back to the mistress. But I'll come and see you, soon as I can.' Tearful again she held Mercy tight in her arms. She seemed reluctant to let her go.

Feeling choked herself Mercy said, 'It's really lovely to see you again, Dorothy. I never got time to say goodbye to you.'

She watched Dorothy's familiar, straight-backed figure move away into the crowd. Dorothy turned more than once and waved her hanky.

'Ever so good to me, she was,' Mercy said, her throat aching. She remembered the red jelly Dorothy had brought her in the cellar and felt as if she were watching her only family walk away.

'She looks a nice, kind lady,' Susan said, a wistful note still in her voice.

'Come on—' Mercy rallied herself to cheer Susan. 'Let's go and see what's going on up New Street, shall we?'

*

Dorothy Finch returned to her employer's house in an elegant street in Handsworth, in a state of turmoil.

As soon as she'd caught sight of Mercy's bright hair in the Bull Ring she'd been certain this was the child she'd lost sight of two years before. The child she had watched so carefully and fondly from infancy.

She went straight to the large sitting room at the front of the house where she found her mistress, Mrs Neville Weston, sitting with the nanny and the two small Weston boys. Robert, a sturdy dark-haired five-year-old, had the florid complexion of his father and Edward, three, was slender, fair and fragile in looks.

Grace Weston looked up, bewildered to see her maid appearing at this time, for this was her afternoon off.

'Could I have a word with you, ma'am, in private?'

Grace eyed the nanny and children, and there was something about the breathless catch in her maid's voice which hastened her to say, 'Would you please take them up and run a bath now?' The boys began a whining protest at the nanny's attempts to hustle them away. Grace went with them to the hall and stood beside the polished bannister smiling up at them. 'I'll come and see you in just a little while. We'll have a story – as a special treat.'

There was still a smile in her eyes as she came in and closed the door.

As soon as they were alone Dorothy began to sob, the pent-up emotions of relief, guilt and sorrow pouring out.

'Whatever's happened?' Grace moved to her straight away, putting her arms round her, her fair head close to Dorothy's dark one. For these women were much more than employer and servant. They had been a close support and bearer of each other's confidences for some years.

Dorothy turned her head at last and looked fearfully

into Grace's pale eyes. She saw anguish seize her mistress's face as she said, 'I saw her – today, when I was in town. I've found her. I've found Mercy.'

Not many afternoons later, Dorothy arrived in Angel Street bringing with her two dresses, one in yellow lawn, the other in soft blue wool, and a pair of boots that she hoped would fit Mercy.

Seeing both her and her gifts, Mercy blushed with pleasure and danced overjoyed round the room with the yellow dress held against her. 'Oh Dorothy, I've never seen anything so pretty before!'

'And this one will be lovely for Susan – look.' She laid the blue frock against Susan, and Dorothy saw the child beam with delight. She'd been about to protest that both dresses were for Mercy, but she kept quiet. Let the other poor kid have one. The dress she had on now was a terrible grey bag of a thing.

'You didn't buy these did you?' Mercy asked anxiously.

'No – the mistress, my employer – she's got older daughters with lots of lovely clothes . . .' She and Grace had worked on this harmless lie together. They were in fact hand-me-downs from the daughters of friends. 'She said I could hand them on to someone who needed them.'

'She's very kind,' Mercy said, trying to imagine such wealth and benevolence.

'You going to make 'er some tea?' Susan asked timidly. She was rather in awe of Dorothy who, although only a servant, seemed to have appeared from a completely different existence where people still had dresses that looked new when they'd finished with them.

Mercy ran out to the tap to fill the kettle. They

talked all afternoon. Mercy could barely keep still in her excitement at having Dorothy there. She told her cautiously about her life in Angel Street, playing on the positive side for Susan's sake. She talked about school, the Peppers, Elsie's kindness.

'Johnny and Tom, the twins, they're my best pals – well, after Susan! And there's little Rosalie, she's nearly five now . . .'

Dorothy listened, trying to keep all her attention on Mercy's face, but she couldn't help her gaze wandering, taking in the rotten state of the place: furniture supplemented with orange crates, the broken floor, and the mean, loathsome smells of damp and mould which she found unspeakably depressing. The more so because it brought back memories of her own childhood. Going into service at fourteen had been her salvation and she was grateful for it daily.

Preparing to leave after their chat she said, 'Let me know if there's anything you need, Mercy. And you, Susan,' she added kindly.

She was moving to embrace Mercy when Mabel came barging in from work.

'I see no one's bothered scrubbing the step.' She was carrying on before she'd even got in. 'Oi – what's going on?' Mercy heard panic in her voice. 'Who're you?'

Mercy stepped forward and said proudly, 'This is Dorothy.'

'Oh yes – Dorothy who?' Mabel's tone was brazen but wary, her arms crossed defensively. She and Dorothy were eyeing each other up with instant mutual distrust.

'She looked after me in the home.'

'What's that rubbish you're talking?' Mabel blustered. What with the NSPCC turning up on her doorstep and now this, Mabel was beginning to feel quite persecuted.

'You're a born liar, aren't you?' Dorothy said, disgusted. 'It were only two years ago, not a lifetime. D'you think I wouldn't be able to remember what someone looks like? Lucky for you she wants to stay here at the moment or I could make trouble for you. But I'll be keeping an eye on Mercy from now on, and don't you forget it.'

Chapter Ten

February 1914

'I've got it – 'e give me the job!'

Mercy tore into Elsie's house to tell Susan. Thanks to Johnny Pepper she had her first job at the bakery in Digbeth where he was employed as a delivery boy.

'Well there you are,' Elsie smiled. She was fixing up her escaping coils of rusty hair. 'You're a worker. You'll get on, you will.'

''Course you got it,' Susan beamed. 'I said you would, didn' I?'

'I might be in with a chance of the odd loaf or bag of stale cakes, you never know!' Mercy was laughing partly with relief as she went to stand behind Susan. It had been her first shot at getting a job and she'd been nervous. 'Hey,' she said. 'That's beautiful, that is!'

Over Susan's shoulder she could see the neat job she was doing mending the astrakhan collar on an overcoat. She was good at it – and not just hand sewing either. Just after Christmas which had been drab and bleak, a miracle had happened.

Mrs White, the miserable, reclusive woman in the cottage across the yard, had dropped dead, aged fifty-seven. Mr White put it all down to nerves. Shortly after, looking a good deal more cheerful than, as Elsie put it, ''e 'ad a right to,' he started carrying a whole load of stuff out into the yard.

'I could cart it off and flog it,' he said, unshaven but chirpy. 'But I thought if any of yer'd give us a bob for anything . . .'

With an absolute lack of sentiment he laid out Mrs White's small selection of clothes over a couple of battered chairs.

'Oh my word,' Mary Jones exclaimed to Elsie. ''E's even brought 'er drawers out. Well I wouldn't be . . .' She trailed off.

'What? Seen dead in 'em? Don't suppose she 'ad that in mind either. Depends 'ow fussy you can afford to be, don't it?' Elsie looked thoughtful. 'Be different if she'd been the least bit pleasant some'ow, wouldn't it?'

There was a small, oblong mirror, a threadbare old coat and Mrs White's few personal bits and bobs: hairpins, a brush, corset, a doll with a chipped porcelain face, old shoes with bunion-shaped hills in them, spectacles. And – Mercy caught her breath – almost seeming to glow in the knife-edged cold as it sat on its wrought iron base across the yard: an old Singer sewing machine. She galloped across.

''Ow much d'you want for that?' Never mind whether it worked. They'd make it work.

'Well 'ow much can yer give me?' Mr White seemed in a celebratory mood.

''E must be as short as anything – no wage or nothing coming in,' Mercy said to Susan after. ''E just didn't seem to care.'

Susan shrugged. 'Looks as if the only thing 'e really wanted shot of's already gone.'

They gave him five shillings for the machine. Mabel stared at it as if it were about to lay a golden egg. Bummy Pepper gave it a clean up and oiled it, humming to himself.

They bought a new needle and spools and Susan was in business. Well almost.

Gradually, by word of mouth, she was getting odd bits of work. When Dorothy came round Mercy showed her Susan's neat skills.

'I'm sure Mrs Weston – my mistress – will know people who need a seamstress,' Dorothy said. 'I'll see what I can do.'

The jobs had already begun to trickle in. Susan was happier than Mercy had ever seen her. Her usually tiny appetite had picked up, she had a pink tinge in her cheeks and an air of purpose.

'I'm so lucky, aren't I, Mrs Pepper?' she said to Elsie one day. And Elsie's tired face lifted into a smile. If someone in Susan's state felt lucky, she was a lesson to all of them.

'Now you've got two earners in your 'ouse,' she said to Mercy. 'Mabel'll be stopping to put 'er feet up.'

When Mercy had been at work for a few weeks she came home carrying a cage in which there was a grey parrot with lead-shot eyes.

''Ere you are, as promised.' She put the cage on the table. 'It was a lark bringing this 'ome on the bus, I can tell yer!'

Mabel would be outraged with her for squandering money in this way but Mercy didn't care.

Susan gasped at the sight of it.

'He's lovely! Is it a boy one?'

'The bloke said so. What're you going to call 'im?' Susan put her head on one side. The parrot did the same and Susan, Mercy and Elsie roared with laughter.

'George,' Susan said, wiping her eyes. ''E looks like a George to me.'

One Saturday evening soon after, Mabel was waiting for Stan again. This time she wasn't in bed but sitting downstairs at the stained table sipping strong tea with plenty of sugar and cursing George who was scratching round the bottom of the cage screeching to himself.

'I'd find a recipe for parrot pie if I 'ad my way,' she growled at him. 'Noisy, stinking thing.'

She soon heard the latch go and there was Stan, dressed only in a singlet and braces with his trousers although it was so cold you could see your breath even in the house.

'What's all this?' All these months she'd been upstairs waiting for him, and here she was fully dressed without even a promising bit of breast showing.

'Shut the door, Stan, I've summat to talk to yer about.'

He kicked the door shut and went to stand by the range, slicking his hair back. Not being very observant, he didn't notice Mabel's excited expression.

'What's up – eh? We gunna go and get on with it in a tick?' He jerked his head meaningfully towards the stairs.

Mabel started to smile, showing her big, gappy teeth. 'It's happened, Stan. It had to in the end, didn't it? I'm carrying your babby.'

Stan's face fell into a study of shock.

'But, Mabel, I thought – I mean we've been at it a long time now. I thought you couldn't no longer – not like Mary . . .'

Mabel had in a roundabout way led Stan to believe she couldn't conceive again, and as the months passed she'd come close to convincing herself as well. All this time and nothing. But now . . . Now she had a chance of hooking herself a breadwinner at last and another babby into the bargain! This time she'd have a proper child. Someone to love her. She'd prove she could be a mother like anyone else. She stood up and went to nuzzle her face against Stan's chest, slipping one arm round him, she unfastened her blouse with the other to show her generous cleavage.

'Say you're pleased, Stan?' she wheedled. 'Your babby. You and me. We can 'ave a fresh start now – get away from all our worries. You can get away from her.'

'Are you mad, woman?' Stan pushed her away, agitatedly pulled his fags out. He lit one and stood puffing away, tapping his thigh with his other hand with quick, taut movements.

'I've already got four kids. You told me, Mabel—' He pointed the cigarette like a gun in her crumpling face. 'You lied to me, you did . . .'

Stan's brain never worked quickly at the best of times and it was on overtime shift now. He'd never questioned Mabel's version of her infertility since his only interest was in getting his leg over. Now she was really putting the wind up him and he couldn't think fast enough what to do.

'I don't know why you're laying the blame on me any'ow, you're that easy. 'Ow do I know who else you've been with?'

He used his indignation to propel himself out of the house. Then he stuck his head back through the door.

'And don't you come laying the blame on me and upsetting my missis. She's got enough on 'er plate as it is!'

When Mercy and Susan got home that evening, depositing bags of scrag-end, potatoes and greens on the table with a pound of sausage, bags of broken biscuits and bruised apples, Mabel was upstairs in her room. Good, Mercy thought, that's her out of the way.

'Mom?' Susan called up to her.

No reply. The two of them listened.

'She's blarting,' Susan said, amazed.

'What on earth can've happened?' Mercy was frowning.

Mabel wasn't a weeper, normally speaking, but today she wasn't taking any trouble to hide her sniffles and mewling noises. She'd really and truly believed Stan would drop everything for her. After all, he did nothing but complain about Mary. But now it was she, Mabel, who was being thrown aside like an old piece of scrap. Just when she thought it might be her turn for some luck for once in life! She was carrying another babby with no husband, precious little money and only that little cow Mercy to help her. Let alone what she'd get in the way of clever comments from smug-faced Elsie Pepper. No – she got up hurriedly off the sordid bed. She wasn't having that. There was only one thing for it.

A few moments later she came heavily downstairs, blowsy and dishevelled-looking. The two girls turned wide eyes on her, the blotchy cheeks and swollen eyes obvious even in the gaslight.

'Mom.' Susan looked away, her cheeks turning pink. 'Your blouse . . .'

'Oh, ah—' Mabel fumblingly buttoned herself back into it. 'I've come to a decision. We've got to move.'

'Move?' Susan said, bewildered. Mercy listened in disbelief.

'Yes, move,' Mabel snapped. 'To another 'ouse. Another part of town, away from 'ere. If yer must know,

I'm expecting Stan Jones's babby and I don't want to bring it into the world around the likes of this lot.'

After a couple of days in which Mabel's house was full of nothing but rows on this subject, Stan's brain caught up with his body and he did some (for him) quick thinking. Here he was, still a young man, struggling, with no real skills to get a decent job, a frail and prematurely aged wife and four brats all trapped together in a rotting house. He was drowning in the difficulties of it, could feel his youth and strength being sucked from him. Didn't he deserve another chance?

And Mabel was offering it – a strong woman, older than him, capable of working. One kid – she wasn't bringing that cripple with her, oh no. They could avoid having any more. And she was a bit of all right in bed, Mabel was – that was the main thing about her.

On the third morning, after retching over the scullery sink, Mabel left for work with a bag and never came home in the evening. Susan was worried to death until they discovered that Stan had disappeared too and suddenly it was clear as anything what had happened.

'I knew she was a scheming, worthless liar,' Elsie raged to Bummy that night. 'But I never thought she'd go and desert that kid of 'ers. And as for poor Mary . . .'

The two of them, and Mercy, spent that evening trying to comfort first Susan – 'How could she go and leave us?' she sobbed, hurt to the very core. 'She's my Mom! And to go with that idiot of a bloke . . .' and then Mary Jones, who was almost hysterical with panic.

'How'm I going to manage? We can barely afford to eat as it is! How could 'e? If I ever see 'im again – or 'er

– I'll kill the pair of 'em with my bare hands.' Her youngest child lay suckling at her tiny breast as she sat sobbing and sniffing. 'Oh Elsie, what in heaven am I going to do? I'll have to move back in with me mom in 'er one room – we'll be in the workhouse else!'

'No.' Elsie's jaw was set and determined. 'You won't have to do that, I'll see to it.'

Bummy, stood in the doorway, hoiked his trousers up from behind with one hand and nodded in agreement. 'Terrible that is, the Parish. D'you remember?'

Elsie nodded curtly. Of course she remembered. The time when they had five young ones, Maryann, Frank, Josephine, Cathleen and Lena, the one they'd lost soon after from diphtheria. Bummy had injured his back so badly that for weeks, months, he couldn't work. He'd lain helpless, watching his vibrant, copper-haired wife exhaust herself.

Finally Elsie went to the local Board of Guardians, timidly asking for help. She was given a weekly allowance of bread but she would never forget the terror and humiliation of it, the rude personal questions, the hard, mistrusting eyes of the people on the board. It was such a degrading time in her life, a reminder of the power others could have over her. Even now she felt panic and disgust thinking of it.

As Bummy had recovered with agonizing slowness, Elsie vowed she would never let herself or anyone else she could save from it have to put themselves at the mercy of the Parish again.

She leant over and took Mary's hand.

'Don't fret. I've got Johnny and Tom out at work now as well as the girls. And there's Mercy and Susan, though God knows they've got the rent to keep up on their own now. But we'll all rally round – I'll make sure of that.

If Elsie said they were going to give help to Mary, then Mercy and Susan were going to do as she said.

'We ought to,' Susan said. 'After all, it's my mom who's caused her all this trouble.'

'The one thing she's good at,' Mercy retorted.

Susan was now earning rather well. Mercy had gone round for her putting cards in shop windows, and she found new customers. Sewing for the poor brought in a very small trickle of money, but far more lucrative was the trade from Dorothy. The clothes she bought for Susan to mend were of much higher quality, sometimes they were awed by the sight of them. Dorothy made sure she was handsomely paid. One week Susan made as much as twelve shillings!

Her confidence was growing and her customers were happy too.

'Imagine if they could see where their clothes are going!' Dorothy said to Grace, holding up a cream satin evening gown with lace straps and underskirt. Its owner wanted it taken in over the hips.

Grace was barely listening. They were standing in the small dressing room which extended off Grace and Neville Weston's comfortable bedchamber. Grace seemed to stare through Dorothy, her expression troubled.

'What is it?' Dorothy asked gently.

Grace looked into her eyes. 'I can't bear it, thinking of her there, in that terrible place!'

If her life had proceeded as her stern, fiercely religious father had planned, Grace's only awareness of the conditions of the slum courtyards, the raucous life of the poor, would have been no more than snatched glimpses as she swept past in a carriage to the centre of Birmingham. The life Mercy was leading, the struggles against poverty and squalor, would have been so distant from her as to be unimaginable.

She could hardly bear to think of her desperate time as 'Lily'. It was an abyss in her experience, those days which had denied her her name, her class, her normally comfortable life, her very sense of self. She had for a short time lived and been part of that other alien life in the wilderness. She recalled even now in her dreams the damp, bug-ridden walls, the fetid smells, the awful sense of enforced intimacy with others. And the terror of that lonely birth. Its memory was all the more horrific in its contrast with her other life. As soon as she could stand after the birth she had fled from it, imagining it would then be over, something she could close the door on as soon as she walked away from the Joseph Hanley Home.

Yet she had not forseen its consequences, that she would never escape the hold those memories had on her, or the tiny child she had brought forth.

'It's worse now!' Her voice cracked. 'Now we've found her – knowing where she is again. At least while she was lost to us we knew nothing, and could do nothing, except hope. And she's older now . . . I find this present situation . . .'

She turned away, gliding into her bedchamber, a lace handkerchief pressed to her face as her shoulders heaved.

'It's unbearable!' Dorothy heard her voice, barely more than a whisper. She saw Grace struggle to compose herself, as she had done so many times over the years, hearing about Mercy when she was at the Hanley Home. She bent her immaculately coiffured head, two golden plaits coiled low behind her ears.

'Dorothy—' She turned, eyes full of tears, appealing to her friend across the white linen of the bed. 'I don't know if I can endure it any more.'

Dorothy went to her quickly, putting her hands on Grace's shoulders. 'Of course you can, Grace, my dear one – you can. You have to be strong for the boys, and you've been so brave until now. The child's a beauty – the image of you. She's fourteen now. If you can just be sure of that position for her ... Just keep yourself together. Good can come of all this, I'm sure of it.'

There was a pause, and both women heard footsteps. Grace pulled her expression into one approaching composure. 'You'd better go. Neville's coming up to change.'

As she spoke, the door opened abruptly.

'Oh – you're here again, are you?' Neville said to Dorothy, pushing past her into the room.

Grace's eyes met Dorothy's, urgently entreating her to leave. Dorothy slipped quietly from the room.

'Forever hanging about, that one, isn't she?' Neville was full of irritation. He sat on the bed pulling his boots off. 'Gets on my nerves.'

'I'm sorry, dear.' Grace spoke in a quiet, even voice, unfastening her hair in front of the mirror. 'I wasn't expecting you up quite so soon. Did you have a pleasant day?' Weston's was Neville's family firm, providing lighting for the railways.

'Pleasant? You think work is pleasant, do you?' He watched his wife from behind, the gentle curve of her hips, that eternal smooth neatness of hers. By God, how he hungered for a woman with hot blood in her veins!

Seeing him watching her in the glass, Grace turned and

attempted a bright smile. Neville ignored her, got up and stumped into the dressing room.

Downstairs, Dorothy thought of the two of them up there, her mouth pulled down in a hard grimace. She had always loathed Neville, had a flesh-creeping distaste for his stocky body, red cheeks and thick brown hair which sat on top of his head with the unsettled look of a wig. Add to that his selfishness and boorishness and Dorothy burned with protective indignation on Grace's behalf, trapped as she was in her life with this ox of a man.

Grace tried to keep up at least the appearance of a civilized marriage, if not a happy one.

'Never mind,' she had said to Dorothy on many occasions. 'I have all I need. I have you and I have my children.

Chapter Eleven

If it hadn't been for Susan's pain over her desertion by her mother, Mercy would have been almost completely happy. She was free of Mabel, could organize the place how she wanted and had kind neighbours. There were Dorothy's visits, every week or two and Mercy had begun to feel she belonged somewhere. No one had set eyes on Mabel or Stan.

Between them, she and Susan were at last making the inside of the house more homely. Mabel, in a perverse way, had refused even to have the rotten stair tread mended, something she and Mercy were constantly having rows about.

'Mr Pepper could fix that soon as winking,' Mercy kept saying. 'I'm fed up with nearly falling through it all the time.'

'We don't need the likes of 'im coming in 'ere,' Mabel would snarl. 'We'll live with it, that's what we'll do.'

'You'd cut off your own nose to spite yer face, wouldn't you?' Mercy snapped, exasperated. She could never get to grips with Mabel's odd combination of self-indulgence and self-punishment.

Now she'd gone, Mercy had had Bummy Pepper in straight away and they had a nice new tread. And bit by bit she was picking up a few bits of furniture: an old settle which Mercy polished until it was a smooth, rich colour, a little cupboard for their few crocks, a comfortable chair for Susan to rest by the fire, and Susan had botched two peg rugs, using old pieces of hessian and scraps of material. They were bright and colourful and covered some of the worst wear on the bricks. Now she was working on some curtains.

The job at Wrigley's Bakery was straightforward enough. Every morning Mercy helped Susan get up. They'd long perfected the art of getting her downstairs. She took Susan in the wheelchair to Elsie's house where she did most of her work.

'I'll bring yer a doughnut!' Mercy sometimes called cheerfully as she set off and Elsie would reply, 'Make it a bagful!'

She walked into town with Tom and Johnny. No longer did she have to hobble along in poorly fitting boots that cramped her feet and chafed her chilblains. Friends of Dorothy's mistress seemed to have a dazzling surplus of clothes discarded by their daughters, and while Mercy didn't wear the prettiest dresses to work, even her plain, serviceable clothes looked quite smart and respectable.

'You're turning into a right toff,' Elsie teased her.

'Well, Rosalie'll be able to have all this lot when she's bigger,' Mercy said.

Yes, life was much better. Elsie noticed Mercy's new softness, a lack of the aggression that had always flared so easily in her before. She was gentle with Susan, tried to comfort her, though knowing there was no true comfort for this kind of loss.

One oppressively grey morning Mercy set off as usual with Johnny and Tom. It was threatening snow and the clouds had already squeezed out a few fat flakes which were drifting down through the biting air. They walked fast to keep warm, Johnny, slightly ahead, impatient as a spring, and Tom beside her, both with their caps pulled down hard and hands pushed into their jacket pockets. Mercy's coat – another offering from Dorothy – was blue with a smooth velvet collar, and she wore a little, old-fashioned bonnet the colour of pigeons' wings. She was beginning to feel small now beside the twins, Johnny especially, who was more than a head taller than her. They walked watching their feet. The pavement was icy.

''Ow's Susan bearing up?' Tom asked 'She don't say much.'

'She misses 'er mom. Cries quite a bit for 'er – nights, you know, when there's time to think about it. But like you say, she don't keep on about it much. She's that busy in the day she's no time to dwell on it.'

'It's rotten when yer come to think of it though,' Tom said, pale face wincing at the cold. 'First 'er dad goes off and leaves 'er, then 'er mom. And that's on top of 'er legs, like.'

Mercy didn't say anything, just walked on, eyes stung by the cold air which seemed to blast up from the hub of the waking city as if from a freezing cauldron. Tom looked round at her with his dark eyes. If Mercy had been looking, she'd have seen the unguarded expression of affection in them.

'I s'pose it weren't any better for you neither,' he said apologetically. They didn't talk like this normally. As a rule it was pranks and gossip on the way to work, the lads sometimes sparring and cuffing each other.

Mercy sighed. 'Never knew my mom and dad in the first place to lose 'em, did I?'

'How d'you get to that home then?' Johnny blurted out.

'Dunno. They never told me. They found me somewhere – in the street. That's my mom, the streets of

Brum!' She tried to make a joke of it. 'Any'ow, that's way back now, and your mom's been so good to us . . .'

Tom peeled off to work at Stern's in Bull Street, and once they'd got to Wrigley's in Digbeth Johnny was off on his rounds with the delivery cycle, red-eyed from the cold and warm breath streaming white from his mouth.

Mercy served in the shop. She loved the clean white tiles, the smells of dough, jam, burnt currants and steamy warmth. It was cosy, and sometimes she hugged herself behind the counter relishing the place, its neat rows of tarts and buns in the glass-fronted cabinets, the aroma of crusty bread, speckled gold of cinnamon and nutmeg on custard tarts, rich dabs of chocolate, coconut snow . . .

'I wouldn't swap my job,' she told Susan. 'It's clean and warm, and all the people coming in – it's friendly like.'

Mr Wrigley was a small, anxious man with an almost completely bald head and a pert moustache on his top lip, who toiled, perspiring constantly, in the bakehouse behind the shop. His wife, red-cheeked and stolid, carried in fresh trays of bread or cakes, dressed in a white apron dusted with flour.

''Ere yer go, bab,' she'd say to Mercy. ''Ere's more for yer!' as if it were Mercy's personal task to eat every cake in the shop.

Mercy served the customers, wrapped warm loaves in layers of tissue paper, pushed sticky buns into bags and rang up the purchases on the huge steel till. She also worked to keep the place looking attractive and orderly, sweeping the black and white tiled floor and rearranging the bread and cakes to fill the gaps.

'It's nice for us to 'ave such a pretty lass serving,' Mrs Wrigley told her. ''Specially one who's as presentable as you. Good for business like, ain't it?'

'Well I'm happy in my work, Mrs Wrigley,' Mercy laughed. 'And if it's good for business, all the better.'

At closing time she and Johnny often set off together again, laughing and joking. She always enjoyed Johnny's cheek. Unlike Tom he seemed energized by his day's work, ready for anything, his freckled face pink and weather-beaten. Tom though, usually looked pale and tired after a day at Stern's. His nails were always black with tarnish and silver polish. Mr Stern, a kindly, prematurely aged man with tiny wire spectacles, a grey beard and a large wife, was teaching Tom the art of engraving and burnishing silver. Later he was to learn electroplating. The shop's windows were crammed with candlesticks, cups, medals and jewellery, and it was very dark inside, lit only by a single gas mantle.

'You look like a mouse crawling out of a hole,' Mercy had teased him one day when he appeared squinting into the afternoon.

Sometimes she felt like slipping her arms through Tom's and Johnny's. They were like brothers to her: family. But she knew they'd say, 'Oi, gerroff, will yer! What're yer playing at!'

That snowy day when she reached Elsie's with a bag of day-old Chelsea buns, she found Susan still toiling away on her sewing machine. Cathleen was sitting close to the fire, lips tinged with blue despite the warmth. Jack was at the table with Frank in his uniform, and Josephine, whose usual expression of discontent had quite vanished (she'd found A Man at last). Dorothy, who'd turned down Elsie's offer of tea, was also there waiting for her.

'You're soon back!' Mercy cried, beaming. 'Less than a week, ain't it?' She opened the bag of buns and they were shared out, Dorothy shaking her head when offered a piece of one.

'She giving you some extra time off?' Mercy asked her, chewing.

Dorothy stood up, her face solemn. 'I'd like a word with you, Mercy. In private like.'

Mercy looked uncertainly at Elsie. So far as she was concerned nothing was so private that the Peppers and Susan couldn't hear it.

'Go round to yours,' Elsie said with chilly tact. 'Then you and Miss Finch can talk without all the commotion.' She wasn't sure that 'Miss Finch' didn't think she was a cut above them all, but Mercy seemed to think a lot of her so she wasn't going to make an issue of anything.

'You come to tell me you're getting married?' Mercy joked as they walked into number two.

Dorothy looked astonished. 'No. What in heaven's name made you think that?'

'You look a bit sort of excited. I wondered—'

'Would that be summat to get excited about?' Dorothy retorted, with such venom in her voice that Mercy was taken aback. Dorothy sat, removed her hat and arranged the powder blue folds of her dress carefully on her knees.

'I have got news for you though, and I think you'll find it exciting when I tell you.'

Mercy stood by the table, clearing the plates from their rushed breakfast that morning. She raised one eyebrow curiously at Dorothy.

'We've – I've found you a position, Mercy. A very good one with a respectable family – well off too. They need a maid of all work. It's a great chance for you, Mercy. You'll live in a lovely house – quite different from here. Good conditions, and I know they'll treat you right. You can start as soon as you like.'

She spoke with complete confidence that Mercy would be overjoyed at the offer.

Mercy stared at her, forehead creased as if she hadn't understood.

'It's a job in service, Mercy.' Dorothy stood up again and leant across the table speaking quietly but insistently. 'A good start in life for you now you're old enough. Grab it and take it quick.'

Mercy's sudden burst of laughter took her completely aback.

'But I don't need a job, Dorothy! I've already got one and I'm happy with that. It's nice of you to think of me and go to all this trouble but I don't want another job just now.'

'But you'd be in a beautiful house – carpets on the floor. It's a job many a young girl'd jump at. And it wouldn't end there. You could work your way up – p'raps even get to be cook there one day if you prove yourself.'

Mercy had no idea just how much she exasperated Dorothy by laughing again. 'Oh, I've been cook here for quite a long while already.' She'd begun bustling around, clattering plates, carrying in vegetables. 'No need for me to go anywhere to do that.'

'She won't take it.'

Dorothy stood in front of Grace, her face red. She had felt helpless when she left Mercy, but now she was furious, and ashamed at the failure of her powers of persuasion.

They were in the comfortable parlour, door closed against the rest of the house, a young fire burning smokily in the grate. Grace moved up and down the hearth, agitated, her dress rustling. Her usually smooth voice took on an edge of shrillness.

'You mean . . .?'

'She said she's happy where she is.'

'Those were her words?'

'She seemed to find the offer all rather amusing,' Dorothy confessed bitterly. 'The silly girl.'

'But she can't want to stay there!' Grace burst out. 'Doesn't she know an opportunity when she's presented with it? There she is, living in that terrible . . . slum of a place, and she turns down a position in one of the most prestigious houses in the city! Dorothy—' Grace's eyes filled with tears. 'This is too terrible. It's just her ignorance that's making her react like this. After all, what does my poor child know of fine houses or anything except an orphanage and a workman's house? You've got to go and make her see how much better it would be for her. Go back tomorrow. You've got to make her take that position!'

'Blimey,' Mercy joked when she found Dorothy in Angel Street again the next day. 'You out of a job or summat?'

'Come in here—'

Mercy had been in the yard with Elsie, and Dorothy more or less ordered her into her own house.

'What's the matter?' She wasn't used to Dorothy behaving so sternly. And she saw a hard expression in the woman's eyes which worried her.

'We need to have words, miss.' Dorothy confronted her once more across the table. 'I come here yesterday and brought you an offer of a good job. A flaming good one, the like of which you'll be lucky ever to see again.'

'Oh Dorothy!' Mercy was relieved. 'It's that again, is

it? I told you, I don't need a job. It was kind of you, but—'

'Take the position.' It was an order, almost spat out. The two women stood staring into each other's eyes. A muscle twitched in Mercy's thin face and she clenched her teeth.

'Dorothy, I don't want it. I told you.'

'Take it!' Dorothy slapped her hand hard on the table, nostrils flaring. 'Who d'you think you are, eh? Turning down summat like that as if you could pick and choose? You're an orphan, you've come from the workhouse or near enough, and life ain't about picking and choosing when you're poor – you take what you're given and you're grateful!'

The look that came over Mercy's face as she spoke filled Dorothy with a sudden chill. She had assumed all this time that this child who so resembled Grace, was in fact a minute replica of her mother, would grow into the same woman with the angelic hair, grey eyes, the soft, yielding personality. But there was other blood in Mercy. It was only now, seeing the glint in Mercy's eyes and her jutting chin, Dorothy recognized she was dealing with a far more flint-like character. She experienced a moment of panic, faced with the strength of this temperament.

'I don't know what all this is to you,' Mercy said, her voice polite but steely. 'I'm grateful for the offer but the answer's no and could never be anything else.'

'But why?'

'Because this is my place here.'

'It doesn't have to be!' Dorothy was growing quite distressed. If only she could tell the girl she was the daughter of a wealthy industrialist's wife, have her see that she didn't truly belong here!

'These're my people,' Mercy said. 'They're the only

people who've ever been anything to me – apart from you. Mrs Pepper's been like a mom to me and I'll never, ever leave Susan. She's all I've got and I've promised 'er. So don't ask me. Everyone else's left 'er and I'm not going to do it as well.'

'But she could go to Mrs Pepper,' Dorothy argued desperately. How could she go and face Grace, having failed again?

'No,' Mercy said simply.

'Yer a stupid little fool.' Dorothy's voice was harsh with bitterness.

'Well maybe I am. I'm grateful, more than, for all you've done for us,' Mercy said, turning away. 'But if you think it's bought you the right to come 'ere telling me what to do you can have back every stitch you've brought. I don't want anything from you if that's the arrangement.'

Chapter Twelve

The summer of 1914 was a very hot one. Smoke from factory chimneys hung in the air. It was a struggle to keep food fresh, the yards in Angel Street were full of dust and the dry-pan privies stank and attracted swarms of flies. Dogs panted in patches of shade under carts or beside steps.

Wrigley's Bakery felt like a furnace by day. They propped the door open to the street despite the dust and grime and Mrs Wrigley kept going to stand by the door in her apron, watching trams on the Stratford Road, fanning herself with a newspaper.

'Phew – this is too much, this is!' she'd say, cheeks a burning red. 'We could do with a drop of rain!'

When at the end of June an Austrian Archduke was shot in Sarajevo, most people had their minds on holiday time. Some would get away to the coast or at least the country. In the Angel Street neighbourhood a few visits were planned for the August Bank Holiday, as far as the Lickeys or Clent Hills. As for Mercy and Susan, they were going as far as Highgate Park where they could lie on the sloping grass with straw hats, eat, laugh, and above all, do absolutely nothing for the day except watch white wisps of cloud edge across a Wedgwood blue sky.

'I wonder what Mom's doing,' Susan said sadly as they lay side by side on the freshly cut grass. She always insisted on having her legs covered.

Mercy reached out and squeezed her hand. 'I s'pect

she's all right.' It was the one despondent moment of the day and Mercy felt helpless, and guilty too, as she so preferred life without Mabel. They were managing. She was determined not to be beaten.

Within days of this sunny respite the air was full of war. Shrill newspaper headlines: War Against the Hun! Flags and bunting, excited queues outside the hastily established recruiting offices taking the King's shilling, young men in khaki with tightly bound puttees, and suddenly the city emptied of horses. They were needed more for the War than they were at home! The talk was aggressive and defiant. Old soldiers of the Boer War gathered in pubs and chewed over events. Men were thin on the ground in Nine Court and Bummy went down the pub with Mr White who was streets more amiable nowadays. A picture of the King and Queen went up in the window of the local huckster's shop. In the name of Honour and of Justice, the Hun were going to be taught a lesson they wouldn't forget!

'It's all very well,' Mercy said, arriving back at Elsie's with the twins one afternoon in mid-September. 'But when's summat going to happen?' She pulled off her straw hat and fanned herself with it. 'We tried to get a paper on the way 'ome but they was all gone again.'

'Summat *has* happened,' Elsie said, tight-lipped. 'Our Frank's only gone and joined up hasn't 'e?'

There were gasps from the twins, of envy from Johnny, more of awe from Tom.

Frank had stood in front of Lord Kitchener's recruitment poster, saw the authority of that pointing finger and the handlebar moustache and speedily decided his country needed him. This being a minor incentive compared with getting away from his missis, he'd hurried to the recruiting station in Great Charles Street.

''E's in the First City Battalion – that's the Fourteenth Warwicks, I think 'e said.' Elsie's face was pale under the freckles. 'I don't know whether to be proud of 'im or put 'im across my knee. 'E's off tomorrow, for training in Sutton Park.'

'Cor!' Johnny was ahop with excitement. 'That's bostin'! I wish I could go!'

'You're too young, and it'll all be over before you get a chance,' Bummy said from the sofa. But there was a wistful note in his voice and Mercy sensed he was envious of Frank too in his way. It was the thing to do nowadays, to prove your manhood.

Mary Jones said, 'Well I hope Stan's joining up and they finish 'im off for us.'

She was battling with financial hardship on top of the daily grind of bringing up four young kids on her own: Lisa eight, Molly seven, Percy four and Paul one. Battling, though not sunk. The Peppers were helping her out with the rent and Elsie, who had no real need to take in laundry any more, passed on her dwindling number of customers. The War was biting people in the purse already. So it was Mary toiling in the brewhouse at all hours now, with the dolly, maiding tub and mangle, little Paul round her legs.

Mary seemed to have found in herself a defiant strength, a kind of exhilaration in 'getting by'. She moved more briskly, face tighter, more alert.

'After all, 'e never raised a finger to do nowt when 'e was 'ere,' she said to Elsie. 'So it don't make much odds 'im going. It's thanks to you we're surviving though. I won't forget yer kindness, Elsie. If there's ever anything I can do in return . . .'

She'd jumped at the chance of helping with Josephine's wedding in May. When they'd begun to despair of ever getting her married off, Josephine had met Fred Larkin, a widower and publican with two kids. They had a white wedding along at St Joseph's. She was now happily queening it in the Eagle in Balsall Heath and talking babies.

Food prices were shooting up. The price of sugar doubled. People were forever moaning about the cost of bread in Wrigley's.

'Anyone'd think it was my fault there's a war on,' Mercy complained to Susan some evenings. 'They come in all in a panic and buy it all up and then everyone else is left to moan.'

Motley dressed groups of men could be seen drilling in the parks, Belgian flags rippled in the breeze outside houses in Birmingham which had become homes for refugees, and newspapers were producing the casualty lists. Yet the names of the battles – Mons, Tannenberg, the Marne, Ypres – were all strange, foreign, the War far away.

Until one morning Tom Pepper went to work as usual, to find Stern's shop had been set on fire and was a charred, still-smoking husk, many of the silver items lying black among the ash and broken glass where they had fallen.

Tom stood there in shock, cap in his hand, as the fire brigade finished dousing the damaged adjoining buildings.

'What happened to 'im?' Tom asked one of them, jerking his head towards the ruined flat above the shop.

The fireman shook his head. 'Died in their beds – the smoke, see. They've been brought out already.'

Tom nodded, sick at heart. He tried to imagine Mr

Stern lying next to his enormous wife, the smoke furling round them.

Passers-by stared, some silent, perhaps not knowing the shop. But Tom heard one say, 'That'll teach 'em. Hun bastards.'

Tom turned away. This wasn't right, none of it. Mr Stern wasn't his enemy!

Putting his cap back on he trudged off along the road. He'd have to spend the day looking for more work. But after, he wanted to talk to someone, to share his sense of outrage. His mom, of course. But as he turned towards the Jewellery Quarter, he knew the person he wanted to see most was Mercy.

He appeared at their door that evening, white-faced and dejected. Mercy wiped her hands on her apron. 'What's up?'

'Can I come in?'

''Course.' She was baffled. 'I'm brewing a pot now – sit down – you look bad.'

Tom took a chair by the table. There was a smell of stew in the room. Mercy lifted the kettle and mashed the tea. She had no idea how her presence had begun to affect Tom, how a look from her grey eyes made his stomach plunge with excitement. It had made him more shy of her and he stumbled over his words as he told them about the Sterns.

'I know they was Germans like,' Tom said. 'But they've been 'ere years and 'e was ever so good to me. Wouldn't've hurt a fly.'

Susan wheeled herself closer. 'What about the business?'

'Well, it's wrecked of course,' Tom said with some impatience. 'Nothing left to speak of.'

'What a terrible thing,' Mercy said thoughtfully. 'It makes all the difference knowing someone, doesn't it? Otherwise you might just say 'e was German and it served 'im right.'

'Can't say I've ever met a German,' Susan said.

'Well you've hardly met anyone, have yer?' Mercy retorted rather sharply. 'Not that that's your fault,' she added quickly. 'So what you going to do, Tom?'

'I've been out all day, over Hockley, trying to get another job in the same line. Either they said they had no vacancies, or when I said I'd worked at Stern's, one of 'em turned quite nasty.' Wearily he pushed his cowlick of brown hair back from his face. 'In the end I gave up on smithing for now. I went over to Dingleys – got a job as a porter.'

Dingleys was a well-to-do hotel in Moor Street.

'Well, there you are then,' Susan said, not quite taking in the disappointment in his voice.

Mercy leant closer and looked into his eyes in a way which made Tom almost overcome with self-consciousness. He was keenly aware of her every move, her small, thin fingers on the back of the chair beside him. Mercy saw him blushing and he couldn't hold her gaze.

'D'you want to stop and have summat to eat with us? We'd be glad of the company, wouldn't we, Susan?'

'Best not.' Tom stood up, stumbling as he tried to push the chair back. He picked up his cap. 'Mom'll 'ave counted me in for tea.'

He paused. 'You managing awright, Mercy? Anything you need you'll come to us, won't you?'

'Yes, ta,' Mercy smiled. When he'd gone she said to

Susan, 'If that'd been Johnny 'e'd just 'ave shrugged it off and that'd be that.'

'I s'pose so,' Susan said. 'Takes things 'eavier, Tom does.'

That night Tom lay awake thinking of Mercy. The very sight of her set his pulse racing. But he was rather in awe of her. She seemed so grown up, so self-contained and untouchable. How could he ever dare tell her how much time he spent dreaming of her!

The War was clearly not going to be over by Christmas. On Christmas Eve Mercy was enjoying the bustle at work, and people coming in asking for space in the bakery oven the next day for roasting their Christmas joints. The oven would be kept working, and Mrs Wrigley did her best to accommodate everyone.

'She's such a kind lady,' Mercy said to Susan that evening. 'Look, she sent me off with this fruit cake, even though things're short.'

Dorothy came briefly that afternoon. Grace longed to send her with gifts, to lavish luxuries on Mercy, but she knew it wasn't fitting, and in any case, such undue expenses would have to be justified to Neville. She had no money of her own.

Mercy greeted Dorothy in the rather more stiff, distant manner which had characterized their meetings ever since the row. Mercy regretted what had happened, but now she'd got a bit of freedom she certainly didn't want anyone organizing her life like that! Dorothy stayed for a cup of tea, admiring the few decorations Mercy had put up to cheer the room. When she stood up to go she stepped forward to put her arms round Mercy, this impulse as much for herself as for Grace. After all, she had watched the child grow up. Mercy felt herself resist for a moment, then told herself she was being silly and hugged Dorothy back.

'Have a Merry Christmas then – see you both soon,' Dorothy said awkwardly.

Mercy waved as Dorothy passed the window. She's nervous of me, she thought. How odd, Dorothy being nervous of me.

While they ate thin mutton stew and spuds, Mercy boiled up water in the kettle and all the pans she could fit on the range. When the plates were cleared she dragged the tin bath over on to the rug in front of the fire, while Susan sat under the gaslight embroidering a little lavender bag and George made whistling noises of interest from his place by the window.

Mercy looked over at him from where she was swirling cold water in with the hot, her sleeves rolled up and steam clouding her face.

'Shush you, or you'll get a dunking in 'ere too.'

George whistled, unrepentant.

'I was thinking,' Mercy said. 'I ought to give this room a coat of whitewash – cover some of the cracks and brighten it up a bit.'

''Ave we got the money?' Susan was always anxious, never confident that they could manage. 'I'm not getting many jobs now. Everyone's cutting back.'

'Oh, I dare say we can manage. Come on then. In yer get.'

She helped Susan undress, pushed the chair right up to the bath and between them, levered her down into the water, Susan supporting herself with her arms and smiling up in triumph as she sank down into the water saying, 'Ah – that's lovely, that is.'

Mercy handed her a sliver of soap, then sat down beside her as she bathed, the two of them chatting idly.

''Ere – let me do that.' Mercy knelt up to wash Susan's back and helped her with her long black hair, supporting her as she lay back in the water as she couldn't steady herself with her feet. Her body, though small for her age, was growing curvaceous, like Mabel's. Mercy watched her with a great rush of fondness as she lay, eyes closed, in the water. Susan's extreme naïveté drove her mad at times, but that kind of innocence was what she also loved most about her.

Soon Susan was beginning to shiver, so Mercy helped her out, drying her on an old, soft piece of sacking. She rubbed oil on her legs.

'Lop a bit off of my hair, will you, after you've had yours?' Susan held up a wet hank of hair. 'It's getting so long I can hardly manage to comb it out!'

Dressed again she watched Mercy tip more hot into the tub and climb in, washing her slight, rosy body in a businesslike way. There was silence, except for the little popping sound of the gas mantle and the light splash of water. Normally Susan was prattling away at such a time, and Mercy looked up enquiringly at her to see her eyes filled with tears.

'What's up with you all of a sudden?'

'You'll get married one day,' Susan said bleakly. It was always there, her morbid fear of being abandoned.

'Nah.' Mercy leant over and squeezed Susan's wrist with her wet hand. ''Course I shan't. Don't talk barmy.'

''Ello, barmy,' George remarked suddenly, and even Susan's stricken face relaxed into laughter.

'Ooh, you're a so-and-so, you are!' she told him.

Mercy was dried and clad in the nightshirt Susan had run up for her, and standing cutting Susan's hair when they heard footsteps outside, the door latch clicked and there was Mabel. She came in, shut the door and stood before them. She had on her old coat and a shapeless green felt hat, was thinner than when she left. She looked both nervous and defiant.

The two girls froze.

Mabel eyed both of them. Mercy's hostility snaked across the room to her.

'Mom,' Susan whispered eventually. She wheeled the chair towards her and Mercy's heart wrung at the sweet hope on her face. 'I thought you'd left us for good.'

Mabel put her bag down. 'It's Christmas,' she said. 'I want to come home.'

Part Three

Chapter Thirteen

August 1916

Mercy pushed past the self-important conductorette, and stepped, heavy-hearted, off the bus into the summer evening. She was dressed in her oldest work clothes, a navy dress with white polka dots, which at work was covered by an overall, her hair taken back under a snood. For she was now a munitions girl, turning out Mills grenades in a factory squeezed between Digbeth and the grey, dripping arches of the railway line.

A few months before Mrs Wrigley had said, 'I'm ever so sorry, Mercy, but what with all the shortages and the price of everything, we haven't the money to keep you on.'

They were crying out for women to go into munitions work then, and the pay! She got a pound a week! But even that didn't go far now, though, and most days she felt she'd more than earned it, standing all those hours in a cramped room lit only by daylight through the windows, bent over a lathe, finishing the opening at the top of the grenades which were piled around her like metal pineapples. The belts on the lathes whirred and slapped round ceaselessly and she breathed in metal dust. Her body was stiff and her feet ached. Still, she told herself, she had some laughs with the other girls. But she couldn't shake off her feelings of worry and dread.

A week ago today it'd been: Jack Pepper rattling at the door after work. 'Mercy – come over ours a minute, will yer?' When she asked why he said, 'Just come!' and ran off.

Mercy got up wearily. At the Peppers' she found Johnny with a grin stretched across his face and Tom, smiling but uncertain.

'We wanted to tell yer—' Johnny was twitchy with excitement. 'We've done it – we've joined up!'

'I like the "we",' Elsie spoke flatly. For once she was doing nothing, just standing. 'I don't have to guess who talked who into it.'

Tom looked solemn.

'You mean they believed the pair of you?' Mercy tried to hide her dismay. 'You're only seventeen!'

'We said we was eighteen,' Johnny bragged. 'No one asked us any different. Any rate, not long now and we will be eighteen!'

Mercy stared silently at them both. Two years ago she'd have been excited for them, proud, but now . . . Week after week the toll had mounted: Ypres, Neuve Chapelle, Loos, Gallipolli, Verdun . . .

''Aven't you seen the death lists?' Now Frank was at the Front Elsie was never quiet, couldn't sleep of a night.

They were so young, all that energy waiting to be spent. Johnny, tall, wiry with boxer's muscles and impish cheek written in every line of his face. And Tom, dark-eyed, pale, serious. Mercy felt his eyes on her, but saw the longing in them as anxiety about what lay in front of them.

'You think you can just go off and leave me, do you?' Mercy said softly, trying to joke.

'I thought you might talk sense into 'em better than

me,' Elsie said wearily. 'But in any case, it's too late now. I s'pose I should be proud.'

'We'll be back, don't you bother yourselves. Bad pennies us, eh?' Johnny punched Tom's shoulder. At his age he knew he was indestructible. He could hardly wait to get into uniform.

'You just as keen to go, Tom?' Mercy asked.

Tom spoke, looking at the floor. 'I thought I would be. Me and Johnny'll look out for each other.'

Mercy swallowed the lump in her throat. 'You'd flaming well better.'

They left a couple of days later, very early, but most of the yard was up to see them go. Elsie was fighting tears, something Mercy had almost never seen her do before and she was frightened suddenly in a way she couldn't have put into words. The tentacles of events in the outside world, bigger and crueller than any of them could have imagined, reached into Angel Street that morning.

Johnny said his goodbyes to her and Susan with a peck on the cheek. 'Ta-ra, Mercy. Take care of yourself, and look out for our mom, won't yer?'

Tom came to her, obviously full of nerves. He tried to kiss her as Johnny had done, but he knocked his nose accidentally hard against her cheek.

'Ooh, Tom!' Mercy half laughed, half yelped, rubbing her face.

'Sorry – sorry, Mercy.' He couldn't look at her for a moment, and stared at the ground, lick of hair falling forward. But then, forced by the urgency of the occasion he looked up and saw the tears in her eyes.

'Oh Lor' – this is terrible – I've got to say it. If I don't tell you now I might never, and I've waited such a long time . . .' Mercy watched as the young man in front of her almost physically screwed up his courage, and amid the general hubbub of the yard, said, cheeks aflame, 'If I've got to die for anyone, I'll do it for you, Mercy!'

'Oh Tom!' She was very moved by his outburst, by his passion and tenderness. 'Would you really? I didn't know . . .'

He'd always been kind and considerate to her, especially as they'd grown older, but she hadn't seen that his friendliness had developed into something far stronger.

'I've got to tell you, Mercy, the feelings I've got for yer – just in case I . . .' He stepped closer to her, his brown eyes looking close into hers, and took her hands in his. She felt him trembling. She was beginning to shake a little as well. 'You're so lovely, Mercy. I love you. I've wanted to tell you for ages but, I dunno . . . we was just kids and I thought you'd – I've never had the courage . . .'

Mercy was so astonished, touched, grateful, bewildered all at once that she couldn't speak. Johnny, heading down the entry with Elsie and a cluster of others was shouting, 'Come on, Tom!'

'Could you say it to me, to take with me? Whether you feel . . .?'

Mercy looked into his sweet, imploring face and was overcome by fondness for him. Her emotions were a storm of confusion, but somewhere in the middle of it all her heart was singing.

'Of course I love you, Tom!'

In a second his arms were round her, pulling her to him.

'I had to do this – just once, before I go, my . . . love.' He pressed his cheek against hers, then quickly kissed her lips. He looked full into her eyes, then pulled away. 'I've got to go. I'll write . . .'

She followed him down the entry to where Johnny was waiting. Everyone stood on the street, waving them off. Tom's eyes met hers. Mercy smiled, going to stand by Elsie, her heart full to bursting.

'Come back to us, you two, won't yer? For God's sake!' Elsie called to them.

Mercy stood with everyone else until the twins reached the corner and disappeared, still waving. She felt strange and shocked. One moment he had been there, so close, now he was gone. She put her hand to her lips as if to seal his kiss.

Walking home that evening from the bus stop on the Moseley Road, Mercy thought of Tom as she'd done almost every moment since he left. At first she had felt only astonishment. Tom, whom she'd known all these years, in love with her! As she grew used to the idea, recalled again and again his look, his words to her, she bubbled inside with the warm excitement this knowledge aroused in her. All this time and she'd never known – someone other than Susan found it possible to love her! More and more she knew she was in love with him in return, loved him for his gentleness and solidity, his kindness. Above all she loved him for loving her.

She'd felt differently about everything since Tom and Johnny left. The War had moved closer, to her doorstep, her heart. She knew that soon they would be sent to the Front, and then all she could do would be worry and pray.

She also felt an enormous sense of restlessness come

over her, as if between them they had prised open a chink in her mind and let in a view she'd never seen before. There was so much more to life and the world than she ever saw, and the twins had stepped out into it.

Turning into the entry, she felt exhausted and prickly with an unfamiliar kind of irritation. She was sixteen, grown up. Was this grimy yard in a grimy city, living with a woman she loathed all she was ever going to see of life?

Perhaps I was wrong, she thought. I should've taken up Dorothy's offer of that job, and I wouldn't be churning out grenades day after day. But that would have meant leaving Susan . . .

She entered the house rubbing her stiff neck and taking a deep breath, preparing herself to be as civil as she could manage to Mabel. Life felt like one long struggle.

'You all right?' Susan asked her brightly, as George shrieked at the sight of her.

'I'll survive.' She sank on to the settle.

'Mom – give 'er a cup of tea,' Susan instructed Mabel who was on her way downstairs. 'This job's wearing 'er out!'

'Dear oh dear,' Mabel said sarcastically.

'Could be worse,' Mercy said, ignoring her. 'I could be shell-filling like Cathleen. I hate to think what's in them shells. I saw 'er again yesterday and she's yellow as a canary, right down to 'er scalp!'

Mercy drank her tea and tried to smile, trying to shake off her restless feelings. After all, this was home. If it meant living with Mabel still, so be it. She belonged here. She had Susan whatever else. And Tom. Each time she remembered there came a rush of joy. Dear Tom.

*

Things had changed a fair bit in Nine Court over the past year and a half. The two cottages with their scrubby gardens had new tenants: the Ripleys and the McGonegalls. Mary Jones complained that the Ripleys were a 'right rough crew', and the yard was like bedlam with all their children everywhere, but she moaned a bit less when they turned out to be good company for her own.

But there had been one change which had taken everyone's breath away. Christmas Day of 1914 after Mabel first showed herself in the yard again, Mary Jones came roaring out of her house and spat in her face.

'Where is 'e then?' she shrieked at Mabel. 'Where's that bastard now?'

Other choice words followed and the neighbours began to open their doors and enjoy a free show on this frosty morning. But it was all a damp squib so far as neighbourhood entertainment went.

To everyone's astonishment, Mabel stood tall, silently drew her sleeve across her face to wipe off Mary's spit and refused to be riled into fighting back. Mercy watched with everyone else. Blimey, she thought. What's come over her?

'I dunno where 'e is,' Mabel said. 'Not exactly any'ow.'

'Did 'e leave yer to join up?' Mary's face puckered into a vicious sneer. 'Went off to do 'is bit and you couldn't stand being left be'ind?'

'Look, Mary,' Mabel clamped her hands on her hips. 'Stan left me for another woman and I don't know where they've gone. 'E just ran out on me. But I know, and so should you – if 'e hadn't left you for me, it'd've been someone else.'

''E never looked at another woman 'til you come along!' Mary yelled, although the wind was fast disappearing from her sails. It was her right, her role to have a go at Mabel, expected almost. But she didn't want Stan back. She just wanted someone to take it all out on, being left alone, the relentless hardship of her life.

'Think what you like,' Mabel said calmly. 'But I've had a lot of hard thinking to do and I've got a suggestion to make to you – for your own benefit.' She looked round, on her dignity at the people strung across the yard. 'Why don't we go in your 'ouse and discuss it where there ain't so many pairs of ears flapping?'

'You – in my 'ouse! You've got some nerve!' Mary looked meaningfully over at Elsie, waiting to be backed up, but Elsie shrugged in her doorway, keeping out of it.

'Come in mine then.'

Mary wavered, though her face was still taut and defiant. 'No.'

'So – it'll have to be yours—'

Mabel, the older and by far the more forceful of the two, ushered Mary Jones into her own house. The door closed. Outside, everyone looked at one another and Susan whispered to Mercy, 'What's come over 'er?'

Stan had left Mabel a fortnight before and in that time she felt she had scraped the rock bottom of her life. Here she was at forty-one, left alone in two squalid, bug-ridden rooms above an Aston fish shop, the stench of it forever in her nostrils. She'd been deserted by the man she'd run after with such paltry hopes. She'd abandoned her only surviving daughter, and her last hope of having another healthy child had ended in a painful, bloody failure at which Stan had shown not an ounce of sorrow or disappointment.

One terrible, grey day when the clouds sat like a heavy lid on top of the city she'd sat in that dreary room. There was a speckled mirror fixed over a battered vanity table. Mabel leant close, peering short-sightedly at her face. She still didn't feel right after losing the infant. Her face was pale and sagging, hair and eyes lifeless. She reminded herself of a corpse and that was how she felt. The living dead. And at that moment she felt enough shame and hatred for herself to go and finish it all for good in the canal.

Her life had had its low points before, no doubt about that. But none of the other things that had happened had been of her own making. What would she say of any other woman who had run out on her child? And she missed Susan. Deep in her guts she missed her and was overwhelmed with grief and shame.

'Why've you come back?' Mary Jones demanded, holding Paul on her lap and keeping up her expression of bitter hostility.

'I've come back to my daughter.' Mabel didn't sit down, but took a stance stiffly just inside the door, arms folded. 'Did you know I was carrying 'is child?'

Mary's hand moved up to her mouth, eyes widening. 'My God – you never—'

'I lost it. Natural. I never wanted to get rid of it. I've two dead babbies already.' Her voice was hard, defiant almost.

Mary lowered her hand and continued to stare mutely at her. She had never known the first thing about this woman before.

'I've had to take a good look at myself and I haven't liked what I've seen. So I said to myself, "Mabel, you can stay 'ere on yer own like a fallen woman for the rest of your life and die lonely, or you can go back there, ask your daughter's forgiveness, and make amends."' She paused. 'What I think is, we should both try and put it behind us and I'll help you out. I know what it's like bringing up babbies on your own. I'm part of the cause, so I'll do my bit. There.'

Mary allowed herself a bitter laugh. 'Oh – you steal my husband and come in 'ere thinking you can eat humble pie and we're all going to turn round and say "Oh that's awright Mabel, welcome back?"'

'I never stole your 'usband. 'E wasn't a child – 'e chose to go and walked right out and as I said to you, if it hadn't happened now it would've later. 'E's a worthless, selfish good for nothing and you know it.'

'Well if 'e was so bloody terrible, what d'yer take off with 'im for?'

Mabel looked her right in the eyes. 'I wanted someone. It's been a long time.'

There was silence as the two woman stared each other out. Finally, Mary shook her head. 'Both got bloody bad taste, 'aven't we?'

When Mabel arrived home, Mercy felt as if she were being put back in prison.

'We need to make a fresh start,' Mabel said to them that same day, her hair brushing Mercy's little home-made streamers. She was struggling to remain calm. She'd already eaten humble pie for Mary Jones and now she'd have to do it again, but by God this was tougher by half. She could feel all her aversion flooding back towards this mardy little blonde child. No, she saw, not child. Not any more. Two young women were before her, who'd struggled and managed to run their lives almost alone.

'I don't want to live out my life with everyone hating me,' she admitted.

'Well it'd have paid you to think of that a bit sooner!' Mercy blurted out. She'd spent the night sleepless with anguish at Mabel's return, despite her relief on Susan's behalf.

'We don't hate you, Mom!' Susan was overwhelmed that her mother had returned. 'Mercy, I know Mom's treated yer bad in the past, but it won't be like that from now on, will it?' She looked at each of them with huge, spaniel eyes.

'I owe you, Mercy,' Mabel said gruffly. She'd known this was going to be damned humiliating and she wasn't going to back out now. Being left alone had been so much worse. 'You've looked out for Susan when I went off and left her. I had my reasons – I want you to know that—'

'Just don't come back 'ere thinking you can take over and start carrying on how you was before,' Mercy burst out furiously, all aquiver. 'There've been some changes around 'ere and we've all managed perfectly well without you.'

'So I see.' Mabel's gaze travelled over the new furniture.

'The wheelchair's indoors for good,' Mercy decreed, as if everything hung on this.

'It's much better,' Susan backed her up, trying to please Mercy and appeal to Mabel at the same time. 'I can do so much more and the sewing's been going ever so well – before the War it was any'ow.'

'I'm glad for yer,' Mabel said carefully. Mercy watched her through narrowed eyes, arms clasped defensively across her body. However hard Mabel's return was to swallow, she was here, and for Susan's sake she was going to have to learn to put up with her.

It was only a matter of time before things blew up. Mercy didn't believe a word of Mabel's claims of repentance and neighbourliness. She had no understanding of the course Mabel's emotions had taken over the years, did not know anyone might try to change out of need and self-revulsion.

Mabel did everything she could to ingratiate herself with Mercy and Susan and with the neighbours, especially Mary Jones. She started to pay attention to Mary's kids. The two women even had a laugh together. But Mercy watched her, mistrustful.

Mabel didn't have a job at this time and was doing the shopping, something Mercy found hard to make time for, except for bread which back then she could still get from Wrigley's.

She'd asked Mabel to get cheap meat for stewing. Mabel not only came home with fish instead but managed to forget about it and burn it almost to a cinder. It was two women, a kitchen stove and so much more besides.

'So you can't get the shopping right and then you serve us up with cowing charcoal for our tea!' Mercy, already living on her nerves, flew straight off the handle as she came to the table.

'Less of your lip – I was doing my best. I just 'ad to nip out! At least I was getting on with the cooking instead of waiting for you.'

'I don't want you doing it!' Mercy's eyes held an icy loathing. 'We haven't needed you for a long time and we don't need you now!'

Without thinking Mabel whipped out and slapped Mercy hard on the cheek. The girl's hand flew up to her face.

'What're you going to do now?' Mabel sneered. 'Call the welfare people? Don't think they'd be interested at your age, do you?'

'No.' Mercy's voice was clipped, chilling. 'This is what I'm going to do.'

She strode round the table, eyes never leaving Mabel's face, and her fist landed on Mabel's nose with all the force she was capable of.

Mabel reeled, eyes screwed shut in pain, gasping.

Mercy put her face right up close to her. 'Just remember,' she hissed, 'you don't hit me, Mabel. Not ever again.

Chapter Fourteen

Mercy stood aghast in the doorway of the Peppers'. Rosalie was lying on the hearthrug letting out heartbroken sobs as Bummy, Cathleen and Elsie stood or sat round the table, faces bruised with shock. The letter lay on the table.

'Frank?'

Their faces told her it was so, but no words would come.

'D'you want—' Mercy's throat had tightened so much she could barely speak either. 'Shall I go for Josephine?'

'Jack's gone.' Elsie's voice had a far away sound to it and she spoke uncertainly, as if she'd forgotten how to use words.

Mercy went to Rosalie, sat beside her and pulled her across her lap. Rosalie was small for an eight-year-old, and skinny. Her hands were clenched to her face and wet from the tears squeezing out between them. 'I want Frankie!'

Mercy felt her body jerking with sobs. 'I know love,' she said softly, rocking the bony little body. 'I know you do.' Cathleen also had tears running down her sallow face.

Bummy Pepper sat at the table, a stunned expression on his face, rubbing his hand again and again over his stubbly chin. After a time he pushed the chair back and walked out of the house without saying a word.

Mercy's eyes followed him.

''S'awright – 'e'll've gone down the Angel. 'E'll be back

after a couple of pints.' Elsie had turned, within hours, from a woman who looked young for fifty to one who seemed much older. She sank on to her husband's chair by the table.

'Oh Frank. Oh God, my little Frankie. I can't even give 'im a decent burial.'

Soon after, in a corner of the yard up by the brewhouse wall appeared a cross about a foot high made from two pieces of smooth wood nailed together. Above it, a Union Jack was tacked to the wall.

'What's all that?' Mercy asked coming in from work. Under the flag lay a bunch of white lilies.

'It's Elsie's,' Susan said. 'For Frank. She's bin out there 'alf the day. I 'ope she's awright – seems to be acting a bit funny to me.'

Mabel peered out at the little home-made shrine across the yard. 'Nah,' she said with authority. 'It's natural enough. She wants to do summat for 'im.'

There were similar little offerings to be seen out on the streets, rolls of honour, flags and flowers for dead sons, fathers, brothers.

Elsie got into the habit of standing for a few moments in front of hers almost every time she passed it, going about her chores. The day after she'd laid her little memorial to Frank and was standing before it, her body one endless ache of sorrow, she heard someone else come up from behind and stand by her. Then Mabel stepped forward, laid another bunch of flowers close by the others and stood straight again, wiping her hands on her apron. Neither woman spoke, nor did they look at each other.

*

Tom and Johnny came home on leave for the first time in November, striding in large as life one wet midday. Elsie fell on them both, drawing them tight into her arms.

'Mom!' Johnny struggled as she kissed his face. 'Go easy – you'll squeeze all the breath out of us!' He shook her off, embarrassed. Tom kept one hand on his mom's shoulder, silently offering comfort, not knowing what to say about Frank.

'You're both bigger!' Elsie cried, wiping her eyes. 'Oh my God, look at the pair of yer!' They seemed enormous suddenly in her tiny house. 'Wait 'til yer dad sees yer! 'Ere – you hungry?'

'When aren't we?' Tom said. 'We could do with some decent grub, I can tell yer.'

Elsie smiled with a mixture of pride and sorrow as her two strapping, now much more muscular sons swung their kitbags on to the sofa and settled themselves at the table. She scurried around preparing food to hide the tears that kept welling up. Tom looked so like Frank now. Cross with herself she wiped her eyes. Enough of this – she had the twins home for a whole week. There'd be time aplenty to dwell on sorrow.

The two of them tucked in, munching like a couple of bulls, Elsie thought fondly. She'd bought all the food they could possibly afford.

'Rosalie's crazy to see yer,' she told them. 'She's taken it ever so bad over . . .' Everything seemed to lead to it. Frank dead, gone. She was weeping, hadn't meant to . . .

'Eh, Mom!' Tom was up, an arm round her shoulders, struggling to control his own emotion. He'd been close to Frank, looked up to him. Both boys did their best to jolly her out of her crying.

'We'll take you out and about now we're 'ome,' Johnny said. 'Give you a break. Don't you cry, Mom. Us two'll look after each other when we get out there. We'll be all right, we will.'

'I'm awright . . .' Elsie forced a smile, pushing them down in front of their plates again. 'It'll be cold else. There's more spud.' She scraped round the pan. 'Come on – let's try and be cheerful.'

After a few moments Tom asked, ever so casually, ''Ow's Mercy?'

A twinkle appeared in Elsie eyes. 'Why – who's asking?'

He'd written to her from the training camp three times since he'd been away. Pictured her in his mind coming home, finding his letter . . . Reading it with a smile on her face. Every night, lying on the hard ground in his tent it was Mercy who filled his mind. Her often solemn little face breaking into a smile for him, her teeth, small and slightly uneven which made the smile special for him. Made her Mercy. But she was still awesome to him now she was grown up. He thought of her startling pale hair, pale neck curving down into a lace collar. He'd started following that curve further in his mind, imagining how she might look. Smooth, very white, except for those two round . . . Tom remembered seeing his mom suckling Rosalie, her breasts huge with milk. He couldn't stop thinking of the tender, swelling shapes under Mercy's blouse. He was certain he was always the last in his tent to get to sleep, dreaming about her.

Trouble was, when it came to writing to her, he couldn't begin to tell her what he was feeling so his letters ended up rather short, just telling her snippets about his training.

'You should've seen us first time on parade – the sarnt

said we was like lambs to the slaughter!' – 'Got our uniforms at last – now we feel like proper soldier boys . . .'

He always told her how Johnny was, asked about Susan and for Mercy to look out for his mom – he said this twice in the letter after Frank was killed. At the very end he'd tried to think how to say what he felt, something soft for his girl. In the third letter he found courage and wrote, '. . . *thinking of you always, night and day. Love Tom.'*

Mercy read these letters with a complete sense of wonder. She'd never received a letter before.

'Who's it from?' Susan wheeled herself over eagerly when the first one arrived.

''Er – Tom,' Mercy muttered, pushing it into the pocket of her dress.

'Well let's see then!'

'Later – I'm in a rush.'

'Well why can't you leave it?'

'It's addressed to me, that's why.'

She read the letter on the bus to work, so absorbed that she almost missed the stop.

'Got summat worth 'aving there, 'ave yer?' a woman teased as she rushed to leap off at the last moment, holding her hat on against the breeze outside.

The letter was strange, she thought. She had no clue what to expect from a letter. Was this a love letter, this little note telling her about a makeshift army training camp? The one spare word 'love' at the end. Was that it? Yet she was stirred up by it, by its very existence. Her man was writing to her. Her Tom! She was learning to think of him differently, not just as a playmate and the lad next door. And while she was a bit ashamed of wanting to keep her feelings secret, she couldn't share this with Susan. This was hers and hers alone. She wrote him brief, affectionate notes in reply.

The day she knew the twins were coming home she could think of nothing but Tom.

'You with us today, Mercy?' one of the other girls in the factory teased her over the racket of the machines. 'I've asked yer twice already!'

Mercy blushed and there were some 'oohs' and 'aahs' from round her.

'What's on 'er mind, I wonder!'

'Nowt any of your business,' Mercy replied with a mysterious smile which only brought on more catcalls and speculation. She took it all good-naturedly and sank back into her day-dreams. What else was there to think of standing in a factory day after day?

She didn't see him waiting as she walked up the entry in the drizzle, her boots rapping a smart clip-clip on the damp pavement. She was dressed in a calf-length grey coat, the collar turned up, and a navy hat with a narrow brim under which her hair was just visible. Her cheeks were pink from the cold.

She caught sight of him and her step faltered. He was there, waiting! He looked broader, more of a man than before. He smiled, with warmth, but shyly. This was all new. They were no longer just childhood friends. Her heart was beating fast. Suddenly she was all nerves.

'Tom,' she said softly. In those seconds, like Elsie she saw Frank's face in Tom's, felt how terrible this war was. But mixed with this, the delicious, warming sense of knowing he had waited for her, had special feelings just for her.

He walked the last few steps to meet her and they stood in the entry, both with a silver veil of water droplets on their clothes.

'How are you?' she said. Seeing his nervous, solemn face, and out of her own giddiness she started laughing. 'Blimey, you're about twice the size you were three months ago!'

Tom laughed as well and the ice was broken, but Mercy felt she was seeing him for the first time, as if through a new, clear lens: everything about him, his brown eyes, shorn brown hair, the shape of his neck, his jaw.

'You look different too,' he said. 'More grown up.'

'Where's Johnny?' She was about to step into the yard when he caught her arm.

'Mercy – can we spend a bit of time on our own like, this week, without Johnny and—?' He nodded his head towards Mabel's house.

'Susan?' Mercy looked guiltily at him. Susan hadn't seen his letters, was prickly about Mercy's secrecy. But Mercy suddenly, desperately didn't want to spend her life feeling guilty because Susan couldn't walk. She wanted to get out, to get some life of her own.

'Come to the pictures – tomorrow?'

Mercy hesitated. It wasn't going to be easy. 'What'll you tell Johnny?'

'I'll just tell 'im. 'E won't mind.'

'OK.' She smiled, bubbling with excitement. 'I'd love to go.'

Tom swooped forward and kissed her cheek. 'I've missed yer.'

So it was real, she thought, touching her cheek. She'd almost wondered if she'd imagined what he said the morning he left, despite the letters. Heart thudding, and with an enormous sense of wonder she said, 'I missed you too.'

'I'm going to the Electric Cinema with Tom,' Mercy announced defiantly to Mabel and Susan, expecting opposition.

Mabel opened her mouth and closed it again, unable to think of a good enough objection. She knew if she just said, 'You're not,' Mercy would take no notice anyway. She'd done a lot of biting her lip over the past year and it was becoming a habit. It was paying her to keep quiet. Mercy was the main wage earner after all.

Susan looked up from laying crocks for tea. 'What?' she faltered. 'Just you and 'im – on your own?'

'Well – yes.' Mercy, seeing the hurt in Susan's eyes, couldn't keep up her tough act any longer and bent down so she was level with her. 'You don't mind, do you?'

Susan put a plate down, concentrating on it very hard all of a sudden. 'No – you go and 'ave a nice time.' She sounded very subdued, near to tears.

They ate thin stew and beans in silence. Susan kept her eyes on her food. Mercy was all knotted up inside and kept glancing across at her. She was sorry, but she wasn't going to go back on it. She desperately wanted to be with Tom.

'I'm going in to give Mary a hand with Percy and Paul in a bit,' Mabel said, laying down her fork.

'Oh.' Susan's voice was bleak.

'You can come too. Paul'd like to see yer, you know that.'

*

As it turned out Mercy went out with Tom that day and almost every other of his week's leave. Johnny, not to be outdone, was walking out with a girl called Violet up the street and one evening they all went out together.

Watching the twins, Mercy saw that they'd both changed. They were both bolder, more manly. But while with Tom this new found confidence made him less awkward but no less kind, she found her feelings for Johnny changing for the worse.

He's getting to be a right cocky sod, she thought, watching him and Violet walking along in front of Tom. He was bossy with Violet, his arm round her, pulling her here and there as if he owned her.

'Let's just go on our own tomorrow,' she murmured to Tom, and he nodded.

'That's OK with me.'

They saw the new Chaplin film, went to the Bull Ring and ate cockles and roasted chestnuts by the illuminated stalls, stamping their feet and cupping the hot chestnuts in their hands to keep warm. Sometimes they walked the streets between high factory walls, or the closed shops on New Street or Corporation Street, Tom shyly taking Mercy's arm, both laughing a lot, new jokes along with shared laughter from the past.

Mercy was intoxicated with happiness.

'You awright?' Tom asked her. 'You don't want to take cold.'

'Ooh yes! I could stay out all night, I don't care!' she told him. She loved the warm feeling it gave her walking out with Tom. He felt a very solid presence beside her, not wild and skittish as Johnny now seemed. She trusted Tom – more than trusted him. She knew she had learned to love him for his kindness and devotion.

When they'd spent two evenings together he found the

courage to draw her close into his arms and slowly, tentatively at first, they kissed in the foggy darkness, conscious of nothing but each other.

'I love you so much, Mercy. I've always loved you, d'you know that? Ever since you belted that girl one for talking nasty to Susan, d'you remember? You're like a beautiful little tiger, you are.'

Mercy laughed, blushing with pleasure. 'You want to watch it then, don't yer?' She joked, making growling noises.

'D'yer love me, Mercy?'

''Course I do.'

He took her hand and they sauntered down the street, in no hurry to get home.

'I've never had anyone before,' Mercy said suddenly. 'Not to call my own. You've made me so happy, Tom.'

'I know you haven't.' The thought made him feel so protective. 'We'll be together and I'll look after yer. I promise yer that.'

Tom and Johnny had schemed to take Elsie out and about while they were at home but the weather was so wet they were more or less stuck at home.

'Next time we'll go out – up the Lickeys or somewhere,' Johnny said to her. He was full of the joys, had been out to a boxing match with his dad like two pals together.

'I don't mind whether we go out or not so long as you're 'ere and I know you're safe,' Elsie said.

The last evening they were all there in the gaslit room, Josephine heavily pregnant and fat in the face, Cathleen much more lively than she was usually, Jack drinking in all the twins' talk, Rosalie running from one to the other and getting playful cuffs and cuddles. And Mercy and Susan.

Mercy sat next to Tom, feeling self-conscious and trying to make sure Susan was included in everything. Bummy went down the Angel for jugs of ale and they had a very jolly evening.

Everyone tried to think of cheerful things. They reminisced, had a song or two, and Bummy asked the lads questions for the umpteenth time about the training, about soldiering.

After she'd wheeled Susan back home Mercy stepped out again to meet Tom so they could say their goodbyes in private. They stood near the brewhouse close to Elsie's shrine to Frank. Tom was solemn suddenly, the reality of his departure the next day seeming so close now. For Mercy, the thought of being physically parted from him was unbearable.

A light rain was falling and it was so dark they could only just make out each other's outlines. Tom put his hands on Mercy's shoulders.

'You know we're going to France, don't you?'

She nodded, then realizing he couldn't see, whispered, 'Yes.' A lump ached in her throat. The War was so strange to her and far away. Now Italy had joined in well. The reality of it came to them in the form of lists. Closely printed newsheet pages of the injured, missing, dead.

'Poor Frank,' she said. He had died on the Somme.

For a moment Tom rested his forehead on her shoulder.

Mercy put her arms round Tom and held him close. They stood in silence until Tom said, 'You mustn't worry. We'll be awright, me and Johnny.'

'Will you go together?'

'I s'pose so.'

She wanted to believe him, that the two of them would get through. All the life that was in both of them, the life she now held in her arms, it seemed impossible it could ever be wiped out. But the next moment the night air felt colder as Tom said, 'Whatever happens, Mercy, my love, I'll always be thinking of you. I'll always love you.'

They held each other so very tight then, not wanting to let go.

Chapter Fifteen

Christmas was over, and a depressing one it had been. Smoke and fog hung over the city streets, there was a permanently damp feel to everything and nearly everyone was coughing. In Angel Street the yards were permanently mired with a slippery mix of filth and water, however hard the women in the courts worked at them with stiff brooms. Each time Elsie laid new white flowers on her little shrine to Frank they soon looked soiled and bedraggled in the dank, sooty air.

It was New Year's Eve, and Mercy was sitting with Mabel and Susan, listening anxiously to Susan's laboured breathing. She'd had a nasty attack of bronchitis and was still suffering a hacking cough. Her cheeks were unhealthily flushed and she sat with her head lolling back in the chair by the fire, under a colourful patchwork quilt that she'd stitched herself. It was quiet apart from Susan's coughing, the shifting of the fire and George grinding his beak against his perch.

'We'd better get you up to bed,' Mercy said wearily. She was exhausted herself, and not looking forward to another sleepless night lying beside Susan's feverish body.

'Just a bit longer, ' Susan said, staring at the flames. She didn't look round, but Mercy could sense how low she was.

'What's up wi' you?'

Susan turned her head and glanced at Mabel who was

asleep at one end of the settle, head resting on one hand and throaty little snores escaping from her mouth. Mabel had gained the weight she'd lost in her absence, her face had lost its look of bitter aggression, and except for some extra lines, she was ripening once more into a quite handsome woman, more at peace with herself now she'd managed to earn some respect from the neighbours and wasn't at everyone's throats. All the same, Susan knew there were things Mercy wouldn't want said in front of her.

'You had another letter from Tom?' Susan kept her voice barely above a whisper.

Mercy looked down at her lap. She'd had a letter that morning and knew Susan was perfectly aware of the fact. 'I have, yes.' She'd slipped out to read it in the freezing privy, the only place where there was ever any privacy to be had. Tom's letters were so sweet, gave her news of where he was – not yet in France – and always ended with great affection. But they were not so demonstrative or personal that she couldn't have shared them with Susan. The fact was – and Mercy was ashamed of this – she just didn't want to. She wanted something all for herself, something just between her and Tom. She kept the letters in the little chest of drawers in their bedroom with the book and handkerchief she had had from the orphanage. Dorothy had told her how it had been left with her on the steps of Hanley's. She took it out from time to time, looking at its immaculate embroidery as if it were a puzzle, a key to who she was. She ached to know whose fingers had stitched the mauve letters of her name.

Susan's expression had turned sulky. 'You used to tell me everything, Mercy. You're full of secrets now and it ain't very kind, being as I'm just stuck 'ere.'

Mercy felt guilty but impatient. 'I'm not. There's

nothing much to tell. 'E just said they're doing more training and 'e doesn't know what's happening next.'

'And I s'pose you've been grinning away like a Cheshire cat and humming to yourself just because he told you that? D'you think I'm daft or summat? I get more out of 'im—' – she jerked her head at George who was staring gloomily across the room – than I do out of you these days.'

'Oh, think what you like.' Mercy was thoroughly riled by the injustice of this. She stood up. 'I'm going to bed, so if you want to get up there now's your chance. No point in staying up, is there? 1917's not looking to be any different from this year.'

'I don't want to go to bed just on your say-so,' Susan snapped, tearful suddenly. 'You're not in charge of everything around 'ere you know.'

'Susan!' Mercy was really hurt. 'That's not like you!'

Susan burst into tears which quickly broke down into coughs. 'I feel so down and useless,' she sobbed once she could speak. 'You've got Tom, and I'll never 'ave anything like that. And no one's bringing me any sewing any more and that's one thing at least I can do . . .'

'But Dorothy was 'ere only the week before Christmas,' Mercy protested. Dorothy's visits had dwindled since Mabel's return, but she always appeared sometime in a month and usually with clothes for them and a job or two for Susan which she'd collect later.

Susan didn't answer, just kept crying, weak and rundown from her illness. Mercy knelt in front of her and put her arms round Susan's waist.

'Look, I'm sorry. I didn't know what to tell you. Tom and I are . . . well, we have got sort of fond of each other, but that doesn't have to make any difference. I'm always going to be 'ere to look after you, you know that.' She leant down, her hair brushing Susan's fingers, and looked up into her face. Susan tried to smile.

'Come on – I'll take you up.'

Leaving Mabel, she helped Susan, step by step, up to the bedroom, on to the pot and finally into bed as she did every night. When she was ready for bed herself she climbed in, leant over and kissed Susan's burning cheek before blowing out the candle.

'Night, night. Happy New Year.'

She pretended to sleep as Susan fidgeted beside her but her mind was wide awake and active. For the first time she was finding all this care for Susan a burden. Mabel was here, she was the one really responsible for Susan yet it was Mercy doing all the work. And Mercy was restless now, increasingly so as each month passed. She wanted something else from life. But what? she asked herself. More experience, excitement? She barely knew what else there was on offer, yet sensed the close restriction of her existence. Going to work, coming home, housework – and now with the War all the extra 'don'ts' imposed on them. She wanted someone to say 'do' for a change. Do find something more to do with your life. Do get out of this place. Do find out who you really are, where you come from. But all these urgent impulses made her feel guilty too. There was a war on, all these lads getting killed. And how could she ever explain how she felt to Susan?

'Get out of my bloody way, woman!'

Grace heard Neville's arrival, as indeed most of the street must have done in the calm of this spring evening, the door slamming thunderously behind him and the howling of her younger son as he roared, 'And get these brats out of the way as well!' She heard Edward crying as their nanny hurriedly escorted them upstairs. Grace clenched her hands until the nails dug into her palms. Neville had very little time for his sons, spared them no attention or tenderness.

She stepped out of the front parlour into the hall where he was standing, so swollen up with fury she thought his shirt buttons might fly off. She glanced coolly at him.

'Damn it – look!'

'What is it, Neville?' He was so prone to outbursts of temper that she had learned over the years to remain absolutely calm in the face of it. This was effortless nowadays since her feelings towards her childish boor of a husband had passed through pain and loathing to an icy indifference.

'Are you blind, or just dim-witted, woman – look!'

In his hand was a large feather, greyish rather than white, but its meaning as it was thrust at him in the street was clear enough.

'Some damn *woman*—' he spat out the word as if it in itself was an insult, 'had the gall to stick it in the front of my coat!'

Grace tried to summon at least a pretence of indignation as Neville hurled the feather down on a polished side table and poured himself a large whiskey. Grace watched him with distaste. Her Temperance upbringing gave her an inbuilt revulsion for his drinking. He took a large mouthful and she saw his florid cheeks suck in and out as he washed it around his mouth.

You are foul, she thought. You disgust me. He was still young – not yet forty – though a little portly, and dressed in the clothes of a much older man: a thick worsted suit with watch-chain and weskit, and a Homburg for outdoors.

‘But where?’ Grace asked.

‘It was in – I don’t know where . . .’ He took another gulp from the glass. The fact that he’d been set upon by the woman – one of those suffragette harridans most likely – as he came out of one of the more notorious brothels on the Warwick Road was hardly something he could tell Grace.

‘It doesn’t matter where, does it? ’Ere I am, working night and day – the factory’s never quiet – keeping most of the British Army’s Motor Transport in supplies, and I get treated like a shirker and a coward.’ He banged the empty glass down on a little rosewood table so hard that Grace jumped.

‘But, Neville, you did say just the other day that shirkers ought to be tracked down and arrested.’

‘Not me though, for heaven’s sake! God knows it’s no good trying to talk to your sort. I’m wasting my time.’

He strode out of the room and went crashing up the stairs.

Grace was left standing alone in the middle of the room. ‘Oh dear, poor, poor you,’ she murmured. The loathing in her eyes and voice was unmistakable.

Two days later he burst into the house again earlier than usual, loud and elated.

‘The Master of the house is home!’ he bawled from the hall. ‘Is no one here to greet him?’

Grace, the nanny, Dorothy and the children dutifully appeared in the hall and stood in a semicircle in front of him. Grace laid her hands on the boys’ shoulders.

‘Well, I’ve done it!’ Neville let out his bellow of a laugh. ‘Come ’ere, boys – your father’s got summat to tell you.’

Robert and Edward stepped uncertainly towards him as Grace gave them a little push.

'Well.' Neville squatted down, pulling his sons between his thick thighs. 'Listen to me. I want to tell you summat.'

The two boys fixed their eyes obediently on his face, Robert with his father's thickset looks, Edward fair and slender.

'Your daddy's going away to be a big, brave soldier.'

Grace gasped, hands going to her cheeks. 'What? What're you saying, Neville?'

'It's all fixed. Joe Grable can run the firm – he's too old to enlist and he's worked there since 'e were a lad. Could run the place in his sleep. And I'm off to the Front, to serve my country.' He stood up, shoving his sons away as if they were tiresome puppies.

'But you could get killed, Neville,' Grace said carefully.

'But you could get killed, Neville,' he mocked her in a prattling voice. 'So the little woman has begun to grasp something about warfare these last two years has she?' He strode over and caught hold of her roughly under the chin. 'Concerned for me all of a sudden, are you?'

'You're hurting me, Neville.' She kept her voice even in front of the children, the servants. 'I'm thinking of our – your boys, our sons. You're their father.'

'Oh yes, I'm their father – at least according to you. Well, boys want to grow up with a father they can look up to, and that's what I'm going to give 'em.' He released Grace's chin, jerking her face aside, and as he did so, caught sight of the expression in Dorothy's eyes as she stood at the foot of the stairs.

'Don't look at me like that, woman.' He looked round at them all with a horrible sneer on his face. 'Hell, to think I've got to leave my lads in the hands of all you namby-pamby, coddling women.'

'So, my wench, your husband's off to the Front tomorrow.'

Neville's body thrust against hers, fleshy and bullying in its force as they lay between crisp linen sheets.

'Hardly the Front.' Grace spoke quietly, evenly, though her mind was recoiling with dread. 'You'll surely be training for quite some time yet?' She tried to inch her body surreptitiously away from his, revolted by his hard maleness forcing against her.

'So come on then—' Neville pulled himself up so he was leaning half over her, his breath thick with whiskey. 'Where are the tears, the "Oh Neville, I don't want you to go?" Some wife you are!'

'I don't wish you to go,' Grace lied, struggling to speak as he was forcing the breath out of her. 'But you chose to do it, Neville. You didn't have to, darling.'

'Darling, eh?'

Suddenly he forced his hand up between her legs, rooting against the folds of her nightshirt. 'Let's see how much feeling you've got for me, shall we, you prissy, bloodless creature. All these years I've spent servicing a dead cow. That's what it's like with you – and less rewarding probably. When I want you panting for me you're there with your eyes shut as if I'm serving you poison, you prim neuter, you.'

Grace let out a moan, automatically squeezing her eyes closed.

'Look at me!' He gripped her cheeks between the fingers of one hand, squeezing hard, and Grace couldn't contain her cry of pain, hands clawing at him to release her.

'That's it – if I can't have you moaning with pleasure you'll have to moan without it instead!'

Releasing her face, he wrenched up her nightgown and forced her legs apart. He started to force a thick finger up inside her, cursing.

'Dry as a dusty attic. Well, see 'ow yer like this then!'

He pushed his face into the most private parts of her, so that all she could feel was the hard grip of his hands on her thighs, his tongue licking, intruding, and the painful rasp of his stubbly chin.

'Oh God,' she whimpered. 'No – stop. Please. I beg you, not this . . .' The most degrading, disgusting . . . She felt sick with revulsion at him, at those unseen, awful parts of her body . . . She wanted to lose consciousness rather than feel any more of this gross nuzzling. She put her hands tight over her face, forced her mind right down into the blackness inside herself.

'That's better – I like a nice wet cunt . . .'

He was hugely aroused now, and she knew her own powerlessness was as much a stimulant to him as the feel of her body.

'Now then, my wench.' He pushed up hard inside her, his face, wet with her juices forced against her own cheeks, his thick-lipped mouth on hers making her sick to her stomach.

'Go on,' he pumped urgently. 'Cry out – you've got to cry out . . .'

Grace squeezed out a few distressed, catlike sounds and he climaxed, arms tensed straight, face puce, the veins on his neck sticking out.

Minutes later he was asleep, prone on his belly, breathing heavily.

Grace crept from the bed and poured water from the pitcher on the washstand into the deep, rose-ringed bowl. She washed all that she could of him away from her sore body, still sick with revulsion. She who had, all those years ago, committed this act of union with a man in such rapture! So long ago, the feelings buried by all that had happened since, that it seemed a life belonging to someone else.

She stood looking at Neville before blowing out the lamp.

Die, she prayed. Die an honourable death in France. The stain be on my soul, but God in heaven, please grant it that he die.

Death was to visit Angel Street, one death among so many in 1917, yet one which was as tragic and untimely as any of them.

Early one April morning, returning from the privy down the yard, Mercy heard a woman's high, grief-stricken wail, a shrill keening that no walls would contain.

She hesitated for a moment, unsure where it was coming from, the sound causing the hair to stand up on her neck and her heart to beat like a hammer. Mrs Ripley was also out there, staring down towards the entry, face as hard as a flat-iron.

'My God!' Mercy cried aloud. 'That's Elsie!'

She tore down to number one and as she did so their door opened and Bummy Pepper tore out pulling on his jacket as he ran heavily, lurchingly down the entry.

She heard Elsie's cries coming from upstairs and stepped inside, relieved to see Rosalie looking the picture of health. Jack was with her.

'What's going on?'

'Our Cathleen—' Jack could barely get the words out. 'Summat's 'appened to 'er.'

'Where's your dad . . .?'

'Gone for Dr Manley.'

It had gone quiet upstairs. 'Should I go up?' Mercy asked, full of dread.

'I think yer should,' Rosalie was trembling. 'None of us knows what to do – she's up the top.'

Mercy climbed the narrow stairs which, unlike theirs at number two, had a thin runner of carpet up the middle of them. The second flight was bare and Mercy felt as if her boots were making the most deafening sound.

'Doctor?' Elsie sprang out of the attic room looking like a madwoman. Her red hair was a wild mass round her head and her eyes were stretched wide and full of terror. 'Oh, it's you. Oh my God,' she moaned. 'I thought you was Dr Manley.'

'What's happened? I hope you don't mind me coming up, only . . .'

Elsie grabbed Mercy's hand and pulled her into the room.

'Look – look at 'er! My girl – what the 'ell's 'appened to 'er?'

She broke down again and began sobbing helplessly. 'I don't know what to do for 'er. I just don't know how to help 'er!'

Mercy's legs turned weak and shaky at the sight of Cathleen. A seeping patch of red half covered her pillow and a very straight line of blood led from her mouth down the side of her chin. Her face was sickly yellow against her red hair, lips a strange blue. Her eyes were closed and she seemed lifeless, lying there on her side, except for an occasional shallow, rasping breath.

'I can't rouse 'er!' Elsie cried, going to the bed again.

She picked up her daughter's limp hand. 'Cathleen, Cathleen, chicken, say summat to me! Open your eyes and look at me – it's your mom. Just show me you can hear me for God's sake!'

Cathleen's head gave the faintest movement.

'There – did you see that?' Elsie shook her suddenly, taking her by the shoulders, the girl's head lolling back, and there came a sudden, horrifying gush of blood from Cathleen's mouth. Mercy saw it spurt up in a thick, scarlet jet. Cathleen's back arched and her eyes snapped wildly open for a second as the blood poured out over her chin, spreading darkly across the bed. Elsie screamed in horror, recoiling from her, and Cathleen fell back like a rag doll and lay quite still. Elsie's screams went on and on.

Mercy felt the blood drain from her own face. Blackness come down on her like a shutter. When she came groggily round from her faint she was propped against the wall, head pushed between her knees and Elsie was beside Cathleen sobbing and shouting, imploring her to speak.

By the time Bummy arrived back with Dr Manley, Cathleen was dead.

'I told 'er. I kept telling 'er to get a job somewhere else.'

The doctor told him over and over that there was nothing to suggest Cathleen's munitions work had anything to do with her death, but Bummy needed to blame something and it was all he could think of.

'I've seen 'em,' he said, distraught, to anyone who'd listen. 'Them young girls all fainting and sick outside them shell factories. It killed 'er, that did. It did for our girl.'

The doctor said Cathleen had died of a brain haemorrhage, a ruptured artery in her head. But when he talked to Elsie during the numb days after Cathleen's death he said, 'You know, Mrs Pepper, I've known Cathleen since she was a young child, and I've often suspected that she wasn't long for this world. That bluish complexion, the lack of strength . . . The child was almost certainly born with a defective heart. If it hadn't been for this, that would most likely have killed her sooner or later.'

'All this time and we never knew.' Elsie was inconsolable. 'Why didn't 'e tell us?'

''E said 'e couldn't've done nothing except for upset and worry us,' Bummy said, fighting the tears which kept welling up in his eyes. His face was shrunken, the life knocked out of it. After a silence he said, 'I don't know. I don't bloody know, that I don't.'

'At least we've got 'er to bury,' Elsie said. 'Not like Frank. Oh Alf, what's 'appening to our family? We've always looked after our kids, tried to bring 'em up right. Now everything's falling apart. And Tom and Johnny going over there . . .' Sobbing, she said, 'I'd cry out before God if I thought there was one, but now I'm not so sure there is.'

Chapter Sixteen

September 1917

They marched into Ypres at evening, along the road from Poperinge, walking in a silence broken only by the clump of boots on the cobbled streets and the thud of guns. It was already almost dark as they crossed the Ypres–Yser Canal, and the silky blue of the sky was lit up ahead by the German counter-attack, shells exploding, flashes of light which quickly evaporated, leaving it seeming a shade darker than before.

Tom marched, half hypnotized by the rhythmic sound of feet around him and heady from drinking rum in the *estaminet* in Poperinge. Johnny was ahead of him along the line, and with them somewhere, two other Midlanders, Billy Cammett from Kidderminster and Fred Donaldson from Erdington. The four of them had been transferred to this company together and were now surrounded by taciturn, undramatic Suffolk men, some of whom had heard the boom of the guns from Flanders across their farmland even before they'd left home. Most were young like himself, no more than lads. In this war you could be a veteran at twenty-one.

The air was rank with smoke and cordite. It was dry tonight. Earlier a hazy sun had shone over the flat Belgian fields as they waited behind the lines, rehearsing campaign strategies, outlining objectives again and again for this push on Zonnebeke, one of the hurdles standing in the way of Passchendaele Ridge. They had eaten well – for here at least – concoctions fashioned from army biscuits, bully beef rissoles, Trench pudding with jam. Johnny had boxed that afternoon against a beefy-faced farm lad from Saxmundham.

And they wrote letters. Tom sent a postcard to his mom and dad. He sat for a long time trying to write to Mercy. Mercy, his girl, his love. He strained to see her face before him, this girl from another existence. He found he had no words. Since August, words to describe anything, to connect in any true way with the life at home, had deserted him. His first experience at the Front, his soldiering baptism, was the Passchendaele salient and even those present were hard pushed to take in the extremity of its horrors. The letter was tucked, barely begun, into the pocket of his tunic, pressed tight to his heart. He kept Mercy's image as a light, a flower in no man's land, a shred of purity to keep him a man.

Tom had known very early on that he was not made for the army: all the noisy camaraderie into which Johnny fitted as if he had been born to the life. Johnny, quickly christened 'Ginger' by the Suffolks, relished the ribbing, the half-friendly brawls, the boxing, drinking, everyone in together.

Almost from the moment he began training Tom had loathed all of it, ashamed though he was to admit it. This was what it was to be a man: soldiering. It had been exciting to get out of Birmingham: Sutton Park, France, Belgium. But he was homesick. Missed his mom and his sisters, even dopey old Cathleen. And with an ache of longing and desire made strong by all the talk of sexual exploits by the other lads, he missed Mercy. He dreamed of her constantly, her face, hair, her bare skin . . . This, all this war was a waste of time for no other reason than it took him away from her.

Tom played football while they were on rest, did his best to join in, but mostly he sat, quiet, on his own. Johnny picked up French or Belgian girls with casual ease, all attracted by his strong muscular frame, his lively cheek, his generosity and jokes. This evening a round-faced blonde had sat on Johnny's lap in the estaminet screaming with laughter, pressing kisses on his cheeks although they shared barely a word of spoken language in common. Tom knew perfectly well that Johnny's relations with women had progressed a hell of a lot further than his ever had.

'You want to get yerself a bird – get cheered up!' Johnny told him. He even thought of it, looked around, sized up a few. But they weren't Mercy.

And tonight, while he put on a show of smiling, cracking jokes as Billy Cammett's chubby face with a little brown moustache grinned back at him, and the little leather-cheeked man played his squeezebox, he had not been able to forget for a single moment what they were being primed for, the place of abomination to which they were being sent back.

'I'll 'ave to go out,' he'd said two or three times as his guts writhed.

'What's up, back door trots again?' Billy guffawed, slapping his leg as Tom nodded grimly, hurrying to the back of the steamy café, face twisted with urgency.

Walking now, he felt weak and nauseous. They'd passed the jagged silhouette of Ypres's ruined Cloth Hall at the centre of this broken, ghostly town and were heading out on the Menin Road. The stench of the salient was already overpowering: of death, of putrefaction, of gas-infused yellow mud. To step into this bulge of land, the foremost tongue of Allied territory held on the Flanders Front, was to walk into hell. It was a place of constant unease and fear.

Since the end of July the fighting had zigzagged back and forth across the ten-mile-stretch of land between Ypres and the ruined village on Passchendaele Ridge. The Allies had speedily taken the first five miles, but had not reckoned on the sophisticated strength of German fortifications further back: iron-reinforced pillboxes defended by hidden gun emplacements. The Allies pushed forwards: were forced back again and again.

It had begun to rain. Then to turn into the wettest August in living memory. This plain of reclaimed Flanders land already existed in a delicate balance, drained by ditches and channels. Bombardment by shells, the constant criss-crossing by carts and horses, gun carriers, thousands of men, and weeks of incessant rain had turned it into a churned-up quagmire, some parts possessing a terrible, active suction which could pull a man down in minutes.

Tom had spent two weeks at the Front, rain falling into his face as he arrived, while he slept on duckboards with the water rising over them, as they fought, moving through knee-deep mud with shells, bullets and water raining down on them. They were never dry. Always rain, rain and stinking mud so that even the rats looked bloated like sponges.

Yet he and Johnny had survived to live with sights that gave Tom no peace in his dreams. And they were going back. He sensed in his guts that he would not come through again. Even now he felt weak and defeated.

He remembered the faces of men he'd seen in the days before marching back from the Front. They had not spoken. Exhaustion weighted their limbs even more heavily than the mud drying heavy and cracked on their uniforms, faces, hands. But it was the eyes. A few, very few, appeared defiantly, almost feverishly cheerful. The rest were vacant, somehow absent in their own bodies as if their spirits had fled in the face of all that had been set before them, the effect of it all the more terrible for being unspoken.

By the time they reached the reserve trenches they were already exhausted. They relieved another company. Tom wasn't sure which, didn't care, but he heard their northern accents, guessed they were Manchesters.

'Good luck, pal,' one said to him. 'You'll bloody need it.' They were desperate to get away to safety, food, to get deloused, to sleep.

There was little in the way of sleep to be had here that night. About a hundred yards behind, the advanced batteries were thundering deafeningly, well before dawn, and the answering bombardment of sound was kept up from behind the ridge. Tom fell in and out of an uneasy sleep, sitting against the side of the trench, head lolling first one side, then the other. He vomited a number of times, too weak and tired even to move, and sat in the smell of it. I ought to report sick, he thought. But even the effort required to do that was beyond him.

They were to wait it out that day. Zero hour would be in the small hours of the next morning. All day, along the line, they waited. Johnny and the others came to see him. The four friends sat drinking tea together, trying to smoke in the damp.

'Marching orders tonight.' Johnny still seemed energetic, while Tom was numb and sullen. 'You awright?'

'I feel fuckin' awful. *This* is fuckin' awful.'

'Shut it,' Fred said with sudden venom, hurling his tea dregs into the sludge. 'None o' that.'

'Everyone got their last will and testament at the ready?' Billy joked, squatting next to Johnny, hands clasped round his cup. He worked in the carpet trade.

'Don't take long, that, do it?' Fred Donaldson was a stonemason, tall and hollow-cheeked. He spoke without humour.

'Got that bit of back pay due to me,' Johnny said. 'What – ten quid? I'll make a note, willing it to our mom.'

Tom's head whipped round, scattering raindrops from the brim of his hat. 'Shut up, will yer? Just shut it. Oh Christ.' He gripped his belly. ''Ere we go again.' He rushed towards the latrines to the raucous laughter of the others.

They spent the day together, watching reinforcement troops arriving, long snakes of them tiny in the distance, bigger at the head. They ate bully beef and bread and Tom managed to keep it down. After a time the rain let up and the sun strained its light through the smoke and cloud. The mud was shiny with water, reflecting the light.

By nightfall a mist had come down. They had the order to move forwards after dark, carrying their full equipment. Tom, as well as his haversack, rifle, gas mask, water bottle, grenades and entrenching tools, was one of the men assigned to carry a shovel strapped to his back for digging in where they were to maintain a position.

They walked, the way illuminated periodically by Verey lights but mostly dark. Tom kept his eyes on Billy in front of him. Johnny was further up ahead. In the mist and darkness, Tom's mind filled with horror at the sea of mud around them and all it contained. He'd seen horses, whole carts with their loads disappear into this foul yellow and grey sludge. He heard frequent shouts of those who had slipped from the walkway and fallen in and his mind almost blanked out at the thought of it. He was still in considerable discomfort, his guts wringing. His equipment felt heavy as lead on him, the shovel making it impossible to bend freely.

'Steady there, Bill,' he muttered as his friend suddenly seemed to make quicker progress in front of him. 'Don't go leaving me be'ind, for God's sake!'

But as he spoke he lost concentration and his feet slid from under him, jerking him off one side of the boards. He fell, rolling in the poisonous, sticky mud, losing control of himself so that diarrhoea squirted from him, warm inside his breeches.

'Fuck!' he cried out, his voice shrill. 'Help me, for Christ's sake!'

'You awright, mate?' He could hear Billy's voice, but see nothing. His feet were in water at the base of a shell hole and he was surrounded by nothing but blackness and slime. Panic engulfed him. They'd go on and leave him in this black stench! He flailed wildly, his legs lifting from the mud with a great squelching noise. He struggled to move up the side, digging his fingers hard and straight down into the ooze, trying to gain a hold. He was making some progress he was sure. A slight change in the intensity of darkness. He must be near the top.

'I can see you!' Billy cried. 'Come on, pal – just a bit further and yer can cop 'olt of my hand.'

Tom frenziedly thrust his hand up again, the fingers jabbing into something tense, inflated, which gave way instantly with a soft belching sound. He smelt the most overpowering, putrid stench. The body must have lain there for many days.

'Jesus! Jesus Christ, get me out of 'ere . . .'

At last he could seize Billy's hand, fingers slipping,

then his wrist and he was up again, plastered in slime outside his clothes, befouled inside.

'I just – fuck. Someone . . . I stuck my 'and in – went right through . . .'

'Come on, come on,' Billy urged him. 'Yer awright, just get going. Just shift yerself. No good thinking about it.'

Only yards later Billy himself tumbled down into one of the drainage channels and Tom had to help him out. They were slipping and cursing all the way along.

By the small hours they had found the tapes marking the starting point east of Frezenberg, and dug into position close to the railway leading to Roulers. A great quiet had come over the place at last. No one spoke. The line of men all waited shoulder to shoulder in position. Tom could just make out the railway embankment to their right, a humped shadow of denser blackness in the dark. Just once he heard the desolate cry of a marsh bird which must have ventured there in the lull.

This is it, he kept thinking. His innards had at last quietened a little. He felt beyond physical concerns now, as if his mind had overridden bodily things and the weakness had left him.

This is it. Oh God, oh God help me, don't let me die . . . He struggled to remember a fragment of a hymn from school:

> All that Thou send'st to me
> In mercy given;
> Angels to beckon me
> Nearer my God to Thee,
> Nearer to Thee!

He couldn't remember any more of it, but that fragment kept going round and round in his head. *Angels to beckon me . . .*

There came a great crashing rent of sound as the barrage of fire started from behind their lines and shells were exploding over towards the ridge.

'Come on, boys!' The whistle blew and Tom, as if dreaming, felt himself move, hauling the burdening weight he was carrying out on to the open ground as the land beyond was lit up by explosions, and flames and smoke rose from the German lines. The men in front of him looked like giants, swollen shadows in the mist and glare, and for a second he thought of Johnny. Johnny's words to him before they parted: 'Keep yer 'ead down, won't you, mate?' Johnny out here somewhere . . . Johnny, someone connected with real life, away from this crashing, screaming nightmare. Then thought left him, and he was an animal surviving.

The German machine-guns were clattering and on all sides he heard the whining of shells, howitzers firing, the hysterical shrieking of horses, the shouts and cries of men. His body felt leaden, the mud not so deep as before, but still clogging every step.

Within moments he was crouching with several other men at the lip of a shell hole. There were no trenches to speak of on the battlefield, just water-filled craters, sometimes so many in a row that they coalesced to form something like a trench, always with a depth of water in them.

'They're fucking miles above us!' one of the others was yelling against the roar of the barrage. 'Got a bird's-eye fucking view – how're we s'pposed to get up there? . . . Where's that bastarding fire coming from?'

The pillbox was their first objective, on a low ridge to

the left of the embankment and the strafing of machine-gun fire seemed to be coming from close to it.

A lull came, seconds only and they decided to break for it, heaving themselves to their feet over the slime. Tom could hear his breath coming in grunts. The fire started again immediately and, as they moved out, one of the Suffolks fell back. Tom, the shovel slung from behind him, was unable to bend or dodge easily. He hovered at the edge as another shouted, 'Come on – leave 'im,' then dived back, following the other man's body. That this was wrong never entered his head. You were never supposed to stop for anyone.

''Ere, I'm coming, it's awright.' Slipping down to the bottom wasn't difficult, borne by his own weight. Tom laboured towards him through the mud which was up to his knees, his hands thick with it. The bloke's face was already under the water. Tom was grabbing him by the shoulders when a shell hit the ground, falling short of their own trenches and he was flung backwards, mud and water raining down on him. As soon as he could he struggled back up, feeling slime creeping down his face, obscenities gushing from his lips, for there was not just mud wherever he placed his hands: sharp slivers of bone, softer bits of flesh or organ. This first section of the battlefield was a churned up morass of human remains. From somewhere near him he could hear moaning.

He seized the feet of his companion and hauled him clear of the water.

'Yer awright – I'll see to it yer awright . . .'

Heaving him up by the shoulders, Tom saw the exploding bullet had blown away nearly all the lad's throat. His head fell back, blood pumping. Aghast, Tom thrust it away from him.

He flung himself out over the top into the murky

expanse of noise and exploding light, instinctively trying to duck, bogged down by his equipment, starting to move in the direction of the railway embankment, looking out the next shell hole for cover. The flash of explosions lit up men running not far ahead through the mist.

Within yards Tom was in the mud up to his waist. An unseen pool of soft, sucking mud. It squelched as he struggled, fast sinking deeper.

'Help! Help me!'

He held his rifle up, trying to throw himself forward but he was in too deep. He could see movement on each side of him, men dodging and weaving, fallen bodies.

'For God's sake, SOMEONE – get me out. Help, I'm going under!' He was roaring with all his strength but his voice was the cry of a small bird against the gunfire. He had to stretch his arms out to the side to keep them clear. The more he tried to move, the greater the appetite of the swampy ground to suck him in. He raised his face, screaming to the sky.

For a few moments looking up towards the smoke-obscured sky, something more chill, more deep and corrosive than panic took hold of him. The possibility of going down into the mud unleashed something in his mind. It was spinning off, already disconnected from its hold on the real world he had known. Here was this black hell of overpowering shocks of noise, of mud and decay, rats, stench, blood and shit, of lice, mutilation, agony. Nothing which linked with what had gone before, the daily reassurance of human life, streets, pubs, washing lines, hearths, mothers, bread, love, life held sacred. Here, he was sinking in this sea of death-filled mud and would be entombed under invisible cold stars.

He was close to blacking out until the sound of rasping, groaning breaths roused him and he knew suddenly that it was his lungs and throat making those sounds. He was a man with a voice, a body, surrounded by other men, and the moment in which he was cut loose, whirling lost, receded.

The butt of a rifle swung towards him. ''Ere – cop 'olt of this, mate, quick!'

Johnny's voice, shrill with terror. In all this, a miracle: *Angels to beckon me . . .*

'Quick – for Christ's sake.'

At first Tom thought it wasn't going to work. Johnny had to keep ducking for although they were in a dip he was still exposed to the enemy fire. Tom could find nothing to push with his feet. Johnny hauled with all his strength until he could reach one of Tom's hands without falling in himself, then both hands. Finally Tom slithered out like a baby from the womb and Johnny flung himself down beside him.

'It's me,' Tom yelled, laughing, drunk.

'Fuck—' Johnny, panting hard, peered into his face. 'So it is! Didn't know . . . We've got to get over there – the railway—'

Their main objective, a spot called Le Moulin, lay ahead of them on this side of the tracks, close to Zonnebeke village which lay on the other.

'Get to the next 'ole, over there—' Instinctively, as ever, Johnny took the lead. Like rats crawling from a riverbank they moved off, stumbling forward through the fire to another shell hole.

'Now!' Johnny cried and they were up and over the edge of the next one and as they did so Tom heard Johnny cry out and clasp his left shoulder. Tom, slightly in front, unable to duck, turned, it seemed to Johnny afterwards, in slow motion, his lips forming the word, 'What . . .?'

Tom fell, mouth still open.

'Tom! Oh Christ, Jesus, no!'

Johnny hauled his brother's body back over the edge of the crater, oblivious to the pain in his own shoulder. Tom's eyes were closed.

'Stay there, brother,' Johnny shouted at him. 'Stay there, mate, awright? I'll be back for yer, I will!'

He rolled Tom on one side and unstrapped the shovel from his back. As he came up over the side of the hole he stuck it into the ground. Rifle clasped under his left arm, and clutching the shoulder with his right hand, he staggered out once more and headed, ducking and lurching, back towards the lines.

Dawn was shrouded in smoke, the sun a blood orange in the sky, guns still firing.

Johnny had made it back behind the lines under cover of the last shreds of darkness. He found makeshift dressing stations along the country road to Zonnebeke, doctors and nurses working in the open. A dark-eyed American nurse wearing gigantic gumboots dressed his shoulder.

'It's a graze,' she said. 'You were lucky – but it's deep – nearly cut through to the bone.'

'Just stick summat on it.' In his feverish state he was ungracious. 'I got to get to me brother – 'e's out there – please, just do it quick.'

'Oh, I don't think you'll be going anywhere,' she said patiently, thinking him delirious. 'We don't want you getting infected, do we?'

But as soon as she'd finished he broke away from her, off along the road, until he met a party of stretcher-bearers lurching exhaustedly towards him, their eyes fixed on the ground, faces shaded by their tin hats. The conditions were so bad in no man's land that it often took a dozen bearers to bring in one of the wounded.

'Steady, steady,' the front one cried. 'Here – get out of the way!'

'My brother,' Johnny ran at them. ''E's out there – get 'im for me, please, pal—'

The men stopped. They were swaying with exhaustion. 'Have you any idea . . .?' another of them said, his voice well-spoken. He pushed his helmet up with a mud-caked hand. 'It'd be like looking for a needle in a bloody haystack.'

'But I know – I can show you, for pity's sake . . .'

'Wait there . . .'

They returned in moments, the stretcher empty.

'Where?' the front man asked.

'Over towards the railway. Look, I'll know when we get there. I'm coming too.'

The sun was paler now, higher, and its rays straining through a sulphurous mist which curled over the surface of the mud and between the blackened stumps of trees. Not a blade of grass, not a hint of any green, living thing remained in this place. For as far as the eye could see was nothing but mud, wounded trees, water reflecting pale sky. The guns had ceased firing except for the occasional report of snipers' bullets. The battlefield was littered with the debris of slaughter.

Johnny walked slightly ahead of the stretcher-bearers, all of them slipping and trying to retain their balance.

They had gone only a short distance when Johnny started to panic, realizing just how difficult it was going to be to find the place. There was nothing to give you a bearing, all landmarks wiped away: woods, farms, villages annihilated in the two years of bombardment. But he wasn't going to show the men that he had scant idea where he was going. Soon he saw the dim shape of the embankment and relief surged through him.

'That way.'

All round them as they waded and hauled themselves so painfully slowly through no man's land, the early morning air was filled with cries and moans. Men lay where they had fallen. Others had taken shelter or tumbled into shell holes, and each hole had its ration of bodies, living and dead, from both armies. As they struggled on, Johnny couldn't look into the eyes of those still alive. They all kept their eyes on their feet. Blood bubbled up from the mud from time to time. The edges of civilization, of decency, of meaning, of the obligation to mercy had simply been blown away. There was nothing here to redeem it, nothing . . . except Tom. Tom's life.

'If you don't find it soon we shall simply have to take someone else.' The stretcher-bearer spoke tersely.

'Sorry – only it was dark. Just a bit further.'

And at last, barely visible, poking up like a tiny matchstick, Johnny caught sight of the shovel. 'There!' he roared. 'See? In there!'

The team of stretcher-bearers, hurrying now, followed him to the edge and stood looking down into the watery morass of the shell hole. They watched as Johnny, with infinite gentleness, hauled the torso of another young soldier into his arms, head bent over him.

There came a small shred of sound from the wounded soldier.

'What's that, mate?' they heard Johnny say.

'Ooom . . . Mo-o-o-m . . .'

Johnny put his head back and turned to them as they stood outlined by the sky where rain clouds were gathering once more.

'Quick,' he said, his voice hoarse. ''E's alive!'

Chapter Seventeen

'Mercy – it's Tom. They've brought 'im home!'

Mercy, only just out of bed with her hair tumbling all over the place, stared at Elsie, unable to make any sense of what she'd said as she burst into their house early one morning.

''E's been wounded – came in on the hospital train . . .'E's up at the university!' Elsie was displaying the first signs of animation that she'd shown for months, and her blue eyes shone with hope. 'That means 'e's out of it. 'E's safe!'

Mercy found herself saying Thank God over and over in her mind. She went out to the privy and had a cry in private, relief and joy flooding through her, overflowing down her cheeks. Only then did she realize how numb with worry she'd been.

Suddenly she felt excited. Tom, home – long before she'd expected to see him! She could visit, help look after him. He was here in Birmingham, only just up the road!

They visited later that day, Mercy with Elsie and Bummy. The bus stopped on the Bristol Road, almost opposite the rather awe-inspiring university building.

'Looks more like a church, don't it?' Elsie said, her worn face upturned as they passed the tall brick campanile in the middle of the university grounds. 'Imagine working here!'

Mercy was trembling with anticipation. In one part of her mind she was preparing herself. Tom was injured: suppose, like a number of the wounded men she'd seen in the streets, he'd lost an arm or leg? Or both? But he'd still be Tom, wouldn't he? She'd still love him whatever, and she couldn't wait to see him, be close to him. As he was wounded he might be home a long time. He might escape the rest of the War altogether!

'They bring 'em in through Selly Oak goods station,' Bummy was saying. He kept clearing his throat with nerves. He and Elsie had put on their Sunday best to come out here and see their son, Bummy in a battered old Homburg which looked too small on his bullish head.

'Ooh!' Elsie took Mercy's arm and squeezed it. 'I feel all of a flutter. I can't believe we're going to see 'im!' She seemed quite light-hearted. Whatever had happened, her boy was home and he was alive.

When they got inside the makeshift hospital, they couldn't find him.

'I'll look on the list for you,' one of the orderlies said, eyebrows puckering as he ran his eyes down the list of names.

'It's a feat of organization, I can tell you. There're a thousand beds here now. Oh – here we are.' He looked up at them solemnly. 'I'm sorry, I hope you haven't come too far . . .' Elsie clutched Mercy's arm as he spoke. 'Tom Pepper? Yes, he's been moved . . .' Elsie let out a shuddering sigh. 'To Highbury Hall – living in style.' He tried to joke, then seeing their bewildered faces added, 'Over in Kings Heath. Joseph Chamberlain's mansion. That's a hospital as well now.'

They thanked him and he said, 'Never mind, just another bus ride.' He watched them walk back towards the entrance. 'Highbury.' He shook his head. 'Poor bastards.'

'When he said "I'm sorry" like that, I thought my heart was going to pack in,' Mercy said as they walked down the road.

'I know, me too.' Elsie was nervy now, tight-faced. The energy had gone from the day and the delay felt ominous. None of them was excited any more, just weary and anxious.

Highbury Hall, though much smaller than the university, felt even more imposing with its long drive and country house splendour, although now there was an ambulance parked outside and the garden was looking unkempt and overgrown.

They walked through an arched doorway into the dark interior of the Hall, the incongruous hospital smell of disinfectant immediately once strong in their nostrils. They could see people bustling about, nurses, orderlies, but the atmosphere was a hushed, careful one.

'Can I help?' A doctor stopped, crossing the hall.

Bummy removed his hat and had to clear his throat twice before he could speak. 'We were told you've got our son.' Mercy felt Elsie take her hand for a moment, gripping it tight.

The doctor was brisk but gentle, obviously aware of the anxiety in their eyes. 'His name?'

He seemed to recognize Tom's name at once.

'Ah.' Mercy saw a tiny movement at the side of his jaw, knew he was clenching his teeth and her stomach tightened further.

'How is 'e?' she asked.

'He's – well, it's very early days.' The doctor seemed uneasy. 'You could go up and see him for a short time, but you should prepare yourselves. He may not recognize you at this stage. He's had a nasty bang on the head.'

They followed the doctor's tall figure up the stairs. He stopped at the entrance to one of the rooms and spoke to a nurse. Even more gently now, he ushered them in.

Crammed in along either side of the room, were rows of black iron bedsteads, and between them, down the middle, two small tables with vases of flowers and a leafy aspidistra resting on lace cloths.

Mercy looked round her, heart hammering. It was very hot in there and she felt overwarm after her walk and suddenly dizzy with heat and nerves. What she saw also began to make her feel sick with dread. In the beds lay young men, or what could be seen of them, so swathed were they in bandages and dressings, and mostly they lay very still and so silent it was impossible to be sure there was life in them. But as they passed, one or two let out chilling cries of anguish. One of them, his face half-covered by a bandage, thrust his arm up above his head, crying in a slurred voice. Mercy didn't know where to look, averting her eyes.

But worst of all, they could hear a loud, inhuman sound, half groan, half gargle, coming from a heavily bandaged figure at the end.

Mercy heard Elsie catch her breath and say, 'Oh Lor,' in a faint voice.

The noise grated on, insistent, nerve-rending. The doctor was steering them towards that bed.

'No!' Elsie stopped, adamant. 'That ain't Tom. That's never my son making that noise.'

There was nothing Mercy could associate with Tom.

So little of the face could be seen. There was no smile, no voice or welcoming embrace. Was this him, this creature lying there, the man she loved? The one in whom she'd invested all her affection, her future hopes? She stood beside Elsie, the two of them paralysed at the end of the bed, as white lights began to flash at the edges of her eyes. She couldn't get her breath: it was stifling in here.

It was Bummy who moved slowly round and bent his red, scrubbed face close to the wounded lad.

'Son?' He spoke softly. 'Son. It's yer dad.'

As he spoke, Mercy felt the heat and flashing lights swell until the lights clicked off and there was only blackness. She slumped to the ground at the end of Tom's bed.

Tom had been taken from the Ypres salient to no. 46 Casualty Clearing Station at Proven (otherwise known as Mendinghem), with a bullet embedded deeply in his skull. After an operation to remove it he was sent home as a cot case on the ambulance train and finally reached Highbury Hall, which had begun to specialize in neurological cases and in a new technique still in its infancy – brain surgery.

'Will he be all right? Will he learn to speak again? Will he walk?' They kept on and on asking the doctors, wanting answers to the main question 'Will he be our son again – our Tom?' No one could give them straightforward reassurance. They were to operate again and see what progress could be made. But it was only right to warn them: damage to Tom's brain appeared to be very severe, perhaps irreversible.

Coming home from that first visit, Mercy still sick and groggy, they were all sunk in shock. They had seen this 'thing' on the bed, hearing the sounds he made, but could barely recognize him as Tom. Mercy felt she was in a waking nightmare.

The next week when they visited she had a few moments with him on her own. Elsie and Bummy had already seen him together and said they'd wait outside. They had operated on Tom on the Tuesday and he was now in a different room. His head was still dressed thickly in bandages but this time they left both his eyes free.

As Mercy walked with weak legs towards the bed he was staring at the ceiling, lying absolutely still. She found herself tiptoeing, afraid to disturb this stranger for whom she'd dressed in her newest, prettiest frock decorated with rust-coloured autumn leaves which set off her hair beautifully.

There was a wooden chair squeezed between his bed and the next, and Mercy sat down, out of range of his view, watching him. His hands lay outside the covers of the bed and the one nearest her was never at rest, the fingers plucking at the turning on the sheet. She knew at last that it was truly him. She knew those hands, had known them for years so that they were now almost as familiar as her own. The hand beside her had gently held hers as they walked in the winter dark together.

She wanted to touch him then, but held back, sitting up very straight to look at his face. His cheeks were thin and pale against the yellowed bandages, and he lay as if he was in a trance.

Mercy could bear it no longer. She leant closer. 'Tom. Tom—' she half whispered, unsure whether any of the other prone figures around her could hear. 'It's me, Mercy. It's me, my love.'

Slowly, he turned his head a fraction towards her and

her spirits leapt with hope. She jumped to her feet and looked down into his eyes.

'Tom, sweetheart – Tom?' She picked up the twitching hand and pressed it to her cheek, her lips. 'Say summat to me – just say you can hear me!'

She saw him watching her, his gaze focussing gradually on her face. But in his eyes she saw nothing of the affection that had been there before when his expression had softened at the sight of her. Now he glared at her, and at the heart of that look she saw a total blankness, a complete lack of engagement with her.

'Oh my God.' She dropped his hand, afraid, stepping back from this terrible coldness. 'Tom? Tom, don't look at me like that – don't!'

She turned her head away, but each time she looked back at him the iron gaze was still fixed on her.

Unable to stand it any longer, she rushed from the ward. Those eyes followed her all evening and into her sleep. Nowhere in them could she see the soul of the man she loved. Wherever it was Tom had been, he had left there the key part of his very self.

Elsie, with a mother's eternal optimism, was certain he would recover.

''E was looking at us, I know 'e was!' she 'd say after their first few visits. ''E knew us awright!'

Whatever Mercy had seen or failed to see in Tom's eyes, Elsie clung to her conviction. 'By Christmas 'e'll be right as rain – the doctor said 'e'd improve, didn't 'e?'

They visited week after week, feet swishing through fallen leaves on the pavements outside Highbury Hall, then the leaves were frosted white, then coated in snow.

As the winter took hold, Elsie's hopes slowly began to dissolve. Mercy went with her each time, dread hard in her as stone.

Elsie would sit at Tom's side, her now fast-greying hair fixed up under her best hat, ankles neatly crossed, chatting to him, holding one of his clammy hands.

'We've had a note from Johnny,' she told him just before Christmas. ''E's in Italy now. Says 'e's awright. You comfy there, love? Anything I can get yer? Just say, won't yer? Your Mercy's 'ere to see you again – look, there she is, over there. Never misses a visit, she don't. You got to get better for 'er, you know that, bab – and for me and your dad. Can't 'ave you carrying on like this, can we?'

Bummy, when he came, would sit silently beside her, hat in hand. Mercy sometimes had to leave the room, choking back her tears on hearing Elsie talk, what remained of her bright hope still fluttering round her son.

By Christmas Elsie had withdrawn from life on the yard in Angel Street. She was thinner, more stooped, and between her grief for her dead children and her concern for those still hanging on to life she had no energy to give to anyone else.

It was to Mabel that everyone was gradually turning for help and advice. Mabel who was seen as the strong one, who had 'come through' and was always there to help Mary Jones and, increasingly, everyone else. Even Josie Ripley, a hard case of a woman who was hardly ever heard to say anything to her six kids unless it was, 'Ger'over 'ere or I'll belt yer one!' had been known to turn to Mabel. Mabel made sure everyone took their turn to clean out the dry pan lavs down the yard, and had their go at washday in the brewhouse. She'd organized the yard women into a 'didlum club', taking pennies from them week by week as savings for Christmas. She'd gained in dignity, walked stately and handsome in her tartan shawl. She had people's respect. She was Someone nowadays.

She even showed sympathy to Mercy over Tom.

'It's a terrible thing, that,' she said to Susan. 'Like a living death. Be better if 'e'd – well, you know – altogether, wouldn'it?'

Mercy didn't want her sympathy. She still couldn't talk about Tom, even to Susan who seemed to feel that now Mercy was in effect 'alone' again, the two of them should be as close as ever. But Mercy didn't feel released from Tom. She had come to dread this helpless wreck of a man who had come home to her, yet she was still tied to him by his suffering, by the past, by guilt.

One afternoon, freezing outside, she sat by his bed looking at him. Once again, he was staring up at the ceiling, hands twitching, an occasional disconnected sound coming out of his mouth. He could do nothing for himself: not feed or walk or clean himself in any way. He had, in all ways that meant anything to her, ceased to be a person, certainly a lover. Yet here he was, this troubling, physical presence that was undeniably in the shape of Tom.

'Are you there?' she asked him over and over. 'Are you still in there? Can you hear me?' She leant over so that her face was level with his eyes. 'Please, Tom – if you can understand me, show me somehow. I can't stand this.' He seemed to be looking straight through her.

'You was everything to me . . .' She began to cry, the first time she had allowed herself to in front of him, though she had many times after leaving the hospital. The old Tom would have been distraught at the sight of her tears, would have done anything he could to comfort her.

This Tom shifted slightly in the bed and let out a low groaning sound, but Mercy knew instinctively that this had no connection with her words. She sank back on to her chair, taking his hand and kissing it, wetting it with her tears.

'I want you back,' she cried. 'I can't bear it. Don't leave me. Come back to me, Tom, my love, please!'

In the end, the only person Mercy could confide in fully was Dorothy. She hadn't told Dorothy about her feelings for Tom, but now she had to talk to someone. She waited until Dorothy was leaving one afternoon and said, 'I'll walk a bit of the way with you.'

'Oh, there's no need,' Dorothy said, gathering up her coat. 'It's ever so cold out.'

'No – I want to.' Mercy eyed Susan, but she was eagerly looking over a dress Dorothy had brought to be altered.

Dorothy saw the desperate look in Mercy's eyes and said, 'Come on then, if you like.'

The two women, both warmly wrapped, walked out along the slushy street in the dusk. Mercy poured out her troubles.

'His mom thinks 'e's going to get better, keeps telling me to hang on. But it just ain't going to happen, Dorothy. He don't even know me now, and I loved 'im, I really did love 'im . . .' She broke off, unable to speak any more.

Dorothy stopped, saying, 'Oh bab, oh Mercy,' and drew the girl into her arms, overcome at seeing her so sad and vulnerable.

'I thought I'd found someone,' Mercy sobbed into her shoulder. 'Someone who could really be mine and be family. And now it's just like talking to a stone. He can't do nothing for hisself, and the way he looks at me. It's as though he's staring right through me, as if he hates me.'

'Oh Mercy, poor babby . . .' Dorothy sounded near to tears herself. 'We – I had no idea all this was on your mind. Why didn't you tell me before?'

Mercy shrugged, head resting on Dorothy's shoulder, still crying, relieved at being able to let out her feelings to someone.

'I know I ought to want to be with him – say I'll stay with him even if he is injured. It ain't his fault, is it? His life's ruined. But . . .'

'There, there – it's a terrible thing's happened to you, and to 'im.' Dorothy's heart was heavy. 'I'm sure no one expects you to stay with 'im forever, course they don't.'

Mercy raised her head, wiping her eyes. Dorothy thought how pretty she looked in the dim light, even in her misery.

'We would've got married, I'm sure of it. I wanted to stay with him for ever, and now I feel I still ought to—'

'Don't!' Dorothy broke in fiercely. She took Mercy by the shoulders, her dark eyes stern. 'Don't ever marry someone unless you want it with all your heart. It'll only lead to misery for both of you. Remember that. I've seen it at close hand and believe me, you're better off without it.'

Mercy frowned, calmer now. 'Where've you seen it?'

Dorothy hesitated, her expression bitter under the rim of her hat. 'If you'd known my mother and father you'd've thought marriage was summat invented by the devil himself. Come on – keep moving or we'll catch cold.'

Mercy walked beside her suddenly seeing how little she knew Dorothy.

'No one's going to expect you to have a married life with a man who can't even speak to you, let alone anything else. Don't be a fool, Mercy.' Dorothy spoke with fierce authority. 'For God's sake don't throw your life away.'

The Weston household had enjoyed a harmonious few months with the master of the house absent. Neville had been sent into a Motor Transport Division behind the lines in France, and wrote home very occasionally.

With him gone, Dorothy lived alongside Grace almost as her equal. The boys were far more relaxed, especially Edward, the younger one, whose sensitive temperament, similar to Grace's, grated on his father who tried to insist that he behave 'like a proper boy'.

When Dorothy returned rather later than expected that evening, Grace was sitting at her little writing-desk looking through the household bills and she turned, smiling, although the smile was, as ever, tinged with anxiety.

Dorothy sat down opposite her. Seeing her sombre expression, Grace's face fell.

'Whatever's the matter, dear? How is she?'

'If only we had more control of the situation,' Dorothy burst out. 'If only you could see her, tell her . . .'

Grace looked down at her lap. 'I can't. I just can't risk it.'

'But while he's away . . .'

Grace gave a wan smile. 'My darling Dorothy, how fierce you are on my behalf . . .'

'Not just yours, Grace.'

'No, I know what Mercy is to you too. But I'm so

afraid. I simply daren't risk such an overturning of all our lives, even with Neville away. There are the boys to think of. If Neville were to find out – and we don't know what Mercy might do, do we? While she is my daughter by birth, I can't be certain of her loyalty and her affections, can I?' Grace stood up. 'Look, dearest, what's happened?'

Wearily, Dorothy rubbed her temples. Grace went to stand behind her, circling her fingers gently along the older woman's forehead. 'Please tell me what's the matter.'

As Dorothy talked Grace stopped her massage and sat down beside her, her expression increasingly troubled.

'She said she thought she'd found someone – real family at last. Not just the young feller – of course, she's close with Elsie, his mother as well. But now . . .'

Grace's eyes filled with tears. 'Now she's been abandoned all over again.

Chapter Eighteen

February 1918

The day they brought Tom home the remains of snow lay on the ground, rounded, filthy cushions of it still bunched in untrodden corners. Mrs Ripley's snotty-nosed kids picked it up to chew mouthfuls as the ambulance pulled up, melting it to metallic soot in their mouths.

Elsie, the only one at home, walked beside the stretcher as they carried him in, clinging to one of his hands, her back ramrod straight. He still had a light dressing on his head and round it his hair was growing back as a brown stubble.

The two men who accompanied him were quiet but gentle.

'There yer go,' one spoke at last as they lowered him on to the bed Elsie had ready downstairs. 'Home sweet home.'

Elsie propped Tom up on what she had in the way of pillows and he lay staring across the room.

'There y'are, love. You can be at home with yer mom now. See – you can watch me while I'm cooking and cleaning up, and whenever you want anything all yer 'ave to do is say. I'll look after you. Now – will yer 'ave summat to eat?'

*

When Mercy came in from work that night Mabel was frying onions in a pan on the range, trying to spin out the meagre amount of food available. Her hair was greying but still more pepper than salt, and was fastened in a thick coil behind her head. When she saw Mercy she pulled her shawl tighter round her.

'I've seen 'im,' she said. 'Bad, ain't it?'

Mercy's face was very pale in the gaslight, her eyes glassy with exhaustion. Even Mabel took in the pinched expression of despair. 'He's home then?'

Mabel nodded. 'I looked in earlier. She's got 'im sat up downstairs like Patience on a monument . . . Be better up out of the way to my mind.'

'What – the way you kept me?' Susan retorted sharply. 'Some people ain't ashamed of their family whatever state they're in, you know.'

Mercy turned to the door again and said in a tone of heartbreaking flatness, 'I'll go and see them.'

''Ave yer tea first – it's ready.'

'No – I'll not be long.' She knew if she went now, she'd have an excuse to leave.

Mercy had not been in to see Elsie and Alf for some time. She'd been unable to face the house, empty of children except Jack who was out at work now, and Rosalie. And Elsie's grief, a black depression she'd slip into for days at a time alternating with a determined, brittle optimism about Tom.

When she walked in there that night, the living room was transformed. Gone was the horsehair sofa, and instead there was only just space to open the door without colliding with the foot of Tom's bed. The table was almost up against the fire and Elsie, Alf, Rosalie and Jack were squeezed round three sides of it. The room smelt dismally of the damp washing which was hanging everywhere.

'Come to see 'im, 'ave yer?' Elsie said brightly. ''E's been waiting for you, 'ain't yer, Tom?'

Mercy's eyes moved from Elsie's thin, exhausted face to Tom's expressionless features. She could feel all of them watching her expectantly. What did they want – that she should run over and embrace Tom as if he were still the same? Would that make them feel better? She knew she couldn't do it – just couldn't. She tried to force a smile to her lips.

'Nice to see 'im back.' She was unable to lift her voice out of the sadness which encompassed not just her own feelings for Tom, but for all of them. They were all so changed, Elsie like an old woman at fifty-two, her face framed by dusty-coloured hair in which almost none of the former copper remained, Alf – for he was always Alf now, his nickname somehow buried with his children – had a redder, coarser face. Jack was the least altered visibly, red-haired and very like Johnny, but he was quiet, had lost his spark. And Rosalie, now ten, who'd always been a rounded, rosy child, was so terribly thin, her face pinched and sad. Mercy, pulling herself together inside, stepped over to Rosalie and put her hands on her shoulders, kissing the top of her head before she went over to Tom. She sat down, hands in her lap. Though she was close to Tom she just couldn't touch him. She felt somehow afraid of him.

'So how's 'e been?'

'Not so bad,' Elsie said as Tom let out a long groan which sounded like water disappearing down a drain. ''E's 'ad 'is dinner. Nothing much wrong with 'is appetite any'ow.'

Tom could eat once the food was in his mouth, but he no longer had the coordination to put it there himself.

Mercy asked a few more questions, tried to be warming and cheerful with this family who had, over the years, lifted her own spirits so many times. But after a few minutes she could think of nothing else to say and she could feel her own distress mounting. Tom seemed to take up so much of the room, filling the place with a sense of all that was broken in their lives. If he had looked very different it might have been easier to accept, but his disfigurement was mostly internal. Added to that, all the empty chairs . . . Cathleen's, Frank's, no Johnny either . . . Mercy suddenly felt she could bear it no longer.

'Mabel's got my tea ready—' She stood up. 'I said I'd only be a minute.'

'Come whenever you like, won't you?' Elsie pleaded. 'After all, you're more or less one of the family.'

That night, when she had blown out the candle in their bedroom, Mercy turned and cried for a long time in Susan's arms.

'Oh Mercy,' Susan said as her friend's sobs finally calmed a little. 'I'm so, so sad for you. But I'm so glad you've come back to me.'

The world was convulsing round them. The end of 1917 had seen more fighting: the remainder of the long battle of Ypres, and at Cambrai. The Tsar had been overthrown in Russia and now the United States was also in the War. At home, they were told the German civilians, their ports blockaded by the Allies, were starving.

'We'll be bloody starving soon too at this rate,' Mabel complained. She'd finally taken on proper responsibility for the house. 'There's hardly any meat to be had, and that stuff they're passing off as bread – like eating chaff, that is.'

For Mercy, the limits of life had shrunk more than ever, so that it was comprised of the grenade factory and numbers one and two, Nine Court, Angel Street. She'd got into the habit of paying a visit to the Peppers every night after tea. They seemed desperate for her to come. Mabel and Mary Jones sometimes popped in during the day, but Elsie, utterly tied to Tom's needs, was isolated and very down. Whenever Mercy walked through their door, their eyes fastened on her hungrily as if she represented normality and hope, things they couldn't keep hold of when left alone together.

Elsie was enormously protective of Tom. She couldn't bear to feel people pitying either him or herself.

''E's awright – 'e'll get better. The doctors said it'd take a bit of time after what 'e's been through.' She toiled day after day to keep him clean as a whistle, fed him, talked to him endlessly.

But to Mercy she complained. No one was doing enough.

'Alf's out all the time, and Jack. I'm left to do it all. And Josephine hardly ever comes over now. It ain't right, keeping a littl'un from seeing his nan. It ain't fair. She ought to come.'

'She's got 'er hands full,' Mercy tried to reason with her. 'What with the pub and that flat and little Janey to look after . . .'

Josephine had come sometimes when Tom first arrived home. She'd turned to Mercy on more than one occasion with a look of desperation in her eyes when Elsie wasn't looking. One day, when Elsie had popped outside she said, 'I can't stand seeing 'im like this.' Looking across at

Tom her eyes filled with tears. 'Look at 'im – 'e's just not 'ere, is 'e? Where's 'e gone? It ain't right, none of it. Would've been better to my mind if 'e'd . . .' She bit her lip, suddenly busying herself picking Janey up and wiping her hands. 'I shouldn't talk like that, I know. Mom'd 'ave a fit . . .'

Her words sent a great wave of relief through Mercy. Josephine was the only one who'd expressed what she herself was thinking. This wasn't hopeful, all this. Tom wasn't a hero. It was a dreadful, heartbreaking hell seeing him in this state day after day, this man whom she'd loved, whose hand she had wanted to hold into the future.

Josephine appeared on rare occasions now, but ever since then Mercy had felt some release. She could begin to let go of Tom, to acknowledge that he really was lost to her. She could visit and try to support Elsie without feeling she had to catch hold of a dream and hang on, for her dream had already dissolved. The man she loved was dead.

It was a long, sad winter. The fighting on the Western Front was held up. No moves could be made before spring, and morale among the troops was low. The casualties at Ypres had been vast and there was a shortage of troops. Johnny Pepper had spent much of the winter up on the freezing *altipiani*, the 'high plains' between Italy and Austria, among the divisions sent to reinforce the Italians. As the snow began to melt, however, and spring came, they were being despatched back to the Western Front. First though, Johnny was sent home on leave.

He arrived in Birmingham at the end of March. A tall, stringy-looking figure now, his shorn hair merely a red haze round the edge of his cap, he strode back into Angel

Street, feeling he was in a dream. This was home, but now it seemed so strange, so alien. It was as if the army, for all the degradation and horror it entailed, had become his true home, the only true way of life.

Elsie would never forget her son's face as he walked into the house that day and saw his twin. Johnny's eyes, already red from lack of sleep, fastened on Tom's face, and Elsie saw burning in them horror, pain and disgust. That sight of hope dying in Johnny's face broke her heart more than she had allowed Tom's condition to do so far.

'Tom?' Johnny swung his kitbag to the floor and went to him. Elsie watched, pulling her old cardigan tight round her.

'Tom – it's me, Johnny. ''Ow are yer, mate?'

Tom was in his usual position, staring intently upwards as if the flaking ceiling was a puzzle which held all the secrets of the universe. When Johnny spoke to him he moved his head a little.

'Tom!' Johnny took him by the shoulders and started to shake him violently. 'Say summat – speak to me, for God's sake. Stop playing about!'

'Johnny, stop it – you'll hurt 'im!' Elsie tried to pull him off. ''E can 'ear yer – I'm sure 'e can. But 'e can't say anything to you – not yet.'

'Not yet!' Johnny stepped back, eyes stretched in horror. He slammed his fist on the table with such force that one of the cups flew off and smashed on the floor. ''E's been home nigh on six month! You wrote and said 'e was doing all right. D'you mean 'e's been like this all the time?'

'Oh, 'e was much worse to begin with—'

'They said to me that day—' Johnny was shouting, completely distraught. 'They said 'e'd be awright – that's what they said. And all this time I thought, well whatever else, Tom's awright . . .'

'But 'e is—'

'You call that awright? 'E's nowt but a vegetable!'

He strode out of the house again leaving the door swinging. He didn't come back until evening.

'Hello Johnny,' Mercy said softly.

Johnny looked up from his tea and saw her in the doorway. She was dressed in her work clothes, thinner, more grown up. But God she was lovely, he thought. Those little white teeth, the deep, inscrutable eyes.

'Mercy—' He put his fork down, wanted to say more but couldn't think of anything. In that moment though, for the first time, he really felt he'd arrived home. She was still Mercy, while otherwise at home nothing else was the same. His mom and dad had turned into old people, and in this short time he'd had to take in Tom's condition, Cathleen's death and the extent of the grief they still all shared for Frank . . . No one and nothing was as it had been. But Mercy . . . Johnny watched as she took off her coat, the smooth way she moved. His mind was skipping on fast. She wasn't Tom's any more – she couldn't be, could she? So why shouldn't he have her?

Mercy said hello to Tom, then sat down at the table between Johnny and Alf.

'You've seen 'im, then?' she said.

'Yeah.' He was looking down at his plate.

'So how are you?'

He looked at her out of the sides of his eyes. 'Awright.' She was so close to him, and he found himself sizing up her breasts as if she were a Belgian whore.

'Good to be home, eh?'

'Yeah. I s'pose.' He didn't know what to say to her, could only think of the excitement rising in him, shaming him. But he wanted her. Sex was his customary way of briefly finding warmth and humanity. He wanted Mercy under him, the hot clutch of her round him so he could come in her and forget.

'Johnny—' Mercy was disturbed by his manner, his short, savage answers to her questions. 'It's – it's been very hard with Tom. We all hoped he was going to get better than this. They operated on his head and that, but – well, it must be a shock to you.'

'I've seen worse.'

'I dare say.' Mercy found she was furious. 'But this is your brother. He's had a bullet in his head and it's done a lot of damage – he was really badly injured—'

'I know 'e was bloody badly injured!' Johnny stood up, yelling with all his force so that Tom made a whimpering noise and Alf protested, 'Eh, son, son—'

'I know what happened to 'im, I was there, wasn' I? It was me brought 'im up out of the mud, and now I wish I'd fucking well left 'im there!'

Mercy went out with Johnny the next evening. He came round and asked and she didn't feel she could refuse.

'Just give me a tick to get changed,' she told him.

'Least he seems more cheerful than yesterday,' she said to Mabel and Susan. ''E was ever so funny with me last night. Must've been the shock.'

'They've all had more than their fair share, that's for sure.' Mabel was clattering plates in the scullery. 'He's come home to a basinful.'

It was a mild evening, and not yet dark. Johnny waited

out in the yard. As Mercy came out he eyed her up, suddenly afraid. She was dressed in matching brown: a calf-length skirt, a white blouse with a little tie at the neck over which her coat was hanging open, button up boots and a little felt hat with a feather in it.

'Posh nowadays, aren't yer?' he said, unable to keep the aggression from his voice.

'Only because of Dorothy. She gives me hand-me-downs.'

She knew his eyes were on her and felt as if her skin was tingling. It was somehow a threatening feeling.

'Where d'you want to go then? Pictures or summat?'

They sat in the picture house together. Mercy had always loved it before, the excitement of going out, a gripping picture to take your mind off things. But now it only reminded her agonizingly of Tom. She kept glancing sideways at Johnny, his profile in the flickering light from the screen. She could not have mistaken the two of them. Johnny's face was thinner, longer, the nose more snub.

Seeing her looking at him, Johnny suddenly reached over and caught hold of her hand. She sat stiffly, keeping her hand in his, their palms going sticky. Once he let go and smoothed his hand along her thigh and she froze. He took her hand again. At the end of the picture he let go. She wiped her palm on her skirt, and knew he had seen her doing it.

It was dark outside. Both of them were subdued, each feeling less and less at ease. Mercy wanted to talk to him, ask him things, but what was there to say?

Johnny was used to women who spoke little English. There were lots of hand signals, giggles from them as he clowned it, he could touch them, each of them knowing how it would end up. But here he felt expected just to walk and talk in the darkness. And Mercy was so grown up now, so pure and beautiful, so well dressed. He felt at sea, and then angry and frustrated.

'So what d'yer wanna do now then?' he asked in a harsh voice.

Mercy was just as much at a loss. With Tom she could walk anywhere, close and comfortable, holding hands, not needing anything outside themselves for entertainment. But Johnny seemed a complete stranger to her now, and one who was smouldering and unpredictable.

'Shall we just go home?'

Each of them looked at the other, desolate for a moment, then in an offhand voice, yet burning with fury inside, Johnny said, 'Oh awright then, if that's all yer want.'

He was used to being courted, women eager for him, his cheeky good looks, the meagre pay he gave them which, close to the front line, they needed to fill their bellies. But now this superior little bitch wanted to get away from him as fast as she could. He felt deeply, terrifyingly lonely.

They were walking quite briskly now, towards the bottom of Bradford Street. There was silence until Mercy could bear it no longer.

'Johnny—'

'What?' His tone was savage again.

'Was it really you – saved Tom's life?'

'Yes.'

There was a long silence.

'Will yer tell me 'ow it 'appened?'

'No.'

'Why?'

'Because yer don't want to know.' He was walking so fast she could barely keep up. 'None of you want to know.'

'I do.'

Even if he had wanted to he couldn't have described Ypres for her. And why should she know, just by hearing of it? Why should she have it so cheap?

'I want to know what happened to 'im, Johnny.'

''E got shot in the head. There's nowt else to say about it.'

She was pleading, desperate to break through his cruel harshness. 'I need some way to feel close to 'im.'

I'll show you, he thought. I'll show you how to feel close to Tom.

'Come 'ere.' He took her hand, pulling her round the corner into Rea Street, walking between steelworks and dark warehouses.

'Where're we going?'

Johnny turned on her, filled again with angry desire. He shoved her up against the warehouse wall.

'Johnny for God's sake—' Her voice was high and frightened. But his need was driving him too strongly to hear her, his body taut. He didn't speak. His hands were in her clothes, pulling, lifting, forcing. Mercy felt the air cold on her legs as he drew her skirt up and she clutched uselessly at it trying to keep it down.

'What're you doing? Don't – oh Johnny, don't!'

She could just see his eyes in the darkness and they were looking, but not seeing her. She was present but somehow cancelled out and this silenced her. Her head was grinding against the wall. Johnny was pushing his body against hers, his breaths sharp and urgent, hands tearing at her bloomers and she fought him, shouting, 'No, Johnny – no!'

Frustrated he pulled at her, unable to reach, to get in. This was no good. Why didn't the silly cow get in the right position?

'Move!' he ordered her.

'What d'you mean? Oh my God, Johnny, what're you doing to me?' She didn't know what he meant, what he wanted.

When she felt him naked, thrusting against her, panic overcame her. What was this . . .? Oh my God, no . . .

He was more than ready, felt himself begin to come, yet thwarted and he clutched her tight, groaning in surrender.

'Johnny – stop it – you're horrible!' She shoved him away from her with every fibre of herself, running, sobbing, towards Bradford Street.

'Bitch!' His cry came after her, distraught. 'Horrible, am I? You don't know nothing, yer stuck up little bitch! . . .' The sound of her running footsteps faded along the street. 'Don't go . . . Mercy . . . don't leave me!'

Chapter Nineteen

When they heard that Johnny had been invalided home, Elsie took the news very quietly, as if she had no spark of hope left in her. The dead or the living dead – what other fates lay in store for her young ones?

Mercy's feelings were very mixed. Johnny had gone back to the Front in March without saying goodbye and with no apology for what had happened that night. She had kept out of his way for the rest of that week, only seeing him with the others, and then they'd barely spoken to each other or exchanged a glance. None of them had heard from him since he'd gone back. Mercy didn't exactly blame him. He'd been like a complete stranger to her, one whose presence would have been disquieting had he really been a stranger, but as an old childhood friend, almost a brother, she had found him frightening and sad.

She felt weighed down by exhaustion and grief. Tom sat there day after day. There seemed to be no future to look to, only the ashes left of her hopes. Her old childhood feelings of uncertainty, of not seeming to fit or belong anywhere, had come back very strongly now Tom had been taken from her. She'd grown into a woman, but the roots of her being, who she really was, were hidden from her. Sometimes she looked at Mabel and Susan and thought, I don't know who these people are, not really. I don't belong to them, or have blood ties with them. I just ended up here somehow.

The spring of 1918 had passed into summer with its own slow, tragic rhythm. Any shred of glory there had been at the beginning of the War was gone and it was now a long, heartbreaking struggle.

'What's the point of all this?' Mercy complained to one of the other girls in the factory. 'Here we are turning out all these grenades day after day just so's it'll all go on and on. The whole thing's just a waste of everybody's life.'

The other girl stared back at her, worried. 'Ooh, you'd better not go talking like that, Mercy. No good, that ain't. You'll get us all into trouble.'

But Mercy found herself thinking: everything's lost. I'm lost.

Johnny was in hospital in London for a time, then they sent him to Birmingham.

'Mercy—' Elsie's eyes were watery, like those of an old woman. 'Will yer go – with Alf. Just this time, and tell me . . .?'

Mercy nodded, heavy-hearted. She knew Elsie couldn't stand any more, was afraid Johnny might be in the same state as Tom.

She and Alf travelled to Dudley Road together, to the Poor Law Infirmary which had also been turned over to nursing war casualties. Alf had no jokes now, to speed them along. He seemed lost too, cut loose from the moorings of his own life.

As the two of them walked the long, scruffy corridors to Johnny's ward, Mercy found she was praying, her lips actually moving. 'Please, please don't let it be bad, not like Tom—' When they reached the door her legs were shaking so much she could barely stand.

Tears of relief poured down her face when they spotted Johnny sitting up, his hair a fraction longer than the last time they saw him, his eyes immediately registering who they were. As she and Alf walked along to him, there came a low whistle from a couple of beds away.

'Hey, mate,' a voice called. 'Yer a lucky fella!'

Blushing, Mercy realized the lad was talking about her. She gave him a half smile.

''Allo, son.'

'Awright, Dad?' Johnny said. He smiled as Mercy said hello as well.

They moved to the side of his bed, conscious of being watched. The long Nightingale ward was packed with rows of beds down both sides, each one occupied by a young man, many of them with dressings and bandages, but the atmosphere was completely different from Highbury. These men had 'caught a Blighty' while fighting and were now fortunately 'out of it' for the forseeable future, more a cause for celebration than anything.

'What happened to you?' Alf asked. Mercy saw his hands were shaking.

The lower part of Johnny's body was hidden by a tent of bedclothes, the covers raised away from contact with his legs by a wire frame.

'Bloke bayoneted me by mistake.' Johnny suddenly let out a gleeful chuckle. 'Before we'd even got started. Stuck it right deep in the back of my leg, 'e did. Reckon 'e saved my life.'

'Thank goodness you're awright.' Mercy was shaking. 'Your mom'll be in – only she just couldn't . . .'

Johnny understood, she could see. She watched him, her embarrassment and anger over what had happened between them almost forgotten now. None of that seemed important, not compared with life and death.

*

Just when life seemed set on a downward spiral into despair, the course of the War changed. Through August and September the headlines were full of uplifting Allied progress, of victories at Amiens, and, at the end of September, against the previously impregnable Hindenburg Line south of Cambrai.

During those weeks Mercy visited Johnny as often as she could, at first out of a sense of obligation and later because, hard as she found him to be with, she could see the acute loneliness in his eyes. She kept her visits brief. She took anything she could get hold of in the way of flowers or fruit. He was always civil enough to her, if distant, and seemed pleased to see her. He was less harsh now he knew he would be home for some time. His mates on the ward interpreted her presence as part of a devoted courtship, and he hadn't apparently contradicted them.

So much of what war had left behind in all these young men was hidden to Mercy, until one day in October when she was visiting Johnny. It was chilly with a cold wind blowing, and Mercy's head was pounding as she walked into the hospital. When she had almost reached the ward she found lights dancing in front of her eyes and knew that if she didn't stop she was going to faint. She leant against the wall and bent over, holding her hat on, until the blood roared in her ears and her vision returned to normal.

'You all right, miss?' a voice said.

Mercy righted herself groggily to see one of the nurses eyeing her anxiously.

''Er, yes. Thanks. Just come over a bit faint for a moment.'

'Oh – I know you, don't I?' the young woman said.

She was blue-eyed and kind. 'You've come to see Mr er . . .'

'Pepper.'

'That's it. He's doing well. One of the lucky ones, I'd say. 'Course, it's not healing quite as fast as it might because of him forever trying to get out of bed, but there we are – same for a lot of them.'

Mercy was puzzled. Perhaps the nurse had mistaken him for someone else. Johnny always sat quite still in bed whenever she saw him. 'What d'you mean?'

'Oh – the nights . . .' The nurse rolled her eyes tactlessly to the ceiling. 'Completely different place. You wouldn't recognize it here at night. Dreams, you see – nearly all of them. It's like a madhouse with them jumping about. Wouldn't think so to see them all joking and card sharping now, would you?'

After this conversation Mercy went to Johnny's side feeling a new tenderness for him. She sat by his bed, still feeling groggy and shaky but trying not to let it show. They talked about the family, how Rosalie was, and then Mercy said, 'Johnny – d'you have bad dreams of a night?'

'No.' He frowned. 'Why?'

'Oh.' She was confused. 'Just summat the nurse said. It doesn't matter.'

There was always a tantalizing feeling that he was holding back a huge reservoir of thought and feeling, and Mercy, still nervous of him, was not sure whether to press him to talk.

Mostly they avoided mention of Tom. His state was a subject too painful for both of them. But that day Mercy told Johnny that Elsie had taken down her little shrine to Frank.

'She said she's got to think about the living,' Mercy

said. 'Mabel says she thinks she's done 'er grieving that way and . . . Johnny, you listening?' She was finding it hard enough to concentrate herself today. The ward seemed stiflingly hot and her head was thumping.

Johnny was staring ahead of him. His hair had grown a lot in the past two months and now almost covered his ears. It made his face look softer, less gaunt than before.

'D'you hear what I said?' Mercy repeated.

'I can't go back there.'

'They say the War's nearly over,' she assured him. 'You won't be in any state to go back for months yet—'

'No!' he said fiercely. 'To Mom. Home. Or what's left of it. I can't go back there and live with 'em. Tom sat there all day. It's no good for you either, Mercy. You ought to get out. Get away.'

She tried to joke with him, though she was having to concentrate harder and harder to talk at all. She was burning hot and the walls seemed to be rippling strangely. 'Oh yes – where d'you think I'm going to go, Johnny, little orphan girl? All alone in the world, me.'

'You'd find your way.' He looked at her with sudden intensity. 'Clever girl like you. It's not that difficult. But—' – he shook his head – 'as for going 'ome – I feel as if I've lived years longer than them already. And walking back in there . . . It's like living in a grave. I'm getting out. Soon as I can walk.'

It took her two buses to get home and as she went, Johnny's words hammered in her mind. Her cheeks and forehead were feverishly hot, her legs unsteady, and as she waited at the first stop on Dudley Road, she longed just to lie down, curl up and not have to move for a very long time. When the bus came it felt horrifyingly hot and stuffy and she had to go upstairs to find a seat. Her throat was very sore, she was dizzy, and sickened by the stench of cigarettes and stale old clothes.

'Get out while you can,' Johnny's voice boomed in her head, riding on the hard throb of her blood.

By the time she had crossed town, caught the second bus to the Moseley Road and was walking home, she was shivering violently and her hands and feet felt like thick chunks of ice, while her head was still overheated and felt heavy enough to snap her neck.

'I feel ever so bad,' she said as she got to number two and almost fell through the door. George let out a shriek at the sight of her from his perch and she thought it might split her head.

'Oh ah, well feel bad when yer've given me a hand,' Mabel said, disgruntled.

'I can't.' Mercy sat leaning her head against the back of the settle. Now she'd sat down she felt she'd never be able to get up. 'I just can't.' She was swaying, floating.

Susan wheeled herself over and peered at her. 'She looks bad, Mom. Like you said about Mrs Ripley. I reckon it's that influenza.'

'Oh well, that's marvellous bringing it in 'ere,' Mabel grumbled unreasonably. 'Best get yerself to bed then – you ain't going to be any use down 'ere, are yer?'

'I can't.' Mercy slumped to one side, her body on fire. 'Can't.'

They had to look after her downstairs. Mabel wasn't prepared to get her upstairs, Susan couldn't help and Elsie insisted that they had the thin old mattress off Cathleen's bed. Mercy was sweating and shivering, burning up with fever, her head pounding and limbs hurting. She had terrifying, shapeless dreams and often cried out in her sleep, too ill even when awake to know how worried they were about her.

She was aware of different impressions of the room: light or dark, the sharp smell of slack as Mabel stoked the fire with their meagre supplies, cooking smells, voices. In the daytime the fever let up a little and her head was clearer but she was so weak she could barely move. The mattress felt punishingly hard under her. Come the evening, the fever raged through her again. Susan laid wet rags on her head and body.

'Can I have water?' Mercy kept begging her. 'More water?' Often she didn't know where she was. Her head felt as if it might burst.

'We should get the doctor, Mom,' Susan begged.

'There's nowt 'e can do. When 'e saw Josie Ripley with it 'e just said to keep 'er comfortable, plenty of water . . .' But even Mabel was getting worried. 'She do look bad though . . .'

One evening Mercy half opened her eyes, aware of Susan sitting close by.

'I'm dying,' she whispered.

'No—' Susan's voice rose in panic. 'No, Mercy, you're not – you just feel bad but you'll get better!'

Mercy fell back into her half-sleeping state, her mind full of odd, buckled images.

When she was alert to what was going on around her she almost always opened her eyes to see Susan beside her, her sweet face, dark hair swept back, fastened now in a bun rather similar to Mabel's. Susan's eyes watched every twitch Mercy made, every shallow breath she took with a caressing devotion. Mercy saw the love in her eyes, felt it wrap round her, holding her.

'She's getting ever so thin,' she heard Susan say

anxiously one night, speaking into a silence which had been punctuated only by the little popping sounds from the gas mantle. 'Look at 'er wrist – like a matchstick. She's wasting away.'

Mercy didn't hear Mabel's reply. But as Susan sat leaning over her, holding and stroking her hand, the one thing she knew was that she was being cared for. She tried to find the strength to squeeze Susan's hand.

'Thank you,' she murmured, before sliding into sleep.

As the fever died in her and she began to recover, Susan brought her thin broth.

'Try, Mercy,' she begged. 'It'll 'elp get yer strength back.'

Mercy attempted to find the energy and will to make her arms push her body up from the mattress. In the end Mabel had to support her as Susan put the spoonful of salty broth into her mouth.

'Johnny's just come home,' Susan said to her. 'Bet you didn't know that, did yer? 'E's on crutches and that, but they say 'e'll be right as rain in a few weeks. Seems awright in 'imself. There's ever such a lot of others down with this influenza now though, all along the street. There's people out there with hankies pressed up to their noses in fear of catching it.'

Mercy looked up at her. She hadn't the energy to reply. She felt very strange and light, purged in some way, as if she were floating. Johnny, all the Peppers, seemed miles away, like strangers.

Johnny came in to see her. His leg was bandaged but he'd managed to get his trousers on over the top, so that except for the crutches and the stiff way he was holding his leg, there wasn't much left to see.

'You feeling better?'

'I'll soon be up and about,' Mercy whispered bravely. 'Feel as if I've been hit by a tram.' She looked him in the eyes. 'You're home then?'

Johnny looked down, tapping the foot of his good leg on the floor. 'Ah. For now.'

As Mercy recovered, moving slowly about the house, Susan started to complain of her head hurting and shivering, and soon she was in Mercy's place on the mattress.

'Getting like the Peppers, we are,' Mabel grumbled, still fit as a flea herself. 'Beds downstairs.'

Now Mercy was having to take a turn nursing Susan, although she was still only just strong enough to move. If she didn't go back to work soon there'd be no money for food, but she barely had the strength as yet to get across the yard. She often lay exhausted on the settle beside Susan in the dying light from the fire, not having the energy to go to bed upstairs. Seeing the frightening severity of Susan's illness she knew just how sick she'd been herself.

When she thought Susan could hear she talked to her, tried to find things to cheer her.

'When you get better, when the War's all over, we'll go somewhere,' she promised her. 'I'll go out and earn some more money and you'll be able to do your sewing again, and we'll go somewhere. We'll go to the sea, shall we? Wouldn't you like to see the sea, Susan?'

She waited, listening for a murmur in reply, but nothing came except Susan's quick, feverish breaths.

Chapter Twenty

For days Mercy's waking existence revolved around Susan. She took turns with Mabel, washing her, giving her sips of water, holding and talking to her. She sang odd scraps of songs or hymns she could remember from the Hanley Home. Remembering the enveloping feeling of love Susan's presence had given her when she was sick, she hoped she could do the same in return.

But by the fifth day Susan was showing no sign of getting better. The fever was raging through her, her face, already thin, was hollow, had taken on a bluish tinge, and she could barely gather the strength to speak. Mercy watched helplessly as she struggled for every breath.

One afternoon she opened her eyes and was obviously trying to say something. Mabel was out looking for work to keep them going and Mercy, who had been half dozing on the chair beside her, immediately leant forward.

'What's that, Susan?'

Susan's eyes opened wide suddenly as if she'd been startled by something. 'I'm going to die.'

Mercy knelt down, heart aching, and took one of her bony hands between her own. She pressed it to her cheek. It felt so cold and fragile. 'No, yer not. That's what I said, wasn'it, when I was that bad? You just wait a bit and you'll soon feel better.'

Susan closed her eyes again. There was something in her face after she'd spoken, such a look of exhaustion and defeat. Her skin looked sallow against her black hair. All that afternoon she seemed to be fading away from them, her breathing more and more laboured. Mercy held her, crying silently, as if she might physically drag her back to health.

'Oh Susan, hold on – for God's sake hold on!'

By the time Mabel got home Mercy was frantic at the door waiting for her.

'She's not gaining – she's getting worse if anything.'

Mabel saw Mercy's frightened eyes and rushed to kneel beside her daughter. She listened, frantic, to Susan's breathing.

'Susan. Susan – love?' Mercy could hear the panic in Mabel's voice.

Susan's eyelids fluttered. 'Mom . . .'

Mabel let out a long, tremulous sigh. 'We're 'ere Susan. Yer going to be awright. Just try for us, won't yer, pet . . .'

As Mabel struggled to her feet again, Mercy saw tears in her eyes, the first tears of sorrow she had ever seen her shed.

'I don't know what to do,' Mabel said, wringing her hands. 'Should I go for the doctor?'

'Yes!' Mercy looked at Susan again. 'And be quick!'

She knelt waiting beside Susan, holding her hand, kissing her, humming softly, her own tears falling into her lap and on to Susan's hand. She willed all her own meagre strength to her, her sweet, placid Susan who'd been her home, her anchor all these years.

'Oh please,' she sobbed, thinking of all the two of them had done together, all the ordinary days they'd struggled and worked and laughed together. She was choked with remorse for the times when she'd found looking after her a burden. 'Hold on. Just hold on. Get better for Mercy, please, Susan. You're my sister – you're all I've got.'

Susan's eyes struggled half open again, seeing only Mercy's face, the grey eyes filled with desperate, loving tears.

'Don't leave me, Mercy.' Her voice was a rasping whisper. 'Don't ever . . .'

Mercy began to cry even harder. It was unbearable. 'Oh Susan, Susan . . .' She lay down beside her, drawing Susan's frail body into her arms. 'You know I won't. I'll always stay and look after you. I'll never leave you, Susan.'

'Mercy . . .' Susan murmered. 'Mercy . . .'

When Mabel returned, panting, with Dr Manley, the two girls were lying there, raven black and golden hair mingled together, their arms wrapped round each other, Mercy's tensed tight as if she would never let go. There was a slight smile on Susan's lips, but when Dr Manley knelt to examine her, she was no longer breathing.

They buried Susan in Lodge Hill Cemetery, under a louring November sky. Alf Pepper came with them bringing Johnny, Jack and Rosalie, and Mary Jones was there too. Everyone was silent, stony-faced as Mabel's daughter was laid to rest, the earth rattling down on Susan's pitifully small coffin, Mercy's posy of flowers fluttering down after it, then the sound of Mabel weeping.

'She's all I had,' Mabel sobbed as they moved away from the grave. 'Three children, all taken from me . . .'

Rosalie crept up beside Mercy and shyly took her hand. Mercy gave a little smile through her tears. Mary Jones walked with Mabel and took her arm as they walked between the quiet trees. To her surprise, Mercy also saw

Alf catch up with them and take Mabel's other arm to support her.

Johnny hung behind to walk with Mercy, swinging along beside her on his crutches as her tears fell. She found his presence a comfort.

'I can't bear it,' she said to him. 'She shouldn't've died. She'd hardly had any life. And she was lovely, she was – I loved 'er . . .'

''Ere—' Johnny stopped, awkward on one leg, and leant his crutches against a tree. 'Come 'ere.'

Mercy loosed Rosalie's hand and felt herself drawn into Johnny's arms like a child. Gently removing her hat, he kissed the top of her golden head.

Less than a week later the Kaiser was forced to abdicate, and in another two days the War was over. The celebrations began, the parties and songs and cheering. Angel Street came alive with flags and bunting, singing and drinking. But in every court along the street there was also so much raw emotion: as much numbness, grief and sorrow as joy and relief. And the need simply to get used to the idea that the War, which had become a way of life for so many, was over.

On Armistice night Mercy was left alone in the house. Mabel had spent most of the time since Susan's death with Mary Jones. She couldn't stand her own home.

Mercy looked round the room, a place so full of memories of Susan there was hardly anything she could rest her gaze on without wanting to weep. *Everything I've ever cared about is gone. Susan, Tom . . .* She could hear cheers from the street. Despite her grief, she put on her hat and coat, feeling drawn to go outside, to be with other people. Staying here alone with her thoughts was too much to bear.

I s'pose I could go to the Peppers', she thought. But the idea of piling more grief on to her already aching heart was too much for her. She stood in the yard, taking in breaths of the dark, smoky air. The celebrations were growing louder. There were shouts and shrieks of laughter, singing. She stood feeling more alone than she had ever felt in her life before. She nearly went back inside, but then came the desolate thought: inside, outside, what does it matter? There's no one for me wherever I go.

The door of the Peppers' house opened and she saw Johnny outlined in the door frame. He came out, awkward on the crutches, and closed the door. She saw a quick snatch of flame as he lit a cigarette.

'Johnny?'

'That you, Mercy?'

She walked over to him. 'Lot of carry-on out there, eh?'

The two of them walked down the entry and stood looking out into the street. A bonfire had been lit in the middle of the road, sparks flying up to the dark sky and a ragged circle of people carousing round it. A woman stood near them, swigging from a bottle. Further down was a piano they must have dragged out of the pub, and the street was full of people milling about in the flickering light.

Mercy glanced at Johnny, propped against the wall. She knew she was never going to hear much from him, of the memories that haunted his mind. But as they stood there she sensed an understanding between them, of the sheer burden of sadness they carried, so at odds with the party going on in front of them.

After a time Johnny stubbed his cigarette out on the wall and threw the butt aside.

'It's no good. I've got to get away from 'ere. There ain't nothing for me. Not any more.'

There was a long silence, then Mercy said, 'Me too.'

Part Four

Chapter Twenty-One

March 1919

'Oh Dorothy, is this where they live? These houses are ever so big!'

Mercy eyed the enormous mansions along the Wake Green Road from under the brim of her hat. She'd never been as far as Moseley before, or seen so many prosperous middle-class dwellings clustered close together. She was churned up inside with nerves.

'This is it. We're nearly there.' Dorothy's hand landed on her shoulder. 'Let's have a look at yer.'

Mercy stood still as Dorothy brushed down her coat for the third time. The two of them were just about the same height now, though Dorothy was ageing to look rather matronly, her face careworn and a little severe. She cast away some imaginary specks from the navy-blue shoulders and straightened Mercy's hat, also navy, but brightened round the brim by a strip of spotted fabric, black on white.

'That'll stop you looking like a war widow,' Dorothy had said, trimming it for her earlier that morning.

But I am a war widow, Mercy thought as she slid the hat on, seeing her own, wan expression in the mirror.

Dorothy finished her inspection by stepping back to look down at Mercy's boots, still bright with much polishing below her calf-length skirt.

'You're making me nervous,' Mercy said. 'Will you stop looking at me like that? You're in more of a dither than I am.'

She leant to kiss Dorothy's dry cheek. 'Look – your hands are trembling! It's me going for the job, not you!'

Dorothy gave her a stiff smile. 'I just want the best for you, Mercy. You know I do. Now remember, try and put your aitches on if you can, and call 'er "Ma'am". It's a companion this Mrs Adair's after, not a maid. And don't go telling 'er exactly where you've come from. Not yet any'ow. No one'd think to look at you you was living there . . .' She gripped Mercy's arm and led her on.

'The woman's rather down in 'erself, I gather, so be a bit cheerful like. Come on – here goes.'

They turned into the gateway of a rambling, gabled house. There was a tall conifer in the front garden. Was she to live in this house? Mercy wondered. Start a new life? She looked up at the brick facade, tilting her head. For a dizzy moment she felt as if the house were swaying towards her, and she stumbled.

'Eh – watch it!' Dorothy caught her arm. 'For goodness sake watch where you're going. We don't need you breaking a leg now, do we?'

She took the brass knocker in two hands and lifted it for two loud bangs.

A skinny maid with freckles and a long nose asked their names and led them into the rear of the house. The hall floor was a mosaic of vivid blues and whites, orange and black, and there was a wide runner of red carpet on the stairs and a well-polished bannister. At the far end of the hall a glass door led out to the garden and Mercy could see trees and a white wrought-iron bench. The whole impression was of colour, light and cleanliness. Mercy looked round in delight, in disbelief. So some people really lived like this – she had never seen a house with anything like such beauty, such comfort!

Her heart was beating very fast, and she took in a deep breath, trying to calm herself. What could the woman be like who was mistress of a house such as this? Dorothy squeezed her arm and she let out a ragged breath.

'Mrs Adair?' she heard the maid say. 'A Miss Finch and a Miss 'Anley to see yer.'

'Ah – oh yes.' They heard a soft voice from behind the door, well modulated but unmistakeably flustered. 'Just one moment . . . Oh goodness.' There was a small sound, obviously from a baby.

'One moment,' the maid said to them unnecessarily. Soon she added, 'You can go in now.'

The room was light and pretty, comfortable chairs covered in a chintz fabric, winter sun casting thin shadows on the richly coloured rug. In front of them, a plump woman with pink cheeks and baby-fine fair hair was holding an infant on one arm and evidently still struggling to fasten the top button of her blouse. On the chair behind her lay a tangle of white linen and a thin, crocheted blanket.

''Er – Emmie—' She called the maid back. 'Please call Nanny to come and fetch Stevie. I must apologize—' She turned to Mercy and Dorothy. 'I must admit, I'd completely forgotten our appointment. In fact I don't know quite what's happening to me lately.'

Mercy eyed her round pink cheeks and generally rumpled air and was relieved. She'd pictured someone stiff and chilly. Immediately she warmed to the flustered, vulnerable woman in front of her.

''Er – do take a seat.' Sounding slightly breathless,

Margaret Adair gestured towards the sofa. Mercy and Dorothy perched side by side on the edge of it. Mercy looked over at the window, entranced by the sight of a ruby glass jug on the sill, glowing in the light.

'No – please sit back and be comfortable,' Mrs Adair urged them. 'We shall have to wait just a moment or two. I'm afraid you've caught me a little bit on the hop . . .'

She jiggled the baby on her hip and he stared fixedly at the two of them with his brown eyes. He had a fuzz of brown hair and a solid, healthy look to him. Not like Mary Jones's babbies, Mercy thought. Scrawny little mites, they were. The only thing marring little Stevie Adair's looks was a wound on his left cheekbone, still pink and not quite healed. He suddenly let out a little belch and Mercy giggled, which made him show his gums in a big smile and kick his legs in excitement. He tried to throw himself forward.

'Stevie . . . Stevie . . .' his mother reproached him. 'Gently now. He's forever bumping himself,' she apologized.

'He's a real bonny babby,' Mercy said. The woman turned to her and smiled, though it was a smile which did not for a moment leave behind the look of anxiety which seemed to haunt her face.

'Thank you, Miss . . . er, oh dear, I'm so sorry. I'm Margaret Adair. You must be . . .?'

'Dorothy Finch.' Mercy felt Dorothy pulling her to her feet. 'And this is Miss Hanley. Mercy Hanley.'

'Mercy – how pretty a name. Do sit down again. I'm so sorry—' She went and peered out into the hall. 'Oh where is – ah, here she comes.'

A moment later, the nanny appeared. Mercy saw a very thin woman, Mrs Adair's senior by about fifteen years, clothed in a black dress topped by a starched white apron.

She stood in the doorway, feet neatly together. She had remarkably thin ankles, even for a woman of her slender build, and wore flat, very pointed black shoes. She was small featured, and could almost have been pretty, had she not pulled her black hair back into such a severe knot behind her head, leaving only a fringe, dead straight across her forehead.

'You wanted me?' Her voice was rather high and nasal, with only a trace of a Birmingham accent. Her eyes took in Mercy and Dorothy across the room. Mercy felt herself being closely, coldly examined. Something about the woman, correct in every way as she was, filled her with an instinctive unease.

'If you could just take him for a time?' Margaret Adair was as apologetic with the nanny as with her visitors. 'I haven't quite finished the feed, but as you see, I have company.'

'As you like ma'am,' the woman said. She moved briskly forward, holding out her arms. Her hands, poking out of the stiff cuffs, were very small, Mercy noticed, like a doll's.

At the sight of her, Stevie Adair's face crumpled with dismay and he let out a roar.

'Oh dear,' his mother said. 'He was so cheerful just now. Perhaps his face is still bothering him. It still doesn't seem to be healing very well, does it?'

'I'll see to it,' the nanny said. She spoke in an even tone, yet managed to imply the younger woman's inexperience, stupidity even. 'As for the state of him now, that'll be colic. Look at the way he's pulling his legs up. Of course, overfeeding a child brings it on. Come along now, Steven,' she commanded, forcing him from his mother's grasp. 'Time for your nap.'

'Oh – do you think he really needs to sleep again?'

Mrs Adair's voice was tremulous. 'He does seem so lively.'

The sounds of distress turned into screams, his face turning blotched and sweaty.

'Now, now, now – tired out, that's his trouble.' Stevie writhed, perched on her angular hip. 'We'll just get you back into a routine, Stevie boy, and you'll be right as rain. That's all he needs. You mustn't be tempted to give in to him.' She gave Margaret Adair a smile which did not warm the frozen depths of her eyes.

'Perhaps if I were just to hold him again, to calm him?' Margaret Adair pleaded, as her son arched his back and screamed in the other woman's arms.

'No need. You have quite enough to do. Leave him to me.'

They heard the screams recede up the staircase, growing ever more hysterical. Mercy saw that Margaret Adair was digging her nails into her palms, her breath shallow and uneven. A door closed, muffling the noise, and she unclenched her hands and tried to compose herself.

Mercy was bewildered. Didn't people have servants so they could order them about instead of the other way round?

'Nanny Radcliffe is very experienced,' she said tremulously, sitting down opposite the two of them. Mercy saw it was herself she was trying to convince of this fact.

'Now, er . . .' She looked dazed, as if she was still trying to hear the sounds from upstairs.

'We've come about the position,' Dorothy said. 'You was looking for a companion, and Mrs Weston suggested I bring her to you.'

'Ah, Grace – Mrs Weston. Yes, of course!' Mrs Adair managed to rouse herself, and for the first time, her round face broke into a smile. 'Dear Grace, how is she? And those lovely boys?'

'She's well.' Dorothy spoke abruptly, and added with apparent reluctance, 'And of course she sends her warmest regards.' Mercy listened with interest. Dorothy seldom said much about her employer. They had concocted an almost true story. 'She wanted to recommend Mercy to you. We've known her for a good while. She's an orphan child who we've taken some interest in . . . although she's young Mercy's already acted as a companion to another girl.'

'Oh?' Mercy found Margaret Adair was addressing her directly. 'Why was that?'

'She was paralysed, ma'am.' Mercy spoke as correctly as she could manage. 'She stayed at home – didn't go to school. So I was there to keep her company, teach her a bit . . .'

'But you attended school yourself?'

'For some of the time I did, yes.'

'And she no longer requires your company?'

'She died last year, ma'am. Of the Spanish influenza.'

To her great mortification Mercy felt tears filling her eyes and she looked down into her lap, clenching her jaw. For heaven's sake don't start blarting now! she ticked herself off.

'How very sad,' she heard Margaret Adair say. 'So you have spent all your working life with, er . . .'

'Susan.' Mercy quickly wiped her eyes and looked up. 'No – I worked in munitions . . .' She looked uncertainly at Dorothy. Was she supposed to tell her prospective employer this? 'I made Mills Bombs in the War.'

'Goodness – you look so young.' Mrs Adair sounded slightly awestruck. 'I've never met anyone who . . . What was that like?'

What on earth did she want to know that for? Mercy glanced at Dorothy again, but Dorothy could give her no advice about what to say. 'It was tiring. Long hours standing up.'

'But you thought it worth it – for the war effort?' The woman questioned her intensely, seemed hungry to know.

Mercy hesitated. She could think of nothing else to say except the truth.

'I did. To start. And the money was good. But then the lads were coming home with no legs – or worse – or not coming back at all. And then I started to think, was we wasting our time? Was it all wrong? But I suppose I was wrong to think like that—'

'Anyway, that's all over now,' Dorothy interrupted.

'Yes, of course – thank heaven.' Mrs Adair pulled her attention back to the matter in hand. 'Now, this position. It's really my husband's idea and of course he's not here. He feels I need a companion in the house, though I do feel a little foolish about it.'

'What are the duties?' Dorothy asked.

'Well . . .' Margaret Adair looked down, a thick roll of flesh appearing under her chin as she did so. 'I hadn't really thought. I suppose I want someone . . . to be a friend.' She looked up into Mercy's eyes.

She looks frightened, Mercy thought. What's she frightened of? She felt bewildered, but drawn to this plump, somehow helpless woman.

'Do you think we can be friends, Mercy?'

'I, er . . .'

'Oh, I'm so stupid, how can you possibly answer a question like that? I should try to explain your duties. Audrey Radcliffe has an afternoon off every week so I shall need some help then. I shall need a few errands done, though of course we do have our maids. Otherwise your main task really is to keep me company, and Stevie, when he's allowed to be with me. To keep me from becoming too glum, that's what James says anyway!' She tried to sound light and self-mocking, but instead sounded sad. 'Perhaps you think me very weak and foolish. Only since Stevie was born, I've been finding life rather a strain.'

Mercy felt she was expected to respond, and fell back on something she had heard Elsie say. 'When you have a babby everyone forgets to ask about the mother, don't they – even if you're tired out. As if it's only the babby that matters.'

To her horror, the fleshy, ungainly woman in front of them burst into tears. Dorothy looked at Mercy as if to say, for heaven's sakes now look what you've done!

'Oh – I'm ever so sorry for upsetting you – oh dear . . .' Mercy stood up, but could think of nothing else to do.

Margaret Adair let out several loud, unstoppable sobs, the emotion seeming to rush out of her like compressed air. Then she wiped her eyes.

'I'm so sorry. Oh dear. This is so undignified of me.' Her face was blotchy. 'But at least you can see, I really don't feel quite myself. James – my husband – thinks that if there was someone here to take my mind off things . . . She tried to collect herself. 'How old are you, Mercy?'

'Nineteen, ma'am.'

'And you have no mother or father – no family?'

'None I've ever heard of.'

'You must be so strong to live so alone in the world, dear. Would you like to come and live here with me?'

Live here! Was she offering her the job? It was like another existence from Angel Street. Almost unimaginable.

'You mean sleep here? Where'd I sleep?'

Margaret Adair smiled gently. 'How solemn you are my dear girl. Don't worry, there's a nice little room on the top floor. Simple, but clean. With a window overlooking the garden. And our maids Emmie and Rose have a room together up there, so you wouldn't be all alone. If you feel you could live here, I'd like to give you the job, from tomorrow, if you can manage that. I feel we'll get on. Do you agree?'

For a moment Mercy was too amazed to speak. She felt Dorothy prod her ankle with the tip of her boot.

'Oh yes.' The smile poured across her face. 'Yes, please.'

That evening, James Adair travelled home as he did in all but the foulest of weather, on one of the cycles manufactured at his own works in Greet, nearly three miles from the centre of Birmingham. In heavy rain or snow he drove his motor car. But he not only designed and built cycles, he loved to ride them, test their metal, the wind rushing past his ears. He reached his own house, dismounted, and paused outside, bending over the cycle and turning a pedal fast backwards and carefully examining the chain.

James was thirty-three years old, a tall man, solid though not weighty, with light brown hair which curled and frizzed a little and was already fast receding from his forehead. His face, if not exactly handsome, had a kind, if slightly austere look to it. His hands, as he made a show of adjusting the bicycle chain, were not built to force or damage: he handled objects with respect and precision.

At this moment though, the cycle needed no adjustment. It was in fact the newest Adair Safety Bicycle for Gentlemen. The mechanics and balance of it were almost flawless, and James had ridden it with excitement, knowing its chances in the fiercely competitive market, even against the big firms – the BSA, Rudge-Whitworth – were excellent.

What he was doing now though, was putting off the moment when he had to walk through his own front door. Family life had come as a shock to him. He had grown up as an only child in a respectable, orderly household, a self-contained boy with a passionate interest in anything mechanical. He had been easy for his parents to entertain and control.

The birth of his own son, Steven, had brought him a sense of joy and renewal he could never have put into words. Even now the child was six months old he watched him with an astonishment which almost touched on unbelief. Every single day of those months, returning from the works, he had felt his heart speed up at the thought of seeing him, of simply being able to look at him, to say to himself, My son. This is my son Steven.

But it was not all pleasurable. What disquieted him, the reason for his hanging about out here with his bicycle, was the abrupt slide into chaos which had accompanied Stevie's birth. He found the irrationality, the unpredictability of family life disturbing. Even in his household with its requisite number of staff – maids, a cook, a nanny, a gardener – James felt his home ensnaring him as he walked in.

There was the child's crying for a start. Surely Stevie shouldn't howl as much as he did? Delightful though he was when cheerful, he did cry for long, grating periods and the noise was almost impossible to escape in any part of the house.

Thank goodness for Nanny Radcliffe! James thought, stowing his cycle in the alley between the house and the garden wall. That woman at least was reassuring. She was strict about order and routine, because without that Margaret would let everything slide into shapeless mayhem.

He went round to the front of the house and rang to be let in, feeling the now familiar sensation of dread.

Let her be all right today. None of that foolish emotion. Just back to normal.

There were times since Stevie's birth when he could scarcely recognize the woman he married. For those five years (it had taken them a long, sometimes despairing time to conceive a child) Margaret had always been well rounded, sensual, with her peaches and cream complexion and pale, girlish hair. During the pregnancy she had bloated and the fat was still piled on her even now, unflatteringly so. It wasn't her size in itself. He found that inviting, sensuous. Yet he was shut out: her lactating breasts which by their swollen tautness seemed to invite his caresses, seeped at his touch, and his wife wrapped herself defensively in her layers of nightclothes and turned away from him. Her emotions were the worst. The agitation the baby seemed to cause her, the weeping, especially at night when they heard Stevie crying.

'He needs me,' she'd sobbed during the early weeks. 'My little one needs me. I must feed him!'

She knew perfectly well that Nanny Radcliffe's regime didn't permit night feeding. That it weakened the constitution and gave him irregular habits.

At times James felt he would try anything to get his old wife back, cheerful and yielding.

'Margaret?' He pushed open the door of the front parlour, his eye gladdened by his beautiful array of green glass in the remaining light through the window. The grandfather clock ticked steadily. But there was no fire and the room was empty.

Then her voice, 'I'm here . . .' came from the back room. She sounded light and cheerful and he felt encouraged.

She was sitting with Stevie on her lap.

'Hello dearest.' She smiled. Stevie turned and beamed at him too.

'Hello there, my two.' Suddenly outrageously happy, he bent and kissed Margaret's cheek, then knelt and played with his son as he lay in Margaret's lap, offering him a knuckle to suck.

'Shall Rose bring in a tray of tea?' Her voice was sweet.

'Oh, I'm all right – dinner will be ready soon, won't it?' He laughed as Stevie sucked hard on his hand. 'What power in that little mouth!'

'I hope your hands are clean – think what Nanny would say!'

He was even encouraged by her scolding. This was the first animated greeting he'd had in weeks.

'And how are you?' He looked up into her eyes, puzzled to see excitement in them.

'I've found someone.'

'Found someone?'

'A companion. As you suggested.'

'You mean – you've already made a decision? Without my seeing her?' He stood up, hands on his waist, frowning in concern.

'Well, darling it's me she'll be keeping company. She was recommended by Grace Weston – you know the Westons, in Handsworth? One of her maids brought her here. She's very sweet, a real breath of fresh air. She's nineteen, and—'

'*Nineteen*?'

'Yes, but ever so sensible.'

James was appalled. He'd pictured Margaret in the company of some staid matron who would bring her to her senses.

'Oh James, don't tell me I've been stupid. I feel sure she'll be all right, and that you'll feel the same about her when you meet her.'

'Well, I hope so.' He went coldly to the door. Honestly, just when he thought she was beginning to see sense! 'I do wish you wouldn't rush into things in this irrational manner, Margaret. We'll give the girl a month's trial, and then see whether or not I think she's suitable!'

Chapter Twenty-Two

'So you're going then – with nowt more to say?'

Mabel stood huddled in her shawl in the doorway of the dank bedroom. Her face was further hardened by grief, hair turning grey. She watched Mercy gathering together her clothes and her few other possessions.

'What else is there to say?' Mercy was folding her grey work dress. 'You mean, no fond farewells? Oh, there'll be fond farewells all right – to Elsie and Alf. They're the ones who've been a mom and dad to me.' She turned to face Mabel. The woman was truly on her own now, but Mercy could find very little pity for her.

'I don't owe you a thing. Eight years you've had me 'ere to act as your skivvy. You stole me, you did. And the only reason I ever stayed in this pigsty of a place is because of Susan and Elsie and the lads. They're my people and they always will be. They looked out for me and took care of me while all you could ever think of was yourself. So don't go telling me I owe yer summat. I don't.'

She laid her book *Cheerful Homes*, and the embroidered handkerchief on top of the little pile of clothes.

'When I came 'ere these're all I had in the world. And there's not much more to show now, is there? Anything else I've ever had's been down to Dorothy Finch or Elsie.'

'But Mercy – you've been like a daughter to me . . .'

Mercy listened to the self-pity in Mabel's voice and felt her temper spilling over.

'No!' She turned on her. 'You never once treated me like a mom should treat a daughter, and in your case it's a good job or I might not be alive to tell the tale, like the rest of your kids!'

Mabel gasped as if she'd been punched and her face took on a terrible, twisted expression.

'You wicked little bitch, saying a thing like that . . .'

Mercy gathered up her bundle and pushed past her. 'And where did I learn to be cruel, eh? I'm going now. I'll be up Moseley, living in a better house than you'll ever set foot in. And I'll be back – to see Elsie. You've got the parrot if you want some company.'

It was far sadder saying her goodbyes to George that afternoon, than to Mabel. Mercy bent and looked into his cage, smelling the sharp odour of him. He was busy burrowing his beak into his chest, cleaning himself.

'Ta-ra, Georgie boy. Make sure she takes care of yer.'

She thought of the hours Susan had spent with him, talking to him. The house felt so desolate now.

She went to take her leave of the Peppers. Time seemed frozen in their house: Tom forever lying there, Elsie with him, shrunken and pinched in the face. She couldn't say goodbye to Alf or Jack as they were out at work, Rosalie was at school and Johnny was gone. He'd joined the police, was in lodgings somewhere across town.

'I'm not really saying goodbye, not for good.' Elsie and Tom looked like ghosts in the dark little slum room.

Elsie came over, opened her arms and drew Mercy into them. Mercy put her arms round Elsie's waist, feeling her thinness, breathing in the greasy smell of Elsie's old green woolly. For the first time Mercy could ever remember, Elsie, once strong, vibrant Elsie, sobbed her heart out there in her arms.

'Oh Elsie, don't, please . . .' Mercy's own tears were falling. She stroked her hands along Elsie's back. 'I'm not really going. I'll come back all I can to see you, and Tom. I'm sorry for leaving you . . .'

'Can't yer stay?' Elsie drew back, wiping her bony hand across her eyes. 'No, I know it's wrong of me to ask you. But you could come and stop with us, away from Mabel. And you'd be near Tom . . .'

'Elsie—' Mercy steered her to the table and gently sat her down. 'You know I can't always stop with Tom, don't you? That we can't be anything to each other now, not as 'e is? I did love 'im, you know I did, with all my heart. But 'e's gone, and I can't – my Tom's not here any more.'

Elsie's watery eyes looked up at her. 'I know, bab. And my Tom too. 'Course I know that. It's bad of me. At your age I was marrying Alf and having Maryann soon after. Never see her from one year to the next, now do I? Not as if Coventry's very far off.' She looked round at Tom. He seemed to be sleeping, his mouth hanging open.

'Sometimes I think about finishing 'im off, d'you know that? My own son.' She started crying again. 'Who's ever going to look after 'im but me?'

Mercy couldn't answer her. She was weighed down by the truth of her words.

'Elsie, can I have a cuppa tea with yer before I go?'

''Course you can. Look at me, wallowing in self-pity. Some send-off for yer.' She went to stand up.

'No – let me do it, you sit there.' Mercy saw Elsie sink back on the chair with relief.

She got out two of Elsie's willow-patterned cups and

laid them on saucers. The two of them sat sipping a strong brew of tea together. It was like old times, yet Mercy could already feel she was slipping away, that her life was elsewhere. She could come and visit, but it would never be the same again. Tears stung her eyes, but she fought them back. No more of that.

Before she left she went to Tom's bed. With a pang she saw that asleep, he looked more like his old self, the accusing blankness of his eyes hidden behind quivering eyelids.

'Goodbye, love,' she whispered. And leant over to kiss him. His face smelt of coal tar soap.

Elsie looked her over at the door, smiling bravely.

'You've grown up to be a right stunner, Mercy. And God knows you deserve a bit of happiness.' She took Mercy's arm for a moment. 'If you run into Johnny, ask 'im to come and see me. I'm not going over there begging.'

Mercy nodded. ''Course I will.'

'Come on.' Elsie summoned all her energy. 'You can't go without seeing everyone.'

She went round the yard, digging them all out of their houses: Mary Jones in her apron, Josie Ripley, the McGonegalls, everyone except Mabel.

'Don't forget us, Mercy!'

'Ta-ra bab – come back and see us—'

''Cos we ain't going nowhere!'

'Give us a kiss . . .'

'Ta-ra – God bless, love – bye!'

They walked down the entry out of the yard as if in triumph, and after all the hugs, pats and kisses, they waved her off down Angel Street. Everyone turned to stare at the beautiful, golden girl after whom the street might have been named, carrying her bundle, a flower in her hat, as she turned to wave a last time, then was gone.

Her room in the Adair house was simple, as Margaret Adair had told her it would be, but she loved it immediately. It was small, squeezed in at the top of the stairs, with just enough room for a bed, a chair and a small white chest of drawers. Resting on it were a pewter candlestick and a bowl and pitcher decorated with honeysuckle. There was a little tasselled rug laid beside the bed on the bare boards, and a high window through which she could only see sky, unless she stood on the chair and looked down across the garden. A small rectangular mirror hung on the wall beside the door, in a white frame.

That evening, as she was stowing her few belongings in the chest of drawers and feeling strange and lonely, she heard a knock at the door, accompanied by giggles.

'Come in?'

More giggles as the door opened and Mercy saw Emmie, the freckly maid, followed by a younger girl with wavy brown hair and enormous brown eyes who Mercy knew must be Rose. Both of them were dressed in plain grey frocks and both had the titters and couldn't seem to stop.

Mercy watched as they sat down on her bed, feeling the infection of their laughter until a grin broke over her face and she was giggling too. The three of them ended up prostrate with laughter on the bed before anyone had spoken a word.

'Ssshh!' Rose sat up after a time, trying to sober them. 'Or she'll be after us.'

'Mrs Adair?' Mercy asked, surprised.

'No.' Rose was scathing. 'The old tartar – Radcliffe, the nanny. You want to watch 'er, she's a right mardy cow.'

Rose jumped off the bed suddenly and strutted about, face like a po'. 'What this child needs is a regular routine . . .'

Mercy laughed with recognition. She already liked Rose a great deal. 'I saw her – when she was here yesterday.'

'We reckon she's a witch,' Rose said, plonking herself down again. 'Don't we, Em?'

Emmie, taller, older, had a lot less to say.

'We just couldn't believe it when she took you on,' Rose said. 'You going to be a companion or summat? We thought 'e'd make 'er 'ave another Radcliffe. Someone all starchy with a face like the back of a tram. 'Ow old're you?'

When Mercy told them they gasped in amazement.

'You're only a year older than me!' Emmie said.

Rose was seventeen, and in charge of cleaning the upper floor, and Emmie worked downstairs. They both helped out in the kitchen. The cook, Mrs Parslow, was apparently all right once she got to know you.

Mercy could see Rose was busy having a good look round at what little Mercy had brought with her. 'You been in service before?'

'Not like this, no.'

'You got a nerve!'

'They awright then – to work for?'

'Not so bad. Mrs Adair's scared of 'er own shadow, 'er is. 'E's awright, when 'e's in a good mood . . .'

'Which ain't been very often lately,' Emmie commented.

Mercy felt thoroughly cheered up by their company. It

was a long time since she'd had a laugh with anyone her own age. The two of them took her to see the room they shared. Rose led them along the landing. On the way she leant close to Mercy, pointing to a third door and whispering, 'That one across there is Radcliffe's – when she's not down there scaring the wits out of that poor babby.'

They sat for a few moments in Rose and Emmie's room where there were two beds and a small window facing the road.

'I think I'd better go down,' Mercy said.

'Eh – if you're 'er companion,' Emmie said as Mercy stood up, 'does this mean we 'ave to wait on you?'

Mercy grinned. 'Oh, I blooming well hope so!'

'I want you to know,' James Adair told her, 'that I am at first only employing you for a trial period of one month.'

Mercy stood before him in the front parlour. Mr Adair turned away and addressed her reflection in the gilt-framed mirror over the mantelpiece. Mercy thought how tall he was. She could see where Stevie got his looks, the shape of the face, brown eyes. He stood there with his legs apart, swaying backwards and forwards a little, one hand stroking his moustache. Mercy did not know how to speak to him. She saw Margaret Adair smile at her across the room, trying to be reassuring, but only managing instead to look more anxious.

'Any trouble,' Mr Adair went on, 'anything missing from the house—'

'James!' his wife protested miserably.

'Any upset in the household routine for which I consider you responsible, and you will have to go before the month is up.' He turned round again and looked at her sternly. 'Is that clear?'

'Yes, sir.' Mercy looked at the rich swirls of crimson, fawn, green, on the rug under her feet. He didn't want her here, that was as plain as anything. At that moment she felt like running back home to Elsie.

'I'll be direct with you.' Mr Adair spoke as if he were addressing a clutch of businessmen. 'I should not have employed you myself. My wife acted rather hastily. I should have looked for someone more mature to be a decent and respectable support to her.'

Mercy felt very deflated and cold inside. Perhaps after all her defiant words to Mabel, she didn't have a future in this house.

Seeing her dismayed expression, Margaret Adair spoke gently to her.

'Mercy – perhaps this is not a good moment to discuss too many things. Come down to me tomorrow morning and we shall talk about your duties properly.' She looked apprehensively at her husband. 'You've finished with Mercy, haven't you, dear?'

He nodded curtly.

'You can go and ask Mrs Parslow for a plate of food, and then if I were you I should have an early night.'

Mercy slunk out of the room. After she'd eaten some cold beef and potato, she slowly made her way upstairs. She didn't know what else to do but shut herself in her room. It felt too early to go to sleep.

The attic stairs were next to Stevie's nursery. Pausing by the door, Mercy heard the sound of splashing water. It must be his bathtime. She pressed her ear to the door, suddenly full of longing. He was such a nice babby. It would have been fun to go in and play with him if he hadn't had such a off-putting keeper! She smiled, hearing Stevie gurgling behind the door. Oh well, perhaps she'd get a chance to play with him when he was down with Mrs Adair.

As she moved her head away from the door, a high shriek came from the room, a sound so sudden and tormented it could only have been of pain. It was followed by a few seconds' silence, in which she heard the nanny's voice say, sweetly, 'There, oh dear, there we are,' before Stevie gathered his breath and began to scream and scream.

The sounds followed Mercy up to the attic. She sat on her bed. His crying went on for a long time. Eventually it went quiet.

Mercy didn't know what to do. It was growing dark and cold. She lit the candle and put it on the chair by the bed. Then she undressed. She got in under the soft, worn covers, reached for her *Cheerful Homes* by Dr J. W. Kirton and began slowly to read,

'*It is the most natural thing*,' the book began, '*for young people to indulge in the hope that some fine day they will fall in love with someone, and someone will do the same thing in return.*'

She turned the book over, lying with it on her stomach, looking up at the candlelight shadows on the white, bugless ceiling. She thought of Tom, of Elsie and the others waving her goodbye that afternoon. This house felt so big and quiet and strange, and it was obvious Mr Adair didn't want her there. Full of sadness and uncertainty, she wanted to run back to all the familiar things of Angel Street. She closed the book and turned over, hugging her pillow. She cried quietly to herself.

The next morning she found Margaret Adair giving Stevie his morning feed in the cheerful back sitting room.

'Do come and sit by me, Mercy,' Margaret said, smiling.

Mercy went and sat tentatively at the other end of the couch. She hadn't been sure what to wear, and had put her black skirt on again. She was also warm inside from eating the nicest breakfast she could ever remember having. It had been slops, it was true, but with all milk and crunchy grains of sugar on top. With her stomach comfortingly full she was ready to take on anything.

'Sit back, dear,' Margaret encouraged her. 'I so want you to feel this is your home. I do have such a feeling we're going to get on. I'm so sorry for James talking to you in that harsh way last night. I'm afraid he does get into a panic when anything the least bit different happens and then he can get rather stiff and starchy . . .'

Mercy watched her carefully, not having any idea that her big eyes and intent stare were making her employer feel quite nervous.

'I really do want you here, Mercy.' To Mercy's astonishment the woman reached across and took her hand for a moment. Hers felt warm and soft.

'I suppose Mr Adair was expecting someone a bit more . . . well, posh?'

'Oh, I don't know.' Margaret sighed. 'Older certainly. He thinks such a lot of our nanny, Audrey Radcliffe. I think she reminds him of the nanny he had as a boy.'

'Poor him then.' Mercy clapped a hand over her mouth in horror, eyes stretched wide. What was she saying! 'Ooh, I'm sorry – I shouldn't've said that.'

But Margaret Adair had hold of her again, was squeezing her wrist, face full of concern. 'Is that what you think? D'you think she's wrong, and unkind?'

Mercy felt out of her depth here. What a strange

household. Why on earth should this woman be consulting her?

'I've only seen 'er the once,' Mercy said. 'I don't know whether she is or not – I'm sure she's very good . . .'

The white hand was still grasping her wrist. Margaret Adair's eyes were pleading.

'I just . . .'

'Yes – what? Please speak frankly, Mercy. I think I shall go completely mad if I can't find someone to speak honestly with.'

Mercy kept looking into her eyes. 'When I was in the home, the orphanage, that is, there were women working there who shouldn't've been within a mile of children. I suppose she just reminds me . . . there's summat about her – but that's just me . . .'

'Oh Mercy, thank you.' Margaret Adair gave her wrist another squeeze and then released her. She seemed triumphant, and carried on speaking in a rush. 'You have no idea what it means to me hearing you say that. She's so harsh and rigid and Stevie's so obviously unhappy with her. But James can't see it. Anything that goes wrong, if Stevie cries or the routine gets upset, he blames me. Routine is his god. Everything Audrey Radcliffe does is right. She knows. That's his way of looking at it. Babies have to be taken in hand and trained. I'm only allowed to feed him when she says, however much he cries. She barely allows me to play with him. You'll see, she'll be down any moment. Some days I feel as if I'll just explode and shout and scream, I feel so helpless and frustrated.'

Her tears started to fall as she finished speaking. She held up a handkerchief to her mouth. Feeling the quivering of his mother's body, Stevie came off the breast and poked his head curiously from under the shawl.

'Oh, and he's such a darling!' Margaret lifted him upright and he kicked his sturdy legs. 'And your nanny isn't such a perfect archangel either, is she, letting you bang your head again. Look – show Mercy.'

The place above his eye where Mercy had noticed the scar before was raw and inflamed, the skin pink around the wound. Mercy thought about the noises she'd heard.

'When he was having a bath?'

'Yes. She said he caught his head. On the corner of the table.'

Mercy frowned. 'Couldn't you get another nanny? I mean, not that it's any of my business.'

'Oh, but I want it to be your business.' Margeret's voice was pleading. 'You must think me a very strange person, but when you came here, even by little things you said, I knew you had courage. Far more than I have. That you'd question things. I need someone to tell me I'm not wrong and foolish. I need you to be on my side, Mercy. Please don't be afraid. Say what you think to me . . .'

Mercy's bewilderment increased. Why was this woman not in charge of her own household? Surely that was how it was supposed to be when you had money? It all seemed very strange to her. She did know though, that she liked her and that she didn't like the look of Nanny Radcliffe at all.

'Well, I'll do my best,' was all she could say.

When Stevie had finished his feed his mother sat him up and he beamed milkily at them both.

'He's beautiful,' Mercy said, drawing closer. She held out a finger to him and he clamped it in his strong fist. Mercy shook her finger and he let out a gurgling laugh.

''Ello there Stevie – you're a fine fella, aren't you? I must say, Mrs Adair, he's one of the bonniest babbies I've ever seen.'

'D'you want to hold him for a moment?'

'Ooh yes!'

Mercy took Stevie on to her lap, holding him upright.

'He'd almost sit by hisself – look how strong his back is!' She jiggled him up and down, playing horsey and making clicking sounds with her tongue and Stevie chortled, his beaming face only marred by the harsh red wound above his eye.

They were so busy playing with him, they didn't hear the footsteps outside. The door opened and Radcliffe stood in the doorway. Stevie, his back to her, carried on chuckling. Mercy, still with Stevie's hands in her own, saw Margaret Adair's face tense up, the smile dying from it.

'Time for a nap now,' Radcliffe commanded. She stared hard at Mercy.

Mercy stared back. I know you, she thought, her flesh creeping. I know your sort.

'I'm sorry – I should introduce you both,' Margaret said. 'This is Mercy who is to act as my companion.' Mercy thought she'd better stand up.

'Pleased to meet you,' she said, forcing a smile.

Audrey Radcliffe smiled, showing small, uneven teeth. 'I'm glad to see you're getting to know Steven.'

'He's a lovely little lad, isn't he?' Mercy said.

'Oh yes, he is indeed.'

What was it about this woman? Mercy thought. She had an air of command, of coldness even when she was pretending to be nice as pie.

'Come along now, Steven, dear,' she said.

'Oh, couldn't he just stay a little bit longer?' Margaret appealed. 'He and Mercy were just getting acquainted.'

There was no reply. The woman just stood there waiting to be obeyed, her disapproval seeping across the room.

Margaret quailed and gave in, reaching over to take her son. 'I suppose time is getting on.'

As she tried to hand Stevie over he clung to her blouse, face crumpling. He'd already begun crying as, without a word, Radcliffe took him away.

Chapter Twenty-Three

Over that first month Mercy settled into the big house on the Wake Green Road. She spent her evenings with Rose and Emmie in the little sitting room at the far end of the kitchen, talking and laughing. She started to feel young again and more energetic, especially as even the servants' food in the Adairs' house was better and more plentiful than anything she'd ever been used to. Mrs Parslow went home in the evenings to a little house in Kings Heath. But she was kind enough when she was there, once she'd decided Mercy wasn't going to get above herself.

But Mercy knew she was still on trial.

'He might send me packing come the end of the month,' she complained to the maids one evening.

'Well, I 'ope you don't go,' Emmie said, huddling close to the tiny fire in the grate. 'It's been a good laugh since you've been 'ere.'

'I hardly ever see 'im, so I don't know how he thinks he's going to know what's going on.' Mercy only ever saw Mr Adair in passing and he never seemed to take any notice of her. This wouldn't have worried her – she didn't expect him to – except that he was the one who would decide whether she could stay or not. And it was growing more and more important to her that she did stay. The thought of going back to Angel Street would come over her like a rainstorm on a sunny day. She liked Margaret

Adair, and her job was easy. She could scarcely believe what a comfortable life she had suddenly found. No more poverty, no more scraping for every penny in that damp, jerry-built house, having to see Mabel's horrible face! It seemed like a miracle. If only she knew for sure she could stay!

But there was one other thing that made her ache for this certainty and that was Stevie. She adored him almost as if he were her own. She looked forward every day to seeing his wide, brown-eyed face and when she heard him crying she had to stop herself running to give him comfort. If only she could get closer to him. She found it hard to understand Margaret letting herself become so cut off from her child.

If I had a babby, Mercy thought, I'd never let it out of my sight.

'I'd love to see Stevie more,' she said to Rose and Emmie. 'He's so beautiful. I wish I could just take 'im off and play whenever I like.'

'You'll be lucky!' Rose guffawed with scorn at the very idea. 'Not with that guard dog 'e's got looking after 'im!'

One day she was passing through the hall when Nanny Radcliffe pushed Stevie's black perambulator in through the front door. It was a windy day and Mercy ran forward and helped her shut the door.

''Er, thank you,' Audrey Radcliffe said, sounding surprised but not hostile. She smiled. Mercy felt encouraged, and bent over Stevie. 'Hello there!' She reached out and tickled him under the chin. 'How's the beautiful lad then?' She looked up at Audrey Radcliffe who was standing, watching. Mercy was taken aback. She had expected the woman to stiffen and tell her to leave off but instead she saw an odd, wistful expression on her face.

Mercy smiled at her again, her heart thudding. What was it about this little woman that made her so uncomfortable to be with? All her childhood nerves around Miss O'Donnell and the others rushed back through her. But this was a chance, and she decided to risk it.

'I, er – I like babbies. I was wondering if I could come up and see him like – I could give 'im a bath or summat for you?'

The woman seemed to tighten up. 'Oh, I don't think so.' She started to push the pram on down the hall. 'No. That's my job. You leave all that to me.'

Soon after, when Margaret had gone out for an hour and the sun was winter bright, Mercy looked out and saw the pram in the garden. Through the glass she could hear Stevie crying. There was no sign of anyone else. Nanny Radcliffe must have put him out for his sleep. She was rigorous about him getting enough fresh air.

Mercy had a great rush of longing. If only she could just go and take a peep at him! She was alone: Rose and Emmie were busy, and she would have loved to play with him or walk him round the park. Perhaps she could just go and rock him to get him to sleep . . .

She went to the back door, unlocked it, and went out into the garden, hugging herself. She had no coat on and it was freezing cold! She could hear Stevie's cries, loud now, and wretched.

When she reached the pram, she gasped, horrified. Stevie had been put outside with no covers on. Not one! He was clad simply in a vest and napkin, his arms and legs bare. He was crying wretchedly, his nose was running and his fingers and lips had a blue tinge.

'Oh my Lord, the stupid bitch!' Mercy reached in without giving it a thought, gathered him up into her arms and carried him back into the house. Sitting by the fire in the back sitting room, she held him wrapped in a shawl and rocked him, warming him until eventually he grew drowsy and slept in her lap. She still carried on humming, looking down into his chubby face, the scar over his eye at last beginning to heal properly. She laid him softly to rest on the couch and sat watching him, mesmerized. Imagine if he were hers. Belonging to someone! Really belonging. Being able to call him family. She pretended to herself that Stevie was hers, imagined trying to build a life for him. How she would work to see he had everything better than her! And she would never, never leave him . . .

'What are you doing?'

The voice at the door made her jump violently. In that split second she had to decide what to say. She wanted to shout, but knew she must be polite.

'He was crying. I just thought I'd give 'im a bit of a love, that's all. He was cold,' she pointed out, trying to speak humbly. She had to keep on the right side of this woman.

Audrey Radcliffe stared at her for an uncomfortably long time. Mercy saw that she, too, was struggling, having to decide how to play this one. To Mercy's astonishment she walked across the room and sat down. She put her feet in their pointed shoes neatly together.

'You shouldn't go against what I say, you know.' Her voice was oddly childlike, wheedling almost.

'Sorry,' Mercy said, controlling her anger. 'Only it is cold—'

'I'm the child's nanny, not you.'

'I know, only—'

'Me. Not you.' She smiled suddenly, eyes fixed on Mercy's face, then stood up again. Mercy noticed to her astonishment that her hands were trembling. In a desperate voice she said. 'Don't tell her.'

'Tell who?'

'Mrs Adair. About this afternoon. It won't happen again, really it won't.'

'Awright. No, 'course I won't.' Mercy smiled up at her. So she was human after all. She was worried about losing her place here! But looking at her Mercy could still only feel the same sense of disquiet. There was something oddly wooden about her. Something not right . . .

'Shall I bring him up when he wakes?'

'All right. Straight away though.' She was on her dignity again now, and went out of the room without another word.

'Well,' Mercy murmured to the sleeping baby, 'she's a rum'un all right, that one.'

'You surely have no objection to her staying with us now?' Margaret Adair pleaded with her husband. 'She's been here a month and she's been marvellous.'

James Adair had arrived home from the works and the two of them were in their bedchamber, changing for the evening. James was sitting on the edge of the bed unfastening his shoes. He hesitated before answering.

Margaret assumed this thoughtful pause was his way of justifying his initial doubts about Mercy, of asserting his control of the household.

'James – darling . . .' Margaret came round the bed. 'Perhaps we could invite Mercy to share our dinner with us tonight? You complain that you don't know what she's like because you scarcely ever see her!'

She turned her back to him, inviting him to button her up. She was dressed in a rather matronly frock, blue, with a maroon paisley pattern, which accentuated her already considerable curves. She had tried to pin up her hair, though wisps of it were already escaping down her back.

'You look nice,' James offered, even though he didn't quite feel it was true. Surely a woman should have more instinct about what clothes would suit her?

'Oh, thank you!' She turned her head, startled. It was a long time since he'd paid her a compliment.

James smiled. Things are getting better, he thought. It was days – no, more than that – since he'd come home and found her weeping and incapable, her clothes all anyhow, some of the buttons left unfastened. And she was definitely smiling more. He stood up and before doing up the dress he slipped his hands inside. Feeling her soft, curving form he wanted her with such a reconciliatory stab of desire that for a moment he felt like weeping. Perhaps all could be well again. He pulled her closer to him.

'James,' she murmured, reassured by his sudden affection. She turned and faced him. James smiled, the skin crinkling round his eyes.

'My love – You seem more . . . yourself.'

'I am! I do feel better. Except . . .' She stopped, chewing her lip.

'What?'

I want her out, she felt like shouting. Get rid of that wretched Radcliffe woman who rules my life and all will be well. But she didn't want to sour the moment.

'Nothing.' She brushed her hands down the lapels of

his jacket, her expression sweet. 'You didn't answer my question about Mercy.'

James laughed. 'You're a strange one, aren't you? Why eat with us? She's a servant! Still, I suppose she's not so much younger than Lizzie. A replacement sister for you, eh?'

'Yes.' Margaret's face was bright. 'Just like that.'

Her beloved sister Lizzie had left her father's Warwickshire farm as she had done, to marry another farmer and settle outside Carlisle. Margaret missed her sorely. 'So may she?'

James's spirits were high, and he could feel the pleasant sensation of wanting her increasing in him. 'Oh, all right, if it keeps you happy. How's our boy today?'

Margaret's face fell. 'He's all right. From what I've seen of him. That woman took him out in a terrible rainstorm. She's obsessed with this fresh air business. I hope he didn't catch his death.'

''Course not. Toughen him up. She knows what she's doing.'

Margaret tried to demur, but she could see James was barely listening. Such close proximity to his wife after the deprivation of months of union with her was overcoming him. Cautiously he ran his hands over her enlarged breasts. The feel of them was extraordinary.

'Oh, my love,' he whispered, leaning to kiss her soft mouth. He was overcome with need for her.

'James, we must go down – they'll be waiting for us.'

'Let them wait.'

Gently, she moved away from him. 'Let us think about – that . . .' A blush spread over her face as she appealed to him. They never spoke of the physical things which happened between them. 'Later – please?'

'Very well.' He struggled for composure, unsatisfied desire bringing him for a moment to the edge of violence. But he must control himself. Self-control was vital, was the mark of civilized behaviour. He turned from her, clearing his throat hard.

'They want me?' Mercy was in the kitchen with Emmie and Rose. She often gave a hand in the evening while Mrs Parslow was plodding round on her big flat feet amid the steaming saucepans.

Rose was grinning. 'Ooh,' she teased. 'Miss La-di-dah. We are going up in the world!'

'Better go and put a clean frock on,' Mrs Parslow commented, testing the potatoes to see if they were boiled. 'You can't sit in there with them unless you're clean.'

'But I haven't got another clean frock!' Mercy was all nerves at the thought of eating a meal in the presence of Mr Adair.

'Ah well,' Mrs Parslow said dryly. 'You'll 'ave to do then won't you? Go on – best get on in there.'

Mercy rushed to wash her hands and then went timidly to the dining room. Why have they asked me? she wondered. Was it to tell her whether she was going to be allowed to stay or not? If they were going to turn her out, would they have asked her to eat dinner with them?

The light was on over the dining table and three places had been set. Mercy thought Mr Adair didn't seem in a very good mood and Margaret Adair was flustered and apologetic in her too-tight dress.

'Come in and sit down, dear,' she said as Mercy slid into the room.

The three of them settled at the well-polished table, Mr Adair at the end with Mercy to his left and his wife to his right. A few moments later Emmie and Rose carried in the food, both smirking at Mercy behind the Adairs' backs and Mercy had to look down at the hunting scene on her place mat to stop herself grinning back. What was she doing sitting here when she should be out in the kitchen with those two clowns as normal!

'So how are you getting along?' Mr Adair asked her once the three of them were alone.

'Oh—' Mercy was startled. 'Er – very well thank you,' she said, unsure how to respond. 'Very nice.' She was watching intently to see what the Adairs did with all the implements on the table. There was a generous slice of belly pork on her plate which smelt delicious.

'Here we are, Mercy.' Margaret passed her the potatoes. Mercy could feel her mouth watering at the sight but the dish was so heavy that in taking it in one hand she almost dropped it.

'Sorry,' she murmured, blushing as James Adair's hand reached out and caught it.

'Steady,' he said. He smiled suddenly, a kind smile. Mercy smiled back, relieved, and for a moment his eyes dwelt on her face as if puzzled, before reaching for the other dish.

'Swede?'

'Oh, no, thank you.'

'Do you not care for swede, Mercy?' Margaret asked. 'I must say I never liked it as a child . . .'

'No, I don't.' Mercy felt her voice coming out very quietly.

She accepted greens, and they all began to eat. The food was delicious, and she was grateful when Mr Adair began to talk to his wife.

'I had a letter today from that Kesler chap – the one in New York.'

'Oh?' Margaret frowned with her fork poised in the air. 'Kestler? Isn't he German?'

'He's an American by birth.' James's tone silenced any argument. 'This is business, darling.' There was a moment's silence.

'And what did he have to say?'

'Well . . .' James laid down his knife and fork, speaking with the kind of animation which only work could bring out in him. 'He's thinking and planning very much along the same lines as we are. That for smaller companies to survive we'll have to get into one of the specialist niches in the market – and fast. And develop that as hard as we can. Kesler's company is on about the same scale as ours.'

'How marvellous,' Margaret said.

James chewed on a mouthful of meat, then chuckled. 'Oddly enough – in fact it seems like fate, almost – he's also putting together a new model of racing cycle. It's rather different from the approach Silkin and I have been working on, but Kesler's full of all sorts of ideas about all these new aluminium alloys – lighter, you see, and . . .'

'That sounds very exciting,' Margaret enthused, just a little too much.

James smiled and looked at Mercy. 'I don't suppose all this kind of business talk is of any interest to you?'

'It is,' she said truthfully. 'What is the name of your company, Mr Adair?' She knew, actually, but thought she'd ask again.

Mr Adair looked a little taken aback at her interest. 'Well, it's Adair and Dunne actually. Dunne's made the parts for the cycles, or a lot of them any rate. So my company bought them up just before the War. We still have to go out to Dunlop for the tyres, and of course your best lamp is a Lucas lamp, but there're local firms too. Of course, during the War—' – he was really getting into his stride now – 'we went over to making spares for military vehicles, which wasn't unprofitable, I must say.' He gave a self-satisfied chuckle. 'But now's our big chance to develop.'

Mercy frowned. 'I always thought the BSA made all the cycles.'

'Oh no.' He laughed again, expansively. He was relaxing, flattered by Mercy's interest. Margaret was visibly relieved. 'The BSA are big of course. But there are quite a few firms. Some of the smaller ones have combined – take Weldless Steel Tubes, for instance. Now twenty-five years ago, they were—'

'James, I can't see that Mercy really needs to know all this,' Margaret interrupted gently.

Her husband looked a little rueful, and sat back in his seat, stroking his slightly gingery moustache with one hand, his fine crystal glass in the other.

'Factory life. There we are. You ever been in a factory?'

'Yes,' Mercy said simply. 'I made grenades – Mills Bombs – for two years. Up Deritend.'

'Did you now?' He glanced at his wife, eyes reproachful. No one had told him he'd employed a factory hand in his house.

Shyly, Mercy began to question him. One question led to another. She was interested, and she also saw her attention pleased him. Margaret was bored by his work. She didn't know anything much, of course. How did he know what people wanted? she asked. How did they know how many cycles to make? And if there were all these other cycle manufacturers in Birmingham, why did he need an American gentleman?

He answered indulgently at first and she was just relieved he didn't laugh at her or become impatient.

'There are nigh on 1,500 employed in the firm altogether . . .'

'Is that big?' Mercy's eyes were wide. As Mr Adair answered she felt Margaret watching her.

'Big enough.' James Adair sat back as Rose and Emmie cleared away the plates and brought in dishes of stewed pears and junket, and pretty ivy-patterned bowls. 'Not big by BSA standards though. 'Course, they can design and produce a whole range. But our route will be through specialized models – racers, leisure bicycles. Now the War's over there's huge demand. And it happens that the most like-minded designer I've come across is over the water.'

For the first time Mercy eased herself back in her chair and sat comfortably, more relaxed. She was not without anxiety though, nervous in case her manners should be found wanting. And were they going to tell her whether she could keep her job or not?

As they finished their sweet, James Adair pushed his chair back, crossed one leg comfortably over the other and lit a cigar, his soft worsted jacket unbuttoned. The room was dark round them, the table a pool of light in the middle.

'So Mercy, are you going to tell us a bit more about yourself?'

Mercy's heart started to pound. Was this it now? Was he going to find out all about her and then decide she wasn't suitable to remain in his wife's company? What in heaven did he want to know? She reddened in confusion, feeling her mouth turn dry.

'Oh James, not tonight!' Margaret intervened.

Mercy looked gratefully at her, knowing she was being protected. 'I'm sure we've tired the poor girl quite enough—'

'Nonsense!' James laughed. 'She's been lively as a cricket – full of questions. Haven't you, Mercy?'

'Well I—'

'Would you like to go to your room now, dear?' Margaret said.

''Er, yes – please.' Mercy couldn't meet Mr Adair's eye. She stood up, gracefully smoothing her skirts.

'You'll join us again, won't you?' James Adair had stood up and was holding out his hand. Confused, Mercy took it, looking up into his eyes.

'Thank you,' she said.

'Goodnight,' Margaret called to her.

Mercy closed the dining-room door behind her and let out an enormous sigh of relief. Well, they hadn't said she couldn't stay yet!

'Good God,' James Adair said as Mercy left the room. He spoke in irritation at himself. What did he think he was doing, shaking hands with a servant like that? He sat down, stiffly continuing to smoke his cigar.

'That was very gallant, dear,' Margaret teased him. 'I see you approve after all.'

'Perhaps,' he said gruffly, 'In fact, yes, she's a great deal better than I'd feared.'

He was left with an unsettled, almost itchy feeling, the image of those large, striking eyes watching him as he'd talked.

'So what do we know about the girl?'

Margaret thought quickly. She wanted to please James, knew that later, in private, she would have to. But in the matter of Mercy she also wanted his approval. Mercy had told her very few things, and those inadvertently, about her past life.

'I only know for sure that she was an orphan – abandoned at birth from what she said.' She watched her husband's face. 'Poor little waif. What a thing to do to a child.'

'Poverty.' James shook his head, leaning forward to knock ash from his cigar. 'The desperation of poverty.' Margaret was surprised and touched by this insight of his.

That night, after they had retired, she didn't instantly turn away from him as they lay together, though she was quiet, listening, he knew, for sounds from Stevie's room.

James caressed her belly through the soft organza nightdress. Felt her sigh, very slightly.

'You, er . . .' He felt he must ask, embarrassing as it was. 'You don't mind?'

'No,' she replied dreamily. 'I don't mind.'

Carefully he moved her nightdress up, at last allowing himself desire, and uncovered her breasts in the soft light.

Chapter Twenty-Four

That Saturday Mr Adair called Mercy into the parlour. Speaking very formally he said that her presence in the house and her behaviour had been satisfactory and beneficial to everyone, and that she could consider herself now employed for the forseeable future.

However serious she tried to look, Mercy could feel a beaming smile breaking out across her face.

'Oh thank you!' she cried when Mr Adair had finished speaking. 'Thank you so much!'

'There's just one thing . . .' Mr Adair looked rather stern. 'Audrey Radcliffe tells me you have taken issue with her on a few matters concerning our son. I won't have that. So far as I'm concerned she's making a marvellous job of caring for Steven. I believe her to be very sound and I don't wish to hear any more about you causing her trouble.'

'But she—' Mercy looked stricken, but closed her mouth again. This was no time to start arguing. 'Sorry,' she mumbled. 'It won't happen again.'

When she was alone with Margaret she said, 'I'm ever so glad. I was afraid you wouldn't be satisfied with me – especially your husband.'

'Oh Mercy, not at all,' Margaret laughed. 'James can see how much you've cheered me up. It's been such fun since you've been here. I do hope you feel happy and settled with us?'

'Oh yes.' Mercy was beaming again. 'I've got used to it here with you and Stevie. I don't think I could stand going back now.'

She had been back to Angel Street though, on her two afternoons off. The first time it was hard. It had only been two weeks after all. In one way she felt as if she'd never left, yet in another, that she'd been away months, years even.

She went straight to Elsie.

'Eh, bab, you're back!' Elsie's face glowed at the sight of her. She was already putting the kettle on.

Mercy went and sat by Tom.

''Ello love.' He was propped upright, awake, but she didn't kiss him. He made a sound, and a sudden movement with his head.

'See – 'e's glad to see you.'

Mercy sighed softly. 'So how've you been?'

'Oh – you know.' Elsie spoke with her back to her, spooning tea from her battered tin with the green lid.

'And Alf?'

'Oh, 'e's not so bad. 'E saw Johnny last week, in town. Said the lad were awright. 'E said 'e'd come over and visit but 'e 'ain't turned up yet.'

She turned round to lay out the cups on the bare, scrubbed table, and Mercy was shocked by the grim, unguarded expression on her face. Was she imagining that Elsie looked a lot worse or was it just that she was now used to Margaret Adair's robust appearance?

'Elsie, are you awright? You don't look well to me.'

Elsie tried to smile but succeeded in something more like a wince. 'Oh, I'll do. Now – ' she spooned condensed milk into the cups – ''ow're they treating you?'

Mercy chattered on to her as they drank their sweet tea, telling her about her first fortnight, how Dorothy had popped in to see her, about Stevie, and Nanny Radcliffe – Elsie tutted as Mercy described her – and about the Adairs. She told her about the house and all the beautiful things in it, Mr Adair's glass collection and the soft chairs and the pretty painted firescreen in the parlour.

'And they've got a great big grandfather clock which ticks ever so loud, and antimacassars on all the parlour chairs . . .'

Elsie was smiling and listening, glad for her, Mercy could see, but a couple of times she saw her close her eyes tight for a moment.

'What's up?' Mercy felt her stomach churn in fright. 'You got a pain, Elsie?'

'What? Oh, no, love. I'm just a bit tired, that's all.' She jerked her head at Tom. ''E were a bit restless in the night so I was up and down.'

Mercy ached for her. She felt as if the walls were closing in round them. Back here. This endless, futile struggle.

'How's she?' She nodded her head towards Mabel's.

'Oh – doing odd bits of work. Mary's 'elping 'er out.'

'Ah – I bet she is.'

'You been in to see 'er?'

'No.'

Elsie gave a long sigh. 'Well, I can't say I blame yer.'

Mercy stayed late enough to see the others come in. Alf greeted her like a long lost daughter which made her happy, and she sat chatting to Jack and Rosalie for a bit.

'Don't forget us, will yer?' Elsie joked as she left.

'I'll see you in a fortnight.' She turned to wave, going

to the entry. As she did so she caught sight of Mabel peering out from the window of number two and turned away. Mabel didn't come out.

Stevie was crying. The sound of it wormed its way into Mercy's sleep until she opened her eyes in the dark. He didn't wake every night now, but on occasion there came a roar from the nursery and then his anguished howling, as if he'd wakened from a terrible dream.

After a time, if it didn't stop, Mercy would hear Audrey Radcliffe's bedroom door squeak open and her abrupt tread going down the stairs.

But that night, though Stevie carried on crying for many minutes, there came no sound from the room opposite. Mercy turned on her back, wide awake now. The baby's cries were pained, or frightened. Those helpless shrieks into the darkness touched something in her, setting her nerves on edge. She felt almost like crying herself. She couldn't lie in bed listening to him.

Moving silently across the floorboards in her bedsocks, she pulled on a cardigan and lit the candle and went down to him. Audrey Radcliffe's door was still shut.

Stevie quieted for a second when she entered the nursery, the light from her candle thinning out the dark. Mercy had to look round to see where the cot was, for Radcliffe kept the room so much as her personal fortress that Mercy had barely even glimpsed inside until now. Then Stevie let out another high whimper.

'It's awright, little'un.' She put the candle on the table by the wall and went to pick him up.

'There – Mercy's 'ere to see you. No need for all that racket now, is there?'

As she held him, Stevie cuddled in close to her, one

hand grasping the sleeve of her cardigan, tangling in her long hair, the other tucked up close to his face, thumb in mouth. He was still gulping and sniffing, but Mercy felt that he was calmer, reassured.

For a few moments she walked round the room holding him, then sat on the rush-seated chair and rocked him, humming, starting to pat his back. Suddenly he stiffened in her arms and let out another great howl.

'Now . . . now . . . there,' she was saying, then looked up startled as the light from another candle appeared at the door.

'Oh Mercy – thank goodness it's you.' Margaret Adair was clad in a long, pale gown. 'What're you doing down here? Do you often come to him at night? I thought it was . . .?'

'No, I don't,' Mercy whispered back. 'Only she didn't seem to hear him.'

'I've not heard him cry like that in a long time.' Margaret looked worried.

'He was awright – I don't know what set him off again.'

'May I?' Margaret held her arms out. Mercy handed the warm, distraught child to her.

'I've wanted to get up to him so often and had to restrain myself,' Margaret said softly. 'I should have just followed my instincts.'

Mercy watched the look of tenderness on Margaret's face as she cradled her son. It suddenly made her feel very sad. This was what a mother was supposed to be, wasn't it? She was supposed to love and cherish her baby and hold it close. The reality of her own mother went through her like a chill. She had left her almost as soon as she was born, dumped her like a parcel on a doorstep. What sort of mother was that?

'She says I'll spoil him,' Margaret was murmuring. 'How could I spoil him? It seems so unkind.'

'What does she know anyway?' Mercy hissed, with a viciousness in her voice that made Margaret look at her, startled. 'Has she ever had a babby?'

''Er – well, I assume not!' Margaret reached out and touched Mercy's shoulder, felt her trembling, whether from cold or emotion, she couldn't tell. 'Poor dear Mercy. You're so sweet with him. With all of us.'

Another light appeared in the doorway.

'What's all this then?'

Radcliffe's tone was frigid. She was wrapped in a heavy wool gown, her hair hanging in a plait down her back. The candle she was holding hollowed out her already gaunt face with shadows. The sight of her set Mercy's heart pounding.

'It's all right,' Margaret said hastily, bending to replace her son in his cot. 'He's going off by himself now.' But as she lay him down, Stevie started to cry again.

'But why do I come down and find people meddling with him?'

Mercy, rage swelling in her, took a step forward. She must control herself, or Mr Adair would send her away, but . . .

'You didn't seem to've heard him. So I came down. What's the harm in that?'

Nanny Radcliffe stared back in disdain at the angelic picture Mercy made standing before her, her pale hair tumbling over her shoulders. The expression on Mercy's face was anything but angelic though. Her chin was jutting forward and her eyes narrowed, arms folded tight.

'It's not your place to interfere.' Radcliffe spoke with exaggerated patience as if they were all terminally foolish, she the only one with any insight into Stevie's requirements. 'Children should not be pandered to. There's nothing he needs for his welfare in the middle of the night. He has to learn not to go attracting attention unnecessarily and inconveniencing other people. You don't want him to grow up into a weak, demanding character, do you?'

''Er, no, I suppose not—' Margaret began doubtfully, when a louder voice said, 'Hear! hear!'

James Adair came into the room, a silky, red dressing gown over his night clothes.

'Margaret – get back to bed,' he ordered, tight-lipped. Margaret scuttled from the room.

'Radcliffe – see to the child,' he said curtly. 'I apologize for this interference. It won't happen again.'

He came and stood before Mercy. With the light of the candle behind her, her face was in shadow so he could not see the defiance written on it.

'I've warned you. You do not interfere with Radcliffe's responsibilities. I don't know why a slip of a girl your age thinks she can come into my house and start transgressing all the established rules. The presumptuousness of it quite astounds me! Now – it'd better not happen again . . .'

Between her teeth, Mercy said, 'Why shouldn't he have what he needs? Making people suffer doesn't make them stronger and better it makes them cruel and nasty.'

James Adair stared at her, stunned, scarcely able to take in that she'd challenged him like that.

'Just leave it to someone who knows,' he demanded. Irritably he turned to the nanny. 'Can't you get that child to stop squawking like that?'

A couple of mornings later, when Stevie was downstairs with Mercy and Margaret for the short period he was allowed with them, he seemed fretful, and even all their smiles and jigglings on knees couldn't seem to cheer him. He cried when they picked him up and he cried when they put him down.

'Perhaps he's feverish?' Margaret said, worried. 'He does feel rather hot, don't you think? She's got him rather well wrapped considering the worst of the winter's over. 'Let's take this off.'

She peeled Stevie's white matinée coat off, but this didn't seem to make him any happier. He grizzled even harder and seemed thoroughly out of sorts.

'He really seems rather unwell,' Margaret told Audrey Radcliffe when she came to take him upstairs again.

'Oh dear,' the nanny said in the sugary voice she sometimes put on to talk to Stevie. Mercy stared at her. You're a nasty cow, her eyes said, however much you act all sweet.

'Let's go and sort you out.' Audrey Radcliffe went to where Stevie was sitting on the floor, surrounded by wooden building blocks. Ignoring his protests, she bent over and briskly removed him. Stevie's face screwed up and he began crying again.

'Oh heavens.' Margaret had tears in her eyes. 'What's the matter with him? He doesn't seem well at all. I've never heard him make a noise like that before.' She saw the taut look of fury on Mercy's face, her fists clenched, arms straight by her side. 'What is it?'

'There's summat not right about her,' Mercy burst out. She had to say it. Her instinct that there was something horribly wrong about that nanny was growing on her by the week. 'She's doing summat to him. I know she is. She's a cruel, scheming bitch.'

'Mercy! I've never heard you talk that way before.'

Mercy's eyes were burning with emotion. 'She made me promise not to tell you . . .'

'What on earth?'

'Back when it was cold, really cold, she left him out there—' – Mercy pointed at the daffodil filled garden – 'with almost nothing on. No covers, nothing. He was going blue when I went out there to get him. And that mark on his head. He never hit it on the table – she did it. I know she did . . .'

Margaret Adair's hand went up to her mouth in shock.

'Let me go up, now . . .' Mercy marched to the door. She was desperate not to lose this job, but if it was a choice between Stevie suffering and her keeping quiet, what sort of choice was that?

'But—' Margaret said.

Mercy was already on the stairs. She went speedily to the nursery door and opened it without knocking.

Audrey Radcliffe was standing by the table with Stevie in her arms. She seemed just on the point of changing his nappy, and while fretful, he was no longer screaming. There was nothing out of the ordinary to be seen.

'What d'you think you're doing?' Audrey Radcliffe spoke in a very flat, quiet voice.

Mercy stepped towards her. 'You think you can do just what you like round here and get away with it, don't you?' Her temper was up, ready to spill out everywhere but she tried to keep a hold on it. 'You may have Mr Adair and her down there dancing to your tune – but not me. I ain't scared of you or of what Mr Adair thinks. I'm worried about that babby and why he cries every time he claps eyes on you. I'm watching you, missis. You don't fool me, so don't you forget it.'

The woman's eyes flickered for a moment with some

odd, disturbed emotion and her top lip curled up in contempt. But she took control of her face, bringing it back to her flat, professional expression.

'Watch away, dear. I'm an experienced nanny and Mr Adair has every faith in me, so I wouldn't speak like that to me if I were you.'

'I've told her you nearly froze him to death in the garden!'

Radcliffe stared at her for a second. 'I don't remember anything of that nature happening.' She turned back to Stevie. 'You should watch me. You might learn a thing or two. Now get out of this room so I can do my job.'

That evening when Margaret Adair went in to say good-night to her son, he was clearly very unwell.

'He's so hot!' she exclaimed, bending to kiss his flushed cheek. 'He looks so poorly, the lamb. Feel him – he's burning up.'

Stevie was moving restlessly from side to side in the cot, never at peace, making distressed whimpering sounds as if he'd even lost the will to cry.

Audrey Radcliffe came to stand beside Margaret. She was wearing her stiff, white apron. Margaret felt as if the woman's eyes were boring into the back of her head.

'It's just a touch of cold,' Radcliffe assured her patiently. 'I've got it well in hand. He'll be as right as rain in the morning.'

'And how did he get a cold?' Margaret turned, eyes full of hostile anger. 'It wouldn't be from being left out to freeze in the garden again with no bedcovers, would it?'

Audrey Radcliffe looked shocked and scandalized. 'Of

course not, ma'am! Who would think of doing such a thing to a child? I'm afraid you may be imagining things again . . .'

Margaret turned abruptly and went to fetch her husband. Standing by his son's cot in his shirtsleeves and braces, James Adair had to admit Stevie was looking very unwell.

'I'll take him down for a while, with us,' Margaret said, leaning over the cot. 'And if he doesn't improve we'll call a doctor.'

'I'd strongly recommend you leave him where he is.' Nanny Radcliffe, as ever when Mr Adair was there, spoke in tones of courtesy and reason.

'Oh?' James turned to her. 'You think . . .?'

'Well, it's only a cold, and you don't want him to start thinking he can just try that one whenever he feels like it, do you?'

'Margaret, perhaps—'

'No, James.' She scooped Stevie up in her arms and he immediately let out a cry. She turned to the nanny. 'If you don't mind, he's my son, not yours. You are simply paid to look after him. You don't own him, nor do you have the right to control our household.'

'Margaret!' James, outraged, followed her down the stairs. 'For heaven's sake, what sort of behaviour is this? She's worth her weight in gold – we don't want to lose her . . .'

'Worth her weight in manure, more like!' Margaret turned, boiling over with long repressed anger and frustration. 'Don't we want to lose her? Don't we? Who doesn't?' She lowered her voice. 'Mercy is convinced she's doing harm to Stevie.'

James Adair's eyes widened, then he roared with laughter. 'Mercy? What in heaven does Mercy know about anything? This is absolutely ridiculous foolishness. What on earth has come over you? You really are getting things out of proportion, darling.'

'I'll tell you what's come over me, what this behaviour is! It's that of someone who has been tyrannized in her own house for far too long, by you and that, that woman up there. She's made my life a misery. Mercy's quite right. I should be able to look after him how I think fit.'

'Mercy?' James said again in angry bewilderment.

'Yes, Mercy. Now be so good as to open the kitchen door for me please – Mrs Parslow?' Margaret called through the open door. 'Could you fetch Mercy through for me, please?'

Mercy appeared, her face still pink and full of mirth, until she saw them. Oh Lord, her expression said, sobering immediately. What've I done?

'Mercy.' Margaret sounded stern. 'Come through here with us, please.'

They went into the back sitting room.

'Light the lamp please, James.'

'I'll do it.' Mercy proceeded to do so, while Mr Adair was still recovering from being ordered around in this peremptory fashion. Margaret knelt down and laid her feverish son on a blanket on the floor and he let out a sound of anguish. Margaret looked up at her husband.

'Mercy has said to me more than once that she believes Radcliffe is not a fit person to look after our child, that she is neglectful, even wilfully cruel—'

'Oh really – look, enough of this,' James snorted. 'Did you really come out with all this tripe, Mercy? I really thought you had more sense. I mean on what grounds are you making all these accusations?'

Mercy blushed, heavily. She had very little proof. But she knew. She just knew. She couldn't speak.

But in any case Margaret held up her hand to stop her as if holding up a train.

'It suddenly came to me this afternoon, after Stevie had gone up, and he was so distraught . . . I took his little jacket off this morning when he was hot. And d'you know, that's about the most I've done for my child since the week he was born? I never dress him, undress him, bath him . . . I'm never allowed to, even if I want to. I barely even know his dear little body. And all those bumps and bruises . . . he's not crawling or walking. How could he hurt himself so?'

As she spoke she started to peel off Stevie's clothes, untying the silky ribbons which fastened at his neck and removing his nightgown.

'Margaret, really.' James stood harumphing beside Mercy. 'This is so silly. But have it your own way.'

'I shall, James,' Margaret looked up at him. 'Whether you like it or not, I'm afraid.'

As she moved Stevie, he whimpered, and when she sat him up to remove his little vest he began to scream frantically. The vest would not come away from his back. It was stuck to him with dried pus.

'Oh my!' Mercy whispered. She had a horrible feeling in the pit of her stomach. James Adair stood, silent now, beside her.

By the time Margaret finally managed to ease the vest off Stevie's skin, his screaming had become hysterical.

Mercy gasped. Her eyes filled with tears. 'No wonder he screamed every time I touched him.'

The three of them stared in appalled silence at his back. There were two huge round welts, the centre of each dark with blood and pus, the flesh around them swollen and angry with inflammation. It was obvious the wounds were sorely infected.

Margaret was shaking and crying, Stevie's head pressed against her. 'Oh Lord. Oh my little boy, what has she done to you?'

'Good God!' James Adair had gone white to the lips. He bent closer, peering at the wounds. 'She must've . . . with a candle! She must be quite . . . insane . . .'

He ran from the room.

Margaret's eyes met Mercy's, her face distraught. 'He's been suffering, all this time and I didn't see it. All those bumps and cuts – she made it look as if . . . Mercy, next time you give me advice, make sure I take notice of it a great deal more quickly.'

They heard James climbing the stairs to the servants' quarters.

Chapter Twenty-Five

The police took Audrey Radcliffe away. So far as they knew she was carted off to one of the city asylums.

Mercy had thought James Adair was going to explode with fury that night. He marched the nanny downstairs, barely even giving her time to pack her bag while he stood over her. Mercy never knew what was said upstairs in her spartan room, but when he came down with her he was shaking.

He made her stand in the hall, and James was still wringing his hands, pacing, unable to stand still.

'Why did you do it?' Margaret asked her, weeping. 'What could have possessed you to do such a thing?'

The woman stared at her. Her expression was impenetrable. In a queer, childish voice Mercy felt she would never forget, she said, 'Well no one ever looks after me, do they?'

'I'll make sure,' James said wagging a rigid finger at her, 'that you never go near another child again in your life.'

The doctor came and dressed Stevie's wounds, shaking his head. By the time they were left alone again, Margaret Adair had seemed to grow in stature and courage. Her instincts had been right all along! They all stood in the hall. James seemed stunned, stood wiping his forehead with his handkerchief.

'She broke all the rules. She just flagrantly . . .' He turned away with an anguished sound, unable to finish.

Margaret was still holding Stevie. No one was going to tell her to put him down now.

'James – now she's gone I'd like Mercy to be Stevie's nanny.'

'But . . .' He turned, catching sight of Mercy by the bannister, blushing with astonishment. 'She's so young, so—'

'Sensible? Trustworthy? A good judge of character? Better than either of us, perhaps?'

'Well . . .'

'Please, James, this makes complete sense. Why employ someone else when we have the perfect person here already? Mercy adores Stevie – don't you?' Mercy nodded, fervently, hardly daring to let herself hope. 'She risked her own position here to make us see what was going on with that evil woman . . .'

James looked at his wife, then at Mercy, standing there so quietly, and as if overcome by the presence of them both, sat down on the stairs.

'I owe you an apology, Mercy. I really believed that that woman was doing the best thing. That she had standards . . .' He looked up into Mercy's eyes. 'Very well. We'll try it.'

Over the next three months, Mercy was the happiest she could ever remember being. She was comfortable, well fed, she had the company of Rose and Emmie to giggle and joke, and the sisterly affection of Margaret Adair. Margaret had taken Mercy on as a project for improvement: correcting her speech, forever telling her things – the names of flowers, birds, capitals of the world (Mercy was proud to show she was good at those already).

Best of all there was Stevie, who grew more delightful each week. His back healed quickly until there were just two little scars. Mercy oiled his skin after she'd bathed him, tickling him and kissing his bare tummy so that he let out his wonderful, free-flowing chuckle which made her laugh too. She played with him, fed him, rocked him to sleep. She adored him and Stevie thrived. No more the pained grizzling, he was a robust, happy boy, pulling himself to stand up now on the nursery chair. The Adairs could hardly get over the change in him.

'Where's my lad?' James Adair often called when he came in from the works. Mercy would see an expression of boyish affection come over his face when he caught sight of Stevie. James would come and pick him up, swinging him into the air as if now free to play himself, until Stevie was breathless with giggles.

Life was much smoother and more contented than it had ever been. The only thing that troubled her was her increasing reluctance to go back to Angel Street. As the fortnightly free afternoon came round, she dreaded it. She'd returned faithfully all spring, found Elsie worn and low, Tom the same, always the same . . . If only there was something I could do for them, she thought. Going there was like walking into a living death which made her own happiness feel selfish and wrong. Gradually, full of guilt, she'd stopped going, and it became easier to stay away.

Margaret Adair, through a mixture of timidity and lack of organization, did not much seek out the society of other women of her class. Nor did she seem disturbed in any way by the fact that most women did not walk out with their nannies and treat them as friends. In her vague way she simply did what came instinctively to her: her need for a true confidante who she could be comfortable with outweighed considerations of class or age.

She and Mercy often went for walks together, each taking it in turn to push the pram.

As they wandered back through Moseley Village one beautiful afternoon in June, Margaret stopped and bought a newspaper. Mercy waited for her with the pram.

'Look—' Margaret opened it out to show her. *Daily Mail* – Golden Peace Number.

'Oh!' Mercy gasped. 'It's gold!'

The burnished ink caught the afternoon sunlight and seemed to glow. A picture of the King and Queen stared glassily at them.

'Look at her necklace!' Mercy smoothed her finger over the choker of pearls fastened high round Queen Mary's neck. 'Ain't they something?'

'Aren't,' Margaret murmured absent-mindedly.

'Aren't. Aren't, aren't, aren't!' Mercy did want to learn to speak better. She wanted to do everything better!

'We'll look at it properly at home,' Margaret said.

They settled in the sitting room with Stevie playing at their feet and a pot of tea. Mercy couldn't stop stroking the pages of the newspaper. 'It's lovely ain't – isn't – it?'

'It's to commemorate the signing of the peace treaty.' Margaret sipped Earl Grey from her delicate, ivy-patterned cup. There was a picture of the crowded Hall of Mirrors at Versailles, of the signed treaty.

Mercy squinted at them. 'They don't write any too clear, do they?'

Margaret laughed, replacing her cup on the polished tray. 'I think once you become really important you can write as poorly as you please. Listen – I'll read you this poem.'

Across the front page was a long poem, 'The Victorious Dead' by Alfred Noyes.

> Now, for their sake, our lands grow lovelier,
> There's not one grey cliff shouldering back the sea,
> Nor one forsaken hill that does not wear
> The visible radiance of their memory . . .

It was a long, sweeping poem, and as Mercy heard Margaret's soft voice reading it, the emotions she was trying so hard to keep down swelled up in her. She took a deep breath, trying to calm herself. But the beauty of the words, the hopes and ideals of the poem for a happier time, a more virtuous nation, crashed again and again in her mind against the thought of Tom, eternally broken, lying in that sunless little room. Of Elsie's old offering to Frank, her shrivelled, sooty flowers, of the fact that she couldn't bear to go there any more. The words hit her like knives releasing her grief for Elsie and Tom, the deep ache in her for all that might have been.

> They have made their land one living shrine. Their words
> Are breathed in dew and whiteness from the bough
> And where the may-tree shakes with song of birds,
> Their young unwhispered joys are singing now . . .

Her heartbroken weeping stopped Margaret before she'd even reached the end.

'Oh, my dear girl – what is it?'

For a time Mercy was unable to speak. She felt Margaret's arm round her, pulling her close.

'What's troubling you, Mercy? This is so unlike you.'

After a few moments Mercy wiped her eyes and looked into her friend's round, kind face. She drew away a little, watched her fingers fiddling in her lap and told Margaret about Tom.

'If he'd died I could've grieved for him, for losing him, then put it away. Started afresh. I know my Tom died in Flanders, the Tom I loved.' Her tears started coming again. 'But his body's still there, day after day. Like a child – no, not even a child. Stevie's got far more life in him. I can't forget him. And I can't stand to see it.'

'Oh my poor, poor girl.' Margaret's eyes were also full of tears. 'Why ever didn't you tell me this before?'

Mercy just shook her head, still weeping.

'Sometimes I feel you've lived a great many more years than I!'

'There's people like the Peppers—' Mercy struggled to speak, gulping. 'Who're so stuck in their lives and nothing ever changes – or if it does it's for the worse. I'm so scared of going back to that. Of getting stuck too . . .'

Margaret squeezed her shoulder. 'There's no reason why that should happen. We'll help you Mercy. And think how strong you are – I don't think you'd ever allow yourself to be trapped by circumstances. Take heart, dear. You're like my little sister now. I'll take care of you.'

As they talked, the sun was going down, the sky glowing pink, and soon they heard James's voice at the front door.

'Hell-o? Margaret?'

Margaret looked at Mercy in amusement. 'Goodness he sounds excited – yes, we're here, dear!'

'Come out here, both of you – I've something to show you!'

They hurried to the front door, Mercy with Stevie in her arms. James Adair was standing in the front garden holding by the handlebar a brand new bicycle. His face was ashine almost as much as the cycle's black paintwork.

'Look – the finished model. The Adair Safety Bicycle for Gentleman, ready for action. This is the first one!'

He moved it closer so they could admire it, childlike with glee. He'd ridden it home and it had gone like a stallion. It was smooth, fast, marvellous!

'Darling, it looks very good!' Margaret smiled at his enthusiasm. She went out and walked round it.

'What d'you think, Mercy?'

Mercy blushed. She was still shy of Mr Adair, kind as he was to her. 'It's beautiful.'

'Goes like anything. I've never been on such a good ride. Here,' he cajoled his wife. 'Give her a try?'

'But it's a man's cycle – I'll never get on!'

'No matter.' He took off his jacket and draped it on the garden wall. 'I'll lift you.'

'Lift me?' Margaret laughed wholeheartedly. 'You'll do yourself a mischief! No, dear – I'm not up to that, I'm afraid. What about Mercy?'

'Splendid – come on, Mercy. Give it a try!'

'But—'

'Oh, go on, put him out of his misery. Here, give Stevie to me and I'll take him in. It's getting cool out here.'

Mercy wished Margaret would stay, but she'd already disappeared into the house. Her stomach started fluttering with nerves. She'd never ridden a large bicycle before, and she was shy, alone with Mr Adair.

'I don't know how,' she said timidly, moving closer to him.

'I'll soon show you – easy as winking. Just keep your

feet on the pedals and push. This is rather high for you, of course. I shan't let go. Look, I'll lean it against the wall to start with.'

Mercy felt James Adair's large hands grasp her round the waist from behind, and lift her high on to the saddle.

'Light as a feather!'

Mercy felt very high up and not especially safe. To her mortification the bar of the cycle was forcing up her skirt, making it ride high in her legs and showing her white bloomers. Thank goodness she had quite new ones on!

'Now, hold still. You put your hands on these.' He directed her to the grips on the handlebars, but it was a long way for her to lean. She felt his arm encircle her waist, his warmth through her thin frock.

As he moved the cycle forwards, Mercy's heart was beating faster and faster. She was wobbling, she was going to fall! The bicycle lurched to one side and his arm tightened round her.

'Steady!' he laughed. 'That's it – now we can have a proper go.'

'Out here?' Mercy protested. She'd expected a quick turn in the garden and he was heading out along the pavement!

'There's hardly anyone about. Don't worry, we shan't knock anyone over.'

Mercy didn't feel she could say she was more worried about whether anyone could see her bloomers! She thanked heaven it was nearly dusk.

The saddle felt hard and uncomfortable between her legs, and the pedals, at their lowest point, were too far down for her to reach. She found she kept losing them on the way round. She was suspended, rather painfully, eyes fixed on James Adair's white sleeve, the hairs on the backs of his strong hand as he guided the handlebars for her.

Yet the feel of the air rushing past her face, blowing her hair back, was invigorating. Once James Adair broke into a trot, leading her along the quiet road away from Moseley Village, the sadness of the afternoon was blown away and she let out her full-hearted, gurgling laugh.

'Nothing like it, is there?' As he spoke, Mercy felt how close he was, his breath on her ear, the foreign, manly smell of him, his arm close round her. She had hardly ever been so close to any man apart from Tom, and was uneasy and embarrassed, but she could do nothing but cling on as he held and steered her.

'Phew!' He slowed down after a time, panting. 'I'm not up to all this – have to turn round – walk a bit.'

'I've – had . . .' Mercy wanted to say, 'quite enough' but she continued, '. . . a good go on it – thanks.'

She turned her head a little to speak to him and he looked round at her, into her eyes. He was so close, smiling at her and she could see perspiration on his forehead. She turned to face the front again with a sudden sense of unease. She liked James Adair and enjoyed being treated almost like his little sister as well as Margaret's. But this closeness, him holding her like that, didn't feel quite right.

'There now.' As they turned in through the gate the cycle gave another big wobble and Mercy shrieked, grasping James's arm with one hand.

'It's all right.' His voice was soothing, almost caressing. 'I've got you, Mercy.'

Carefully he propped the bicycle back against the wall and lifted her once more into his arms with a lingering lack of haste. He held her high for a moment, almost as he did with Stevie, and Mercy laughed, exhilarated.

James looked up into her face, smiling broadly, eyes crinkling at the corners, then lowered her to the ground.

'Little scrap of a thing, aren't you? So – what d'you think?'

He laid his hands on her shoulders and she could feel their damp heat. She couldn't look him in the eyes.

'It's lovely. Thank you.'

'She is, isn't she? A little beauty. I'm glad someone was game to give her a try.'

He released her with sudden abruptness and turned to the machine.

'I'd better go in,' she said, relieved. 'Thank you again.'

Chapter Twenty-Six

How had this come about? James Adair mused to himself as he walked behind Margaret and Mercy, who was pushing Stevie in his pram, down the hill to the park.

'Mercy's never been boating,' Margaret had implored him. 'And it's such a beautiful day.'

It was indeed, a burnished August day. Holiday season: an atmosphere of Sunday afternoon languor pervaded. They had attended church at St Mary's in Moseley, eaten a good lunch of tender lamb and mint sauce, and now James felt a great sensation of wellbeing surge through him.

After all, what could be the harm? He was going out in public with his wife and his son's nanny. He would not be alone with Mercy: he could enjoy the afternoon in a pure attitude of companionship with a clear conscience. He knew, as he had known for some time, had had confirmed that evening when he held her in his arms during her cycle ride, that he must not be alone with her. She was a temptation, a thorn in his conscience, a tune which played insistently through his head. The memory of touching her made him ache with desire. This went against all the rules of the code by which he lived. He wanted to believe that he was upright, scrupulous, faithful. Since then he had gone out of his way to minimize his contact with her.

He watched the figures of the two women – my

women, he found himself thinking – swaying gently in front of him. Margaret was in a fussy dress of sky-blue and white candy stripes, looked plump and overdressed. She had on a wide-brimmed, white hat with a cascade of blue flowers tumbling from it. James found himself wincing at the acid colour of them. She was still a country girl by instinct. In contrast, Mercy was all slim simplicity in her white dress with the sailor-suit collar, white button shoes and a simple straw hat. Her hair was gathered up loosely in a plait which swung between her shoulder blades.

By heaven she was lovely! He found his eyes hungrily following her every movement, the twitch of her plait as she turned her head to talk to Margaret, the lean curve of her as she leant over Stevie, the light, eager walk. He imagined peeling off the dress, slowly, over her head, unveiling her, the wondrous, magical shape of her . . .

For heaven's sake, he railed at himself, pull yourself together, man! What sort of thoughts were these for a married man to be indulging in?

But fantasies of her had gradually begun to bombard him: at home, at the works, even when she was nowhere near, until he was thinking of her a great many times a day.

He stopped for a moment to remove his blazer and fell a few paces behind, freeing his arms, flinging it boyishly over his shoulder by the collar.

These feelings had crept up on him so gradually he had barely known it was happening. Mercy's wide, serious eyes turning on him when he spoke, her interest in him, her untutored intelligence. The way, Margaret had told him, she'd confronted that Radcliffe woman. Margaret would never have had the guts to do that! And further still, he had learnt from his wife of the girl's tragic past, of her maimed lover. The thought of her sadness and devotion moved him unutterably.

Margaret and Mercy stopped at the gates of the park and turned, both still laughing at something.

'Come on, James!' Margaret called. 'You're dawdling!'

'Coming!' He beamed at them both: at Margaret's new serenity, at his son's happy, tanned face, at Mercy, fresh and sweet as a spring flower. What a blessed life he had!

As they neared the lake they could hear excited voices, shrieks of laughter, the plash of oars and their creak in the rowlocks and occasional indignant quacking of a duck hurriedly taking flight. The small expanse of water was crowded with rowing boats and paddle boats, their passengers clad in bright summer clothes.

James paid for the hire of a rowing boat. 'We'll have to wait our turn. They're all taken at the moment.'

They stood contentedly in the shade. Margaret poured lemonade for them to sip. They helped Stevie to throw some crusts to the ducks and watched the other pleasure-seekers until a boat was ready for them.

'I think I'll feel safest if I hold Stevie,' Margaret said, lifting him from the pram. She handed him to Mercy. 'I'll get in and you can pass him to me – and then you can relax for a bit.'

James helped his wife climb in in a rather ungainly fashion, waiting until she'd sat down in the stern and readjusted her hat.

Mercy carefully handed Stevie to her and Margaret settled him on her lap.

'Take my hand,' James said.

Mercy gave her uncertain smile. 'I've never been in one of these before.'

'It's quite safe – Here—' Gallantly he took her little hand, melting inwardly at her inexperience. 'There's a first time for everything.'

She settled on her seat in the bow while James moved to the rowing seat, sitting with his back to her.

'Off we go!' The oars were ready and they pulled away, in and out of the shade of trees, James leaning forward and back, forward and back with an easy, rhythmic stroke.

'All right?' He turned his head, conscious that his back was sweating from his exertions.

'Yes, thank you,' Mercy said dreamily. The sunshine seemed to make her glow.

James tried to concentrate on watching Stevie who, wide-eyed, was letting out shrieks of excitement and struggling to get down from Margaret's lap and throw himself over the side.

'Dear, oh dear!' Margaret laughed. 'I'd never have believed a small child could be so strong – my arms are aching!'

After a time James stopped and turned round. Mercy was sitting sideways, the brim of her hat pulled low to shield her eyes from the bright, sunlit ripples.

'Have a try?' James invited softly.

'What? Rowing the boat!'

'Of course, why not? Come on.' He spoke more briskly than he meant to and cursed himself inwardly for sounding like a sergeant major.

She came to him, hand over hand, instinctively adjusting her weight with the tilt of the boat until she reached him.

'You sit here.' He patted the space beside him. 'We'll try one each to begin with.'

He gave her the right hand oar and showed her how to

manoeuvre it, up, back, down, then spooning the water away. His right leg and her left touched, side by side. Mercy frowned with concentration, and James kept watching her, smiling. He longed to lean round and kiss the furrowed brow, to smooth it with his fingers. He found his mind shaping extravagant words of adoration to her.

All he said was, 'That's good. You must come from a seafaring family.'

'Well . . .' Mercy smiled without irony. 'I s'pose I could've done.'

'Oh – yes, of course.' He was uncomfortable at having highlighted her uncertain origins. 'Anyway – how about trying both now?'

He stepped behind the seat and gently urged her to move to the middle, kneeling behind her.

'Now – take both and do the same.'

She dipped the oars in and pulled with her wiry arms. The boat made a promising surge of progress.

'Good!' he cried. Then she forgot to lift the oars and pulled so the blades stumbled in the water, ruffling it up, slowing them right down. The left oar flung out of her hand and James lurched over to catch it for her.

'Never mind. Here, let me help, just 'til you've got it.'

Reaching round her he laid his hands over hers and as he did so, breathed in her smell, a mixture of soap and warm flesh and hair, a warm animal smell which caught him by surprise.

'That's better.'

She half-turned her head, animated. 'I think I can do it now.' He released her, desire raw in him.

'Perhaps she'll row all afternoon!' he joked, turning to Margaret, afraid that his feelings were plain in his face. But she was taken up with Stevie's antics.

'Here – please, darling.' She handed him over. 'He's exhausting!'

James busied himself with his son, gladly sitting him in his lap in order to conceal the gross outward sign of his desire, distracting both Stevie and himself, talking to him, showing him the ducks, letting him wet his hands.

All the time though, he was conscious of Mercy's every move, her legs stretched out in front of her so that sometimes his ankle brushed against her as he moved, her lithe frame bending back and forth, her dazzling smile of happiness as he caught her eye.

Oh God, James thought. God help me. He would have to put a stop to it. He couldn't live like this, with this constant longing gnawing at him. He didn't know how long he could control himself in her presence. He couldn't get rid of her – however could that be explained to Margaret? He must struggle for self-control – bury himself in his work. What sort of man was he otherwise?

'Do take over again,' Margaret urged him eventually, as he sat staring ahead. 'Mercy must be quite exhausted by now!'

That night James Adair made love to his wife with an energy and urgency that startled both of them. He was more passionately aroused than she could ever remember, and at the height of it he cried out loudly as if the release of it was painful to him. Afterwards, still startled, she held him, caressing him as he lay in her arms, his eyes tightly closed.

'I had a wire from Kesler today,' James announced a few weeks later, as the three of them sat round at dinner one evening. Margaret insisted that Mercy ate with them still at least once a week and couldn't understand why her husband was being so awkward about it recently, trying to insist that as Mercy was an employee she should be treated as such and kept in her place.

It was a mellow evening in early autumn, the light dying over the now tarnished leaves in the front garden.

'D'you mean the American?' Mercy asked, passing Mr Adair a well-filled gravy boat.

Margaret looked at Mercy in some gratitude that at least she had remembered who her husband was talking about as her own mind had a tendency to flit on to something else as soon as he began to talk about work. James also smiled appreciatively at her.

'That's the one.' He nodded to Emmie to indicate they had everything they needed. She left the room with her usual smirk at Mercy. She and Rose were always cross-questioning Mercy – 'What did they say? What do they talk about?' – but were habitually disappointed by the information.

'Didn't they talk about anything else?' was usually Rose's complaint when Mercy reported conversations about the health of the cycle market or Stevie's daily doings. 'Don't they ever 'ave a good fight?'

But the Adairs didn't. Most of what passed between them was a low current, under the surface. To Mercy they seemed calm, which she took to mean contented. Tonight, by their standards, James was animated.

He accepted the gravy, then picked up the delicate glass beside Margaret's plate to pour water into it, then Mercy's. Mercy was still nervous of drinking from the long-stemmed glassware, but James disdained drinking out of anything of lesser quality, even though he was abstemious and seldom drank alcohol.

'Kesler's planning a new works outside New York – in Rochester. They should be moving out early next year, and he suggests—' – James sat back, holding his glass with an air of triumph – 'that when things have progressed a bit further, I visit him in New York!'

Margaret, who had been eating with a hungry sense of purpose, looked up startled.

'You – go to America!'

James laughed youthfully. His moustache shifted when he smiled, making the smile appear broader. 'And why not? It's not the moon, you know. It's only a few days' voyage, and I gather Cunard will be taking passenger bookings again before too long. I think it's a splendid idea. Kesler and I will have a hugely productive relationship, I'm certain of it. He has all that New World drive and enthusiasm, and with all our technical know-how put together . . . Ideally I'd go sooner, of course, but if we're to travel on the best ship in the world, we shall have to wait until she's ready for us.'

Margaret was frowning at him.

'The *Mauretania*, of course – she's undergoing a complete overhaul. They had to convert her for War service—'

'Yes, yes,' Margaret said. 'But you said "we"?'

'Of course you must come with me! You're forever saying you never go anywhere or do anything.'

'But James – Stevie.'

'Oh, Stevie will be perfectly all right with Mercy here. My mother can come and stay for a few weeks. She'd love it – we'll be gone a month at most. What harm could come to him?'

'James,' Margaret spoke with unusual resolve, 'I am not going to travel to the other side of the world and leave my son. Least of all with your mother. He barely knows her and she's as cold as a dead herring. I'm just not. I'm sorry. You'll have to go alone. After all, it is business.' She popped a piece of potato in her mouth as if to emphasize that she wasn't going to say anything else.

Mercy listened expectantly. Was she now going to have something approaching a row to report to Rose? After all, she did just call his mother a dead herring . . .

'But, darling—' – James was stroking his moustache with his left hand as he tended to do when irritated – 'Kesler has a very nice wife – and children. And he's requested that you come.' (The final phrase of Kesler's telegram had read 'Bring wife.')

Margaret looked defiantly at him, swallowing the potato. 'How on earth do you know she's nice? Whatever this American has requested, I am not leaving my son. He's had quite enough to contend with in his short life already. And that's that.'

'Oh to hell with it. Let Stevie come as well then.'

'And Mercy.'

'Mercy?' A momentary look of alarm swept over James Adair's face. But of course, the child could hardly travel without his nanny. She could travel second class, somewhere well away from him . . .

'Very well,' he said with dignity. 'Mercy too.'

'D'you hear Mercy?' Margaret was overjoyed. The thought of being alone with James and a collection of strangers for weeks at a time had filled her with panic. She was maladroit socially, and what on earth would she and James have to say to each other all that time? She thought it a sad but inevitable truth that husbands and wives had very little conversation beyond the common interest of their children. At least in normal circumstances there were other people. But now, if Mercy was coming, and Stevie, she would have familiar companions.

'We're going across the sea to America, the first chance we get!' James said.

Mercy was so astonished she couldn't take it in. 'I've never even seen the sea!'

'Well, you'll be seeing plenty of it soon!' James laughed. Suddenly he seemed full of joy.

Part Five

Chapter Twenty-Seven

March 1920

'Mercy – Mercy dear. You'd better wake up!'

Margaret Adair was leaning across from the opposite seat of the train. Feeling the warmth of the hand on her knee through her dress, Mercy slowly opened her eyes. Stevie was asleep on top of her, crunched up like a crab, his damp head resting under her chin, making her hot and sweaty inside her clothes. She had a dry mouth and a bar of dull pain stretched between her temples. The seat was rocking gently, the train chugging, der dum der dum . . . Wherever was she?

'We're coming into Southampton.' James Adair was sitting up very straight, peering with boyish enthusiasm out through the sooty window. 'Soon get a look at her!'

The ship – of course! She was on a train going to the sea and they were travelling to America! Mercy was wide awake suddenly, gently sitting up and trying not to wake Stevie.

'Bless him.' Margaret Adair looked fondly at her son. She had seen James smiling at the two of them as they slept and was moved by the tender expression in her husband's eyes. What she had achieved in giving him a son!

Stevie, eighteen months old, was very active once

awake, but now, oblivious of her adoration, let out a shuddering little sigh in his sleep.

'I don't suppose he'll remember any of this,' Margaret said. She stopped speaking rather abruptly and Mercy saw her close her eyes and rest her head back as if in discomfort.

Mercy looked out as the train snaked between warehouses and factories. She saw rows of dwellings, church spires, occasional faces topped by workmen's caps turned up to watch the boat train hurtle past. She was surprised to see these familiar things, as if, having left Birmingham for the first time, she was expecting a completely different world.

'We must be about the last train.' James's watch hung on a gold chain from his weskit. 'She sails at noon.' He was trying to sound like an old sea dog.

When the train came to a halt with a groaning of brakes, Mercy eased herself and Stevie out of the comfortable first-class seat. She wrapped a blanket round him carefully as he stirred and carried him out into the chill spring air.

The platform was full of excited crowds. From first class spilled gentlemen in expensive suits, trilbys, bowlers, even the odd top hat, and their womenfolk, stylish gowns covered by fur-trimmed coats and stoles and a dazzling variety of hats, feathered and flowered, some outrageous with wide brims and decorations of fruit, others pared down, elegant skullcaps trimmed with a single gorgeous feather. Mercy felt small and poor and bewildered amid the loud ring of upper-class voices, some with foreign accents, all so ripe and confident. They found a porter, and negotiated their way through the heaving mass of people shuffling along, slowly, to the dock.

'Smell that!' James cried, leaning close to her ear.

She breathed in, and through the thinning smoke from the trains, smelt for the first time the salt of the sea. As they moved out, the bracing air hit her face. She felt an odd sensation go through her suddenly, tingling, excitement and wonder making her breathless. Such beginnings she had come from, she who was nobody to anyone in the world – and now this!

James Adair looked as if he might burst with pride when they saw the *Mauretania*. Over and over again during the past weeks he'd told them, as if for the first time, 'D'you know, she's held the Blue Riband since 1907 – fastest passenger ship across the Atlantic – never beaten in all that time!'

'He seems to think it's one of his bicycles!' Margaret murmured to Mercy with a wry smile.

But Mercy barely heard her. Her head was back, her eyes, at least as awed as James Adair's, taking in the massive bulk of the ship. The huge black hull stretched way above them like an endless wall, topped with white which was interspersed by the hundreds of windows of the ship's prime living quarters. Crowning it all were the four enormous red funnels. Everyone was looking up, exclaiming.

'Look, Stevie,' she said, leaning him back in her arms and pointing. 'Look at the big boat – and up there, red chimneys. Chimneys, Stevie!'

The little boy's eyes were wide and solemn.

The place was swarming. Mercy felt herself jostled at times and held tight to Stevie. James stood protectively close to her. Once she found herself looking into his eyes. He smiled at her. She heard people exclaiming, laughing, some weeping, many hugging each other farewell for a short time or a long, perhaps even for ever. Mercy started to notice many other sorts of people, the poor as well as the rich, some dressed in odd, foreign-looking clothes and shawls. Smoke from cigarettes and cigars was quickly blown away by the brisk breeze.

'Come along.' James guided her arm, speaking over all the commotion. 'We'll take you to second class and we'll come and find you after. Stay close to me . . .'

They made their way gradually to the second-class embarkation point, amid a more soberly-dressed, respectable gaggle of people, many businessmen in Homburgs, some with anxious-looking wives beside them. High above them, the rails were lined by passengers who had boarded earlier and now had the leisure to watch the proceedings below, calling down and whistling to friends or relatives on shore.

There was a smell of tar. Mercy felt her face buffeted by moist air and thought for a moment it was raining, but it was a damp, brackish gust from over the water and it subsided. As they drew near the gangway and the clatter of feet grew louder, she felt her stomach tighten. The dark, deep gap between the ship and the dockside, with its gurgling strip of water, appalled her. She wanted it to be over now, to be on board.

'Go to the steward at the top,' James instructed. 'He'll give you directions to your quarters. We'll find you . . .' He smiled reassuringly as she stepped up, tightly clutching Stevie, then he turned back to join his wife.

Halfway up the gangway, as she slowly followed an elderly couple, the man leaning on a stick, a gust of wind lifted the front of her hat and carried it over the back of her head where it hung, flapping from its pin. She was flustered and afraid of it flying right off, but didn't dare loose Stevie to fix it. She'd see to it when she reached the top.

But suddenly the hat settled back on her head, the pressure of a hand on top of it. She turned, startled.

'Allow me.'

She found herself looking into a young man's face, long and pale, with deep grey eyes, a wide mouth and striking, dark eyebrows which were pulled into a slight frown of concentration as he straightened the hat. Briefly Mercy also took in details of a baggy tweed suit on a tall, but thin body.

'Thank you.' She was taken aback. 'Trouble is,' she said timidly, 'I've got my hands full.'

'So I see. That's quite all right.' He smiled, the rather mournful face brightening for a second. 'I often forget how windy it is on the coast as well.'

'Two pins from now on,' she agreed.

'Go on – get a move on!' someone called grumpily from behind, and it was only then Mercy realized they'd stopped and turned to scurry on upwards.

A smartly-dressed ship's officer stood at the top to welcome them all aboard. James had booked her a fine room – a second-class state room on C-deck just for Stevie and herself so she would not have to share with a stranger. It was close to the Nursery and Children's Dining Room.

'Oh look, Stevie! All for us!' she gasped with delight when she saw it.

It was like a little house all in itself: two beds, one on each side of the room, a table and two chairs, a little cupboard, a basin and her own WC . . . Her luggage, which they'd sent in advance, was already waiting for her in the middle of the floor. She put Stevie down and the two of them scurried round, looking at everything. Soon after there was a knock at the door.

'Ah – this looks very good,' James said. Margaret

followed him into the room. She steadied herself against the wall for a second, then sank down abruptly on one of the beds, her face nearly as white as the paintwork.

'Whatever's the matter, dear?' James peered at her, concerned by the pallor of her face. He sat down beside her and took her hand. Mercy went and knelt on the floor beside her.

'You feeling poorly? Must be all the travelling. Takes it out of you, doesn't it?'

Margaret leant dizzily against her husband, who removed her hat and helped her loosen the neck of her blouse.

'It's been getting worse all morning – I feel so faint and hot . . .'

'Put your head down.' James and Mercy helped her lower her head between her knees, Mercy fending off Stevie who was all for tugging at her hair. Eventually she sat up, her complexion a little pinker.

'Oh dear,' she smiled weakly. 'Perhaps I'd better go back to our room and have a little lie-down. I keep feeling so strange.'

James helped her to her feet. 'I'll take her to rest,' he told Mercy, 'and then come back here. We'll be off fairly soon. It'd be a great pity not to be up to see it.'

James Adair pulled back the silky eiderdown in their sumptuous first-class stateroom and helped his wife ease herself on to the bed. She looked very pale and shaky still. The brass bedstead creaked gently as she settled herself down and closed her eyes.

'Shall you be ill, Margaret, d'you think?'

James stood over her, eyes on her plump face, concerned but not without a little exasperation. He didn't want anything to mar this precious journey – Cunard's very first passenger voyage with the *Mauretania* since the War!

Margaret opened her eyes, a half smile on her lips. 'Darling, it's early days – I'm not sure, but I think we might soon be giving Stevie a little companion.'

'Oh, my dear!' A glow came into James's eyes and he knelt down beside her. 'You think – it's possible – again?' They had taken so terribly long to conceive Stevie.

'It seems very like it to me – I feel even more ill than last time.'

He leant over, overjoyed, newly powerful, and kissed her cheek.

'Then we must take the very, very best care of you. Should you like something to eat or drink?'

'Just a little water . . .' Margaret seemed mown down by exhaustion. 'Food . . . perhaps later . . .'

'You'll miss the departure,' he said, standing up. But she was already lost to sleep.

He would go and fetch Mercy and Stevie. Who better to share this experience with than his son – and Mercy with her naive enthusiasm for life? She mustn't miss it. He went to the little bathroom and looked in the mirror, ran damp hands over his hair and straightened his tie. He could feel that illicit, eager excitement rising in him at the thought of being with her, standing close to her, giving her a new experience in life. How he had worked to avoid the lure of her presence through the winter months! There had of course been moments of temptation, of huge intensity of feeling. But he had plunged into his work. He had been strong and controlled, even averting his eyes at times when coming upon her so as not to disturb his thoughts.

But now he would be alone with her. His pulse quickened. He could feel himself beginning to slide, surrender to the force of it. Of course though, he wouldn't be alone with her, he reassured himself. There would be crowds up there . . . His behaviour was perfectly within bounds.

Mercy took Stevie up to the first-class promenade deck, where James said they should join him as they'd have a good view. Stevie was bright and frisky after his long sleep on the train and toddled along, wanting to run off here, there and everywhere.

'Here – let me take him!' James picked him up and strode off, his unbuttoned camel coat sweeping behind him.

Mercy was glad of a few moments' respite from Stevie. There were already a lot of people waiting out on the deck, and Mercy felt overwhelmed by the opulence of the furs and jewels she could see displayed around her. Once again she was humbly aware of the simplicity of her blue wool coat and little cloche hat – she'd taken off the one with the brim. Her clothes were respectable enough and new, the hat even rather fashionable, but she still felt drab.

'Am I allowed up 'ere?' she asked.

James turned, looked tenderly at her. 'Of course. You're with me.' As if reading her thoughts he lowered his voice and said, 'Don't you worry – you look lovely. Not like some of these overdressed peacocks.'

Mercy blushed at this personal remark. She had been confused by his behaviour towards her of late. In front of the other servants he addressed her as one of them, which was of course what she was. When she was alone with the Adairs he had previously been more relaxed, brotherly almost and teasing. But recently he had been home so little, forever working, only appearing for dinner, and then he had often seemed remote, if not actually cold. When Margaret insisted she join them for dinner, which she soon realized made things easier for Margaret – it made the two of them make an effort together – he confined his conversation with her to questions about Stevie. Mercy had almost forgotten his former friendliness, the cycle ride. But it had relieved rather than troubled her. He was her employer after all and she knew where she stood.

But now the light-hearted, friendly Mr Adair of last summer was resurfacing, now he was not so preoccupied with work. He seemed younger, a spring in his step.

'Come – let's find a space where we can see.'

Still carrying Stevie, he led Mercy to the rail. They were so high up! As they nudged into a space there came the brisk sound of a bugle, though it was hard to tell from which direction.

'Ah look.' James freed an arm and pointed. She saw an orderly flurry of activity as a group of men hurried down the last remaining gangway. 'Those'll be the chaps who work on shore.'

Mercy knew he loved all this, relished telling her about it. He leant over, supporting his little son between his chest and the rail, and pushed his brown trilby on harder. 'Don't want to lose it,' he smiled at her.

The last gangway was being pulled into the ship.

'Bang on.' Once more James pulled out the well-polished gold watch. The two hands were exactly on the twelve. A few moments later they heard the bugle again. The tugs had already cast off. There came a great, soulful burst of sound from one of the funnels and James laughed as Stevie's head shot round, his eyes peering upwards, astonished.

'That gave you a shock, didn't it?'

The ship eased itself away from the dock, girded by its

tugs. There was much waving and calling out to the crowd below.

Mercy looked down at the dark water. It was astonishing to think that all the way to America, for days and days, would be water. She thought of little Amy Laski, so small she would barely have been able to see over the rail as their ship bound for Canada slid out of Liverpool harbour. Where was her sweet friend Amy now?

The people, then buildings, wharfs, cranes, docks, began to fade, blur and lose colour until even squinting Mercy couldn't make out their shape. As the view faded a quiet fell over the passengers. With majestic lack of haste the *Mauretania* nosed along Southampton Water and they began to feel the wind quicken on their cheeks. She was bound for the short call in at Cherbourg before turning west across the Atlantic.

There came a sudden release of tension, of anticlimax, as if separation from the land was a trauma now passed through and they were free to get on with everything else.

James straightened up, taking in deep breaths of air. Stevie kicked his legs against his father's stomach. 'Marvellous, the sea – gives you an appetite. Time for lunch, I'd say. How would you like to join me?' he asked her recklessly.

'I don't think – not with him,' she said, uncertain, holding out her arms for Stevie.

James's face fell. 'Ah no, perhaps not. Silly of me. Look, I'll accompany you down.'

'How's Mrs Adair? Will she want anything to eat?'

'She said all she wanted was sleep, thank you,' James said. They went down the first-class staircase to B-deck where he drew her aside. 'Look – you'll have to know soon enough. The fact is—' – He seemed hugely embarrassed suddenly, covered in blushes – 'Margaret is, in fact . . .' What on earth? Mercy was thinking. Surely he wasn't going to tell her that Mrs Adair had her monthly at the moment? She wouldn't know where to put herself.

Mr Adair seemed to be struggling for words. 'She – well, soon, quite soon, you, er – you'll have more than one little one on your hands.' He was red to the ears.

'Oh! She's having another babby?'

'Ssh!' He looked round as if he were imparting state secrets.

'Sorry,' Mercy whispered, beaming at him. 'That's wonderful news, Mr Adair! I'm ever so happy for you both. And it'll be lovely for Stevie to have a brother or sister.' She shifted Stevie on to her left hip, balancing him with one arm. 'Won't it, pet?'

James smiled bashfully, thrusting his hands into his pockets. 'There's something about this kind of news. Makes you want to tell someone. I know some women are superstitious about it – in case, you know, but I can't think of anyone better to tell than you, Mercy.'

'No – well I'll be the babby's nanny, I mean—' – it was her turn to blush – 'that's if you think . . .?'

He looked deep into her eyes. 'Of course I think.'

On impulse he took up her spare hand and pressed it to his lips. She felt them, warm on the back of her hand, and the slight prickle of his moustache. She was touched, but very embarrassed. What was he doing! She had no idea what to say.

He was also overcome by confusion again, dropped her hand and became abrupt all of a sudden. 'Come this way,' he said, striding off along the corridor. 'I'll show you where Stevie can be fed.'

*

He knew when he left Mercy that he should go and see how Margaret was, but he was too agitated, full of a restless desire to walk, to be out on the promenade deck in the fresh air. He returned to A-deck, nodding to a few other passengers on the way, but walking briskly to avoid any attempts at conversation. A coastline was still visible, the green and chalk white of the Isle of Wight, like a hazy mirage in the distance.

'Help me, oh Lord, to do what's right.' He leant looking out, his lips moving in a childlike chant. 'Help, oh Lord . . .'

What in heaven had he kissed her hand for like that? She must have thought him so peculiar, unbalanced even. Yet he wanted so much more of her! And hadn't he seen an answering warmth in her eyes – surely that was what it was?

At home his feelings had seemed monstrous. It was unthinkable that he should harbour such intentions, such a force of desire for anyone but his wife, and towards a servant at that . . . Away from home, even now so freshly cut loose from the coast, he felt altered, freer. As if, even with his wife and son on board he was – could be – a different man. Images he had for so long tried to keep at bay flooded through him. Mercy's parted lips moving to meet his, her eyes languid with need of him, his hands removing her clothes, peeling open to reveal what he had until now only imagined, her shy, eager, wanting . . . His fancy drove him on to caress her white thighs, the wet, silky opening between them parting for him . . .

He put his hands over his face, afraid that anyone passing should read in his expression the content of his thoughts.

I will ask her, he resolved, to dine with me tonight.

The boy would be asleep by then and could be left. With us – quickly he corrected himself – with us. For surely Margaret would be recovered by then? This fact came to him like a chill shower of rain.

Chapter Twenty-Eight

'Hello again.'

Mercy turned, closing the door of her room very quietly. She had finally lulled Stevie to sleep. The ship had left Cherbourg and was picking up speed, and she had to brace her legs so as not to lurch across the corridor.

For a moment she didn't recognize him. A tall man stood in front of her in working-man's overalls smeared with grease, and his hands and face were blacked with it too. But the smile was familiar, and the voice.

'I – er – your hat, on the gangway. Remember?'

'Oh yes!' Mercy laughed. 'I didn't know you for a minute. Whatever's happened to you?'

He joined in her laughter, ruefully. She saw him keep looking over his shoulder to see if anyone was coming. Most people were already at dinner.

'I shouldn't be seen up here in this state, of course. We're supposed to clean up down there but I forgot to take a set of clothes to change into. I haven't got into the swing of it all yet.' He held his hand out. 'Paul Louth – oh!' He withdrew the hand. 'You can't really shake that, can you?'

'I'm Mercy Hanley.' The ship rolled and she found herself lurching towards him. Paul instinctively put a hand out to steady her, catching her by the wrist and leaving a black oil smudge on her sleeve.

'Oh my goodness, I am sorry!' He looked perturbed. 'How ridiculous of me.'

'No – you're awright.' Mercy smiled. 'It ain't – isn't – the end of the world, is it? The pattern hides it and it'll wash out.' She held her hands behind her back as if to give him permission to stop worrying about it. 'How did you get in that state then?'

'I'm a student, in London – Imperial College. Well, I've nearly finished there actually. Engineering. I was lucky enough to get the position – experience the working of a real ship. So I'm spending a lot of the time seeing her in action, learning on the job.' As he spoke his eyes flickered towards her and away repeatedly, his expression serious, earnest. He rubbed nervously at the oil on his hands.

'There's another student – from Cambridge.' Paul's expression suddenly became wry and he lowered his voice. 'He's travelling first class. Not really my scene. The silly thing is, I actually come from Cambridge and his people live in London. Quite daft when you think of it.' He looked nervously up and down the corridor. 'Look, someone's bound to come along. I shouldn't really stick around here.'

But he still didn't move away, and stood bracing his legs in a relaxed way against the sea's motion. Mercy was learning to do the same. She was flattered that he seemed to want to talk to her.

'Was that your little boy I saw you with?'

'Oh, no, I'm not married! I just look after him for Mr and Mrs Adair. They're upstairs.'

'In first? Now, where're you from? No – let me guess. Birmingham, by any chance?'

She smiled. 'Right first time. Am I that broad?'

'No more than anyone else. That's what a stint in the

army does for you – you learn to pick out all sorts of accents. Great city, Birmingham. An engineer's paradise. Is this your first voyage?'

'Never been out of Brum before.'

'Oh well, in that case I could show you around,' he said enthusiastically. 'She's a great vessel. I could show you parts of her that no one else would . . .' He looked stricken all of a sudden. 'I'm sorry, Mercy – I mean only if you'd like, and you're able?'

'I'd love it. Would you really – are you allowed?'

Paul looked surprised at this notion. 'I've really no idea! Don't see why not. Would you like to tomorrow – if it's convenient?' He seemed reluctant to let her go. 'In fact I'll be dining soon, alone, unless you'd like to join me?'

'Oh, no, I can't. I've got to go up and have my – and dine – with Mr and Mrs Adair.' Mercy rolled her eyes comically as if it was all a bit of a trial eating in first class. At that moment it did rather feel so. It was nice to talk to someone of her own age. 'But I'll see you tomorrow?'

'That'd be very nice. ' He sounded surprised she'd agreed. 'I should be free soon after five-thirty tomorrow. Where shall I find you?'

'Oh, I don't know . . .' She had no routine yet, barely knew where anything was. 'Shall I meet you here? Quarter to six?'

'I'll look forward to it.' Paul slowly backed away. 'Better go down and make myself look respectable now!'

Margaret Adair was sufficiently well by the evening to dress for dinner. She wore an elaborate gown stitched in panels of eggshell blue and café creme silk with a low waist and floating panels of the same materials falling from waist to ankle. Her feet were squeezed into elegant blue shoes. James had refrained from mentioning that the subtle pastel colours made her already pale skin look even more washed out.

'You look delightful, my dear,' he told her, adjusting his collar. 'I'm so glad you're well enough to come down. I've invited Mercy to eat with us – just for tonight.'

'Oh good,' Margaret said, dabbing a last-minute touch of powder on her nose and cheeks.

'Yes – I thought it'd be an experience for her, first class.'

Mercy felt quite overpowered walking into the first-class dining room. It was the most sumptuous, luxurious room she had ever seen. She followed the Adairs as they walked with extra sedateness between the comfortable swivel chairs to their table, past a glittering array of evening clothes.

Thanks to the grease mark on her best dress she had changed into a soft woollen frock patterned with pretty blue flowers which she liked very much normally but in here it felt very plain and run of the mill. She had twisted her hair into a rather elegant knot, but even that felt rough and childish now. She sank down thankfully into the chair James Adair indicated for her. He looked very smart in a new, crisply pressed evening suit. At the far end of the room a group of musicians was playing soft, but cheerful music.

'Well this is something, isn't it?' James looked round the room, lined from floor to ceiling with beautifully carved wooden panels. 'They say it's in the style of Francois I – King of France in the sixteenth century.'

'No two panels the same,' Margaret said. She sounded rather weak and quiet.

Mercy looked about her at all the wood and the

beautiful ceiling, elegant furniture. She felt all lumps and bumps, awkward under the eyes of the stewards in their starched jackets and very conscious of the posh voices and extravagantly dressed people around her. Talk about fish out of water! Many of them in their jewels and lace and fur made James and Margaret Adair look very staid.

'Don't worry, Mercy,' Margaret leant closer, seeing her alarm at the amount of cutlery. 'Just start outside and work inwards. Then you can't go wrong.' Mercy saw she was nervous as well.

A steward handed them menus printed on thick, good quality paper. Seeing him eyeing Mercy a little askance, James Adair said rather sternly, 'Miss Hanley is our guest for this evening.'

'Yes, sir, of course. Quite so.' The steward seemed offended that he felt it necessary to justify himself. James smiled across at her reassuringly, but Mercy rather began to wish he'd thrown her out so she could go back to second class, third even, where she'd be far more comfortable. It was too hot and she wished she could roll her sleeves up.

James Adair selected from the menu for her.

'No swede here, don't worry!' he joked. He seemed to take delight in choosing for her a bewildering array of food. She sat nodding solemnly, clenching and unclenching her sticky hands on her lap. He kept looking at her and smiling. Even when she was talking to Margaret she could feel his eyes on her, so intensely that his gaze almost seemed to burn her skin. She wondered if he was watching to see if she behaved properly. It made her even more uncomfortable.

They ate oysters, poached sole, capons, a delicate selection of vegetables: asparagus (what's this? she wondered), glazed carrots shining with butter, parsley potatoes, slim green beans dressed with lemon which squeaked a little against her teeth.

'Let's order some wine,' James said, and a bottle of chilled white wine was brought to their table in a starched white cloth.

'Not for me, thank you,' Margaret said. She was struggling with the food.

'You'll try some, Mercy?' He filled her glass.

Mercy sipped the wine curiously. It was strong and fruity. She thought it tasted like cough medicine and decided a few mouthfuls would be enough. But she smiled back dutifully at James Adair as he raised his glass to her, beaming. If only he'd stop watching her all the time she might be able to relax a bit.

'Good health to you both. We're in for a marvellous voyage and a great adventure!'

Drinking more than he was accustomed to, James Adair grew red in the face, his forehead beaded with perspiration, and he was very talkative. He went on and on about the ship as if it were necessary to fill every second with words, despite the violins playing softly in the background.

'She was at Gallipolli you know,' he said rather loudly. 'Hospital ship – picking up the wounded. Quite a thought, Mercy, isn't it, that this very room was probably full of hammocks containing injured fighting men. Imagine that!'

Mercy felt she'd rather not imagine it. The thought made her stomach turn. Long before they reached the cheeses and the orange and lemon soufflé she was already full and longing for the second-class dining room where she could enjoy something like a chop with spuds and carrots and have done with it.

'I'm sorry about this afternoon,' Margaret Adair said

when she could get a word in. She was only picking at her food and had refused the roasted capon altogether. 'I gather James has told you . . .?'

'Yes, he did.' Mercy touched Margaret's hand for a moment. 'I'm so pleased for you. And Stevie'll love having a babby to play with.'

'I feel so foolish,' Margaret said. As usual, strands of her soft hair were coming down and she kept trying to press them up with her fingers. 'I'd begun to wonder – but I was showing no sign and I couldn't be sure. But it was like this with Stevie, only rather less extreme. Perfectly well one day, and the next, bang! Sick as anything. But what a catastrophic time for it to happen!'

'Maybe you'll be all right tomorrow,' Mercy said. 'You never know.'

'Never mind, darling.' James was in a very genial mood tonight. 'You'll still be able to experience the voyage and we'll take good care of you, won't we, Mercy?'

''Course we will. Oh!' Mercy remembered suddenly. 'I met someone ever so interesting tonight. He's a student, working down with the ship's engines and that. He said he'd show me round the ship and all sorts.'

James frowned. 'Well, who is he? We can't have you – and Stevie for that matter – just knocking about with any old person.'

'He's not just any old person, by the sound of it,' Margaret pointed out gently. 'Mercy said he's a student and I expect he's far too busy to be thinking about a small child.'

'He's from Cambridge,' Mercy said, eager to prove Paul's respectability. 'And some college in London – I forget now. He talks ever so nice.'

'Which is more than can be said for some people,' James retorted. 'Sure he's not a bit above you?'

'James!' Margaret was incensed. 'What on earth has got into you?'

'Well, we don't know the first thing about him, do we? We can't have her going off with just anyone.' He put his dessert spoon down petulantly.

'Honestly, darling, I've never heard you talk such nonsense,' Margaret said quietly, but with the firmness she occasionally mustered. 'It's not as if he can actually take her anywhere far, is it? We're on a ship. And I'd say it'd be nice for Mercy to make a friend – he sounds very kind. In case you've forgotten, James, Mercy is really rather a good judge of character . . .'

Mercy watched the two of them in alarm. Mr Adair seemed to be getting so angry all of a sudden and she didn't understand why. How had she offended him?

He took another mouthful of wine and looked across at her. After a moment, more calmly, he said, 'Just be careful. It's Stevie I'm concerned for. Don't want him associating with the wrong people.'

'I wouldn't dream of letting him come to any harm.' Her feelings of hurt were plain in her voice.

'Of course you wouldn't,' Margaret said. 'Now don't you worry. When I was expecting Stevie I wasn't much company for a few weeks and it may well be the same this time. So if you meet a nice friend your own age, dear, then I'm pleased for you and so will James be when he stops this old fuddy-duddy mood he's got into. You spend far too much time with us old things as it is. Well it's true, James,' she added, seeing her husband's disgruntled expression. 'Mercy may be in our employ but that doesn't mean she doesn't deserve to have some life of her own.'

The steward loomed over James's shoulder. 'Shall you require the cheeseboard, sir?'

James looked round the table. Both women shook their heads emphatically.

'I feel like a stuffed chicken,' Mercy said, before realizing that the first-class dining room was probably not the place to admit such a thing.

But Margaret laughed. 'Quite a meal, wasn't it? We shall all have more flesh on us when we reach New York.'

As the diners finished their meal the musicians struck up dance tunes and the stewards began to shift the empty chairs and tables back, creating a dance floor.

'It's no good,' Margaret said. 'I'm sorry, darling, I'm not up to any more tonight. I must retire to bed.' She looked pale still, unusually fragile. James stood up courteously when his wife did. Mercy stood up as well.

'There's no need to come,' Margaret said. 'I know my way. Goodnight, Mercy.' Suddenly she leant over and her soft lips touched Mercy's cheek. 'See you in a little while, darling,' she said to James. Then she was gone.

Mercy felt James's hand on her back, its heat. She stiffened, wanting to step away. She was already too hot, and could see how he was sweating.

'How would you like to dance, Mercy?'

'Me? I can't dance!' She tried to laugh off the suggestion.

'Oh, you'd pick it up in no time.' He caught her hand. 'Let me teach you, my dear.'

No, she thought. Please. She was even more uncertain of him after his harshness earlier. But she sensed he was trying to make it up. His eyes were pleading.

'I should go and see if Stevie's all right.'

'He'll be perfectly all right.' He still clasped her hand. 'Sleeps like a log once he's off, the little fellow, doesn't he? Just one dance – for me. Please?'

A few couples were already on the floor, their feet moving expertly to a waltz.

James took her in his arms, his right hand pressing her close at the waist. She could only shuffle and stumble after him when she knew he longed for her to whirl, to match his expertise. All the time she had to look down at her feet.

'One, two, three; one, two three,' he counted. If she glanced up his eyes were always fixed on her face. It made her feel uncomfortable. She felt he wanted something from her and she didn't know what it was.

When the music finished she left him with enormous relief, after he had kissed her hand and said, 'Goodnight, my dear.' She wanted to be back in her stateroom with the little light on and Stevie's little breaths coming to her across the room.

On the promenade deck, moist air rushing past his flushed face, James Adair stared, unseeing, over the dark ocean. After a time he raised a clenched fist to his mouth and bit on it so hard that his eyes started with tears.

Chapter Twenty-Nine

Mercy padded round the stateroom in her bare feet. Her oil-stained dress was drying over the back of the chair. She had rubbed the smudge with soap and done her best to scrub it out.

She undressed and slipped on her white cotton nightdress, still able to marvel that she possessed such a garment. The little electric light was burning on the table, shedding a soft glow round which the rest of the room was a circle of shadow. It was not bright enough to disturb Stevie. It had been decided that he should sleep in one of the beds with pillows tucked along the side. If conditions grew rough they could ask for a cot for him.

Mercy was still like a child with a new doll's house. She went and stood by the basin, turned the taps on and off, drank from the tooth mug and leant forward to look closely in the mirror. She brushed her hair out and plaited it into one thick braid. Even in the subdued light she could see her colour was high. Her cheeks looked quite swarthy, though she had drunk only a little of the wine, heady after a few sips. She'd left the rest.

'You'll have to watch it, eating and drinking wine with all them toffs!' She grinned cheekily in the mirror. 'Bet some of 'em wouldn't've wanted me up there if they knew . . .'

She washed herself then sat on her bed, pulled her knees up and hugged them, full of wonder. Everything felt so soft, so comfortable. She'd sleep like a princess tonight.

But her happiness never came unmixed with guilt and sorrow. Every time she'd been to see Elsie she'd looked worse and worse. More drawn in the face, more exhausted. When she had begun visiting regularly again in the autumn she was terribly shocked. She found Elsie in a chair, weak and shrunken, barely able to move.

'Elsie—' With a tight feeling in her chest Mercy rushed to her side.

'Oh – oh Lor' – Mercy—' She tried to raise herself in her chair, giving a whimper of pain.

Mercy was really frightened. She felt as if the breath had been knocked out of her. Elsie's face was so pinched and thin, barely recognizable. Her hands clutching at the arms of the chair were bony as twigs.

'What's the matter, you look terrible! Oh Elsie, I'm sorry. I meant to come more often. I didn't know things were this bad.'

'You're awright.' Elsie's voice had changed. It sounded high and reedy. 'I know yer busy, bab. I just ain't been too bright lately.' She tried, unsuccessfully to laugh. 'As you can see, I've got a bit be'ind with myself.' She jerked her head in Tom's direction. 'With 'im and that. Rosalie does 'er best to 'elp like, but you know . . . 'Ere, let's 'ave a cuppa tea.' The range had all but gone out and the room was dank and cold.

'Don't move, Elsie.' Mercy was fighting back tears. The sight of the two of them, mother and son, stranded in this room together was so pitiful she could hardly bear it. She wished she could knock the rotten house down and rebuild it, warm and clean and comfortable for them.

'I'll make tea. I'll cook for you. And let me sort Tom out . . .'

She fetched a bucket of slack and stoked the range, noticing as she moved round the small room the dirty state of the place, the grimy floor, bugs in the crevices, running up the walls.

'I was going to stove the place today,' Elsie said, seeing Mercy looking round. 'Only I just never got round to it some'ow.'

'What's wrong with you, Elsie?' Mercy asked gently, but the only reply she got was, 'Oh, nowt worth wasting breath on, bab.'

It took a long time for the kettle to boil. Mercy got the broom out and briskly swept the room, swishing bugs from the corners.

'And I'll come and sort you out in a tick when I've got some hot water,' she said to Tom.

She handed Elsie a cup of tea and prepared a pail of water, soap and a rag.

The bed was in a filthy state, the smell of it overpowering. Tom had been settled on a collection of rags to try and preserve the sheet, but they were badly soiled and the stained sheet was wet from edge to edge.

'There's a spare.' Elsie pointed to a sheet hanging over the chair beside the dead fire. 'Might still be a bit damp.'

Mercy moved the chair next to the warm range and stood the bowl on another chair near the bed. By the time she'd made all her preparations, Elsie was dozing again, the cup of tea forgotten on the table. Her clothes were holed and stained, stockings crinkled down her thin legs.

Using all her wiry strength, Mercy rolled Tom over. He let out a groan. His body was so much thinner now, the limbs pale and wasted. She turned him on his side. Even in his soiled state she could see the sores at the base of his back, the skin chaffed away from pressure on the bed to form two deep wounds.

'Oh my God.' She stood holding him, aghast. For a few moments she was overwhelmed, felt as if her sorrow would drown her. Tears coursed down her cheeks. 'My poor, poor boy,' she whispered. 'Oh Tom, what's happened to you, my love?' For those moments, soiled and vulnerable as he was, he was once again the quiet, kind lad she could still remember with great tenderness.

She wiped her eyes with the back of one hand. In a fury she pulled all the filthy rags out from underneath him and bundled them up by the door to be thrown out. The mattress was so wet and foul. If only she could get him on to another bed! But there was nothing, and even if there had been she had the strength only to roll him over and pull the sheet out from underneath him as she'd seen Elsie do so many times.

She wrung the cloth out over the pail, pushing wisps of hair away from her face with her wrists. She set about washing him with a bar of carbolic. With great gentleness and care she soaped his body, massaging his stick-thin arms, the pale, almost hairless chest. He made no sound, though when she turned him on his back he was watching her with a puzzled look on his face. His belly was soft, sunk inwards. Very gently she washed the small shrunken part of him that should have fathered her children and felt in it not a flicker of life. She dried him, put the other, still damp sheet on the bed and tucked a bottle between his legs. Of course he'd move and it would spill, but it might help preserve the sheet. Mercy kissed his soap-smelling cheek, emptied the bucket, and sat spooning tea into his mouth. All the while he looked sternly at her.

'Mercy?' Elsie looked round at her with the dazed eyes of a much older woman. 'Oh, you're still 'ere. I must've dozed off.'

She reached for the tea and Mercy rushed to help. 'It's gone cold – I'll get you some more.'

'Rosalie'll be in soon.' This was an important moment of the day, Rosalie's return from school.

'There must be a place, you know,' Mercy said very gently, moving her chair closer to Elsie's. 'Somewhere you could get Tom looked after.'

Elsie ignored her. She seemed far away, as if nothing anyone said fully sank in. Her face puckered in pain. Hissing through her teeth she reached under her left arm, moaned, eyes streaming.

'What's the matter, love? Let me look.'

She didn't protest as Mercy, hands trembling, unbuttoned her blouse. The skin under Elsie's arm and round her breast was taut and blackened.

'Radiation.' Elsie stared down at herself as if at a stranger. 'That's what it does to yer.' Covering herself again she looked into Mercy's eyes. 'I want Johnny. Can yer find 'im for me?'

She tried Johnny's address in Aston. He'd moved on. His second landlady was not many streets away.

'Johnny Pepper? Ar – 'e were 'ere. Ain't no more though. Went more'n a month ago. 'E couldn't afford the rent like, after the strike.' The police strike had ground on through the summer. Mercy had hardly given it more than a passing thought. ''E were one of the ones they let go. Quite a few of 'em with no job at the end of it. S'pose it serves 'em right really,' she said complacently. 'Any'ow, 'e couldn't pay the rent no more.'

'D'you know where he went?'

'Can't say I do, bab, no. 'E said summat about the country at one time. Moody lad, 'e was. Nights 'e'd be up moving about, in and out all hours. Used to walk the streets. I don't know. Sorry not to be more 'elp though. 'E yer brother?'

'No, just a friend.' Mercy tried to smile, despite her sinking heart. 'Ta any road.'

She told Elsie. 'The woman said 'e'd gone to the country. I s'pect he'll be in touch. She said 'e'd got himself a really good job on a farm somewhere.'

'Ah well,' Elsie said. She seemed cheered. 'That'll be nice for 'im. 'E always liked to be out and about.'

Elsie died in the December. With Margaret's permission Mercy had visited every week and helped as much as she could. She knew Elsie was not going to get better. She was in bed through November and they watched her sink until she could no longer speak and didn't know anyone. They took her to hospital where they gave her morphine, and after two days she was gone.

Rosalie gave up school and stayed at home to look after Tom. The funeral was at St Joseph's and Margaret gladly granted Mercy time off to go.

'She was like a Mom to me,' Mercy told Margaret. She felt clenched up inside with sadness.

The sun shone in weakly through the long church windows, panels of light dancing with dust. They sang 'Abide With Me' and 'Safely, Safely Gathered In'. Rosalie leant on Mercy and sobbed and Mercy stroked her auburn head. Poor kid, only twelve and the woman of the house now. She was a brave little thing. Maryann had come from Coventry, and Jack was there, but they hadn't found Johnny. Josephine was there, pale and tired-looking. Things were strained with her husband. Alf's hair was almost white but he still looked strong, upstanding. At his side, Mabel, in her smartest dress, hair piled high under her hat.

Mercy shyly kissed Alf as the organ played at the end of it.

''Allo, wench.' He seemed stunned. 'You're looking very nice. Thanks for coming to see 'er like. It meant a lot to 'er.'

Mabel, who seemed to be a fixture beside him said, 'I 'ear you're doing very well for yourself, Mercy. That Dorothy Finch still looking out for you?'

'Yes thanks. I see Dorothy from time to time.' She was very taken aback. She expected to hear rancour or sarcasm in Mabel's voice, but there was none. She even felt a little ashamed for harbouring so much bitterness towards her when she'd helped Elsie. This was Elsie's funeral and she must behave nicely.

'How're you, Mabel?'

'Oh, I'm awright.' She smiled a fond, gap-toothed smile at Alf. 'You know – going along.'

The neighbours were all there: the Ripleys, McGonegalls, Mary Jones and her kids. Everyone acted pleased to see her, was kind. She'd seen them in snatches on her visits to Elsie. But Mercy had felt strange, known their distance from her in their exclamations about how well she was looking.

The sadness of the funeral was deepened by her own sense of being an outsider. Thinking back on it now in this seaborne room so far from Angel Street, she knew it had been Elsie who had tied her to the neighbourhood. She'd changed, moved on from them. She couldn't share their day-to-day concerns. The realization was one of melancholy and loss mixed with excitement. Her life was opening out, it had possibilities which she could never have dreamed of in Angel Street. It seemed her future lay with the Adairs.

Chapter Thirty

Chilly now, and feeling sleepy, Mercy slipped out of bed to switch off the light.

She heard a low knocking at the door. She stood still holding her breath. Had she imagined it? The knock came again, still restrained but a little louder. Without stopping to think she went and opened the door a crack.

'Oh goodness, I didn't think you'd have gone to bed this early!' Mr Adair sounded very flustered. 'Margaret's feeling very queasy again, so I said I'd come down and see Stevie instead. But I suppose', he added lamely, 'he's asleep and peaceful?'

Mercy was confused. Margaret usually came to see Stevie much earlier when he was awake. James never usually came at all.

'Well, yes. He's sound asleep.' She was speaking very softly. 'Seems happy enough on the bed for tonight.' She didn't know whether she should open the door wider. She was acutely aware that all she had on was her nightdress. 'D'you want to see him?'

James looked agitatedly up and down the corridor. He was holding his hat, circling the brim round between his fingers. 'Perhaps, as I'm here. If you don't mind.'

She stood back to let him in, his coat brushing her arm. Immediately she'd shut the door she pulled a cardigan on over her nightdress, for the sake of both warmth and modesty.

He stood in front of her. The fiddling with his hat went on. He stared at his hands, looked as if he was about to speak, closed his mouth again, sighed.

Mercy felt terribly awkward. His presence was so large and imposing in the small room and she, despite the wool garment she was pulling tight round herself, felt naked and foolish. She clenched her jaw to stop her teeth chattering. Why on earth didn't he look at Stevie and then go away again?

'He's there.' She pointed.

James stepped over and looked down at his son. Stevie was flat on his back, arms stretched out, his cheeks pink, mouth a little open. He looked adorable with his long eyelashes and dark curly hair. Mercy smiled. She stood with her arms tightly folded.

'He looks perfectly comfortable.' James spoke in a forced, jovial tone, which softened as he turned to her and said, 'And you, Mercy? Is everything all right for you?'

'Oh yes, thank you, Mr Adair. It's lovely.'

'Good. Good. Very well.' There was a note of appeal in his voice as he said, 'Is there nothing you'd like?'

''Er, no, thank you,' she said, bewildered.

'Right then. Good. I may come another night. Margaret's still poorly.'

In that case, Mercy thought, she'd make sure she remained dressed until he'd been. It was all very strange. Perhaps as he was on holiday he thought he should see as much of Stevie as possible?

He put his hat on and went to the door. 'Goodnight,' he said tenderly.

'Goodnight, Mr Adair.'

*

As Mercy closed the stateroom door behind him James Adair had to resist an impulse to lean against the wall of the rolling ship and bang his head on it at his own folly. But there were people coming, a respectable-looking couple in modest evening clothes earnestly reading the numbers on the doors.

He couldn't bear the thought of the smoking room, or reading room. He didn't want other people, nor could he possibly be still. He stormed along the passage and climbed one staircase, then another. The promenade deck: blast it, he was in second class still, of course, but the deck was more or less empty so no matter. It was too late, too bracingly cold out there for most people.

He went to the side and looked out. From inside he could hear the sound of a piano. It struck him how odd it was to hear a piano in the middle of the ocean. The ship's lights dimmed quickly into the far greater darkness beyond for it was cloudy, moonless. He could sense the sea rather than see it, except for occasional riffles of white foam which appeared and vanished so quickly, he felt he might have imagined them. The wind was scouringly cold against his cheeks, but he welcomed it. He raged at himself.

Stupid, deluded imbecile. What the hell has got into you? What must she have thought of him turning up like that when she'd already retired to bed? It was asinine, it was insane!

He leant his elbows on the side and rested his head on his upturned hands, letting out a groan. The expression on her face! She must have thought him deranged! But no, damn it, he justified himself. He could call in and see his own son if it suited him, couldn't he, for heaven's sake?

He ought to be thinking of his plans and projects, of Kesler, of how they would work together. That was the entire purpose of the voyage – the business; his life's work. Instead of which he knew he would not sleep for the ceaseless longing in him which ached for relief. Never in his life had he experienced such helplessness. He knew, whatever his rational mind told him, that he would go to Mercy again. Somewhere in him the battle was already lost.

'Oh Mercy – oh, help me . . .' he groaned into the buffeting Atlantic wind.

'Good evening.'

A young man approached, smoking a cigarette. The glowing tip of it moved in his hand. James jumped, heart pounding. How long had he been there? Had he heard?

'Evening,' he replied brusquely. Under the low lights he could make out a long face, deep-set eyes, a baggy suit. He was about to turn away when the young man spoke.

'Queen of all ships, isn't she?'

James relaxed. Perhaps he hadn't heard. The wind was strong. And even if he had, civility would prevent him from commenting.

'Yes, indeed,' he replied, attempting geniality. 'A real privilege to travel on her.' He held his hand out. 'I'm an interloper along here. Really should be in first class. James Adair.'

The young man seemed unmoved by the information but he returned the handshake. 'Paul Louth.' He frowned. 'Adair? I believe I met your – would she be nanny? – earlier on. I offered to show her around. I hope that's acceptable?'

James bristled inside. This must be the student! He felt a violent rush of resentment.

'Mercy? Oh yes – she looks after our son. So you're

the student? She said she'd met you.' It stuck in his throat to mention this, but he wanted to find out more about him.

'Yes, I am,' Paul said, brightening. 'I just had the opportunity to work this round trip. Fascinating to see her in action, though of course the work's filthy and rather repetitive. I did see round the *Olympic*'s engine room once. Marvellous – 'course she's a triple screw, whereas they put the quadruple screw propellers in this one . . .'

They spent a good half hour sharing engineers' talk. They discussed the workings of the ship, its construction, the intricacies of the Parson's turbine engine. James told Paul about his business with Kesler. He relaxed. Watching the young man's pale profile, his serious expression as he spoke, he could not harbour dislike for him. He had intelligence, expertise. There was a sadness about him, as of so many of the remaining young men of his generation. It was when he talked of his trade, of the ship, that he became animated.

When they parted for the night James strolled back to first class feeling calmer, mellowed, ashamed of his earlier jealousy. Mercy had only spoken to him once after all. What did that signify? He was a pleasant young man. An odd mixture of charm and melancholy. And hard to place somehow – well-spoken, clearly educated, but travelling second class and without the kind of well-heeled assumptions of superiority James would have expected, which would have made him bridle. Bit of an oddball perhaps, he thought, but certainly a well-informed one. He mustn't mind Mercy seeing the boy or whatever would she think of him? His display of temper at dinner had been bad enough. He was being a fool.

The door of his stateroom creaked as he opened it.

Margaret was moving restlessly in the bed, her face white. Once in bed, against his expectation, he slept immediately.

The next day was one of cloud broken by occasional bursts of sunshine. Mercy spent the day chiefly with Stevie. They went to see Margaret but she was so sick they left her in peace. She took Stevie out on deck, well wrapped up, letting him run up and down on his sturdy legs, pointing and babbling. His red muffler streamed in the wind like a flag. He could say few words clearly as yet but compensated with a great many inquisitive and expressive sounds. He was very intrigued by a stack of folding deckchairs, not in use as it was too cold to sit out. Mercy had to put one up and down several times to show him, and herself for that matter, how it worked.

'Come on, my lad,' she said eventually. 'That's enough of that. Let's go and see if we can find some toys, eh?'

She picked him up, both their cheeks cold and glowing.

He was on a rocking horse in the nursery, crowing with delight, when James Adair appeared. He stood at the door in his coat and hat, smiling.

'Dadada!' Stevie yelled, pointing. The nurse in charge smiled indulgently.

'Just thought I'd have a look in.' James came over to them. 'Everything all right, Mercy?'

'Yes, thank you.' She smiled shyly. 'Is Margaret any better?'

'Not much, I'm afraid. And the motion of the ship's not helping. She said she'd like to see you both later – just for a few minutes. She's very fed up of course.'

'I know.' Margaret had been tearful when she went in earlier. 'Poor thing – what a time to feel bad.'

'I, er—' – James pushed his hands into his pockets – 'I met your friend last night.'

Mercy lurched over to support Stevie as he began to slide off the horse. 'Who?'

'Paul Louth.'

'Oh – yes!' she smiled. 'He's going to show me round later on!'

'Good. That'll be interesting.' He spoke with determined enthusiasm. 'You'll have to tell me about it. He seems very nice. Quite put my foolish fears at ease!' And he laughed, long and loud so that Mercy felt obliged to laugh a little with him.

She met Paul at a quarter to six. He had already washed and changed back into his too-large suit.

'I'll have him with me—' – she indicated Stevie – 'at least for another hour or so. Will it matter?'

''Course not!' Paul squatted down. 'Hello, Stevie. Are you going to come and have a look round with us?' Looking up at Mercy he said, 'Tell you what. If we take him down with us now we can have a quick look in the engine room. He won't be frightened by the noise, will he?' Mercy shook her head. 'Then perhaps after dinner we could look at some of the less dramatic bits?'

'That sounds lovely!'

'Come on then.' He stood up. 'The tour begins here.'

She picked Stevie up and they moved down through the ship, through a warren of narrower, much more rudimentary corridors the passengers never normally saw. The throb of the ship grew louder each time they moved down a deck.

'Are you s'posed to bring me down here?' she asked, following Paul's eager stride.

'Don't know really.' He turned to her, looking quite unconcerned. 'They can hardly throw us off the ship, can they? I shan't keep you down long. It's pretty filthy lower down, and noisy. But it'll give you a sense of what goes on below decks, what keeps it all ticking over . . . Would you like me to carry him for a while?'

'No – I'm awright for now. He might not go to you anyway, as he doesn't know you.' But she was touched by his protectiveness.

The powerful, vibrating hum grew more insistent. She could feel it through her feet. The floors were metal now, clanked as they walked on them. There was no natural light down here. All the work was done under electric lamps. Stevie sat quite still in her arms now, head turning this way and that, a finger in his mouth.

'Now – look in here,' Paul said.

They stood at the threshold of the main engine room. Mercy looked up, up at the working puzzle of steel girders and plates, levers and tanks, dials and chains. So enormous and complicated, so much weight in all that throbbing, churning metal. She gave a gasp of awe and amazement.

Stevie's eyes were like giant marbles. Mercy felt his tight grip on her shoulder.

'It's enormous!' Mercy shouted. 'Don't know why – it reminds me of a church!'

She saw, rather than heard Paul laugh. 'Quite right too!' he shouted back. Suddenly he took her arm. She was warmed by the familiarity of it, as if they'd been friends for years.

'You must see down here . . .' He had to put his mouth close to her ear for her to hear him. 'I'm afraid it's pretty filthy . . . Coal gets in everything.'

'Well I'm learning not to wear my best clothes when I see you!' she yelled.

'Oh dear – didn't the oil come out?'

'Yes,' she replied, hoping it would eventually.

Holding her elbow he led her down another staircase, then stopped.

The floor was black with coal dust, the air stiflingly hot. All around she could hear the clang and rattle of metal, shovelling sounds, bangs and shouts and the trundle of wheels as the trimmers shifted loads of coal from the bunkers ready to be shovelled into the furnaces. There came the sound of a gong banging loudly amid all the other noise. From the stairs Mercy caught glimpses of men clad only in singlets above their trousers, their faces and muscular bodies black and shiny with coal and sweat so that they looked as if they were made of iron.

Mercy and Paul stood poised on the stairs. Mercy could feel the heat beating against her cheeks. She pressed Stevie's head protectively close to her. The air smelt evil and was full of ash and dust, and within seconds the three of them were all coughing. It was like hell down here, Mercy thought, holding her hand as a shield to Stevie's face. Those people in first class ought to see this, to make them realize what kept their luxurious saloons and dining rooms churning across the sea! The inside of her throat was burning.

'Come away,' Paul said, taking her arm.

They retreated very gratefully upstairs, longing for a drink of water.

'D'you know,' Paul said – there was no need to shout now – 'each of those men shifts about five tons of coal a day.'

'I couldn't stand it even for five minutes,' Mercy said. 'How the hell do they put up with it?'

'Beats me,' Paul said. 'But they do. Do it well too.'

They reached C-deck and stopped between his room and hers.

'I'll get this little'un to bed now,' she said.

'He's been very good, hasn't he? Not a murmur.'

'Thanks ever such a lot, Paul.' She hesitated, not sure if he'd still want to see her later.

'Pleasure's all mine.' He hesitated. 'Would you like to join me for dinner? Not quite like first class, I'm afraid, but it'd be good to have some company.'

'I'll eat with you,' she said happily. 'I'll turn up your sleeves for you too if you want!'

Paul held his arms down straight at his sides. The cuffs dangled halfway down his hands. 'I think I'm still supposed to be growing into it,' he said ruefully. 'If you would . . .'

'Give it 'ere. No – wait. Let me get the door open first.' Paul took her key and unlocked the door for her. She put Stevie down inside.

'See you then?' Paul handed her the jacket. 'At seven?'

'Better say seven-fifteen,' she said. 'What with the sewing.'

Chapter Thirty-One

She saw him outside the dining room before he saw her. He was standing sideways on to her, his thinness more obvious without the jacket. He was looking into the dining room as if watching the diners there, but she sensed that his mind was far away, his expression one of deep melancholy. The sadness she saw in him almost stopped her in her tracks. Before, with her, he had appeared cheerful.

'Oh hello!' He saw her and the smile blazed across his face.

'Here you go.' She had speedily unpicked his cuffs while waiting for Stevie to fall asleep, and sewn them up almost an inch shorter. 'I damped them down a bit, but they need pressing – I couldn't do that in time as well.'

He slipped on the jacket and tried the length. 'That's marvellous – thank you! I'll press them myself. I'm so grateful. So – are you ready for food? I'm absolutely ravenous.'

They settled themselves at a table beside the wall.

'You look – very nice,' Paul said stumblingly.

She smiled. 'Thanks.' She'd put on the dress with the blue flowers, plaited her hair simply. She'd wanted to look nice.

'Sorry – I'm not used to much conversation. I don't see many people who aren't engineering students!'

They turned their minds to food.

'Ooh, lovely – roast beef!' Mercy brightened further. 'They have all sorts of odd stuff up in first class, I can tell you.'

'Yes – it'd be too rich for my palette, I must say. Especially several days in a row. Stanley – he's the other student – has been full of praise for it all.' Paul grimaced. It was obvious he was none too keen on Stanley.

They ordered food and then fell silent as if something in the air had shifted that prevented them talking. They each looked down at the table, looked up smiling, fiddled with the simple provision of cutlery. For a moment, in this silent, face-to-face awkwardness, Mercy was acutely aware of the difference in their class. He was obviously educated, better off, superior. What on earth were they going to talk about?

Paul, who seemed for the moment equally at a loss peered into his cuffs and said, 'Thank you again. It's a very neat job.'

'Oh – not really. I'm not much good at sewing. It was . . .' She was about to say Susan. Susan's the one who can sew. But that was the past now. She didn't feel like explaining. 'Doesn't your mom do that sort of thing for you?'

'Oh no – my mother's dead. She died before the War.'

'Oh dear,' Mercy said.

'Yes. We miss her.'

'Are you a big family?'

'Only myself and my brother Peter. Two little dickie birds, we were, growing up together. He was three years older than me.'

He paused, sitting back and opening his napkin, spreading it on his lap. 'He joined up as soon as he was old enough. Desperate to go. He was killed at Loos.' Paul looked across the room. Mercy kept her eyes fixed on his face, willing him to keep talking.

'My father stayed in Cambridge throughout the War – at the university. He's a linguist – French and German. We were never close. Certainly aren't now. The War somehow put paid to any sort of communication – it was precarious enough before. It was another life over there . . .' He paused as if looking for words. 'You brought it all home in your mind but you couldn't talk about it.'

Paul stopped, obviously feeling he'd said too much, unsure what was right, to talk or not talk. He lit a cigarette, smoked in nervous little puffs. Once more he looked away across the room and Mercy could feel his unease. She thought of Tom and Johnny. Both of them before the War. Just ordinary lads. The sadness that bled eternally from those years of war.

'So you left home?' she asked hesitantly.

Her question seemed to put him at ease, to show him his talking wasn't a burden and he was able to look at her again, if shyly, drawing on the cigarette.

'I can't abide being in the same house as my father. Don't seem to fit in the way he wants me to. He'd have liked me to be an academic, a man of letters . . . He just has a housekeeper now.' Paul shrugged. 'Still, all you can do is go on.'

'Yes.' His simple statement hit home. Her own life: her mother, Tom, Susan . . . but she had to go on. 'I s'pose so.'

'Are you close to your family?'

'Me?' Mercy gave a bitter laugh. 'I ain't – haven't got a family.' It was always a difficult admission.

'What, no one?' He sounded startled, and sorry.

She shook her head, took a sip of water from her tumbler, not like the elegant cut glass upstairs, then looked up into his eyes.

'My mom, whoever she was, left me on the steps of the workhouse – well, orphanage – when I was just a few hours old. All she left with me was a little hanky with my name embroidered on it – least, that's the name they gave me. Hanley came from the name of the home – the benefactor was a Joseph Hanley. But I've looked at that hanky so many times and wondered whose fingers stitched my name; why she couldn't keep me . . .'

'Poor woman,' Paul said. 'How terrible.'

'Yes, I know, but . . .' Mercy felt her emotion boiling to the surface, the hurt and anger. 'But to just throw away your own child as if she were a bag of rubbish!' Tears stung her eyes and she wiped them away furiously, hanging her head.

'Oh dear,' Paul said wretchedly. 'I'm sorry. The last thing I want is to upset you.'

When she looked up his eyes were full of concern. She tried to smile.

'No – it's all right. I'm glad I told you. I don't know why it is, it always feels like summat to be ashamed of. I've tried so many times to think what it must've been like for her. I don't know whether she was too poor to keep me. She might've had a whole host of other kids. She might be dead . . . I just wish I knew who she was, that's all.'

The soup arrived, leek and potato, plentiful and tasty. Paul put out his cigarette. For a time they chatted more lightly, about the ship, the voyage.

'We're not up to speed, you know,' Paul told her. 'Barely managing twenty knots. She used to be able to average twenty-six before the War – more sometimes.'

'Does that mean the journey'll take longer?' She'd been told they'd be five days on board.

'A few extra hours at least.'

'Oh well – I won't complain about that,' she smiled. 'I'm enjoying it all too much to want to hurry.'

The dishes were cleared, and plates arrived arranged with slices of well-cooked meat and generous servings of potato, carrots and greens.

'This is the nicest beef I've ever had,' Mercy said.

'It is good.' Paul spooned horseradish. 'Makes you appreciate good food when you've done without it, doesn't it? In the army we were all obsessed with the food – well, when nothing much was happening. Food and dry boots!'

'Where were you, Paul?'

'The Somme area. I joined up towards the end. I was there five months – not that long really but it felt like a whole lifetime. Ended up near le Cateau. I went in with two friends – with the Lincolns.'

She waited, seeing he had more to say.

'Neither of them came back. John went first, early on. Eric and I – well, he said I had a charmed life and I suppose it turned out to be true. He was shot. I don't know how exactly, or where. I found out afterwards. And I–'

'You got through without a scratch?'

'Well, no, I didn't as a matter of fact. That was the extraordinary thing. I was hit twice. The first time it came from a long way away – the bullet caught the rim of my helmet. Must have been that far from my eyes.' He held out his finger and thumb. 'The second time I was holding my rifle, like this, elbows out. A bullet zipped straight through here, under my left arm and out the other side. Burned a lump out of my arm as it went. I remember looking down and my uniform was smoking – there was a whopping hole in it. The arm bled like anything, but in fact there was no serious damage. Again, a few inches further across and it would have killed me.'

'What fantastic good luck!'

'Yes, but the worst of it is, it makes you feel responsible. I don't know what for exactly. But hundreds, thousands of men had the same luck in reverse. It didn't miss. And you start thinking, why me? What's so bloody special about me? Oh, look – I'd better not get going on this.'

'I don't mind. I'd like to know.'

He couldn't look at her and she could sense in him a shame which matched her own.

'What about other friends?' she asked.

'I don't seem to have too many now. Everything's different . . .' He gave a hugely weary sigh. 'Look, let's not go into that. Go forward from every day, that's my motto. Tell me some more about yourself.'

'I can't think of anything much. I'm not very educated or anything. Just ordinary, you know. I mean I'm not . . .' She stumbled to a halt.

Paul picked his knife and fork up again. He leant towards her. 'Not what?'

Mercy felt herself blushing. 'Just that I'm not your class of person, am I?'

'And what class of person am I? Do tell me, because I'm damned if I know any more.'

She stared back at him. In Paul's eyes she could see a sad, hungry expression which moved her deeply.

'People are just people, Mercy. That's all. If there was one single thing the War taught me it was that. So please . . .'

So she talked. About the home. About Mabel and

Susan, Elsie, Tom, Johnny. And Paul listened, intently. The waiter brought a steamed marmalade pudding with custard and they ate, barely tasting it.

'Johnny said the same as you when he got back, that he couldn't stop at home. I don't know where he's gone now.'

Paul looked sorrowfully at her. 'You've had so many losses.'

'I've been so lucky working for the Adairs though. Dorothy found 'em for me. They're ever so good to me.'

'You were lucky in Dorothy too.'

'Oh yes – she's awright, Dorothy is. She's a good sort.'

'You don't think . . . Perhaps I shouldn't say this . . .' Paul eyed her sideways on, hesitating.

'What?'

'Well, that Dorothy might actually be your mother?'

Mercy stared at him in speechless astonishment. She started to laugh. She laughed so hard that people stared and her bubbling mirth eventually made Paul join in as well.

'Dorothy? You mean – oh no. No!'

'I'm sorry. I didn't realize the idea was that absurd!'

'She's just not. No . . . Oh dear no. She's just Dorothy.'

'I'm sorry. Shouldn't have even said it.'

'D'you know, it'd never even crossed my mind.' Mercy wiped her eyes. She looked thoughtful for a moment, then shook her head. 'No. No, she just isn't.'

'Ready to explore now?' Paul asked impishly when they'd finished.

'Let me just look in on Stevie. He's a very good sleeper but I must make sure.'

Paul waited as Mercy tiptoed in and replaced Stevie's

covers which he was forever kicking off. She leant over and kissed him.

'He's so beautiful when he's asleep,' she smiled, re-locking the door. 'All warm and peaceful. Where're we going then?'

'Let's just follow our feet, shall we? Hmm.' He stopped as they reached the third-class staircase. 'I suppose just meandering round inside might get a bit dull. Shall we go and get our coats?'

'OK.' Mercy didn't mind in the least where they went. It was all fun. More than fun. She surprised herself with the thought: this is the best night of my life!

They were just turning back when someone came running up the stairs behind them, three at a time.

'Eh – eh!' There came a loud burst of a language Mercy had never heard before.

A man, swarthy-faced with a black moustache, a cap, and black workaday clothes seized Paul's arm, talking urgently: 'Daktar – daktar . . .'

'No, I'm not a doctor!' Paul said. 'I'm sorry . . .'

The desperation on the man's face was unmistakable. He made dramatic gestures, sweeping his calloused hand over his stomach and talking frantically.

'What the hell's this language?' Paul said exasperated. 'Is it, are you . . . Polska? Polska?'

The man nodded emphatically and flooded them with more incomprehensible language.

Mercy watched his hands. 'Someone's 'aving a babby,' she said suddenly. 'That's what. Down in third class.'

'Wait – I know who can help. Stay there – DOCTOR,' Paul said to the Polish man, and ran off.

A few moments later he returned with a dour-faced young man dressed in white with almost painfully prominent cheekbones.

'He's the kosher cook,' Paul panted as the two other men spoke. 'Speaks bits of all sorts – English, German, Yiddish – Polish too, thank heavens.' Mercy's eyes were intent on the Polish man's face.

'He says', the cook informed them disdainfully, 'that his wife is with baby and he needs a doctor.'

'See!' Mercy said. The cook disappeared, shaking his head.

'Get him to show you where and meet me back here.' Paul was already moving away. 'I'll find the ship's surgeon.'

The man beckoned her down the stairs, then down again until they were on F-deck. Their feet clattered on the steps.

In one part of the corridor a small crowd of people, mostly women, were huddled anxiously near one of the doors. Mercy could see they were poor, their skirts made of thick, workaday cloth, clutching shawls round their shoulders. They reminded her of a cluster of starlings. The man spoke to them, pushing past to the cabin door. 114F. Mercy memorized the number. She could already hear the sounds of the birthing woman.

To her great surprise the man indicated for her to enter. She pointed back down the corridor. She had to meet Paul. But he insisted, taking her arm, motioned her inside. The other women outside all stood round the doorway. Mercy began to wonder if they thought she was a nurse but since she had no way of explaining she followed the man in.

The room was lit by one small bulb and was stuffy, full of cloying, intimate smells, especially sweat. Two narrow berths were squeezed in down either side, and Mercy saw that the young woman, barely more than a girl, was lying, panting, on the one to the right. At her head, on the edge of the bed an older woman was perched, talking endlessly in a low voice, a string of beads dangling from her fingers. It took Mercy a moment to see she was praying.

For the moment the young woman was quiet and the man beckoned Mercy forward. Mercy felt timid, confused. What did the man want? She couldn't speak any Polish. She knew nothing about having babies.

The young woman turned her head and Mercy saw that her black hair was drenched in sweat. Such a sweet face, but so exhausted and frightened. She put her hand out and muttered something. Mercy took the hot hand and squeezed it.

'The doctor's coming,' she said. 'You'll be all right. You'll 'ave your babby soon.'

Pain gripped the young woman again and she began to writhe and groan horribly, her body lifting from the bed. She loosed Mercy's hand and clawed at the thin bedcover, her cries becoming a long, sobbing wail. Mercy felt her knees turn weak. She motioned to the man that she was going up to meet the doctor. She saw in his eyes, then, that he loved his wife and how afraid he was. He had needed her to see. She spoke English: she would be able to speak to the doctor when he was unable to.

Paul and the doctor were coming down the stairs as she reached them.

'This way.' She ran ahead of them.

'What's the trouble?' The surgeon was a middle-aged man with a bushy moustache and a brisk air. He smelt of whisky.

'She's pretty far on by the sound of it,' Mercy panted as they clattered along F-deck. 'I think summat might be wrong but I'm no expert, doctor.'

'I hardly supposed you were,' he replied dryly.

'Here.' The crowd stood back respectfully to let him through. The door opened, letting out the woman's distressed cries.

'Poor thing.' Mercy leant weakly against the wall on the other side of the corridor. The sound of such suffering made her feel faint. The other spectators were eyeing her and Paul curiously.

'Well, we've done our good deed,' Paul said. 'Would you like to go up on deck now?'

Mercy looked at him as if he were a madman. 'Of course not! I'm not going anywhere 'til I see how she gets on. I want to know if she's awright and if she has a boy or a girl.' She folded her arms adamantly.

It took another two gruelling hours. Mercy ran back up twice to check Stevie was still asleep. Several times Paul suggested tentatively that they go up and have a cup of tea before resuming the vigil.

'You go if you want. I'm staying.'

The young woman was clearly having a very difficult time. At every agonized outburst Mercy tensed, folding and unfolding her arms across her chest, hands clenched, listening. 'God, I hope she'll be OK. Oh my ... oh dear ...' she kept saying over and over. She felt as if her own innards were being torn out. The sounds of pain were terrible to hear. Paul paced helplessly up and down, seeming just as bothered by Mercy's distress as the Polish woman's. Towards the end it seemed everyone in the corridor was willing her on with every fibre of themselves. They all stopped talking. Almost stopped breathing. There came a final, terrible bout of screams which had Mercy bent double and almost tearing out her own hair. Everything went quiet. After a moment they heard the wild, outraged scream of a newborn child. There was a collective gasp from all the other women, relieved talk and laughter and embraces. Mercy found herself sobbing.

'Hey, hey . . .' Paul felt in his pockets for a hanky but failed to find one. After a moment's flustered hesitation he put his arm round her shoulders. 'You don't even know her!'

'No . . .' Mercy found her own hanky and wiped her eyes. 'But she looked at me and took my hand.' She tried to smile. 'Daft, ain't it?'

After a moment the doctor put his head round the door. 'Could someone—' – he spoke tersely, looking at Paul – 'go up to the galley and fetch some hot water?'

'Is she all right?' Mercy cried.

'Yes, yes . . .'

There was toing and froing with water. The stooped, elderly woman carried a bundle of bloodstained bedding from the room. Eventually the doctor left.

Soon after, the dark-haired man came out of the room, a smile under his moustache. His face looked more youthful with relief. He beckoned to them. Mercy and Paul looked at each other and stepped inside. The crowd of Poles followed until the room was full.

The young woman was sitting up, hair plastered back on her head. Her eyes were like dark pools in her exhausted face, but there was a gentle smile now on her lips. The baby lay wrapped in her arms.

'Oh!' Mercy cried, tears filling her eyes again. So much pain, she thought, for such a miracle!

The woman gently held out the little one for her to see. Mercy looked into a crinkled but perfect face with a tiny shading of barely formed eyebrows. Its eyes were closed as if to cling on to the secrets of life before birth.

'I wonder if it's a girl or a boy,' she said to Paul.

As if the woman had understood, she unwrapped the baby for a moment. Mercy saw where the umbilical cord had been cut and bound.

'A girl! Oh Paul, she's a real picture!'

She saw his eyes appraising the new child, seriously and with complete attention, and was filled with tenderness for him. Everything was full of wonder tonight.

She felt her hand being grasped and the young mother raised it to her lips, kissing it again and again. Mercy was startled, but then pulled the linked hands back towards her and kissed her new friend in return.

The father presented Paul and another man with a tiny glass, hardly bigger than a large thimble, full of liquid. He handed another to Mercy. They must have brought these glasses with them, among what looked like pitifully few possessions. The man threw his head back and gulped his liquor down. Paul did the same and gagged and spluttered until tears ran down his cheeks. Everyone else laughed heartily, slapping Paul between the shoulder blades. Mercy took a cautious sip. The stuff tasted explosive. Even that small amount was like a fire in her throat! Paul was still recovering, wiping his eyes.

The man held his hand out and Paul took it.

'Petrowski,' he said. 'Tomek Petrowski.' He pointed at his wife. 'Yola Petrowski.'

Mercy and Paul told them their names, and then felt the time had come to leave this new family in peace. With a great deal more nodding and smiling they departed.

It was only when they began to climb the stairs that Mercy noticed a long, oval stain on her dress.

'Oh no – look, blood!' The mark was nearly the size of a hand. 'Must have been off the side of the bed.' She turned to Paul. 'Honestly – next time I go anywhere with you I'm going to wrap myself in an old sack!'

'Oh Mercy,' he laughed. And she heard a wealth of fondness in his voice.

'Where on earth have you been?'

James Adair was pacing the corridor, his expression livid. 'I've looked all over the place for you!'

He was full of pent-up emotion, a mixture of jealousy, frustration and self-righteous anger. He'd known Mercy was with Paul. She should be here, damn it, looking after his son! But then he noticed her dress.

'What's happened? Are you all right?'

Mercy explained. 'I kept coming up to see Stevie was asleep though – every hour or so. He's been perfectly all right!'

'Yes, yes.' James felt his ire melting away. His besotted imagination had tortured him with images of her and Paul alone together . . . but this had clearly not been the case.

'Well—' – he tried to speak lightly – 'how very exciting. I'd better get back to Margaret. She's not at all well tonight. I'll see you tomorrow. Will you be dining with us, or with Paul here? Up to you of course.' He forced himself to sound jovial, an old fuddy-duddy joking about the fact that she might choose to spend time with him.

Mercy looked at Paul.

'It'd be my pleasure,' he said.

'Paul, I think, Mr Adair.' He didn't fail to notice the flush in her cheeks.

'Right you are then.'

He turned away in an agony of contradictory shame and longing.

Chapter Thirty-Two

Mercy tried to spend a short time with Margaret each day, taking Stevie to see her. She called in mid-morning the next day. Margaret seemed no better. She tried to sit up and play with Stevie who wanted to crawl all over her and roll on the bed. Her face was very pale, and her soft, peach-coloured nightgown only seemed to make her complexion look more sickly. Her hair hung down limply and she was weak and lethargic.

Mercy chatted to her, telling her about the Petrowskis' baby and she tried to smile.

'You went down to third class? How brave!'

Mercy refrained from saying she had felt far more at home down there than in first class.

'I'm sorry,' Margaret murmured after a short time, her head lolling back on the pillows. 'You'll have to take him away. This terrible nausea . . . If only I could be somewhere calm and still.' She lay down, grimacing as she moved, and closed her eyes.

'Come on, Stevie.' Mercy lifted him from the bed and he protested for a moment, wrapping himself round her like a monkey. She noticed his nose was running. Perhaps she'd kept him out in the air too long yesterday?

'Could you pass me a little more water?' Margaret barely had enough energy to speak.

Stevie on one arm, Mercy poured a glass of water and passed it to Margaret's outstretched hand. She took a few sips, then whispered, 'James should be back soon. Poor chap – I'm really cramping his style. He'd like to be staying up, dancing, out and about. Perhaps you could dance with him tonight, Mercy? I just can't . . .' She slumped down again.

'It's not your fault, is it?' Mercy said, trying to cheer her. 'Nobody asks to be poorly. I s'pect he's enjoying himself anyway – the ship and that.'

'But he's been so grumpy and out of sorts . . . oh dear . . .' She was slipping into sleep.

Mercy could scarcely wait for Paul to finish his day's stint down in the bowels of the ship. Now it was the third day of the voyage, the ship and the constant circle round them where dark sea met pale sky were losing their novelty and everyone was beginning to need a little more stimulation.

She whiled away the day with Stevie, passing time with some of the other nannies who visited the nursery. Scarcely any were as young as herself, but there was one not much older who was friendly. Ruby was a thin, bright-eyed young woman from Leeds who'd moved south to work for a London family and the two of them chatted idly.

James Adair called in twice to the nursery and Mercy noticed throughout the day that no other fathers did this. Both times he saw she was busy and left again looking ill at ease.

'Funny bloke,' Ruby said the second time. 'You'd never find 'er dad—' – she jerked her head at Charlotte, her two-year-old charge – 'coming down to see if she's all right. Or still alive for that matter.'

'Oh, Mr Adair's very fond of Stevie.'

'Oh yes – is that all 'e's fond of?' Ruby gave a chesty laugh.

'What're you on about?'

'Don't act all innocent. You know what I mean full well.' Ruby rushed off to rescue Charlotte who had fallen bang on her face.

Mercy frowned. Did Ruby mean ... was she saying ...? Uncomfortable thoughts came to her mind of the look in James Adair's eyes when he held her on the bicycle those months ago, of occasions when she'd seen the same look in his eyes since ... But no. What did she know about how men should might look at you? She actually shook her head to dismiss these thoughts. What was she? A servant, that was all. It was just ridiculous.

That night James Adair dined alone again, despite Margaret telling him that she was sure Mercy would come and join him.

Mercy met Paul for dinner and they talked and talked, and laughed together.

After dinner he said, 'Shall we go and see how the Petrowskis are getting on?'

'Ooh yes – I want to see that babby again. But first—'

'You need to look in on Stevie?'

She smiled. Happiness gave her face an extra glow. 'I ought to. That is what I'm here for! And I'll get my coat.'

They found the Petrowskis in the third-class sitting room. The place was furnished for very basic comfort, with slatted wooden seats round the walls. The air was full of smoke, tumblers of ale stood on the tables, round which there was a loud buzz of conversation in different languages, games of cards and dice and in one corner there was a sing-song going on, someone playing a fiddle. Mercy stood on the doorway with Paul looking round at the mass of people with their mix of nationalities and felt rather intimidated. It was if she'd just walked into another country altogether.

But Tomek Petrowski noticed them almost immediately and strode across, talking fast, shaking Paul's hand over and over. He motioned them to come and join his friends. They were a group of Poles, mostly men but a few women also. They all smiled and made welcoming gestures. Work-roughened hands were held out to them. Mercy saw Yola sitting watching her.

She stepped over to sit beside her and everyone made room. Tonight Yola's face was still tired, but relaxed. She welcomed Mercy happily. The baby was lying asleep in her lap, only her tiny face visible.

'Hello,' Mercy smiled. She felt such affection for this woman, strange as it was. 'You look better.' And Yola smiled and nodded back.

Mercy leant round to look at the baby and for a time she and Yola communicated in a universal language of smiles and coos and baby conversation. They sat with their heads close together, Mercy as fair as Yola was dark. When Mercy told her how beautiful the baby was, Mercy knew she understood her meaning.

Yola pointed at the sleeping child and said, 'Peschka.'

'Peschka? Is that her name – Peschka?'

Yola nodded.

'It's very pretty. She's very pretty.' Once more lots of nodding and smiling and appreciating. Yola lifted Mercy's hand and kissed it until Mercy felt quite tearful at receiving so much unbidden affection.

Paul found himself plied with more of the fiery liquor by the men and this time he took miniscule sips. Mercy saw Tomek hand him a slip of paper and a photograph. Paul looked at them and nodded before handing them back. After a time he stood up, looking across at her, asking with raised eyebrows if she was ready to leave. She said goodbye to Yola and joined him.

'I think I'd better go before they get me too tight to move!' he said.

They took their leave, smiling until Mercy felt her face might crack.

'Let's get some fresh air,' Paul said. 'Goodness – I don't know what that stuff is, but it's like drinking lava.'

'What was it they were showing you?' she asked, pulling her coat round her.

'Well—' – He stood back for her to go ahead of him up the stairs –'it seems they've got some relative in New York already – the chap in the picture. A brother or cousin maybe? His is the address Tomek showed me and they're hoping to join him.'

'What d'you mean, hoping?'

'They don't just let everyone in, you know. They have to have all sorts of checks – health and suchlike. They look robust enough to me though. They're from a village near Katowice – at least, I think that's what he meant.'

'They're a lively lot, aren't they?' Mercy said. She found herself feeling anxious for them. 'Imagine travelling all that way, starting a new life somewhere you don't speak a word of the language. I s'pose she hoped they'd reach America before the baby came. I think they're ever so brave.'

'Yes.' They stepped out into the dim light of the promenade deck. 'Sobering thought, isn't it?' He chuckled. 'Maybe that's why they're not keen to stay sober very much of the time!'

They strolled along, passing a few other couples out to

take the air. When they'd walked the length of the second-class promenade deck they stopped, as if of one mind and leant on the side to look out. Mercy breathed in the salt air, the wind buffeting her cheeks. Ever since she'd been aboard the ship her cheeks had taken on a healthy glow. They stood close together, hearing dance music drifting to them from inside, soft, then louder, according to the shifting wind.

Mercy looked at Paul beside her, his pale profile, a lock of his hair moving in the wind, dark against his forehead, the long, slightly crooked nose, wide mouth. At the end of this, she thought, I'll never see him again. And the thought was suddenly unbearable.

'D'you think you could do it?' she asked eventually.

Paul turned to look at her. 'What?'

'Just up sticks and go, like the Poles. Leave everything – your house, family, country – everything you know.'

Paul thought, staring out over the sea, biting his top lip.

'Yes. I really think I could. It's a peculiar thing. Before the War I felt British. English, let's say. It seemed unthinkable that anywhere but England could be home. It was the centre of my world – *the* world come to that, so far as we were concerned. Now though, I feel I could live almost anywhere. It wouldn't make that much difference.'

He snorted. 'We British are so self-important. I suppose instead of feeling English now I just feel human. Like one tiny dot in the human race.'

Mercy listened to him with a strange mixture of emotions. Often when he talked she felt his sadness, the sense that through the War so much had been lost forever. Yet now there also rose in her a pounding sensation of euphoria. That was the other thing he made her feel – he gave her freedom, a heady feeling of excitement! Here, on this ship, she was not trapped by her past, her class, her circumstances. The ship was as class-ridden as anywhere else, but with Paul she could be anyone. She could simply be herself and that was all he required her to be. She moved a little closer to him.

'How long will it take now?'

'A couple of days.' He spoke rather absently. 'As I say, she's not doing her best, nothing like, the poor old girl.'

'I don't really want to get there.'

Paul remained silent. He continued to stare out into the blackness. She felt he had slipped away from her into the world of his own thoughts, leaving her bereft. They had so little time left and she wanted to talk and talk, but he suddenly seemed so distant from her.

'Shall we go in?' she asked eventually, in a flat voice. He agreed with a sigh, and as he followed her downstairs she was acutely aware of his presence behind her. She longed to know why he had gone quiet so suddenly.

They stopped outside Mercy's room. She had been afraid of finding Mr Adair pacing up and down again but there was no sign of him. She looked round at Paul.

'What's up?' she said gently.

His hands were thrust into the pocket of his greatcoat which was, like his suit, too capacious for his build. He stared at her, seemed to be looking deeply into her.

'Paul?' She moved closer, stricken by the look of him. 'What on earth's the matter?'

He shook his head and looked down at his shoes. 'Nothing. Nothing that I can explain anyway.' Looking up again he forced a wan smile. 'Sorry – I can be a moody so-and-so. I don't mean to be.'

'No, you're not,' she said, not quite truthfully.

They stood apart, paralysed by the intensity of feeling in each other's eyes.

'Can I – I mean, shall we eat together tomorrow?' Mercy asked uncertainly.

'If you're sure you'd like to.'

'Paul . . .' Lost for words to describe quite how sure she was, she said, 'I'd like to. Yes. Please.'

'Goodnight then.' He turned away, towards his room. Then he looked back and said softly, 'Sweet dreams.'

Mercy's hands trembled as she unfastened her dress. She felt churned up. She knew how strong her feelings were for Paul with far more certainty than she ever had with Tom. She had wanted to go to him out on the landing and take him in her arms.

But she was very anxious and unsure. His melancholy eyes seemed to look at her from every corner of her mind. She didn't know if he returned her love. Life had given her so little love, and she didn't dare to expect it from anyone. Why should he feel the same? she thought. It had felt as if Paul was drawing away from her tonight and it all made her unsettled, full of longing, and afraid.

She tucked Stevie in and lay down in her own bed, her cheeks burning. The pillow was not sufficient to cool them. She turned on her back, the light still on, casting a soft circle on the ceiling. All she could think of was Paul, his thin body wrapped somehow pitifully in that enormous coat, the way he looked at her, how tender his eyes had been at the sight of little Peschka, how she could speak about anything to him and feel safe, how kind he was. But maybe that was all it was – kindness? Even though he seemed to look at her with such feeling.

She tossed from side to side. Time I turned the light off, she thought. But how ever am I going to get to sleep in this state?

Eventually she got up, went to the mirror and unfastened her hair to brush it out. Her face was glowing with health, the reflection of her large eyes seeming to burn back at her. She brushed her hair forward over one shoulder.

'I love you, Paul,' she dared to whisper. 'I really, really love you.'

She put the brush down and brought her hands together, close to her face as if praying, giggling quietly at herself for her silliness. Then her face sobered. 'Goodness only knows what he thinks of me though.' She longed to feel certain, for the strength that would bring.

A knock on the door made her jump. She listened, heart thumping hard. Could it be Paul? She flung her hair back and went to the door, not thinking of anything but that he wanted to see her again.

'Please. Let me in. Just for a moment.'

James Adair's tone was so urgent, distraught, that she stood back immediately and he stepped into the middle of the room. He had no coat or hat on and his tie was pulled askew. Mercy closed the door and stood with her arms folded.

'Whatever's the matter? Is it Mrs Adair? If you're worried about Stevie, he's perfectly all right. I know he's got a bit of a cold but look – he's not even feverish or—'

'No.' He turned away from her. 'No – none of that. Margaret's asleep.'

He sank down on the edge of her bed as if his legs had given way. 'I was just getting ready to retire for the night and I . . .'

He looked across at her and Mercy was startled by

the anguish in his face. She stood before him, completely unaware of her effect on him, how in his eyes she looked like an angel in her white nightdress, the curves of her breasts, the mass of gold hair tossed down her back.

'Mercy – oh God, God,' he groaned, burying his head in his hands. She was appalled to see him begin to weep, dry, desperate sobs shaking his whole frame.

'Oh goodness – whatever's the matter? Please don't, Mr Adair.' She paced up and down in front of him, clasping and unclasping her hands, completely unable to think what to do.

He raised his face and she saw tears in his eyes. He held out his arms.

'Save me.' He was past holding back now. Whatever was moral, seemly, correct, he was quite beyond all of it. 'Please say you'll come to me. I can't stand it any more. I love you, Mercy. I can't sleep. I can't rest or work for thinking of you. Look at me! Before you came, I was a man asleep. I didn't know it was possible to feel like this. All I can see is you until sometimes I think I'm making myself ill with it.' He covered his face with his hands again.

Mercy stood in front of him quite still, eyes wide and frightened. Her mind was in complete confusion. What Ruby had said . . . No, she had fallen asleep and this was a dream. James Adair sitting on her bed saying these things, crying over her, it wasn't real.

'If I can't touch you I'm going to go out of my mind.' He looked up again. 'The very sight of you . . . I can't go on like this, Mercy. You've got to save me.'

Her mouth had gone dry. 'Save you?' She could barely get the words out. 'What d'you mean?'

'Margaret wouldn't mind, if that's what you're thinking.' He stood up, words flooding from his lips which he'd said over and over to himself in justification. 'She doesn't really like – any of it. And she's ill. You'll be helping her, though of course she mustn't know. It's not wrong, Mercy, believe me . . .' She was shrinking away from him, holding herself very tight. Blood pounded in her ears.

'Wrong?' she whispered. 'I don't know what you mean.'

He seemed to loom over her and she felt tiny beside him. He put his hands on her shoulders. She saw his face twitch with emotion, his forehead perspiring.

'It's the best thing in the world, a beautiful thing. Oh, whatever it is, I can't be obedient any longer. This has to be right!'

Her mind seemed to have stopped working. She felt completely paralysed, unable to speak or think, she was so afraid. Surely he didn't mean . . . She remembered Johnny pushing her up against the wall that night . . . Mr Adair wouldn't . . . No, he couldn't mean . . .?

He turned her round to face the mirror. Her stunned face stared back at her. She felt it was someone else, a stranger.

'Look at yourself. You're the most lovely, perfect thing I've ever seen.' He leant down and put his face beside hers. 'Look at us, my loved one.' She felt his breath hot on her neck. He pushed her hair gently aside and his lips brushed the flesh just behind her right ear. She could feel the prickle of his moustache. Somewhere in her mind a voice – not even a voice, an impulse – hammered, stop him . . . This is wrong. Wrong! But she felt hypnotized by the strength and authority of his desire. How could she argue? How could she go against Mr Adair? She should do something, say something, but she couldn't speak or move.

His hands moved round her, enormous and dark against the white nightdress. Trembling, hardly daring at first, then feverishly, he began to fondle her breasts. She heard his breath catch behind her and he gave a groan of surrender. She was mortified by his touch. It started to hurt and she gave a whimper – 'Please!' – which made him grasp her even more firmly. Her cheeks were burning. She felt dirty. This was wrong, all wrong, horrible . . .

Help me – please, God Almighty, help me, she prayed. Help me tell him to get off . . .

'Mr Adair!' Tearful, she tried to turn and face him. 'This ain't right—'

'Oh it is . . .' He held her tightly. His body was strong, taut with need. 'It's the rightest thing that's ever happened. I love you, Mercy. I adore you. This was ordained by the gods . . .'

He released her and began to fling off his clothes.

I should run . . . She eyed the door. But where to? To Margaret? Paul? How could she go out there, half dressed, and admit this to either of them? It was impossible. And still she couldn't scream, shout. Not to Mr Adair. She was trapped by his desire, his power over her.

'I want to see you,' he was saying. 'To be naked with you. Adam and Eve in the garden . . .' He was feverish with impatience, flinging his shoes across the room.

Naked, he presented himself to her, walking towards her, proud, his body as a gift. Tears poured down Mercy's face. She was shivering, wretched, afraid of him with his acrid, foreign smell, that cloud of hair at his groin, his . . . his . . . she couldn't even say the word to herself . . . standing up like that . . .

'Oh no – no!' Her voice cracked. 'I don't like this. Please, Mr Adair, get dressed again. This is all a mistake. I don't know how I've given you wrong ideas, but this isn't right! You can't mean to . . .'

James came to her, arms outstretched and she shrank away, sobbing. 'My dear, sweet, Mercy.' He was a fraction calmer, and spoke soothingly. 'Don't be afraid, my lovely, my darling one. Don't you see how much I feel for you? I'm going to help you. I want to be the first to teach you, to give you all the pleasure in the world.' He bent to lift the hem of her nightdress.

Pleasure? She found herself looking down at the back of his head where his hair was thinning. What did this have to do with pleasure?

'Raise your arms,' he instructed firmly.

She resisted for a moment, but then half raised them. He pulled the garment roughly over her elbows. Mercy gasped as the cool air brought her body up in gooseflesh.

'There we are, my love.' He took one of her hands and held her away from him to admire her slim, curvaceous body. 'How could anything so beautiful be wrong? You must believe that.'

'What're you going to do to me?' she said in a small voice.

'Come here.' He pulled her into his arms, letting out a sound of pleasure as he felt her against him.

'Please, just let me go . . .' she sobbed. 'I don't want to have a babby!'

'No, no – you won't, my dear one. It doesn't happen just straight away, you know, it takes some time. Believe me.'

Her view of him was level with his collarbones and the sprinkling of sandy, curling hairs on his flushed chest. She turned her head up to look into his face, her eyes wide and welling with tears. Perhaps if she looked into his eyes, she thought, he'd see how much she wanted him to stop.

But his hands were moving on her buttocks, pressing his body, jerking, against her, hard into her stomach. His eyes closed. He wasn't seeing her any more. She cried out, horrified at the feel of his fingers between her legs.

Abruptly he made her lie down. The bedcover felt cold against her back. She knew she couldn't fight him. She must do as she was told and it might be over quickly.

'That's it – I need . . .' He forced his way up hard inside her, instinct driving him. Mercy screwed her eyes shut at the tearing, burning pain. She whimpered, then it eased a little and he was thrusting, panting, groaning, anguish and relief at once flooding his face. His climax was intense, silent. Then he fell into her arms, half laughing, half weeping, twitching faintly inside her. Her tears trickled back into her hair. Every trace of her freedom and euphoria with Paul was wiped away. For those moments she was Mercy Hanley, rubbish off the street, something to be taken and used by everyone. She had never felt such despair.

He kissed her wet face again and again. 'You see? I told you, didn't I? You angel. Oh, my little angel.'

After he'd dressed himself and gone she lay, damp and burning between her legs. Her body felt very cold. She couldn't stop shaking and weeping.

Eventually, teeth chattering, she got up and washed herself, tears still rolling down her cheeks. She couldn't bear the thought of ever lying in her own bed again. Climbing in beside Stevie, she wrapped her arms round him, curled up tight beside his innocent, oblivious warmth.

Chapter Thirty-Three

Stevie woke her the next morning, poking his fingers experimentally in her ears and nose, trying to prise open her eyelids, enchanted at the novelty of finding her in his bed.

Light filtered through the curtains. The soreness between her legs was a reminder of what otherwise would have seemed a crazed dream. That she had seen James Adair in that state, what he had done – what she had allowed him to do – seemed impossible in the morning light. Thinking only of himself he had taken from her the innocence a woman was supposed to prize.

But her body had taken in the enormity of what had happened. Her head ached and her limbs were like lead. She felt numb and shrunken inside.

'Stevie – don't,' she pleaded as he kneaded at her face. She rolled over, shielding her head with a moan. If only she could just lie here all day, bury herself and hide from everyone. Most terrible was the thought of facing Margaret Adair. Their friendship now could never be as it was: she could never confide this to her. If only she could just disappear and never see either of them again! But she knew that somehow she had to rally herself, act as if nothing had happened, look after Stevie.

Once she left her room, the night before did seem to fade into unreality, especially when James Adair came to find her in the nursery. He drew her out of the door so they could still see Stevie pushing a little wooden trolley. He was his usual reserved, courteous self.

'I came to invite you to dine with me tonight,' he said politely. She saw he was nervous, left hand smoothing his moustache, which increased her feeling of bewilderment. 'If you would like to join me?'

'I . . .' She felt like weeping and couldn't meet his eyes. Was he completely barmy? Even his look seemed to contaminate her. She spoke very quietly. 'No – no, thank you.'

'I see.' He became curt. 'Are you dining with Paul Louth?'

Mercy nodded. She knew Ruby was watching them.

There was a pause, then he said, 'I could order you.'

She couldn't look up. She just stared at the floor in silence.

'Very well then,' he said savagely. 'I'm glad to know you've made such a fine friend.'

Mercy watched him stride away. What have I done? she wondered. Everything felt desolate, as if nothing good could come of anything now.

She moved over quickly and picked up Stevie's little coat to go outside. She didn't want to be with anyone today.

James Adair found himself pacing the promenade deck alone for the umpteenth time of the voyage.

When he thought of the night before, need stirred in him again, the relentless, imprisoning gnaw of it. Yet that piercing mixture of agony and shame he had seen in Mercy! She who had always been so clear-eyed, sunny-faced, looked so drained this morning, was unable even to meet his eyes.

He slammed his fist down on the side. Damn her! She'd wanted him all right last night, hadn't she? It had been – he smiled grimly – extraordinary. Not just the satisfying of his desire but the fulfilment so longed for by his hungering soul. So what the hell was the matter with the girl, giving him those hangdog, hostile looks?

He turned, touching his hat to a couple walking towards him. Very queer fish, women, that was the truth of it. All he knew was that it was right, what had happened. Intended. It was an experience that had burnt through his life, brief, illuminated. And it had had to happen here. At home it could never be. Not in his real, morally confined life. This period on the water was his special gift from life, his epiphany . . .

A surge of panic interrupted this lofty thought. He hadn't made her promise not to say anything to Margaret! Of course she wouldn't, surely – how could she? It would cost her her living, she must see that! But he knew he must say it. 'You mustn't say a word to Margaret, you know, Mercy. You do know what would happen, don't you?'

He felt euphoric again suddenly. The supple loveliness of her moved in his mind's eye, still his, for a short time yet, left to enjoy.

'Are you all right?'

Paul looked closely at her across the table, dishes of tomato soup and crumbled bread on plates between them. Mercy could barely eat.

'Yes. 'Course I am,' she said dully.

'You look tired,' he said, so kindly that her eyes filled with tears which had waited all day to be shed.

'Oh dear.' Paul sounded really concerned. 'Mercy what is it?'

'Nothing – honest.' She wiped her eyes and forced a smile. 'It's just tiredness. Stevie was restless last night, sorry. Look.' She tried to divert him, holding out her arm. 'The oil all came out.'

It was almost true. The mark was hard to detect now amid the soft-edged pattern of leaves.

As they ate she tried to pull herself together. Nervously she asked Paul questions about his day, trying to be jolly, joking about Stanley who was of course dining in first class.

'And did Mr Adair want you to dine first class tonight?' Paul teased.

Mercy felt herself freeze. 'Yes.' She kept her eyes on her plate. 'I said I'd rather be with you.' She spoke so fiercely that Paul frowned for a moment.

'He's tolerant.'

'Yes.' She was only just short of snapping at him.

'I thought you liked him.'

'What d'you mean?' She cursed herself for sounding so alarmed.

'I don't mean anything! I just thought he was a kind employer. Mercy, what is the matter tonight?'

'Nothing.' Nothing, except that everything, everything was spoilt and dirty.

They didn't find the Petrowkis that evening. Mercy was disappointed. She was longing to be alone with Paul yet dreading it at the same time, afraid. There may be only one night left after this, she thought, as they went up on deck. And then he'll be gone.

'Let's stay out all night,' she said. Nothing would induce her to return to that terrible room early tonight.

Paul gave his chuckle. 'What, and have them find us frozen to death in the morning?'

I shouldn't mind if I was with you, she thought.

The future, the idea of going on without him, returning with the Adairs, was utterly desolate. She found herself unable to joke any longer and fell silent.

They walked along the boat deck, the lifeboats lined up between them and the sea. It was blowing hard tonight and Mercy and Paul both took their hats off for fear of losing them.

'Let's sit here!' Paul said. A bench facing the stern of the ship offered a small respite from the buffeting. They had to sit close to hear each other speak.

'Reminds me, when I come up here, of going to France.'

Mercy looked round at him. Their faces were in the shadows. She was relieved to hear him talk. She desperately wanted things to be right between them. Here, in the darkness, she willed herself to think of nothing but Paul, so that these moments were the only ones that mattered, unspoilt by James Adair.

'D'you think about the War a lot?'

'Yes – even though I try not to. It never leaves you.'

'Paul,' she said, suddenly, 'please don't ever leave me.'

For a second he was still. Then with a fierce motion he pulled her to him, almost knocking the breath out of her, and she was pressed into his arms, her head resting under his chin. She felt his trembling, the hard beat of his heart.

'I love you.' She knew somehow she must speak first. 'I love you, Paul.'

Afraid, she looked up. But everything she needed to see was there. The emotion in his face overwhelmed her.

'Mercy—' – his eyes were serious – 'I was afraid that—'

'What?'

'That I felt too much, that you couldn't possibly feel the same, not so soon. I've become so used to being alone – I mean, deeply alone, within myself. I had begun to think this was how it would always be. But you just came and . . . you make me feel complete – more human. As if with you is the only place I fit.'

'Yes,' she said, hearing him describe her own feeling. 'Sort of coming home. I've never had a home before – not a proper one.' She began to cry suddenly, brokenly. Paul rocked her, stroking her.

'Perhaps with each other is the only way we can fit. I don't know how – we'll work out a way somehow.'

When she had calmed a little, his face moved down to hers and their lips met, warm, searching, arms holding each other with such tender force. Mercy could hear a pounding in her ears as if her blood and the sea were one. She felt Paul's frail frame in her arms, his eyes closed, face intent. She wanted to stay in this moment for ever, where no other thoughts and feelings, no other person could intervene.

He rested his cheek against the top of her head and gave a huge sigh of joy and relief. She reached up and stroked his face.

'You're too gentle to fight, Paul. Too kind.'

'No.' His voice was profoundly sad. 'No – I'm not. That's the worst of it. It'd be good if we were all too gentle to fight. Mercy—'

She turned her face up to him.

'That's better.' He cupped her cheeks in his hands, wiping her tears away with his thumbs. 'You're so, so lovely . . . every time I see you I feel weak just looking at you.'

She smiled. 'Do you? I couldn't tell.'

For a few seconds their lips met in quick, playful kisses, then at length, urgent, passionate, the strength of their feeling expressed wordlessly.

Later they walked together again, arms wrapped round each other. They strolled back and forth, along the gently rolling deck, amid all the noises of the ship. There was a half moon tonight, as if it had been rubbed away as in a child's drawing. Nothing else mattered to Mercy, not the coldness of her hands and feet, nor James Adair or even Stevie. The only important things were Paul and what the two of them felt for each other.

He stopped her in the middle of the deserted promenade and took her in his arms again, smiling joyfully into her face.

'You look happy,' she said.

'Happy isn't even an adequate word.'

'Paul.' Her face became painfully anxious. 'Am I good enough for you? I don't feel ... you know, I've done things I'm ashamed of. I'm not ...' The reality of last night crashed back in on her. It was so raw, recent. I'm not what you think, I'm spoilt, she wanted to tell him. I'm not worthy of you.

'A good enough person?' His tone verged on anger. 'How can you ask me that? You're the only person. You've made me feel whole again – I can't get near anyone else. Nobody. But with you everything's different, I love you Mercy, more than I thought I'd ever be capable of loving anyone again.'

'But I'm not good,' she insisted. She couldn't look at him. However much she wanted to put it out of her mind, the stain of James Adair was on her. Her face burned with shame.

Paul shook her lightly to make her look up. 'Mercy,' he said gently. 'Don't think like this, please. Whatever could you have done that's so bad? Isn't it that things have been done to you? And perhaps you should think about whether I'm good enough for you. I've killed other men. Not perhaps, but certainly. I've seen men fall under my fire and that's the truth. Think of that and ask yourself if I'm worthy of you.'

'But—' She was glad he couldn't see the red in her cheeks. She had had her innocence taken from her.

'What is it?'

She looked into his kind, loving eyes. 'Nothing.'

'Look, what difference does anything make here – where we've come from, what we've done or been? I told you, we're all just people. All the same fundamentally. That's all that matters.'

She gave in, falling into his arms. 'I love you so, so much. This is the happiest I can remember being ever!'

'Yes.' He kissed her eyelids, nose, lips. 'Me too.'

They stayed out very late, as late as Mercy could possibly waylay him, though that took very little effort. Neither of them wanted to let the other go. When they finally returned inside their hands were stiff with cold, cheeks raw from the wind. They talked and touched, kissed, warmed each other for hours. Time fled past.

Mercy felt her insides turn with apprehension. Stevie! She had completely forgotten about him! But when she reached the door of her room all was quiet.

'It's nearly twelve fifteen!' Paul said.

'Marvellous nanny, I am.' Mercy rolled her eyes. 'Still, it sounds as if there's been nothing wrong.'

'I should have reminded you.' He rested his hands on her shoulders. 'On a night like tonight though, it's hardly surprising we forgot.' Mercy looked up, loving his smile, his wide mouth, loved every atom of him. She reached up to kiss him and they held each other again.

'Goodnight,' she said. 'I'm so happy, Paul.'

'And me. I can't believe how much.' He squeezed her tight, then released her. 'Tomorrow night?'

'How can you even ask!' She poked him, teasing. 'I wish it was now.'

He went to his door and she watched him. They blew each other a kiss. He waved before he closed his door.

Mercy turned to go inside and saw James Adair moving fast down the corridor towards her room.

In panic she rushed inside and shut the door, locked it, and stood inside, panting loudly, her heart racing.

In a moment she heard his knock.

No! She was trembling. It was so late – surely he hadn't been waiting, watching them even? She stood with a fist clenched to her lips. A terrible helplessness washed over her. What could she do? He was her employer. If she didn't do as he asked could he refuse to let her back on the ship for the return voyage? Leave her stranded? She could run out and shout for help, but then everyone would know – Paul would know. She was trapped. Unless she just ignored him – perhaps he would be shamed into going away.

Another, sharper knock followed.

'I need to see my son,' he said, with icy politeness. 'Open the door, please, Mercy.'

Eventually she opened it a crack, starting violently at the sight of him even though she had known he was there.

'What's the matter?' He sounded livid, pushed his way in straight away. 'Expecting a knock from someone else?'

'No.' She could barely speak. She was shaking all over. At least she was fully clothed. She couldn't be said to be offering temptation . . . If only she'd told Paul, if only – but how could she have done? James pushed her out of the way and closed the door, standing against it.

'Please – no,' she implored him. 'Stevie's not really asleep. Not in front of your son. It's so late, and . . .'

'And?' The chillness of his voice gave her no clue to the reservoir of pent-up emotion which had built in him all evening, as the night grew later, knowing she was with Paul. 'What's the matter, my dear? I thought we'd come to an agreement?'

'What? What agreement?' What was he saying?

He went and stood over Stevie, half-whispering so as not to disturb him.

'Just for the voyage, we shall enjoy this little arrangement together. You won't say a word to Margaret because if you do, when we reach England you'll be without employment or references. When we get home, we shall resume life as it was and I shall not come to you again.'

She could see his high colour, knew he'd been drinking and in some quantity.

'Does that sound fair?'

'Fair?' she asked faintly. 'How can it be fair when you ain't – aren't – giving me any choice?'

'Oh, I think you have a choice, Mercy. You could just go now, out of here. Go on – go.'

She looked desperately at the door. 'Should I spend the night outside then?'

'If you consider being with me a worse option, then yes.' He stepped towards her as she was still wildly eyeing the door, and gave a heavy sigh. 'It's a torment to me, seeing you look at me like that, knowing you've been with him all evening.'

'Mr Adair—'

'James, for heaven's sake!'

'I'm in love with Paul Louth!' she gabbled. 'And he loves me. I don't want this. You're spoiling everything. It's wrong of you—'

James actually flung his head back and laughed loudly. Mercy looked across at Stevie, praying he would wake, but there was no sound from him.

'Paul Louth – you can be sure – wants just the same from you as I do, my dear. That's students for you. Anyhow – if that's what he wants at least I can give you some practice!'

He put his hands on her shoulders with a kind of confidence which said he owned her. Hatred and fury surged inside her. She collected saliva in her mouth and spat it into his face, her eyes narrowed with loathing.

'You don't deserve your wife. She's kind and sweet and a lady. But you – you may be a gentleman on the outside, but underneath you're just filth, worse than filth.'

Slowly, as if in a daze, James wiped her spittle from his nose and cheek.

'I see.' His voice was so cold with fury, Mercy felt herself go rigid with fear. 'So it's going to be different today is it, angel?'

He was on to her before she stood a chance of moving, tearing at her, hurling her back on the bed, half winding her. His face was a grotesque mixture of lust and fury. He pulled her legs in the air and stripped her as she tried to kick at him.

'Stevie – Stevie, wake up!' she shrieked. 'Look what your daddy's doing. This'll make you proud of him, won't it?'

'Shut up.' James's red face loomed close to her. He was holding her down with one hand, unbuttoning himself frantically with the other. 'Just shut your mouth.'

He lunged into her, face straining. 'That's it – now I'll have you . . .'

Mercy lay under him, squeezing her eyes closed. She was dry-eyed with loathing and disgust. Hold tight until he's finished, she thought. Just hold on and it'll be over and he's never, ever going to do this again . . . Over and over she repeated it in her mind to his lunging rhythm: never, never, never . . .

He rolled off her, leaving her curled up, wet with his sweat and juices and, at last, with her own tears pouring from her in a torrent of shame. He enclosed his sticky body in his clothes, disgust and horror settling on him like extra garments. He looked down at the pitiful little body on the bed.

What had happened to his glorious ideals of their love, his fantasy of her gratitude and devotion? She was lying there, naked and vulnerable, curled up with her hands over her eyes, unable even to bear looking at him.

He let himself out of her room without a word and walked disconsolately back to his own. What a fool he was! A naive, ridiculous idiot, seeking paradise between the thighs of a servant like many another boorish master! That his behaviour fell into the realms of such a run-of-the-mill cliché only increased his despair.

All of it was finished, he knew. He would avoid her from now on – in America, once he was busy with Kesler this would be easy. And once they were back in England she would have to be moved on. He couldn't have her there, knowing, reminding. And Margaret – the thought of her knowing how he had behaved, he who always saw himself as superior to her! Oh, the humilation! The thought was too appalling to contemplate.

He did not think though, that she would tell Margaret. He tried to rally himself. Why should he let her have this power over him? Who was she, anyway? A servant, dross from the workhouse, a nobody! He should just forget it.

But his last sight of her would not leave his mind, her utter dejection as she lay there on her bed. He burned now with contempt, with remorse for his grotesque behaviour. And he was weighed down by sadness – for his loss of innocence: for her bitter tears.

Chapter Thirty-Four

'This is our last night,' she said to Paul the next evening with a heavy sigh. She was longing to leave the ship: her room now filled her with abhorrence. What had happened in there with James Adair could not be undone. He had shamed and abused her, and while she was on the ship she could never get away from the fact. Once off the ship it would be over. Finished. James Adair's madness was something conjured by the sea.

But she was also afraid that with the landfall something else would evaporate: the magic wonder of Paul loving her. She was afraid he would see her with new, more critical eyes. She knew she would love him whatever.

They sat after dinner in the second-class saloon. First class and James Adair felt like another existence. Raw and fresh as his forced visits to her were, Mercy had grown used to pushing things she couldn't bear to think about into the darkest pockets of her mind. She didn't want any sadness or pain to colour her time with Paul.

They talked of what Paul was to do next.

'I'll be on the return voyage of course. The next main thing will be to look for a job.'

'On a ship?'

'Oh no – not actually on a ship. I'm best at design, I think, so it could be marine engineering – I'll have to see what opportunities there are. So – the future's rather uncertain. Shall you mind that?'

Mercy's heart stepped up its pace. He was including her in his future!

'No! All I'd mind is not being able to be with you.'

Paul laid his hand gently on hers. 'You're so sweet and trusting. But it may take a little time before I have a living.'

Mercy looked up earnestly at him. 'Paul – knowing that I've got you – somewhere – that we love one another . . . They're the things that matter most. The only things.'

Eventually, as usual, they went outside, where a quietness overcame them both. It was a clearer night than the three before, the wind gentler, and they kept their hats on, Paul's misshapen trilby, Mercy's hat with the brim. Paul smoked a cigarette.

After a while, Paul said, 'I wonder where we'll be in a year.'

'Don't!' Mercy shuddered.

'What's the matter?'

'I don't like talking like that.'

He stamped the cigarette out and put his arm round her shoulders, pulling her close, then gently removed her hat, freeing the pin and pushing it carefully through the brim to keep it safe. He kissed her hair. Mercy closed her eyes and leant against him.

'All I want', Paul said softly, 'is to look after you. Care for you. It's all that matters. Both of us seem to be so alone in the world.'

She opened her eyes and wrapped her arms round his neck, felt his round her. He was still holding her hat.

'Do you really love me?' she asked urgently. 'Really?'

'Of course. More than I can say.' He went to kiss her but she held back.

'You could forgive me – anything?'

'Mercy.' He stroked her face. 'Why do you feel so bad and unworthy? Of course, my love, anything.'

She held him tight, kissed him, overwhelmed by his care and trust.

'Listen,' he said after a time. 'You can hear the music even better tonight. Can you dance?'

'Me? No!'

He laughed. 'No, nor me. But let's do it anyway!'

He laid her hat on a chair and, oblivious of two men pacing the deck, they grasped each other awkwardly. Mercy couldn't forget being hauled around the dance floor by James Adair. Paul held out his left hand and Mercy placed her right hand in it, looking uncertainly into his eyes.

They started off swaying and shuffling, each trying to move in different directions and stumbling over the other's feet. By trial and error they made up their own half-galloping, half-twirling dance up and down the deck until Mercy was panting and whooping with joy. Ignoring the music, they linked hands and spun round and round, counterbalancing each other, until the windows, cables, funnels, sky, became a spinning circle of lines and blurred light.

'Stop – my head's gone all funny!' she begged.

Laughing like children, they held and steadied each other, Paul's back resting against the side of one of the lifeboats. When their laughter faded it was replaced in his face by a solemn, hungry expression. He took her cheeks between his warm palms, gently stroking her face and looking at her with such a longing intensity that she felt awed.

'I love you,' she said, afraid for a second.

'I never thought . . .' He paused for a second. 'I never thought I should ever feel anything this strongly.'

She looked into his face and saw her whole world in front of her. For a long time they stood in each other's arms on the deck of the *Mauretania*, a tiny island of love and hopefulness in a dark, hurtful world.

Much later, dizzy with happiness from Paul's embraces, she lay in her room.

'I don't want to go back in,' she'd said. 'I want to stay out all night.'

Paul squeezed her shoulders. 'Anyone'd think that room was haunted.'

Mercy gave a pained frown in the darkness. 'It is.'

If James Adair came tonight, he could knock the door down before she opened it. He could do no worse to her than he had already done.

But the night was undisturbed. He didn't come. She slept.

She was woken by knocking, gentle, then louder and more insistent.

She could tell by the sound that it wasn't James Adair.

'Mercy?' Paul hissed as she opened the door a crack. 'We're coming in. You can see land. Come up on deck!'

'What time is it?' She felt disorientated.

'Only seven – will you come?'

She wouldn't miss it for anything. 'But I'll have to bring Stevie . . .'

She dressed herself hurriedly, then the sleepy boy, wrapping him warmly. Paul waited for them outside.

'Let me take him,' Paul offered. 'He's such a weight for you.'

Stevie went to Paul without protest, and sat quiet and

wide-eyed as they went up on deck. Mercy followed, smiling at the sight of Stevie's little hand draped over Paul's shoulder.

It was chilly and damp, the early morning sky rubbed with smudges of darker cloud. Mercy felt the air stinging her nose. There were already a number of people up on deck, all looking in the same direction, some raising a hand to their brows as if better to focus their vision.

Paul led Mercy to a space where they could see. And there it was, already closer than she had expected, there, with sea all around her, the statue on her plinth in the mouth of New York harbour. From here she still looked grey and indistinct. Beyond her they could just see little puffs of steam from boats further into the harbour.

'Lady Liberty,' Paul said.

'Is that what it is?'

'The Statue of Liberty. She's holding up a torch for freedom.'

The end of his sentence was lost in a massive blast of sound from the *Mauretania*, as if in salute, as she rode majestically into the harbour.

'Look,' Mercy said. 'Look at that.'

It was as if they'd entered a fairy tale. A magical, unpredictable land was rising out of the sea to greet her. Her stomach fluttered with expectation. Between the shifting water and pale sky, the uneven line of buildings, high, pointed towers, square, blockish constructions, too distant as yet to see their detail, some tall, some squat, seemed flat and melded together from here as if in a painting, with its unique proportion and beauty. Mercy narrowed her eyes, trying to see it more clearly.

'It's hard to imagine there are streets and people behind there, isn't it?' Paul said.

'It looks lovely.' Mercy leant her head against his

shoulder. His old coat felt soft and worn. 'Let's stay here, shall we? Just live in America and never come back.'

Everything felt different now land was in sight. There was a new purposefulness in the air after the languor of the crossing. She and Paul would soon have to part: he was wanted at work downstairs.

'But we shall see each other,' he said as they climbed down from the deck. 'I'll make sure of that. You're staying with this Mr Kesler, aren't you?'

Mercy could not hide the dread his words aroused in her. She would have to live in the same house as Mr Adair. She wouldn't be able to avoid him as easily as she had done on the ship. A wave of terrible emotion passed through her as land drew closer.

'I don't know where. I'll ask Mrs Adair to write the address for you and put it under your door,' she said, subdued.

'Cheer up.' Paul squeezed her hand. 'Things'll work out. Have faith.'

'Oh,' Mercy said wanly. 'Yes. I s'pose.'

'You know,' we ought to go and say goodbye to the Petrowskis! They won't be going the same way as us.'

'Won't they? Why not?'

'They take all the steerage immigrants over to Ellis Island to be processed, I gather. To see if they're going to be allowed in.'

'You don't really think they won't be allowed to stay?'

'It's possible. They do turn people away. But they must have a good chance.'

They went down to third class, Mercy carrying Stevie. The Petrowskis were, as ever, pleased to see them, but enormous anxiety now showed in their faces. They looked as if they'd been too worried to sleep. Yola was tearful. She was sitting in the overcrowded, smoky third-class saloon holding Peschka, a pitiful little bundle of belongings tied in a shawl, resting at her feet. She grasped Mercy's hand and pulled her down beside her, with Stevie on her lap. Mercy could see the mingled hope and desperation in her eyes. She squeezed Yola's hand, kissed it. Tomek and Paul were shaking hands, hugging. Tomek showed Paul his precious slip of paper again.

Yola started talking in agitation, the Polish words cascading from her lips.

'Oh Yola, I wish I understood you better,' Mercy said, trying to show with her own eyes all she hoped and prayed for this new little family. She reached over and stroked Peschka's forehead. Yola looked down at the baby, pride, love, fear all clear in her eyes.

'Yola,' Mercy said, 'I wish you and Tomek and Peschka all the luck in the world. I hope you find your family and everything goes well for you.'

She suddenly knew a way to make Yola understand all she hoped for them. Awkwardly, touching her fingers first to her forehead, she made the sign of the cross. Yola flung her arms round her and they held each other in a tight embrace.

On the way upstairs, Mercy burst into tears in earnest, all her gathered emotions coming to the surface.

Paul gently touched her shoulder. 'Don't worry, my love. They have a good chance, and so do we.'

They had to part. Even though she hoped it would not be for long, Mercy felt her heart was being torn out. She looked up at him with huge, sad eyes.

'I love you, Paul.'

'I love you,' he said, kissing her. 'Don't worry.'

*

Margaret Adair was still very weak and groggy.

'I'm sure I shall feel better just for being off this ship,' she said. Mercy helped her wash and clothe herself.

They all sat in silence together in the first-class saloon, waiting to disembark. James Adair was very distant, businesslike. Just once, Mercy felt his gaze on her, but when she looked at him he immediately turned away. In that second, Mercy was chilled by the disgust she saw in his expression. The same emotion, and more, had showed itself in her own.

She wanted passionately at that moment to be away from them both. Now she had met Paul she could only feel diminished by them. To them she was a servant – Margaret was exceptionally kind, it was true, but he had shown what he thought of her. She was something to be used, like an old rag, then thrown away. And both of them were deceiving Margaret. Mercy sat full of shame and revulsion. But here, now, thousands of miles from home, she could do nothing. Margaret needed her to care for Stevie more than ever before.

'I don't think I'm going to be able to walk far, I'm afraid.' Margaret's voice was thin and feeble. She had visibly lost weight during the voyage, eating very little and then not keeping it down.

'You won't need to walk. Kesler said he'd send a car.' James spoke so abruptly he almost snapped at her. He picked Stevie up and went to stand by the window, making a show of talking to his son. Showing what a marvellous father he is, Mercy thought savagely.

'Oh dear,' Margaret put her hand to her head in distress. 'I do feel so ill. And I feel such a fool letting James down like this, but really I can't help it. And he's so angry and tense – look at him. I know it's my fault.'

No, Mercy wanted to assure her. You haven't let him down. It's the two of us who have let you down, and far, far more badly than you know.

'Stay with me, Mercy,' Margaret implored. 'I'll be able to bear it all if you're with me.'

''Course I will.' Mercy squeezed her arm. 'Where else would I be going?'

'But you must see him while he's here, my dear.' Mercy had asked her earlier for Kesler's address. 'That young Mr Louth. I insist. I want you to have a happy time, Mercy. Some freedom. You'll only be young once.'

Kesler's driver was a talkative fellow with a stocky body, a jauntily angled Homburg and a thick accent Mercy couldn't at first identify.

'A warm welcome to the United States of America,' he said, after James had spotted him among the throng outside the Battery, holding a piece of card which had, ADAIRS FROM ENGLAND printed on it. He introduced himself as Tommy O'Sullivan, shaking their hands with his huge, brawny one.

James said curtly, 'Do we have far to go?'

Margaret had only just endured the formalities of arrival.

'No, sir,' Tommy O'Sullivan said, not seeming to notice James's rudeness. 'Not far at all. Well, hello there little fella!' His stubbly cheeks shifted into a wide smile at Stevie. 'We'll have to find you some candy when we get on home.'

The road was busy, but Tommy had managed to park the car remarkably close.

'Nice machine Kesler's got there,' James said, thawing a little at the sight of the stylish black motor car.

'Yes, sir,' Tommy said. 'Ford T – nothing but the best for Mr Kesler.'

Between them they helped Margaret into the back seat and she sank into it gratefully, closing her eyes. Tommy stowed their bags. Mercy sat Stevie between herself and Margaret, and James removed his hat and took his seat at the front. He did not turn round.

Mercy stared at the back of his head. He sat very stiff and upright. Beside Tommy O'Sullivan's easy lounge at the wheel he looked rather foolish. Mercy could see his pink flesh glistening through his sandy-coloured hair. The thought came to her of his head close to hers, the rasping cheeks, his heaviness on top of her as he strained into her. A horrible blush spread all over her body.

I wish you didn't exist, she thought. That I'd never met you. She sensed he was feeling the same.

As they left the Battery at New York's tip, Tommy O'Sullivan nudged the Ford through the cars, carriages and streetcars of Manhattan with some aplomb.

'Mr Kesler says I'm to show you a thing or two on the way up,' he said, his hairy hands expertly manoeuvring the wheel.

He gave a running commentary on the journey, turning his head as if he was addressing Mercy, had picked her out. She felt easy with him, as if there was a bond between them. They were both servants of a sort. She listened, craning her neck to see the things he was talking about.

'We got the tallest buildings in the world here in New York. Space, you see – saves space. Beautiful, aren't they?'

And they were, dizzily tall, stately skyscrapers crammed in between the other buildings, dwarfing the bustle of life on the streets below.

'This your first time here?' Tommy jerked his head round to look at her.

Mercy was so excited, so busy trying to take in all the new impressions, she almost didn't reply.

'Yes,' she said, and at the same time James replied, 'It is, yes,' sounding as if he didn't like to admit it.

'If you look out this side—' – he jerked his head to the right – 'that's the East River. This here's Manhattan Bridge.'

He stopped at a junction with the second bridge. Traffic wormed across its gigantic, metal span. The car turned into a busy mesh of streets and Mercy was already beginning to feel drunk on all these new sights and sounds. She found herself wondering what Paul was doing. The thought of him sent an excited rush of feeling through her.

Paul, I love you, she thought. She missed him, ached to see him. Would he find her? Would he come?

Names spilled from Tommy O'Sullivan's lips: Park Avenue, Grand Central Terminal, and then the park moved past their windows to the right. They were still passing it when they turned into a side street and Tommy drew the car up outside a gracious brown-stone dwelling.

'So – here's home,' he said cheerfully, opening the car door. 'Mr Kesler's waiting for you.'

As he spoke the front door opened and a rather short, stout man with ruddy cheeks and spectacles, wearing a tight brown suit, bounced down the steps, beaming.

'James, my dear friend!' He was shaking James's hand through the window before he had even had a chance to get out. Mercy saw James Adair relax visibly, and felt herself do the same, for how could you not in the cheerful face of William Kesler?

'My wife Margaret . . .' James managed to extricate himself from the car and step round to her door. 'I'm afraid she is feeling rather unwell.'

Margaret roused herself, managing to sit up and give a strained smile. Mercy climbed out, lifting Stevie into her arms.

'Oh – and your beautiful son!' Kesler enthused. 'My children will be so pleased. You must come and meet Gerder, my wife – ah, here she is! Gerder, come on down!'

Gerder Kesler was a slight, dignified woman, also not grand in height. She came shyly towards them and Mercy felt immediate liking for her. She was relieved. The personality of the woman of the house always seemed to be what made it homely and welcoming or not. Mrs Kesler wore simple, rather old-fashioned clothes – a grey skirt which reached almost to her ankles and a white blouse embroidered with small blue flowers. Her voice was soft and sweet, the American accent gentle and very different from Tommy O'Sullivan's.

'We'd like to welcome you most warmly to our home,' she said smiling.

'Mrs Adair needs some assistance.' Kesler nodded meaningfully at his wife, who peered into the car.

'Oh my dear,' she said. 'What a terrible ordeal for you. We must take you indoors and make sure you are made very, very comfortable.'

At hearing the wonderful kindness in her tone, Margaret Adair covered her face with her hands and began to sob.

Chapter Thirty-Five

The Keslers' was an elegant, orderly home, every well-upholstered chair in its exact place, Kesler's collection of china all perfectly dusted on shelves and in a glass cabinet, shining mirrors, and a smell of polish as soon as they walked through the door. Gerder Kesler was its deceptively soft-spoken, efficient organizer.

They had four children: Konrad, fifteen, Lise, twelve and Karl, eight, who were all at school, and little Andreas who was five and was looked after by Helga, a pale, plain woman in her twenties. She barely raised a smile at Mercy, but as soon as she saw Stevie, her face shone with happiness.

'A baby!' she cried, in a strange, guttural voice. 'Oh – let him come to me, won't you? Andreas is getting such a big boy now – he'll soon be away to school!'

To Mercy's surprise, as personally she thought Helga a wee bit odd, Stevie went to her straight away with absolute trust.

Margaret Adair wept even more at the sight of the immaculately made bed in her room, the piles of pillows encased in stiff, white linen. Gerder Kesler was all concern, and Margaret immediately confided in her the nature of the problem.

'I shall feel better later, I feel sure of it,' she said, once she was lying down. 'I just need some time to recover . . . Mercy—' – She reached her hand out and Mercy took it

– 'Paul Louth asked my permission to see you during the days the ship is in port . . .'

Mercy waited, nervously.

'Is that what you'd like?'

'Oh yes,' she replied fervently. 'Yes please, if that's . . .'

Margaret looked at Gerder. 'Mercy is my very special friend as well as Steven's nanny. Owing to my illness on the voyage she has been working very hard. I wonder if Helga would mind . . . ? For a day or two?'

Gerder smiled at Mercy. 'You could see, I think, how delighted Helga would be! She's a simple girl, but you'll find she is nothing but kindness and she has a rare gift with small children. So please, Mercy, feel relaxed here. I can see—' – she sat down on the end of the bed with a graceful movement – 'that Margaret and I are going to be firm friends. And I don't suppose we'll be seeing very much of the men, do you?' She laughed softly.

Margaret squeezed Mercy's hand and then let go. A spasm of nausea passed across her face. 'There you are – and you deserve some time to yourself.'

'Oh, thank you!' Mercy went to find Helga, her heart singing.

As soon as James Adair stepped into the Keslers' house a huge tide of relief swept through him. His emotions during the voyage had reached such extremes of agony, desire, relief and shame that his life had felt like a shattered glass, the pieces distressingly scattered and misplaced. Quite apart from what had taken place with Mercy, Margaret's sickness had confined him. He had been reduced, on the ship, to a kind of passive, semi-domestic situation. But he could reassemble himself here with Kesler, step back into the comforting, manly world of work.

He dined with the Keslers that night at an oval, rosewood table, a silver candelabra unlit at the centre. To his relief he found that Mercy was expected to eat with Helga and the other servants. He enjoyed the simple but flavoursome meal of soup and beef and fruit tart, and questioned Kesler about the ornate pieces of china he saw arranged round the room.

Once Gerder had excused herself, he and Kesler spent the evening discussing business. Kesler, ruddy-cheeked, offered him brandy and a cigar, and the two of them sat back into slippery leather chairs so large they looked as if they might swallow them up.

'What I propose', Kesler said, resting one plump leg on the other and blowing smoke towards the ceiling, 'is that we take a few days here in New York City. After that we can go on down to Rochester and I'll show you the new place. It's coming on. Another couple of months and I'd say we'll be on the move. But I'm glad for you to visit now. Of course, New York City has far more to offer a visitor.'

James appreciated Kesler's directness and enthusiasm. He gave off an air of anything being possible. 'That all sounds very satisfactory to me.'

'So—' – Kesler leant forward – 'while you're here – let's sit down and design the greatest damn racing cycle the world has ever seen. Agreed?'

James blew out the smoke from his cigar and grinned, suddenly boyish. 'Agreed.'

Retiring to bed that night, James was full of drive and excitement from his conversation with Kesler. After the afternoon's rest and all this enthusiastic talk the last thing he wanted was sleep. He'd like to have been out on the town, dancing, laughing, throwing off the constraints of his life again. He was restless, amorous.

Very quietly he opened the door of his room. Margaret was awake, to his surprise, watching him as he stepped close to the bed.

She wrinkled her nose. 'Goodness, you smell of cigars.'

'Kesler's a generous man.'

'You had a good evening then, darling?'

'I did!' He spoke with rather overdone enthusiasm. 'He really is rather marvellous. And are you feeling better?'

She thought about it. 'I'm not sure how permanently, but yes, at this moment I don't feel too bad.'

He could feel her eyes on his as he undressed for bed. Then they lay together, in a rare, companionable position, each on the left side, he wrapped round the back of her.

'I've given Mercy permission to spend some time with Paul Louth,' Margaret murmured.

His jealous, at odds feeling returned. 'What, go gadding off? But she's a servant for goodness sake. And you need her more than ever . . .'

'Nonsense. Helga, that pale creature downstairs, will take over Stevie. Mercy's in love. Haven't you noticed? But then no, I don't suppose you have!'

He was silent. Of course he had noticed. He felt relieved, in some way vindicated. He nuzzled Margaret's neck. Her rounded, soft body pressed against him made him harden with desire.

'Won't she need a chaperone?' he murmured.

Margaret elbowed him playfully. 'Don't be such an old fuddy-duddy. And anyway, Paul seems very nice and responsible to me. She arched herself against him, surprising him with her sudden, slightly wanton energy.

He reached round for her lolling breasts, sculpting

them into peaks while she squirmed. He let out a groan of relief and pleasure. Kissing her hair he slid up into her, feeling her, moist, taut, enclosing him. In a fraction of a moment, before thought ceased his mind said: at last, something proper, something right.

The next morning Mercy was sitting restlessly with Helga, Stevie and young Andreas Kesler in the nursery when the doorbell rang. Helga, oblivious to the effect this was having on Mercy, continued to chatter on.

Mercy found she was holding her breath and wishing Helga would do the same. She strained to hear the voices downstairs. Her heart was racing. Surely – she just caught the sound of it – that was Paul? A moment later she heard footsteps in the passage and Gerder Kesler appeared smiling at the door, her spectacles catching the light from the window.

'Your friend is here, Mercy dear.'

'Oh – thank you!' Mercy scrambled to her feet in confusion. Gerder Kesler was even more informal than Margaret and barely treated her like a servant at all. 'You shouldn't have had to come . . .'

'Not at all.' She smiled at the obvious elation on Mercy's face. 'I'm only sorry the weather's so inclement for you.'

'Oh . . . well,' Mercy said. Weather? What did weather matter! 'Never mind.' She hesitated, awaiting permission of some sort.

'It's all right, dear, you may go. Helga is perfectly fine looking after little Steven.'

Mercy kissed Stevie's cheek hurriedly with a 'Be a good boy now, won't you?' smiled gratefully at Helga and dashed for her hat and coat.

He was waiting for her in the hall and the sight of him, slightly dishevelled-looking as ever, filled her with immense tenderness and joy. He was real! He had come for her!

'Hello,' he said, with a shyness that suggested he, too, might be afraid she'd changed her mind.

'They're letting me off – the days you're here. Isn't it marvellous?' she whispered.

Paul's face fell a fraction as he picked up his sodden umbrella from the stand behind the door. They went out into the rain and he opened it and held it over her. 'The thing is – I'm afraid I've only got two days.' He sounded apologetic. 'They want me back on board the day after tomorrow.'

Mercy took his arm and squeezed it. 'Two whole days though!'

He looked down at her fondly, relieved. 'Yes! Let's make the most of it.'

'How about saying hello properly then?'

'What – here?' He looked round the respectable Upper West Side street.

'No one knows who we are, do they? And anyway, I thought you didn't care about what people think.' She felt euphoric in the rain in this great, exciting city.

Laughing, he scooped her closer to him and their lips met, finding each other hungrily.

Paul rested his forehead against hers for a moment and gave a loud sigh of happiness. 'Everything feels right again as soon as I see you. I can somehow make sense of things. See a point to it all.'

Mercy took his face in her hands. 'I've missed you' – kiss – 'missed you' – kiss – 'missed you!'

They set off with more purpose, arms linked, elated at simply being together, and further intoxicated at the thought of this place to explore freely.

The rain fell steadily, the sound of it all round them. They walked the distance of a few blocks through Riverside Park, smelling the pungent scent of wet spring flowers and hearing the doleful blast from the hooters of steam boats chugging along the brown water of the Hudson. Then they turned east again. Paul had a plan of the city which he opened while Mercy held the umbrella.

'Let's come back through Central Park later, shall we? It'll be interesting to look at more of the streets.' He glanced down at her. 'Are you all right? We're going to get soaking wet.'

Her pigeon grey eyes beamed back at him from under her blue hat. 'I don't care!'

They walked on, stopping to admire grand buildings, talking, exclaiming, swerving round the puddles which were forming everywhere.

'I tell you what though.' He stopped abruptly as they made their way towards Fifth Avenue. 'I think I can remember the address – shall we go and see if we can find the Petrowskis?'

Chapter Thirty-Six

Paul was certain that Tomek's scrap of paper had said Broome Street. When they reached the Lower East Side, they found themselves in streets edged by high, dingy tenements between which streetcars rattled and cars hooted. The buildings were astonishingly shabby with shutters hanging off and ancient, peeling paint. From the windows spilled hanks of bedding, and laundry festooned every possible spare hanging place. Racks of clothes for sale splayed across the sidewalks. And there were people everywhere, teeming through the streets, sitting on steps, standing in doorways, yelling from windows. Mercy looked round in fascination at the men in shabby black clothes like dishevelled crows with their hats and beards and ringlets, and the shawls and embroidered blouses, the stiff, old-fashioned dresses and assortments of garments and materials worn side by side that she'd never seen in her life before, on people of a kind she'd barely ever seen either, with their high cheekbones and raven hair. And a pandemonium of different languages, guttural sounds shouted along the milling streets where you had to shout simply to be heard at all.

Broome Street was as crowded with activity as anywhere else. Paul remembered that Tomek's number had been forty-three. They walked slowly along the row of poor tenement houses, amid a curious gaggle of ragged children, and found a house with forty-three chalked on the door. They looked uncertainly at each other. A man sitting on the step of a house two doors away stared at them, then hawked and spat into the gutter.

'I think this is right,' Paul said. 'Can you hold this a minute?' They had bought bread and spiced meat in the Italian Quarter on their way, and Paul handed the bag of food to her.

Going to knock, he found that the door shifted a little and he nudged it with his shoulder. When it opened he turned and grimaced comically at Mercy.

'Well, here goes.' He led her inside.

When the door swung shut again they found themselves in almost total darkness. The air was thick with smoke and there was an overpowering stench of lavatories mixed with stale smells of cooking and a general frowstiness.

'Ugh,' Mercy said. She was afraid to move. But then she said, 'Listen, Paul – that's a babby crying upstairs! Could be little Peschka.'

'It could.' Paul went and opened the front door again to let in some light. It was then they noticed that the walls and ceiling of the hallway were also very dark and seemed to be covered with some sort of pattern.

'Good Lord!' Paul tapped his hand on the wall. 'I do believe it's lined with – tin, it feels like. Embossed tin! How strange. Bit wasted in here, isn't it? It's like the Black Hole of Calcutta. I tell you what – let's see if there's anyone in here.'

He went to an inner door off the hallway and knocked softly. After a moment it opened a crack and a woman's face, very pale and gaunt, peered out at them. Mercy could just make out an arc of frizzy red hair round her forehead which was wrinkled with suspicion.

'Er, Petrowski?' Paul said to her. 'Petrowski? Polska?'

Without altering her expression she opened the door a little wider, pulling the ends of her shawl round her. Mercy heard a clicking sound behind her, comfortingly familiar, and realized it was a sewing machine. The woman pointed silently up the stairs.

It was Tomek who opened the door. His face remained blank for a moment as he peered at them in the gloom. It was then transformed with joy as he recognized them and he pulled Paul into his arms, chattering madly.

Two young children also peeped out through the door at them.

'Yola – Yola!' Tomek shouted.

Yola came to them from what appeared to be a second room behind the first. As she walked across the bare boards of the dingy room and saw them, emotion immediately welled in her dark eyes. She clung to Mercy, weeping, kissing her and clutching her hands, as if she were a true sister who'd come all the way from Poland to find her.

The Petrowskis' living quarters, which they shared with Tomek's brother and his wife and children, consisted of two rooms, where they had to cook, wash, live and sleep, amid the smoke from the range. Yola showed Mercy the little back room in which a bed was curtained off from the small amount of space remaining. She indicated that she and Tomek slept on the floor in the other room.

Yola's sister-in-law Zanya, who spoke some broken English, explained haltingly to Mercy that her husband was finding Tomek a job at the docks, that soon he and Yola might be able to find a place of their own. She was taller than Yola, with a lighter complexion and more pointed face, her hair fastened back in a green scarf. When Yola told her who Mercy was she smiled and kissed her.

Yola looked exhausted, Mercy thought, but did not seem downhearted. The four of them and Zanya's children shared the food that Mercy and Paul had brought and Zanya brewed coffee on the stove. Tomek insisted that Mercy sit on one of the chairs and Yola, suckling Peschka, had the other, while the others sat round on the floor. The Poles exclaimed to each other over the Italian meat, which was as strange to them as to Mercy.

They communicated in the usual way of nods and gestures, and with a little help this time from Zanya.

'Is Yola happy to be here?' Mercy asked her.

Zanya asked the question of Yola and the two women laughed.

'She is happy,' Zanya said. 'She is . . .' She struggled for the words. 'We have help here – she not alone. Not to be hungry now . . .'

Mercy nodded, understanding.

'She will be sewing,' Zanya said.

Yola suddenly got up and went into the other room for a moment. She returned holding a brass candlestick which she unwrapped from a piece of soft cloth, and a photograph. The woman who stared back from it had a face as lined as bark on a tree. Mercy looked up and saw that Yola's eyes were once again full of emotion.

'Her mother,' Zanya said.

She didn't need to explain that they would never see each other again. The candlestick was evidently also one of the few precious possessions she had brought from Poland.

They sat for some time. Mercy held Peschka and fussed

over her, and then they left, promising to visit again the next day.

Mercy's two days with Paul passed with terrible speed. That first night she lay in bed across the room from Helga, praying that the woman would soon cease her continual chatter, fall asleep and leave her alone with her thoughts.

When Helga did eventually sleep, Mercy turned on her back, the bed creaking as she moved. It had been wonderful to see the Petrowskis had fared well on Ellis Island and now had hope of a new life. Their bravery, the risk they had taken, filled her with burning determination. She, like them, would leave her past behind and look forward. Whatever James Adair had done, she would leave it behind. She would not let it mar her future. Like the Petrowskis she was going to begin again.

When we get back to England, she thought, I'll look round for something else. I'll get away from him. She would be sad to leave Margaret after all her kindness, but her presence in the house could only mean trouble for Margaret. She would wait for the right time, for something suitable. Then she would go. She would wait for Paul.

The day she had just spent with him seemed the most perfect she had ever had. When they parted that night they had held each other for a long time in a shadowy spot round the corner from the Keslers' house. They touched and kissed and he spoke such loving words to her. Her body filled with desire for him, seemed to have a will of its own. For a moment she couldn't forget the revulsion she had felt with James Adair, but she forced him out of her mind again.

I loved Tom, she thought, I can love. I feel even more for Paul, love him with all my heart, mind, body . . . His words of affection, of passion, were still fresh in her mind and she was full of wonder.

'I want to be with you always, Mercy. I want to spend my life with you. Life would be nothing without you now.'

She was almost too thrilled and excited to lie still.

I must be, she thought, the happiest person in the world.

The next evening they had to part. When they met in the morning this still seemed far off – they had a whole day in front of them! But it rushed past.

Once more they walked, talking and laughing all day. They watched the almost imperceptible movement of the East River from Manhattan Bridge, bent their heads back to look up at New York's most soaring buildings, and once more visited the Petrowskis to say, for the time being, their goodbyes. Amid the hugs and blessings and tears, she and Paul promised that they would keep in touch, and they left them in their cramped little rooms which held so much hope for the future.

Late that afternoon, Mercy and Paul walked back, with painful reluctance, towards the Keslers' house.

'Now's our chance to see more of the park,' Paul said.

'Slowly,' Mercy added wretchedly. 'Oh Paul, I wish we could just stay here. Forget about everything else and start a new life ourselves.'

'I know. I wish too.'

The closer the time to part was approaching, the more difficult they both found it to speak. Mercy's heart was weighed down by the thought of not seeing him. They were to be in New York another two and a half weeks and even when they got home Paul would be in London and there was no telling when they might meet.

'You will write to me, won't you?' he said. 'Letters from you would keep me going.'

'I'll try. Only I've hardly ever written letters before!'

'Just write the way you talk to me. I'm not up to much at it either, but at least it's something.'

They passed along the winding paths of Central Park, eyes full of green grass and spring leaves. Paul's arm was round her shoulder, hers at his waist, now it was dusk and they were away from the streets, and few people were in the park.

They stopped at the lake and stood together, looking across the wrinkled water, at the black, spindly trees beyond.

The lake seemed to hold secrets, Mercy thought, the unknown spread out in front of them, like their future.

She was acutely aware of Paul close to her, could feel his heart. The city was beating distantly around them, but here it was quiet, serene, a breeze riffling the water.

Paul took a deep, nervous breath.

'Mercy?'

She turned to him. He looked tense, eyes full of longing.

'I know things are very uncertain. I can't offer you much, not with any guarantees . . .' He trailed off, watching for her reaction. 'Could you – will you marry me?'

Mercy's hand shot to her mouth.

'O-o-o-h!' She reached out for the support of his shoulders, lest her legs give way. 'D'you really mean it?' But she could see that he did. 'Yes,' she said softly. 'I'll marry you, and cherish you with every bit of my heart.'

With a cry of joy he held her tight to him. 'Thank you – oh God, thank you. My beautiful, beloved Mercy!'

Too happy then, for words, they stared across the water in each other's arms. Mercy took off her hat and rested her head against Paul's shoulder.

How lovely everything is, she thought. The New World. A new life, new tomorrow. With this man whom I love. New beginnings are possible, and I'll make this one the best of my life.

Part Six

Chapter Thirty-Seven

May 1920

Mercy knelt on the linoleum in the Adairs' bathroom, resting her forehead against the cold rim of the bath and closed her eyes.

'He said it couldn't happen!' The words escaped as a desperate whisper from her lips. She was too sick and exhausted even to cry.

Screwing her eyes even more tightly shut she prayed, 'God in heaven help me! What am I going to do?'

It had begun gradually, with a slight feeling of queasiness which she put down to something she'd eaten. But it had got worse and for three weeks now she'd been bad in the mornings, and all day long was plagued by exhaustion of an intensity she'd never experienced before. She felt as if she'd turned into an old woman, barely able to get through the day, and it was frightening. Whatever was the matter with her?

The truth was too terrible to think about. If it wasn't for the way she felt she would have shut it right out of her mind. But she couldn't pretend to herself any longer. She'd seen the state of Margaret, and while she wasn't anything like as bad as that, she grew more and more certain that she, too, was carrying a child by James Adair.

She turned slowly and sat on the floor, resting against

the bath, shivering, arms hugging her knees. Her head ached, and the small amount of breakfast she'd managed to eat didn't feel at all safely stowed in her stomach. Nausea rose in her like water filling a bucket.

'Mercy – are you there?' Margaret called through the door.

'Just coming,' she managed to reply.

'That's all right, dear, no hurry. Stevie's ready whenever you are. You might take him out this morning as it's such a fine day.'

'Yes—' Mercy lurched forward on to her hands and knees, trying to stand up and catching her foot in her pale blue frock – 'I'll do that.'

She heard Margaret move away, and got up, feeling dreadfully sick. Her innards clenched and she retched miserably over the basin until her eyes and nose ran and she was panting. But she felt better after and washed the basin thoroughly.

She met Rose on the landing, carrying an armful of dry linen.

'Blimey – you look bad.'

'No.' Mercy pulled her foul-tasting lips into a smile. 'I'm awright. 'Course I am.'

Rose frowned, watching her as she walked determinedly towards Stevie's room. Whatever she said, Mercy looked terrible. It was obvious she was putting on a brave face.

'You're such a help to me,' Margaret told her all the time. She was at last beginning to feel better. She had been unwell, in patches, through most of their visit to the United States. For a day or two she might be all right, and then the sickness would return and she was laid up.

Mrs Kesler had been kindness itself and the two women grew very close. On days when Margaret was weak and sick, Gerder and Mercy took it in turns to keep her company. When she had the strength to venture out they had taken gentle walks in the city, strolling the avenues and the park. When James and Kesler were there at the weekend they had motored out to Long Island, to a place called Westhampton. It was a long drive, but when they arrived they picnicked by the ocean, the sand piled in heaps behind them and stuck with sharp, papery grass. James Adair did not speak a word to Mercy all day, did not even meet her eyes.

But she was full of excitement and euphoria at the sight of the sea. She and Stevie frolicked on the sand and watched the Atlantic swoosh up on to the beach, hearing the pound of it against the shore, feeling it rush cold over her feet. *Paul*, *Paul*, the breakers seemed to whisper, and through their roar and mutter she heard his voice, 'my beautiful, beautiful Mercy', and she smiled and laughed, running in and out of its lacy edge.

'Another letter for you,' Margaret said when Mercy eventually carried Stevie downstairs. 'Mercy – are you still feeling unwell? Perhaps we should call a doctor?'

'Oh – no!' Mercy forced a smile and pretended to be surprised. 'I'm on the mend, thanks.' She took the letter and put it in her pocket. The sight of Paul's sloping, untidy handwriting sent an agonizing pang through her, and she tried to hide her tears, busying herself with Stevie. 'We'll go straight away. Get the best of the day.'

She was glad to be out in the fresh air. Stevie sat in his pushchair, left thumb comfortingly in his mouth and his little grey rabbit snuggled up to his face. Mercy pushed him down the hill to the park. She felt weak and light-headed, but her thoughts seemed to hammer in her mind. Not for one second would they leave her in peace. A babby . . . a babby . . . inside her, and it was going to get bigger and bigger. Margaret Adair was four months gone with child and her belly was already growing. When she grew like that she wouldn't be able to hide it any more, and then what would become of her? Everything she'd hoped for, a new job, new life, would be lost to her. James Adair had torn into her, made her dirty, a disgrace. Now she was home again, where everything felt different and she could no longer block out what had happened, her shame and regret were enough to overwhelm her. She hated herself. She should have run out of that state room, screamed for help from Paul, suffered disgrace then, instead of being left to live with the consequences for ever.

As for Paul . . . the letter in her pocket nudged against her leg insistently with every step . . . The very thought of him filled her with anguish. She couldn't help it, couldn't stop herself weeping even as she walked down the road, keeping her head down to hide her face under the brim of her straw hat. She felt as if her very soul were pouring out, flooding the street.

She'd been such a ninny, thinking she could start afresh, that she could lift the curse of her beginnings and put the bad things of the past behind her. Everything had seemed possible when she was with Paul, but how could she have forgotten who she really was? That all her fresh hopes had always ended in suffering and loss?

She passed through the park gates with trembling legs and a leaden heart. The beds of bright spring flowers seemed to mock her. She began to sob so hard that Stevie craned round to look at her.

'Here—' – She bent over him, trying to sound normal – 'you can have a little run round now, can't you?'

He was still at an age when he wanted to keep her in sight. Mercy sank down on a bench and, steeling herself for fresh pain, took out Paul's letter. Once again it was from Cambridge. Paul had returned to London after his post on the *Mauretania*, but shortly after, Mr Louth had been taken seriously ill and he had been forced to go home. Mercy's heart had gone out to him. She knew how hard it would be for him to be with his father.

My dearest Mercy,

Another week and I'm still in Cambridge. Father has been out of hospital for several days now, but is still very weak and incapable. His right leg is not making the progress they hoped and as yet he can barely utter a word that anyone can understand. The doctor came to see him this morning and said he should be sent back to hospital, that they had allowed him home far too soon. I agree really, but the agony in his eyes when he heard those words! It's terrible to see him. The horror for a man like my father – a teacher, a linguist – of not being able to make himself understood, is almost beyond imagining. I can imagine enough though, and feel in a constant state of unrest, impatience and sadness seeing it. I looked after men in France in far worse condition, but there's something impossible about it when it's your own father. If only you were here. I miss you. Perhaps it would all make sense if I could see you . . .

Mercy broke off as Stevie ran to her carrying a flower.

'Oh dear.' She managed a watery smile. 'Thank you,

darling – but you mustn't pick any more flowers, Stevie love. No more.'

He ran off, wide-eyed. She saw him stop, eyes following the looping flight of a yellow butterfly.

. . . I have had some time to think, Mercy, and I wonder whether, when this is over, the best thing would be for me to come to Birmingham and find work. Not ships of course, but I haven't gone far down that path yet. Birmingham couldn't be a better place for an engineer. The more I think of it, it seems the very best thing. As soon as I can safely leave Father.

What I know is that life is very short and fragile and the best things in it have to be carefully cherished. All that matters is that we can be together, and I long for that. Apologies: today finds me in a rather mournful, philosophical mood. Do write soon, my love . . .

He finished the letter with more loving greetings that started Mercy's tears afresh. She put her hands over her face. 'Oh Paul, Paul . . .' If only he were here! If she could only weep in his arms and tell him all her pain and troubles. But he was the very last person she could be with now or confide in. She was racked by a multitude of emotions. Everything was wrong. It should have been his child that she carried, he who should have touched her and bound their lives together. But no. It could be no more. He'd said he could forgive her anything that had gone before. But this wasn't before – it was now and for the future. No one could forgive her that.

'Oh,' she sobbed. 'I can't have a child! I haven't the strength to do it all on my own.' For she would have no help from James Adair. He and Margaret must never, ever know. His knowing would only compound her shame and humiliation, and Margaret would find out that she had been betrayed by both husband and friend. She knew that from now on, she was alone.

Stevie toddled up to her and patted her knee when he saw her crying. The sight of his sorrowful brown eyes made her sob even harder. For he, dear, lovely little boy, would be lost to her too. She would have to leave him as completely as she left his parents and the thought broke her heart.

'It's awright, bab.' She scooped him up into her lap and held him tight, resting her wet cheek against the top of his sun-warmed curls. 'Mercy's awright, don't you worry.'

She clung to the soft, warm flesh in her arms, kissing him. For a moment she was overcome by utter astonishment. Inside her, another child was growing. It was part of her and she was its mother. Joy passed through her, just for a second, like a fork of lightning. She was going to have to survive, to struggle alone, and at this moment she had no idea how. But however hard it was, she was going to do right by this child. With burning determination she thought of her own mother.

I will never desert you, she pledged. I'll never abandon you as my mother abandoned me. You'll be mine and I yours, and whatever it takes, come hell or high water, we'll stay together.

Every day, for the rest of that blossom-filled week in May, she did her jobs for Margaret Adair, and hid her sickness. At night she tossed and turned in her attic room, rigid with fear and worry. Her mind spun round and round. How much longer can I stay here? Where can I go?

On Saturday evening she made a bundle of clothes. She lay on her bed fully dressed, knowing she was never going to sleep. Late on in the night she slipped down into Stevie's room, her heart hammering so loudly she felt it might wake the household. It was still very dark and she had to feel her way across the room towards the sound of his breathing. She couldn't reach far enough over the side of the cot to kiss his face, so she kissed her palm and stroked it against his warm cheek, held his curled hand for a moment. She had cuddled and kissed him that night for a long time before he slept. Now the time had come she had to be quick.

'Goodbye, darling Stevie. Mercy will always love you, wherever you are. Have a happy and blessed life.' With one more kiss, she left him.

The clock downstairs chimed four thirty. Almost dawn. With great care she drew back the bolt and turned the key of the door. She took a last look into the hall, just able to make out the shadowy shapes of its furnishings. Already, with the leaving of it, the place felt distant from her.

'Goodbye, Margaret,' she whispered. Her throat ached with unshed tears.

Carrying her bundle, she stepped out into the misty garden.

Light began to finger the edges of the city as she walked down the Moseley Road and the mist slowly cleared. She didn't hurry. No one was awake, she wouldn't be missed, and besides, she hadn't the strength. She pulled her coat round her in the cool air. She hadn't been able to bring all the clothes Margaret had generously supplied her with, but she kept the blue overcoat.

Down the hill she walked, into Balsall Heath, and how much it felt as if she was sinking down! As the light grew firmer it highlighted the grime and delapidation of the place, the filthy cobbled road, the smoking chimneys which coated everything in muck. The buildings shrank to small, menial dwellings, shops and workshops, houses with yards squeezed in behind. She had left her temporary dream life of the big, well-appointed house, and as her feet trod the road towards Birmingham, she felt as if the streets were closing in on her, claiming her. A slum child, returning to her rightful place in the slums. She found herself thinking of Yola Petrowski, the kinship she felt as if they were sisters, even though they hadn't a single word of language in common. They were two of a kind: poor and needy. She remembered baby Peschka and felt a moment of exaltation – she too was going to have a child! – followed by a sinking desolation. She had no Tomek. There was no one for her.

She stopped for a moment, slipping her hand inside the bundle. A car backfired, breaking the silence and she jumped violently, heart pounding. Its engine chugged off down a side street. From the bundle she pulled out a letter and walked on. At the next posting box she would send it, and that would be that. The future cut away from the past.

Dear Paul,

I'm going to say this quick, because I don't know how else to. I can't marry you or ever see you again.

I'm sorry. Don't come to Birmingham, there's nothing for you here.

Forgive me. Forget about me now.

Love,

Mercy

She hadn't been able to sign off without the word 'love'. Anything less seemed so callous and abrupt. And she did love him. She ached with love and longing for him.

Fifty yards further along she saw a pillar box. She stopped, the envelope resting against her lips and closed her eyes for a second. Taking a deep breath, she quickly pushed it through the slot.

Angel Street looked just the same: the sloping, cobbled street, huckster's shop on the corner, that tilted street lamp just along from their entry. Mercy paused. She had to face Mabel. Whatever the humiliation it might mean putting herself through, instinct and common sense had driven her back to the one place she might find a roof over her head. She pulled her shoulders back and went into the yard.

She saw Josie Ripley's eldest son John coming out of their house. He stopped, putting his cap on, and stared at her as she went to Mabel's door.

'Awright?' he said, coming over. He had a thin face and narrow, squinting eyes. 'Mercy, int it? You're 'ere early.'

'Well, you're up early too.' She felt horribly conscious of what a pathetic waif she must look standing there with her little bundle of all she possessed in the world.

'If you're after Mabel, yer won't find 'er there – there's

a new bloke in now. She's over there.' He pointed at the Peppers' house.

'Oh, she is, is she?' Mabel hadn't wasted any time.

John was still hanging about, kicking at an uneven corner of brick.

'All right then, ta,' Mercy said tartly. 'I think I can manage to knock on a door by myself. Ta-ra!' She waited until he'd gone off down the entry.

'Who's that?'

Mabel's voice was the first she heard through the window as she knocked loudly several times. From upstairs, eventually, came the sound of someone yanking at the sash but it would only open a crack. 'Who's making all that racket? What d'yer want?'

But the door opened a second later and Alf stood there, bare chested except for his braces, looking blearily out at her. His eyes were red, cheeks covered in pale stubble, but he still looked a strong man.

'What the – Mercy? Is that you, wench?'

'Can I come in?'

''Course yer can, course yer can . . .' He stood back. She could hear his chesty breathing, smelt the sweat on him as she squeezed past.

'What's up?'

'Alf, I need somewhere to go. I'm in trouble.' She put her bundle down on the table, speaking very fast in the hope that she could talk to him before Mabel got down and stuck her oar in, tell her where she could get off. Her heart was beating very fast. 'Can I stay here – for a while, anyhow?'

But Mabel was down by then, without her blouse properly fastened up and Mercy could see her wide, flaccid chest and her cleavage above the top button. Her hair was all hanging round her face and she looked like a witch.

'My God.' There was already a note of triumph in her voice. 'What the 'ell d'you want then?'

'Mabel,' Alf commanded her sternly. 'Don't start on the kid. 'Er says 'er's in trouble. 'Ere, have a seat, Mercy.' He pulled out one of the chairs by the table.

Mercy sat, chin stuck out as she looked up at the two of them. They'd have to know soon enough. Best to get it over with. 'I'm 'aving a babby. And I've nowhere to go.'

She expected Mabel to rant and shout, laugh even. Instead, she sank down on one of the chairs by the table, pulling the neck of her blouse together.

'I'd've thought you'd've had more sense. What happened?'

'What d'you think happened?' Mercy retorted fiercely. To her fury she felt tears welling in her eyes. Mabel hadn't immediately cast her out. There was hope. It was such a relief to be back in this familiar place among her own people, even George there by the window, on his perch.

'But who's the father?'

'I don't want him to know. Never! It wasn't my fault. It was all a mistake.'

Alf stood by, at a loss, breathing heavily.

Mabel leant forward, eyes narrowed. 'Was it that Mr . . . what's his name?'

Mercy nodded, looking down on her lap, her cheeks burning red. Oh, the shame of having to admit such a thing to Mabel of all people!

'Did 'e take advantage of you?'

Mercy hesitated.

'Well did you want it too?'

'No! Never!'

'So 'e took advantage.'

He did. Yes, he did. Mercy nodded again.

'Ought to be ashamed of hisself – young kid like you. You could be 'is daughter . . .'

Alf suddenly laid a warm hand on her shoulder for a second. ''Course yer can stay. You've always been like one of the family. Can't she, love?'

Mercy slowly raised her head and looked at Mabel. Instead of the mean exhaltation, the crowing she'd expected, she looked up and saw tears in Mabel's eyes.

'You can stay,' she said gruffly. I know I never treated yer right as a kid. It were a rotten time of my life that, and I want to put it behind me. But I'll try and do right by yer. You were always good as gold with Susan. You're my daughter, sort of, even though it were never regular like. And nothing's regular about this child that's coming, is it?' She wiped her eyes. 'But I've always loved having a babby in the 'ouse, that I have.'

Mercy rested her head on her arms on the table and burst into tears.

Chapter Thirty-Eight

'Where's Tom?'

Mabel had brewed tea and they sat sipping it from the chipped willow-pattern cups that reminded Mercy so much of Elsie. The room looked the same, although George was there, pecking at his feathers, but now there was so much more space in it. Mercy had only just fully taken in this fact.

'Have you moved him upstairs then?'

Alf looked shamefaced. 'No, we, er—' – he glanced at Mabel –'Tom's not 'ere, love. 'E's being looked after over at Hollymoor. 'E was in a terrible state, what with Elsie being bad and . . . and that . . .' For a moment he seemed unable to speak. 'They took 'im up the 'ospital and they said 'e should be looked after proper like, somewhere where there's nurses to see to 'im.' He took a big breath. 'Any'ow – it's for the best.'

'We don't know if 'e knows any different,' Mabel said.

'Thing is – we'd best tell 'er Mabel.' They looked at one another for a second. Suddenly Mabel smiled. Mercy saw, like a revelation, that she was happy. 'Mabel and I are getting wed.' Alf rubbed a beefy hand over his stubble. He spoke the words like a confession. 'Next month like . . .'

'Oh,' Mercy said. It stood to reason – they'd already set up house together, and Tom would've been in their way. She wanted to be angry with them. Didn't she owe it to Tom to stick up for him, with them having him put away to suit them? But if all the doctors said it was the right thing . . . And she, too, could feel the relief of his not being there. Guilt too, but yes, relief. She had to believe he was all right, being well looked after.

'Well,' she said, 'I hope you'll be happy.'

'Oh, we will,' Mabel said.

Rosalie and Jack came down after a while.

'Mercy!' Rosalie ran straight to her for a cuddle, even though when Mercy stood up she saw Rosalie was almost the same height as her now.

'You're like a beanpole, you are,' she said. Rosalie was thin and gaunt, auburn hair scraped back, cheeks pale, wrists like sticks. 'Barely an ounce of flesh on your bones!'

'Yer back at school now any rate,' Alf said to Rosalie.

'You stopping?' Rosalie asked.

Mercy blushed. 'Yes. I'm stopping for a bit.'

Rosalie beamed. 'Oh good – ain't that lovely. You not working up Moseley no more?'

'No,' Mercy said quietly. 'I'm not.'

Jack, twenty now, was tall, his hair still a bright ginger and for a moment Mercy almost thought he was Johnny, except he was broader, more stocky, like Alf.

He nodded to her and they exchanged a few friendly enough words, but she could tell immediately that he and Mabel didn't get on. He acted as if she wasn't there. He'll be leaving home soon, Mercy thought, and they'll be lucky if they see much of him again. She was surprised to note that Rosalie seemed all right with Mabel.

Mabel stood cutting bread with the loaf under her arm. They ate a bit of breakfast before Alf and Jack went off to work, Jack with barely a word, and Rosalie to school.

'Take the ticket for Chubb's,' Mabel said to her as she

left. 'And don't go and lose it. I want yer to get yer dad's suit out for Sunday on yer way 'ome.'

'Awright.' Rosalie tucked the pawn ticket in her pocket. 'You will still be 'ere when I get back, won't you, Mercy?'

''Course I will. See you later, love.'

Rosalie departed, smiling.

'There's no need to breathe a word to anyone – not yet,' Mabel told her once they were alone. She stood riddling ash out of the range. Mercy watched her. Mabel's body had thickened and spread, but had kept its curves. She now had a rather stately figure, and was a handsome woman, despite her sluttish ways. Mercy could smell her, that ripe, sweaty odour which always hung about her.

'Why're you being so nice to me?' Best to get it over, know where she stood.

Mabel straightened up, brushing ash off her sacking apron.

'Look – I'm not all bad, yer know. You used to rile me as a kid. Always looking at me as if I were the devil's mother or summat. And I didn't always treat yer kindly, but can't we let bygones be bygones?'

'Awright.' Mercy still felt wary. Old feelings, years of cruelty, weren't so quickly overcome. But she also felt queasy again, and absolutely exhausted. She rested her head on her hand, elbow on the table.

'Alf's a good man and 'e's giving me a chance, even if I don't deserve it . . .'

'You helped Elsie,' Mercy said grudgingly.

'I did what I could.'

Mercy was silent for a moment. Stevie would be awake now. They would know she was gone.

'Mabel – I need to go to sleep.'

Mabel pushed a chair in under the table. 'Yer look all in. Go up on Rosalie's bed – sleep all day if yer want.'

Mercy passed an odd, restless few days of sleep and sickness. She kept dreaming of Stevie, of the daily routine at the Adairs', and she'd wake, bewildered to find herself in Rosalie's bed in the bare little back bedroom with its cracked ceiling.

The first day she slept almost all the time, prostrate with exhaustion. Mabel brought her up water and tea and she was too far gone even to be surprised. In the evening Rosalie made herself up a bed on the floor.

'No,' Mercy protested weakly. 'You must have your bed!'

'Don't be daft,' Rosalie said. 'You're poorly. I can sleep down 'ere easy. It's the best thing having yer back, Mercy.'

'Is Mabel awright to you?'

'She ain't so bad.' Rosalie sat on her bedding on the floor, unplaiting her hair. 'It felt a bit funny at first – 'er and Dad like, yer know. As if it was wrong some'ow. She was really good to our mom when she was bad and that. Sometimes I don't like 'er being 'ere, as if she thinks she's taken Mom's place, but Dad'd be lonely without someone. It's for the best really and she's awright to me. It's Jack can't stand having 'er 'ere – not that quick.'

'I could see.'

'But even Mom said, life has to go on. Mabel'll never be my mom but it's nice to have someone 'ere. I was all on my own with Tom before, see.'

'You've been a real good kid, you have.' Mercy was

drifting off again. She didn't even seem to have the strength to move an arm or leg.

It was such a relief to be able to lie down for a time, and not pretend any more. She wouldn't be turned out on the streets, she was safe for the moment. But now these immediate needs were met she kept thinking of Paul. She dreamed of him too, kept seeing herself in New York with him, everything happy and undisturbed. She felt that enormous warmth and joy in the knowledge of his love and woke with tears streaming down her cheeks into her hair. Once she woke like this to find Mabel standing over her.

'What's all that about?'

'Don't know.' Mercy wiped her eyes, trying to sit up. 'Just everything.'

'You'll be all right.' Mabel handed her a cup of tea. Mercy still felt she was dreaming this, Mabel being kind. At that moment it was all too much and she burst into tears again.

A week passed. She got up, had to get out and face the neighbours.

'I'm looking for a new job,' she told them. She simply couldn't bear to tell the truth. Not yet. But each time she saw anyone, Mary Jones, Josie Ripley, Mrs McGonegall, blushes flamed in her cheeks. She wasn't going to be able to keep this up for long. But after their initial surprise they all treated her as if she'd never been away. There was a new man called Samuel Formby living in number two, the old house, but he was out at work all day and in the pub most of the rest of the time.

'I shall look for a job,' Mercy told Mabel. As soon as she felt a bit stronger she helped out round the yard, maiding and mangling on wash days, cooking, scrubbing. But she was still being sick a bit, on and off.

'Wait till you've got over that,' Mabel said. 'We'll manage.'

Mercy watched Mabel's new happiness and wondered at how much of a person's nature was built on circumstances.

Of course everyone soon found out about her. One morning Mercy was out in the yard and felt nausea rushing up in her. She dashed down to the lav, just making it, and stood heaving in the foul-smelling privy. Josie Ripley was in the one next door. As soon as they both stepped out, Mercy walked off trying to pretend nothing had happened, but Josie strode up behind her and tapped her on the shoulder.

'Mercy!' She looked round into Josie's crooked face. Even Josie couldn't fail to see the agony and shame in the girl's eyes.

'You in trouble?'

'Trouble?'

'Yer know what I'm saying. In the family way?'

Mercy nodded, looking miserably at her dirty work pinner.

'Thought so!' Josie was triumphant, hands on hips. 'Coming back 'ere sudden like, I knew there had to be more to it. Bit of a comedown eh, after what you're used to miss?'

Mercy didn't answer her.

'Does Mabel know? 'Cos if she don't yer'd better tell 'er right quick.'

'She knows.'

'So—' Josie was always one to get things straight. 'You're no better than the rest of us then are yer?'

Mercy shook her head and looked up indignantly.

''Course I'm not!' She'd never thought she was – had she?

'Any'ow—' – Josie softened suddenly, backing away – 'if yer need anything . . .'

Mercy folded her arms over the pinner and walked slowly back to the Peppers' house. She could see her future spread out in front of her. Angel Street, work, the babby. She'd grow old like Josie, Mary, Mabel, among all these people she'd known almost all her life. It was good enough for them, she told herself. And it would have to be good enough for her. But as she looked up at the drab, mean-sized little dwelling, she felt as if her very soul was dying inside her.

She got a job at the Futurist Cinema in John Bright Street, sitting in the little wooden booth selling tickets.

'Your pretty face'll bring the punters in,' the manager said. Not that people needed bringing in. They came in droves, especially Saturday afternoon. The job was easy. Tickets 3d, 6d, 1/6d, 2/6d. She could sit down and do it. She smiled as sweetly as she could at everyone. No one would have guessed at the shattered, lonely heart inside her.

On the second Sunday she caught a bus down the Bristol Road to Hollymoor Hospital. Her sickness was easing a little now, leaving room for her enormous loss and loneliness. Rosalie was good company, of course, and the neighbours were all right. But she hungered for someone she could really talk to.

Hollymoor seemed like a world of its own, shut away

behind its high walls like a self-contained village, the forbidding hospital buildings clustered together.

Eventually she was directed to where Tom was, out in the grounds. He and several others were sitting in an oval-shaped ring of chairs, round which two nurses in starched uniforms came and went, fetching, carrying, cajoling. The men mostly sat still, some with their heads lolling, some just staring, one with bandages across his eyes. Mercy's heart contracted with pity.

There were a couple of other visitors here, sitting patiently beside their sons, brothers or lovers in half-concealed desperation. Mercy picked up one of the spare seats and placed it beside Tom's bath chair, facing into the sun. He didn't register her presence and she reached for his nearer hand and held it in hers so that he stirred slightly. His eyes were watering in the bright light.

'Hello, Tom.' She spoke quietly, feeling self-conscious. 'It's me, Mercy. You're looking well, love.' He was, compared with the last time she saw him. He was clean, shaved and groomed and his cheeks and nose were turning a faint pink in the sun.

'I've moved back home now.' She wondered if anything she said ever reached him. 'Living with Alf and Mabel and Rosalie. They're all going to come and see you again very soon. Everyone else is much as usual . . .' She watched a woman across the circle from them clinging to what must have been her son's hand, staring at him with tormented eyes. A moment later she got up suddenly, as if overcome by emotion, and left.

Mercy sat in silence with Tom as he made odd sounds and fidgeted. She needed him so badly that day, needed to believe he could hear her and offer friendship and comfort as he had in the past.

'We've both got a life sentence, haven't we?' She didn't look at him as she spoke. 'There's you here and me back where I started when you and me was kids. Shame we can't put the clock back, eh? I'd give anything for you to be back like you were.'

One of the nurses approached with a cup of cordial for Tom to drink through a straw.

'Would you like to help him with it?' she asked Mercy. She seemed stiff and formal, yet not unkind.

Mercy held the straw to Tom's dry lips. He knew what to do and there were soon loud slurping noises as he drained the cup. When he finished he said, 'Ahhh,' loudly. Mercy smiled.

'Was that nice?' She felt as if she were talking to Stevie. She put the cup down on the grass, took her hat off and laid it in her lap.

'See, if I don't talk to you, Tom, there's no one now. And I know you'd be kind to me and understand.' She drew closer and quietly poured out all her troubles to him.

'I've tried so hard with my life,' she finished. 'You know that, don't you? I can't make sense of it. Everything seems to happen before I'm ready for it . . .' She found she was suddenly weeping again, warm tears coursing out. She'd never cried so much in her life as in these few weeks. It was as if all her defences had been trampled down.

'I don't know what I'm going to do. I just don't know how I can bear it . . .'

Tom moved his head suddenly and let out an 'Er-r-r-r' sound which she found comforting, as if he'd heard and wanted somehow to reach her. She kissed his hand.

'You were always so kind and good. You don't deserve this, Tom, none of it.' There was nothing else she could say to him that she hadn't said over and over. 'I'm so sorry. I wish, I wish . . .' If only he could talk and yell out all the horror and injustice of being trapped in there forever, in his useless body. But he sat silent now, like an inscrutable puppet.

She said goodbye to him, promising she'd come back.

It was as she left the hospital that despair hit her fully, a great surge which washed through her. She leant against the wall outside and closed her eyes, the rough brick against her forehead, crumpled with agony inside.

Tom would sit there like that for the rest of his life. How long? Ten years, twenty, thirty, more? And Paul – she saw his eyes looking into hers with all his pained tenderness, his need of her. She loved him so much. However often she tried to convince herself that she could be strong, could move forward, it was not true.

'I don't want to spend my life alone . . . I can't, I need someone. I need you, Paul. I can't bear it.'

But she'd told him there was nothing for him here. She was no better than a tart, a trollop, carrying the child of a bullying, selfish man. She was alone in the world, nothing to anyone, and that was what she had always been. She thought of the railway, of lying across the track, hearing the train thrumming faster and faster towards her, the singing, the thundering roar of it. Then blackness. No more. Her troubles would be over, and who would care? She could have peace, blessed peace . . .

'You all right, missy?'

She turned, bewildered, and found herself looking into the watery eyes of an elderly gentleman with white hair tucked under a smart black Homburg. He was rather stooped, carried a stick, and his face wore a sad, gentle expression.

'Yes.' With an effort she straightened up. 'Thank you. I just came over a bit dizzy.'

'It's a warm day.' He looked at the sky for a moment, with a sideways swivel of his head. 'I saw you visiting one of the young men, didn't I?'

'Yes – my, er, friend. ' She remembered the old man now, from among the visitors. 'I'm just going for the bus.'

'Perhaps I could give you a lift somewhere, my dear? I've got my car. My sons say I shouldn't be driving any more at my age but I can't see the harm. I don't go at any great speed.'

'Oh – it'll be out of your way. I live right near the middle of Birmingham.'

'Not at all, my dear. Let me help you – look, just along here . . .'

The idea of being driven was very attractive. He opened the door of the motor car and Mercy saw the blue veins standing out on his hands. She sank gratefully into the leather passenger seat.

The gentleman's driving was perfectly in order, though he must, Mercy saw, have been nigh on eighty. Now and again he wiped his eyes with a handkerchief. They drove in silence for a few moments, until he burst out, 'That was my grandson in there. Was. Like a vegetable now.' She could hear all the grief pressed into his quavery voice.

'Only eighteen he was, when it happened.' He punched the air impotently with one hand and the car swerved. 'Arras. That's where it was, curse it! If only I could take his place—'

'I feel that too.'

'You?' He glanced round at her, eyes wide. 'Oh no – not you. You're much too young, my dear. It's us old, useless things – he should be out working, prime of his life . . . And you – lovely girl like you. I don't know how you can even think such a thing.'

'The way things are, it'd be easier.'

'Now, now, now – nothing can be that bad, surely? Not compared with them in there. Young slip of a thing, life all in front of you. No war on now, nothing like that . . .' He reached out and patted her hand. 'Only thing to do, you know – keep putting one foot in front of the other and you're sure to get there.'

Mercy managed a little smile. 'Yes. I s'pose so.'

She got him to pull up on the Moseley Road, saying she'd walk the rest of the way, and thanked him sincerely.

'I'll perhaps see you there again. What's your name, my dear?'

'Mercy Hanley.'

The old gentleman let go of the steering wheel and slapped his thighs in amazement.

'Extraordinary! Well, well, d'you know, my name's Hanley too? Joseph Hanley – delighted to make your acquaintance. No relation, I don't suppose!'

Mercy's heart started to thump harder. No, surely it couldn't be – he must be long dead . . .

'You're not – surely – that Joseph Hanley – the Hanley Homes?'

'Yes, my dear. The very one – they're still going strong, I'm happy to say.'

'I can't believe it!' She clasped her hands to her cheeks. His face was much more shrunken now, softer, with an innate sympathy, and she could barely see that it was the same person. 'I grew up in the home in Aston,' she told him. 'They gave me your name because I had no one—'

'Did you, my dear?' Mr Hanley's face creased in wonder. 'Well I'm proud to know you! This is a great day for me, seeing how you've grown up into such a fine girl.'

Mercy swallowed. 'I, er – I was the one that bit you.'

Mr Hanley's forehead wrinkled. 'My, my – now you come to say it, I do remember that. Tiny little blonde thing – eyes like a cat. I had a mark on my hand for years after . . .' He glanced at his thumb, then back at her. 'It's gone now though!'

'I'm sorry, Mr Hanley. I wasn't cross with you, not really. You gave me a roof over my head. But they sent my friend Amy to Canada and I felt I was all alone . . .'

Mr Hanley shook his head, still astonished. 'Well well. I shall look forward to telling my family I've met you, Mercy. And I hope we shall run into each other again.'

Mercy climbed out of the car and looked in through the window, smiling. 'So do I,' she said.

Chapter Thirty-Nine

Dorothy Finch waited on the step outside the Adairs' house the next Saturday morning, a perplexed frown on her face. Emmie opened the door, and seeing her, clapped a hand over her mouth.

'Oh – sorry, Miss Finch – only we've been so worried about Mercy. D'you know where she's gone?'

'What d'you mean, "gone"? Ain't she here?'

Margaret Adair appeared, her face pale and tired. She immediately recognized the woman's rather old-fashioned clothes and her dark, soulful eyes.

'Thank goodness someone's come at last – we haven't known what to do. Please come in, won't you? Emmie, you can go now . . . We're all rather at sixes and sevens without Mercy.'

In the sitting room, Dorothy could see the woman was quite distressed. She motioned Dorothy to sit but remained standing herself, moving restlessly round the room.

'I imagined she must have come to you. I just don't understand it. She had seemed just a little unwell, but – is she all right? Where is she?'

Dorothy felt dread spreading through her. She clenched her teeth for a moment to quell her anger. How could they have just lost her!

'It's news to me that she's not here, Mrs Adair. I expected to see 'er last Thursday. She comes to meet me about once a month as a rule, as you may know. I thought I'd come and see if she were awright like . . . When did she go?'

'Nearly three weeks ago!' Margaret wailed. 'We all got up one morning and she'd gone – just bundled up some of her things and walked out in the night. For a terrible moment I thought she might have taken Stevie. That's what's so odd – she was so fond of him! What could have induced her? We thought of calling the police, but then it seemed she must have wanted to go, and the trouble is—' – Margaret sat down suddenly beside Dorothy – 'she talked occasionally about the home she'd grown up in, but I've been thinking about it and I don't ever once remember her saying the name of the street. There've been letters coming for her too, I think from that young man. He even telephoned . . . I don't know if all this had anything to do with him, but if she'd gone with him he wouldn't need to write to her, would he? And I can't even send the letters on. I do feel so very worried about her. And rather let-down to tell you the truth. It's so out of character . . .'

Dorothy stood up, stemming the flow of Margaret's agitated chatter.

'You should give me the letters, Mrs Adair. Don't worry,' she added grimly, tucking the envelopes into her pocket, 'I'll find her. Good day to you.'

'But . . .' Margaret stood up after a moment. 'Where are you going to . . .?'

Dorothy had already gone.

'So, miss – what d'you think you're doing back here?'

Dorothy's voice was harsh with worry. She'd come

straight from the Adairs' and caught Mercy an hour before she was due at work. But Josephine had come to visit with her three kids and there was nowhere for them to talk in private.

Mercy didn't look especially pleased to see her either. She seemed quite put out at her arrival. Dorothy saw how thin she was, gaunt and tight-lipped, a dull expression in her eyes. She'd last seen Mercy after her return from America, blooming with health and happiness. Whatever had got into her?

'I'm just off to work,' she said curtly, picking up her cardigan.

'I'll walk with you then.' Dorothy's tone brooked no argument.

'I'm in good time,' Mercy said. 'Let's go round Camp Hill way.'

She didn't speak as they passed through the streets of St Joseph's parish, wouldn't answer Dorothy's agitated questions until they reached the bustling thoroughfare at Camp Hill. Mercy was almost choked with nerves. She had to tell Dorothy, 'course she did. But it was the hardest thing yet. Dorothy had known her all these years, had tried to help her live a good life. She would expect better of her.

'I didn't think I'd see you,' she said lamely.

'And why not, pray?'

Mercy shrugged. Angel Street felt like a completely different existence that she'd slunk back into to hide, expecting everyone to just leave her alone to get on with it. She wanted to be left alone, to forget she'd ever had any hopes.

'What's going on, Mercy?'

They stopped by an ornate street lamp across the road

from the Ship Hotel. There were trams passing, bicycles, people bustling along. The bell of Holy Trinity struck one.

Mercy folded her arms tight, looked into Dorothy's eyes and told her. She expected disgust, scorn and anger. Instead, Dorothy's face lost all its colour and she had to lean against the lamp-post for support.

'Oh Mercy. Oh my Lord, you mean he . . .? Of course you couldn't tell Mrs Adair why you were going! Oh, Lord above.' She put her hand over her eyes. 'I knew summat terrible must've happened.' She turned, face hard for a moment. 'Tell me you didn't encourage 'im.'

'On my life.' Mercy's lower lip was trembling. 'You've got to believe me, Dorothy. I hardly knew what he was doing before it was too late, and I just couldn't think that he was going to . . . It was all so strange and horrible . . .'

Dorothy breathed in and out deeply, trying to steady herself. Mercy was moved by her emotion. Dorothy really did care about her, almost like family.

'What're you going to do, Mercy?'

'Have the babby. What else?'

'But there are places – well, like Hanley's – after, you know . . .'

'No!' she shouted, so enraged she didn't care who heard. She could hear blood throbbing in her ears. Lowering her voice a little she said, 'Are you saying I should just throw my babby away the way my mother did me? She didn't care, did she? She just did what suited her. But I'll never cast my child off!' She laid a hand on her belly. 'It's my babby – the first person I've ever had who's related to me by blood. Blood tells in this world – or it damn well should anyhow. I'll look after my own, not like some.'

The two women stood glaring at each other for a moment, then Dorothy reached into her pocket.

'You're not telling me everything, are you? Mrs Adair said—'

'You went to see her?' Mercy was filled with panic. 'You mustn't, Dorothy – don't tell her! She must never know. It'd destroy her and I don't want him knowing, making any claims, or—'

'He won't make claims!' Dorothy said scornfully. 'I'd've thought you could at least work that one out for yourself. He'd run a hundred mile rather than admit that babby's his, in his position. But if you was to tell just him, you might get some money out of him.'

Mercy stared back at her as if she were deranged. 'I don't want his filthy money! I don't want anything to do with him!'

'You might think different when it's born and going hungry.'

'Alf and Mabel won't let us go hungry.' Mercy pulled herself up straight, making a show of strength. 'And I'm going to provide for it too. I can survive. I've always had to, haven't I?'

A tram rumbled past on the street beside them. Dorothy pulled Paul's letters out from her pocket and held them out. Only then did Mercy's face crumple. Her eyes widened before filling with tears. She covered her face with her hands.

Mercy sat in the ticket booth at the cinema while the first showing was on. She could hear the music from inside. She slit open the envelopes containing Paul's letters, her hands trembling so much she could barely manage.

The first, two weeks old, contained the usual news from Cambridge. Paul's father was deteriorating, had had another slight stroke. Paul was caring for him continuously. The sight of his handwriting wrung her heart.

By the second letter he had received her last note, posted on her flight from the Adairs'. Mercy began reading, then looked up, unable for a moment to go on. In the dim light she could just see her pale face reflected in the glass. When she looked down again to read the letter, the pain and bewilderment contained in his few quiet words seemed to burn from the page.

My loved one,

I can feel – I hope – the distress of your last letter to me. I have read it over and over many times, trying to make sense of it. How could you imagine for a second that I could ever forget you? Or perhaps there is another reason, another person in your life, and that is why you want to forget me? What is it, my love? What could have made you write a letter like that all of a sudden, as if I could just stop feeling what I do for you and that everything between us was nothing? If only I could see you, I'm sure we could make ourselves understood so much better.

Until I hear from you again I shan't be able to believe you meant your letter. Please write and tell me it was a mistake, that the future is not just the bleak nothingness it feels to be now.

Yours ever,
Paul

*

'She says she's going to keep the child. Won't hear of anything else.'

Grace had gone to the window as Dorothy talked, standing in the shadows by the long curtains, looking, but seeing nothing of the street outside.

Dorothy waited, knowing Grace had heard everything she'd said. The carriage clock on the mantelpiece ticked, deafeningly, it seemed. The sound of time passing. Dorothy watched Grace's profile, her fashionable, jaw-length hair caught neatly behind her left ear. Standing like this she looked quite youthful, still slim, in her white pleated skirt and a soft blue blouse. But as soon as she turned towards Dorothy, every day of her years of suffering showed in her face. It was not the suffering of physical deprivation, of hunger or the grinding lack of money and warmth. But Grace had never known a day in the past twenty years without emotional pain.

'It's the worst.' She spoke barely above a whisper. Her face had suddenly taken on the creased look of an old woman's. 'I can't think of anything – if she dies it could scarcely be worse. To think of her having to endure the pain, the shame and hardship . . .'

'You did it – you survived it.' Dorothy wanted to reach out, to give comfort, but Grace was untouchable. 'She has people round her who are perhaps more forgiving than you did.'

'I ran away. But I always knew I could go back. He said I could always go back so long as there was no child. I was a coward. But she has so little to go back to – not wealth or comfort as I had.' After a moment she said in horrified wonder, 'James Adair . . . are you sure? My memory of him is of a rather kind, stuffy fellow.'

'I can only go by what she says, dear. But there is someone else – was. In America. But she said she'd had to put him off.'

'What did she say to you? What are her thoughts?'

Grace stepped forward, desperately. 'Oh, I feel I know her so well, and yet . . .'

'She said she'll never give up the child. Whatever happens she's sticking with it.'

Grace paced the room, unable to keep still. 'No one knows better than you what I've been through, my dearest Dorothy. You know never a day has gone by without my thinking of her, praying for her . . . But I've asked myself over and over again whether I was wrong, whether I should have faced every shame and denial that would have been handed out to me. I could have stayed in that room, with that Mrs Bartlett, while I still had a little money.' She shuddered. 'I suppose somehow I should have survived. But Dorothy, I was so young, so very frightened. I felt I'd sunk beneath the level of life itself when I was there, into an appalling hell . . . But Mercy has lived most of her life in such places. I condemned her to that. And she has strength – oh God, that I had had her courage! If they hadn't made me – if I hadn't let them make me . . . If he hadn't gone away – I should never have abandoned my own flesh and blood . . .'

As her distress mounted, Dorothy went to Grace and took her gently in her arms. If only she could take this pain from her! Grace sobbed brokenly against her shoulder.

'He would've been no good for you. Not in the end.'

'My life has been one long pretence – this parody of a marriage . . .' She looked up, wet-eyed, into Dorothy's face. 'D'you know, before Neville left – in the War – I prayed for him to die?'

'Yes, well – so did I.'

The two women looked at each other solemnly. Grace suddenly broke away and sat down.

'I have spent my life safeguarding all the wrong things.' Dorothy saw in her a moment of the steeliness that reminded her of Mercy. 'Even now, to protect my sons I am a stranger to my daughter. To protect this facade of a respectable marriage which suits my husband I tolerate him spending more time in common whorehouses than he ever does with his sons.'

She straightened her back, her chin jutting out. 'Mercy must know who her mother is. I owe her that, and so much more.'

'What about Neville – if he were to find out?'

'I think', Grace said calmly, 'I shall probably kill him.'

'Grace!'

'It's all right, Dorothy. I don't think I mean it. I don't wish to rot away in prison for the rest of my life. All I mean is, I have to be prepared to pay the price, whatever it may be. But now the boys are old enough, they see their father with clear eyes. I'm certain we can trust them to support us.'

'What's up with you, wench?' Neville said when he got home that evening. His voice, as ever, was sneering. 'Didn't the wind blow the way you wanted it to today?'

'I'm quite all right, thank you,' Grace said mechanically. She knew her eyes still showed signs of tears, and she evaded his brief, insolent glance.

Neville had returned from the War a much leaner man. Over the past year and a half though, he had bloated into middle age, with a complexion ruddy from over-indulgence. His cheeks were loose and flushed and merged with his thick chin with scarcely a hint of jawline present. His body was short and stocky and he walked, legs apart, with a swagger. Lately he grew more quickly short of breath. Over the years his catalogue of charming habits about the home had grown in number and intensity: bawling about the place, hawking phlegm in his throat, drinking regularly to excess, cursing, belching and passing wind with orchestral loudness. And despite Grace's barely concealed revulsion for him, he hadn't left off his intermittent, gross mauling of her in bed.

She had learned early in this loveless marriage that he could be two different men. Out of the home, or in company, he could be gregarious, charming, humorous. He had a generous side to his character and a loud, infectious laugh. This was how he had appeared to Grace's father when their marriage was arranged. They had not been married more than a few weeks when, with her, he became moody, foul-mouthed, out of control. Both of them were unhappy. Grace knew that nothing she could do ever seemed to give him satisfaction and never had, since the very earliest days, though she had tried and tried.

That night he flung his hat down in the hall and went, as usual, straight to the whisky decanter. He poured half a tumbler of the burning strong liquid, downing it in gulps. Grace usually avoided him, but tonight she stood at the threshold of the parlour, watching.

'I don't know why you've bothered to remain in this marriage.' She spoke with such cold objectivity that he turned, mouth swirling a gulp of whisky, startled to find her observing him. He narrowed his eyes and swallowed.

'It's the thing to have a wife. If I have to have one it might just as well be you. Out of my way.' He pushed past her and stumped heavily up the stairs.

*

'Boys, I have something important I want to talk to you about.'

She sat on Edward's bed. He, the younger of the two, was now ten. He sat up, grey eyes fixed solemnly on her face. Robert, twelve, was puppyish and full of often misdirected energy. He hurled himself across from his bed and landed on Edward's legs.

'Ouch!' Edward yelled. 'Get off, you great lump of a thing!'

'Boys, please just sit still,' Grace said, her voice sharp with nerves. 'I want to tell you something important.' For a moment she wished that Edward, the one most akin to her, was the older.

Once they were sitting quiet, sensing her seriousness, she told them what she had to say, her tears coming unbidden. She felt she was confessing to them, her own children, laying bare her shame.

'You see,' she finished, looking up at them bashfully, 'perhaps Mummy isn't quite the person you thought she was.'

'So—' – Robert was frowning, attempting to take in the implications of this – 'you mean we have a sister . . . somewhere?'

'That's right. Her name is Mercy.'

'And she's much bigger than us and she's never going to live with us?'

'Yes, dear, both those things are true too.'

'Oh,' Robert said, beginning to lose interest. 'Well, that's all right then, I suppose.'

'Mummy,' Edward said, 'can I carry on reading *Treasure Island* now?'

Grace smiled. 'In a moment. There's something else, just as important, I need to say to you. I don't often ask you to keep a secret, though this is a very special secret that I thought you were old enough to know. But this is something I don't ever want you to breathe a word to Daddy about. Ever. It would make him very, very angry. Can you understand how important that is, my darlings?'

'Oh yes,' Edward said dismissively. 'Daddy never listens to anything we say anyway.'

Grace knew this was true. And even when the boys spoke to their father it was never a relaxed interchange. It was a risk she had taken, but it was unlikely anything would slip out in an unguarded moment of jollity, for such moments did not exist in their household.

'And Robert – listen to me now, very carefully.' She had a special task for Robert to perform, and he was going to have to be very grown up about it.

Chapter Forty

'Miss Hoity-toity's been 'ere again.'

Mabel stood across the table from Mercy who was ravenously eating bread and scrape. She'd just got in from work and was, as ever, nearly dropping from hunger. Rosalie was brewing a cuppa and Alf and Jack'd be in from the pub any minute. Soon as they arrived Mabel'd be sweet as pie to her, Mercy knew.

'Dorothy, you mean?'

'Left you this. In an envelope too.' Mabel held out the note. Obviously the sealed envelope rankled with her as she couldn't have a nose at it. Mercy examined the back of it to see if she'd tried to steam it open, but there was no sign. She took another mouthful of bread, longing for the comfort of food in her grumbling stomach.

'Aren't you going to open it?'

'In a tick. Give us a chance to eat. Ta, Rosalie.' She stirred sugar in her tea, feeling Mabel's eyes still boring into the letter.

Despite Mabel's grand speeches and her attempts to be kind, the two of them still only just managed to get along. Mercy knew Mabel wanted to show herself in a good light to Alf, her husband-to-be. Maybe she'd even meant it all, wanted to be kind, be liked. The fact was, they still rubbed each other up the wrong way.

She looked at Mabel who was stirring a pot of broth. Elsie's range, Elsie's room. The place was still full of ghosts: Elsie, Tom, Frank, Cathleen, Johnny . . . No wonder Jack wanted out and Rosalie's little face was so sad, so grown up before her time. No wonder Alf wanted a new start.

She stopped eating for a moment as a lump rose in her throat. Why was she worried about letting Margaret Adair down? She did miss her, it was true, and she'd been so kind. But Margaret could soon hire herself another servant. What these people – her people – here had endured was so much greater.

Alf and Jack came in then, both smelling of ale and heavy under the eyes with fatigue.

As Rosalie gave the men their bit of supper, Mercy sloped off upstairs and lit the candle in Rosalie's room. Dorothy's writing was a stiff, rather childish copperplate, but her spelling was good:

> Mercy –
>
> There's an urgent matter I need to talk to you about in private. Meet me, Saturday 11 a.m. near the gate in Highgate Park. Don't let me down.
>
> Yours,
>
> Dorothy Ann Finch

Mercy sighed and tore the letter into tiny pieces. It didn't say anything much but she wasn't going to give Mabel the satisfaction of a look at it. Truth to tell she felt irritated with Dorothy. What was she making such a to-do about?

I suppose I ought to be grateful to her, she thought, preparing herself for bed. She laid her skirt over the chair, smoothing her hand over the soft, wrinkled cotton. It was cream, sprigged with leaves and yellow flowers. A bit old-fashioned-looking though, that length, she thought. I'll hem it up a bit . . . She stopped herself short.

What'm I going on about? For a second she almost laughed. What the hell's fashion going to matter when my belly's pushing everything out at the front and I can't get into it anyway?

She looked down at herself in her blouse and bloomers. Was there anything to see yet? She must be, what? Between three and four months gone? She moved her hands round her slim waist, then down over her belly, feeling the warmth of her skin. Wasn't it just a tiny bit rounder? She kept her hands there for a moment. There was nothing she could do – it was going to grow inside her, bigger and bigger until she had to let it out. She felt very solemn. So this was what it was to be a woman, to find your future lay in the hands of your child.

My mom must have looked at herself like this, she thought. Must have hated me for being in there, come to ruin her life. For a moment she felt a sad sympathy with her, that young, terrified woman, whoever she was. For the first time it occurred to her to wonder where her actual birth had taken place. Had she borne her child in the gutter? Was she alone, penniless, sick? Did she die in the throes of birthing and someone else take the child from her, carry her to safety where she could at least survive? Was anyone else present at her arrival? The old feeling of being lost, abandoned in the world, swept over her. It wasn't right, any of it. Everyone should have a chance to know where they came from.

What did Dorothy want? she wondered, pushing her thin arms through the sleeves of her nightdress. She felt very weary of it all suddenly, didn't want Dorothy planning for her, trying to rescue her. Not again. That would only lead to more trouble, more pain. She just wanted to be left alone to struggle with her life in her own way, come what may.

When she set out there was a light, mizzling rain, but the clouds had an insubstantial look to them and the sun was already trying to break through their swirling veil. Mercy had put her coat on but immediately felt too hot. She peered at the sky, unbuttoning the coat.

Just stop blasted raining, she thought. Then I can take it off.

There were plenty of people out Saturday shopping, going to get stuff out of pawn for Sunday, kids playing out along the pavements. She walked along Stanley Street, crossed Catherine Street, where a young man on a rough, wooden crutch was making his way along with terrible slowness, gripping a paper under his spare arm which ended at the elbow in a stump. He shuffled along on his one leg, unshaven face turned towards the ground. Mercy had seldom seen a face look more desolate. She wondered where Johnny was. Whether he'd found somewhere he could be at peace.

Before she reached the park the drizzle stopped and it grew even warmer. Mercy took her coat off, leaving her navy-blue cardigan over the white blouse and floral skirt.

The entrance to the park was opposite a row of big, posh houses on the Moseley Road. Mercy stepped inside, looking across the sloping grass. She wasn't sure of the time.

'Mercy.'

She jumped, hearing Dorothy's voice, and, as she turned, heard St Joseph's clock in the distance begin striking eleven.

Dorothy had a boy with her, a solid, rosy-cheeked lad dressed in good quality short trousers, a jacket and shiny black shoes. He was staring at her with a pointed curiosity which verged on insolence.

Mercy looked from one to the other of them. Dorothy appeared to be in a right state. She reached out to touch the boy's shoulder and Mercy saw her hand was trembling. She was breathing fast and for a moment seemed unable to speak.

'Who's this?' Mercy asked. 'One of your mistress's, is 'e?' Dorothy couldn't have anything much to say to her if she'd brought a child along as well.

The boy opened his mouth to speak when Dorothy put her fingers urgently to her lips and shushed him.

'Yes, this is Robert.' She spoke very quickly as if afraid for the words to linger in her mouth. 'And we've got summat to show you, haven't we, Robert? Mercy, I think you'd better come and sit down, dear.'

Mercy felt her heart thump harder. She was bewildered, and Dorothy's tone made her feel very nervous. Her hands began sweating and she had to wipe them on her skirt.

They went to a bench beside a flower bed of mixed pansies and sweet william. Dorothy sat the boy between the two of them. She took a deep breath and held it for a second.

'Now,' she said finally, on a rush of exhaled air, 'Robert is going to show you . . . Go on, Robert.'

Obviously aware of the solemnity of the occasion, Robert pulled a soft handful of something creamy-white from his pocket. Mercy frowned. As he opened it out it began to look familiar. She thought her heart was going to hammer its way out through her ribs. She gasped, clapping a hand over her mouth.

The boy opened out the handkerchief and laid it across his knees. Embroidered in one corner in a blue thread, with exquisite neatness, was the name ROBERT. He unfolded the second and in almost the same cornflower blue she read EDWARD. There was a third square of linen, older, more yellowed, just like hers, embroidered, just like hers, in a faded mauve: THOMAS. She stared and stared. She couldn't make sense of anything. Here were the very same linen squares, the same stitching as on the only small possession she had had since birth. The one tiny clue to her identity. And here this stranger, this young boy . . .

With her hand still pressed to her lips she looked uncomprehendingly at Dorothy. Dorothy's eyes stared back at her, full of mingled fear and tenderness.

'If you'd been a boy,' her voice trembled, 'you'd have been called Thomas. She had it all ready for you, long before . . .'

A winded, choking sound escaped from Mercy. She dragged her hand from her face and pressed it over her heart as if to contain the violence of its beating. Her whole body began to shake.

'What d'you mean, Dorothy? What in heaven's name are you telling me?'

The boy looked up at her. 'Mother says, and Dorothy says that you're my sister. Well, half-sister at any rate.'

Mercy felt her head had been filled with smoke, thicker than that billowing from any factory chimney. She couldn't see through it who the boy was, make sense of what he was saying, or why Dorothy was here with him. She felt dizzy and hot. The fog grew darker and darker, until only a few lights were flashing somewhere at the side of her vision, confusing her further, until the darkness began to fold in round her.

'Mercy? Mercy! 'Ere, get your head between your knees and you'll feel better.'

Dorothy's hands were pressing on her shoulders. The darkness cleared and she could hear blood pounding in her ears until the pressure of it was too much, her belly felt cramped and she had to sit up. She was sick and groggy.

'Stay here with 'er,' Dorothy instructed Robert, patting Mercy's shoulder. 'I'll go and ask up there for a drink of water.'

Mercy closed her eyes. This was all too much. She wanted to sleep, not hear any more. Go back to how things were. But she could never go back, she knew. Her life was tumbling round her and she was powerless to stop it.

'Are you all right?' Robert asked courteously.

She opened her eyes. 'I'm OK now. Thank you.' She examined his face as she might have done a mirror, looking for traces of herself, but she found nothing. Robert sensed this, had seen the same look in his mother's eyes.

'She says I'm the image of my father.'

Mercy noted that he didn't say 'Daddy'. Nothing that sounded affectionate.

'What's your mother's name?' she asked faintly.

He had to think for a second. 'Grace Elizabeth Weston.'

'Grace Weston.' Hearing her name, Mercy did recognize it, faintly. Dorothy had named her before. She turned the name round in her churning mind. Grace. Grace. What did this Grace have to do with her? Of course she had considered that her mother, a real flesh and blood person, might exist somewhere. But in her heart she had never believed it fully. No! Not a living, breathing person, who did ordinary, everyday things like anyone else.

Dorothy came back with a jam jar full of water and handed it to Mercy. 'They said we don't need to take it back. Big of 'em, eh?' Her dark eyes were full of anxiety. Mercy drank, then sat gripping the glass jar, head bowed.

'Tell me, Dorothy.' Her hands, legs, every part of her was still quivering.

Dorothy sank down on the bench.

'When your mother had you she wasn't wed. She comes from a respectable family. Religious, God-fearing sort of people. Her father was a lay preacher – Methodist – very strict man, he was. Any road, when she was forced to tell him he as good as washed his hands of her. Said she was to come home when she'd got rid of it, one way or other. He didn't want to know nothing about it. He'd've packed her off there and then if her mother hadn't persuaded him to let her stop at home 'til nearer the time it was due. They kept her in like, so no one'd know. Hid her.' Dorothy told the story in a flat voice as if she could hardly bear it.

'I was her maid then. We're of an age, see. When the time came near she went out and didn't come back. None of us knew where 'til after. It was her way of punishing herself, I think. Otherwise I might've gone with her.

'She went off, somewhere no one'd know her and soon after she had . . . you. She knew if she kept you she'd have no roof over her head. Her mother, Mrs Bringley, had given her a bit of money to help her get by. There wasn't a lot else she could do. Mr Bringley was a stern man, had her right under his thumb. Grace would've been on the streets else, or in the workhouse. No home, soon no money, no way of earning a crust – nowt.

'She'd seen the Hanley Home. You were born somewhere around there. It was the only thing she could think of – you'd be taken care of. They might've sent you to Canada – they started that soon after you was taken in there.'

'Amy . . .' Mercy said faintly.

'Yes, like Amy. She thought it was the only way the both of you could survive. After two or three months she sent me over there asking for work. When a job came up they gave it to me as I wouldn't leave 'em alone. So there was always someone there, someone watching over you . . .'

The smoke cleared out of Mercy's mind as suddenly as if a tornado had swept through it. Her fists clenched tight.

'You mean . . . you're saying . . . all this time, ever since before I can even remember anything, I've had a mother? And you've always known who she was and where she was?' She gasped, memories flooding through her. 'And you brought me clothes – from her? And those jobs you got me – all her, and you?'

Dorothy nodded, her expression full of pain.

Mercy stood up as if propelled by an electric shock. Rage seemed to crackle through her, making her limbs turn rigid, her jaws stiff. She turned on Dorothy, eyes ablaze with outrage and fury.

'All this time, the pair of you kept it from me, my own beginnings, my family! All these years I've felt like . . . like nothing – thrown in the gutter because no one wanted me, and all the time . . .' She could barely speak, reeling under the violence of her hurt and anger.

'You and she have dressed me in the clothes she thought right, you nearly forced me to take that job and leave Susan, who was the only person who ever showed me any real love. You both treated me like a – a puppet, organizing my life, pushing me here and there as if you owned me . . . And she hid behind you and never had the guts to come out and own me as her child . . .'

She stopped abruptly, feeling she might be sick. She swallowed, panted. Robert stared at her, frightened.

'She abandoned me,' she said in a hard, quiet voice. 'And then she still wanted to run my life, giving me nothing of the things a mother should give a child. I had nothing. I was starving from lack of love and protection, and when did I ever see her eyes looking at me with worry or love—'

'But I saw them—' Dorothy interrupted, pleading.

'When did I ever feel her arms round me? Knowing this is worse . . .' She began to weep suddenly, weak and overwrought. 'It's far worse than thinking she might have been too poor or sick to keep me, or thinking she might be dead . . .'

Dorothy stood up, her face full of anguish, and reached her arms out, 'Oh, bab . . .'

Mercy backed away. 'Leave me, you deceiver,' she spat. 'You hid her. Why did you do that, all this time? What did you owe her that you don't owe me? You could have told me. You're just her servant, aren't you?'

Dorothy made as if to speak, then helplessly closed her mouth.

'I'm going,' Mercy said, holding out her hand as if to stop Dorothy in her tracks. 'I'm sorry, Robert.' She was suddenly aware of the child. 'I don't know what you thought – that I'd just come running? Leave me, Dorothy. I'm going home. I don't want to see you again. I may have a mother, but she's left it too late by a long way. I've got my own child to bring up now.' She started walking away.

'It's going to cost me, like being a mother should,' she

said, turning, walking backwards for a moment. 'Never cost her much, did it?'

'Oh, it did,' Dorothy implored her. 'Believe me – it did.'

But she was gone, a bright-haired, solitary figure, striding across the park.

Mercy cried all the way back to Angel Street. She couldn't help it. Loud, racking sobs she couldn't have prevented even if she'd wanted to. Her emotions were so mixed, so overwhelming, that she had not even the strength to fight for control. Anger, humiliation, a sense of betrayal, of huge loss and sadness were all mingled together. And the old, deep emptiness inside her. It felt as if her grief was bottomless and she would never be able to stop its flood. It was as if all her unshed tears of childhood were pouring from her now.

At home she couldn't stop either. Couldn't hide it. She had to tell them. Jack was off somewhere, but Alf, Mabel and Rosalie were all home. She had their absolute and rapt attention as she sat gulping out her story, and after, there was silence for a moment, all of them standing round.

'I always thought there was summat queer about that Dorothy Finch keeping on coming round, that I did,' Mabel said in a tone which suggested she'd known the truth all the time. 'In fact, it crossed my mind to wonder at times whether she wasn't yer mother 'erself – 'cept there was nothing in the looks, of course.'

Just what Paul had said, Mercy remembered.

'So you've got a little brother?' Rosalie said timidly.

Mercy's eyes welled again. 'Two. They said two . . . How could she – all these years – deny I ever existed?'

'It's a disgrace,' Mabel said, arms folded self-righteously over bosoms. 'Abandoning a child like that.'

Alf cast her a look which plainly said, 'Shut yer great big trap, wench,' and Mabel subsided.

'You're not going away, are yer?' Rosalie asked.

'No, 'course not,' Mercy said fiercely. 'Why would I be?'

'But it does mean—' – Alf leant forward and Mercy could see the white stubble on his cheeks close up, the red veins in the curves of each nostril – 'somewhere you've got a family, Mercy. Blood ties of your own. That means summat, don't it? You can't just forget that.'

Mercy's eyes widened with dismay. 'D'you want me out – is that it?'

'No – no, wench.' Alf closed his hand awkwardly over hers for a second. 'It's just – well, she must've had 'er reasons like, for doing what she did. No one gives a babby up easy. And one day, when you've 'ad time for it all to sink in, you might want to know more about her and where you come from, that's all.'

'Where does she live, this mother o' yours?' Mabel asked.

'I don't know.' Mercy's brow wrinkled. 'Handsworth, I suppose – that's where Dorothy works – if she works for her now. I s'pose she does. I never asked.'

A week passed. Mercy gave up her job at the Futurist for something which didn't mean working evenings. She looked for work in a shop, and went back to Wrigley's Bakery to see if they might take her on again as she remembered it fondly. Mrs Wrigley recognized her at once but said she had a regular girl in now and couldn't let her go.

So she went from shop to shop along the Moseley Road, Ladypool Road. In the end she found a job with a Miss Martin who owned a draper's at the end of Camp Hill. Miss Martin's health wasn't any too bright and she needed help. Mercy was tempted to say, 'That makes two of us,' but wisely buttoned her lip. It'd be a nice quiet job, regular, with a half day on Mondays. And not hard: cutting from the bolts of cloth in the dimly-lit little shop, selling cottons, spools, zip fasteners, pins, buttons and all the other little cards of things Miss Martin had on her racks. Seeing them reminded her of all the evenings she and Susan had spent carding.

All that week as she walked the streets, her head was full of Dorothy's disclosures. Over and over, round and round it all went like the clothes in a maiding tub. The truth. Her truth. At first all she could feel was the raw hurt and an enormous, violent anger. She'd been treated like something of no worth, like a clockwork toy, expected to live her life according to her mother's desires and ideas. She wondered exactly what this woman had had planned for her before Mabel came along and mucked it all up, taking her off where they couldn't find her. Served her right!

As the week passed her anger gradually calmed and began to seep away. She found herself thinking as much about Dorothy as her mother. Maybe she'd been wrong to be so angry with Dorothy. After all, who else had ever shown her such devotion and care? Paul might have done – but she tried to push the thought of him away, the pain of it. She hadn't answered his last letter, felt completely unable to. Dorothy had been the one who protected her as a child, had displayed genuine emotion when she found her again, and genuinely cared for her.

The more Mercy thought of this, the more baffling it

was. Who was she, in the end, that Dorothy should bother with her? And what about this shadowy mother Dorothy was protecting? Grace Weston. Mother. She found herself repeating it over and over. Mother. My mother.

Gradually mingled with the hurt and bitterness came a surging curiosity which at first she could barely admit. When once she did voice it at home, 'I wonder what she's like . . .?', Rosalie said, 'Well aren't you going to go and see 'er? Swallow yer pride. I would. I miss my mom like anything. It's not too late for you, is it?'

'Oh no!' Mercy's voice was adamant. 'I'm not going barging into her posh little life. Not after all this time. She's never wanted me before, has she? Why should she now? I'm not giving her the chance to throw me out again. Oh no. Never.'

Chapter Forty-One

Mabel and Alf's wedding was a fortnight off and a woman down the street was making Mabel's trousseau. It wasn't being kept any great secret though.

'I had all that caper the first time,' Mabel said. 'All of them superstitions and none of them brought me much luck.'

'I should keep it plain and simple,' Alf had said, obviously worried how much she might be thinking of forking out.

'Don't fret, I will. But we'll make a good day of it all the same.'

Rosalie was to be her bridesmaid, and the same needlewoman was stitching a frock in pretty pink sateen for her.

The other women in the court, knowing there was a wedding afoot, were in and out of the house discussing, offering help. Mary Jones was out at work now her children had reached school age but she was round as soon as she'd fed them enough to keep them quiet.

Mercy, so many causes of distress tugging at her heart that she could scarcely think clearly about any of them, kept out of the way. Not that everyone wasn't kind. Her news spread round the yard like a blaze and there was no one who didn't know what had happened. All of them had soft, sympathetic words for her and questions. But she couldn't stand talking about it, not to anyone. It was still all too raw.

She went to see Tom again. He was outside, as before. Always as before, she thought. Nothing changing or moving on. That was the awfulness of it. She sat holding his hand and just once he gripped hers in return.

'I've got such a lot to tell you.' She spoke very quietly, pouring out everything that had happened. It surprised her how much better she felt after talking to him. He couldn't respond, but knowing he'd loved her once, that he likely still would if he were able, warmed her burdened heart.

After a time she saw Mr Hanley shuffle across the grass on his thin, bowed legs. He noticed her immediately and raised his hat, giving her a sweet, wistful smile. She waved back, full of unexpected excitement at seeing him. Her mind was still trying to marry this stooped old man with the fat fellow she'd felt so much aggression towards at the age of seven.

Mr Hanley drew himself up a chair beside that of another inmate about Tom's age. He had light brown hair and a round face. Mercy saw him turn his head for a second and thought ah, he's all right, he can recognize his grandfather. But the head lurched round again to face the other way, then back and forth in a convulsive motion and she could see the blankness in his eyes. She saw Mr Hanley take his hand as she had done Tom's, and begin gently to talk to him.

When later she got up to leave Tom, kissing him goodbye, Mr Hanley rose as well.

'Hello my dear.' His voice was thinner than she remembered. 'How nice to see you again.'

'How are you, Mr Hanley?'

'Oh – bars of iron, bars of iron.' But his eyes were sad and watery. 'May I have the privilege of transporting you home again?'

They walked down to the gate together.

'It's so hard coming here, isn't it?' Mercy said.

'Hardest thing I've ever done I think,' Mr Hanley agreed.

'Does anyone else come to see your grandson?'

'Oh yes, on other days. His mother, of course, and his sisters. I do Sundays – it's become a sort of routine. Now – just a moment, dear.' He stopped, fumbling in his jacket for a pipe and a pouch of tobacco and spent a little while obliging it to light. Eventually he managed and the sweet smell of the smoke reached Mercy. 'Ah, good. Now – how are you, my dear? Life treating you well?'

His Austin was parked not far from the gate and he opened the door for her. Mercy turned to him, feeling a great need to tell him. After all, he wasn't just anyone. He'd seen her as a child, too, and he was kind.

'Mr Hanley, d'you know what? I found out I've got a mother after all.'

Joseph Hanley nodded gently. 'Well, of course, my dear. Many of our unfortunate children aren't orphans in the strict sense of the word.'

'No, but I was,' she said fiercely. 'I was the one left on the doorstep. The one who didn't even have a name so they gave me yours. I had no one in the world . . .'

She poured the story out to him as they slowly made their way into Birmingham, and he listened intently. However many times she told the story it came out raw, angry, bewildered so that it seemed to her that she would always feel the same.

Mr Hanley stopped in the same spot on the Moseley Road. He reached over and took one of her young hands in his gnarled ones, turning to look into her eyes.

'I can see you're in distress, Mercy. Shocking for you, of course. Perhaps you'll be able to forgive your mother eventually for her difficulties. You know what they say, my dear, to know all is to forgive all. Whatever happens, I wish you all the luck and good fortune possible.'

He squeezed her hand for a second, then released it.

Another week passed. On Sunday afternoon Grace caught a bus into Birmingham, resolved to walk the rest of the distance. She had thought carefully about what to wear. So unimportant in one sense, yet it seemed vital for her first appearance. She was presenting – offering – herself. She dressed simply: the white mid-pleated skirt – white, to go to such a place! Yet she wanted to show her confidence, not arrive in some murky-coloured garment looking as if she were afraid of dirtying herself. On top, a white, lacy blouse covered by a soft wool cardigan in her favourite colour: cornflower blue. Her shoes were two-tone – white and navy, with an elegant heel.

Dorothy said goodbye to her, her face tense with worry.

'She's stubborn, you know. I don't know that she'll've calmed down yet. Don't be surprised if she . . .'

'Rejects me?' Grace looked back at her steadily. 'I'm certain I must do this. Mercy's right. I have risked nothing all these years. Always what Father wanted, then Neville. Believing they knew what was right for me. And yet my father married me to a man who is scarcely more than an animal. Now, I'm truly going to do the right thing.'

Dorothy seized Grace's shoulders and kissed her forehead. Grace raised her right hand and laid it over Dorothy's where it still rested on her shoulder.

'I'm so terrified, I can't tell you,' she said, eyes cast down.

Dorothy said nothing, squeezed her shoulders.

'But I must go.' Grace raised her head, the pale hair brushed immaculately round her face. Her eyes were wide and sad. 'Living with myself has been hard enough these twenty years. But now . . .' She pressed Dorothy's hand, then released it, stepping back. 'I've thought about it endlessly and I can't carry on – not like this.'

She was not accustomed to travelling on buses. Inside it was warm, stinking of smoke and old beer. She got off in town, hatless in the warm sunshine of early July, and walked across the Cathedral Square.

She felt a heavy-headness come over her. After her sleepless nights of turmoil when her mind seemed to protest, 'No more!', she was now filled with a fatalistic calm. What would be would be. She could only follow her conscience and her instincts. Her child, her flesh and blood, was in trouble and this sharpened her own memories of being alone, carrying a child, in desperation and shame. She wanted to make reparation. Give comfort. Make peace.

She walked briskly and purposefully through the centre of Birmingham, past the smart shops and banks towards New Street Station. Around Smithfield Market factories and workshops clustered in increasing numbers, hemmed in by the warrens of slum housing. The air was acrid with the smells of smoke and swarf, chemicals and grime.

The horror of it flooded back to her. Those days in Aston, where the same smells were mingled with that sickening, vinegary tang from the HP Factory. She knew, logically, that she had survived it, come safely through, but the terror and degradation her twenty-five-year-old self had suffered was engraved on her very soul.

Dorothy had described the route to her many times, and she had been here herself just once before. Just to look, to be able to picture it. Perhaps catch a glimpse of

. . . But she had not seen her. From her memory, nothing had changed: pubs, houses, everything timelessly the same. She knew that where she wanted was down on the right.

'Nine,' she muttered under her breath. A man pushed his cap further back on his head and stared at her.

'Oh God, give me strength!' Here it was, the dank, mossy walls of the entry. Nine Court, Angel Street. Her heart seemed almost to rise into her throat.

They were all there when she arrived, except Jack, who was always out if he could be, these days, Mercy, Mabel, Alf, Rosalie and Mary Jones, talking about food for the wedding. The door was open to let a breeze in, even though it meant they could smell the drains every time there was a fresh waft of fetid air.

They heard the footsteps, the light, ladylike clip of her heels, their hesitation as she approached the door and found it open. She didn't need to knock. She could see the ring of people inside, all quite still now, watching her, Alf and Mabel with their heads screwed round to look.

For a moment no one said a thing. Mercy could barely even breathe. She was paralysed, felt as if the room had begun to sway around her. There seemed to be a spell on them all. The moment went on and on. She saw the woman's elegance, her pale skin, gold hair, the deep grey eyes. Those eyes fastened immediately on her, and in them she saw the intensity of her sorrow, longing and fear.

Then Mabel said quietly, 'Oh Lor',' and stood up, scraping her chair. 'You'd best come in then.'

The woman stepped, with humble attitude, over the threshold and stood in front of them all. For a moment she couldn't seem to think what to do. Then, visibly gathering together every last ounce of courage she possessed, she stood tall, jutting her chin out a little.

'You know, don't you, who I am?' She spoke gently, entreatingly to Mercy.

Mercy just had the wits to give a small nod. Everyone else's eyes bored into them.

'I've come here because – because Dorothy said – you could feel nothing but anger and disgust towards me, and I . . .' For a moment she seemed about to lose control, her hands covering her face convulsively for a second. She removed them, clawing back her composure and returned them to her sides, gripped tight into fists. 'I knew that if we were ever to meet it was right that I should be the one to come to you.'

Alf stood up suddenly too. 'Come on,' he instructed the others. 'This ain't no time for us to be 'ere. Let's get out and leave 'em on their own.'

'Why should we get out?' Mabel griped. 'If 'er's got summat to say she can say it in front of us, and not before time neither.'

'You're Mabel?' Grace turned to her. 'You're the one that . . . took her?'

'Ar, I did.' Mabel folded her arms aggressively. 'And I gave 'er a home to grow up in and took 'er back when she came 'ere in trouble like. And I never deserted none of my kids, that's for sure.'

Mercy roused herself for a moment and turned her head. 'Oh, didn't you?'

Reminded of her absent months with Stan Jones, Mabel flushed an ugly red.

'Come on.' Alf jerked his head again. 'Out.'

They trooped to Mary's house leaving a sudden, engulfing silence between Mercy and Grace.

Mercy was still sitting, her hair loose and falling round her face. Grace stood, her eyes fixed with yearning on Mercy's bowed head, willing her to speak.

The silence went on, during which the conflict of Mercy's emotions was so acute she couldn't move or speak. She sat trying to summon up all her pain and anger, all the loneliness and hurt of the past years, but instead found herself overcome by helplessness, a sense of dream-like unreality. Her mother, the woman she had never been able to imagine was standing in front of her. Had come to find her. Flesh and blood. An unassailable tie which drew her like a magnet however hard she tried to resist. There Grace stood, looking at her with her own eyes, her hair the same straw gold. But she couldn't quite bear it. Not yet.

In a voice unmistakable in its hostility she said, 'So you're my mom then?'

'Yes.' Grace's voice began to break. 'Yes, Mercy. I am.'

Chapter Forty-Two

Grace pulled a chair out. 'May I?'

Mercy nodded, still not looking at her.

'So what d'you want off me then? Decided I exist after all, have you?'

Silence followed, for so long that she was compelled to look up. Grace's eyes were fixed on her, sorrow spilling in wet lines down her face.

'Oh Mercy, how callous and wicked you must think I am!' She wiped her eyes, though more tears came immediately. 'How can I explain to you that I did the cruellest thing a mother could do to her child, and yet I loved you so much – still love you – so that never a day has passed when I haven't ached to be able to have you properly in my life?'

Mercy felt a tightness take hold in her chest, a hard ache like a gigantic sob trying to escape. It was a sensation so overpowering it filled her with panic. Don't let her reach you! her mind screamed. Keep her at a distance . . .

'So why now?' She made her voice as bitter and sarcastic as she could. 'All of a sudden, out of the blue.'

'Because I know that you, my daughter—'

'Daughter!'

'That you are also carrying a child. And I couldn't live, knowing the suffering you would go through without . . . support. Family. I can't describe to you how it has been watching you from a distance all these years. Knowing all your difficulties. And then when we lost you . . . When Mabel . . .' She ran a hand over her face. 'My life has been tied to yours since the moment you came into the world.'

Mercy tore her eyes away from Grace's face, from her anguish. The tension inside her increased further. Her sense of being lost, rejected, worthless, tussled with her enormous, unsatisfied longing to mean something to someone else, for family bonds, to belong. But she mustn't let it surface, mustn't allow herself the prospect of being satisfied, and she moved her hands under the table to hide their trembling. She was shaken by all the hungry needs of a child, so many and so intense. She was the tiny, bereft creature in the cellar who could not help herself.

'I'd like to tell you,' Grace said, 'May I?'

Mercy nodded, swallowing hard. Her teeth were chattering again and she had begun to shake all over, so much that she couldn't hide it.

'Oh, my dear,' Grace said, seeing her. She moved to get up. 'I—'

'Just tell me,' Mercy interrupted savagely. 'Tell me and then go.'

Grace leant back in her chair again. She spoke in her soft voice, looking away from Mercy, giving her a chance to compose herself. From the corner of her eye she could see her shuddering attempts to do so.

She described the wretched house in Aston to which she'd resorted in desperation, the women who had birthed her, and her departure, still shaking from shock and exhaustion, in the middle of the night.

'When I reached the home, it was very late. Three o'clock – the clocks were chiming, I remember. The streets were so very dark and I was terrified. I'd never been out at that time before and I was afraid that someone might see me. A policeman perhaps. Then it would have all been impossible.

'It was so cold. There were icicles hanging on the railings. I'd wrapped you in everything I had, but I was worried it wouldn't be enough, that you wouldn't last the night. I thought I must just leave you, once I'd put you down on the steps. Leave you and run right away, or I'd never be able to give you up.

'But I found I couldn't. Simply couldn't physically leave. It was as if you were still attached to me. I went and sat on the steps of that school – your school – across the road, and all the time I was straining my ears to hear if you made any sound. Every so often I crept across and made sure you were still breathing. After a time you started crying. I was just on the point of getting up when I heard voices along the street. I couldn't imagine who it could be. I hid behind the wall with my cloak pulled over my face.

'There was a lamp outside the home, so there was a pool of light. When they came I saw there were five of them. Boys, no more than that. All rather oddly dressed – big boots, cravats and bowler hats with a peculiar pointed bit at the front.' She gestured, making the shape. 'I realized after a moment what they were. There were a few of them about in those days, boy gangs calling themselves "Peaky Blinders" – to do with the hats, I s'pose. I'd heard snippets about them because they were notorious for terrible, vicious fights . . . Anyway, they were only young really, but their voices sounded so rough and threatening to me.

'They started arguing – it was because they heard you crying. "Here – what's that?" – "It's only a cat." – "No, it's a babby." – That sort of thing. One of them bounded up the steps. I was biting my hand so hard I drew blood. He said, "Eh – it is an' all! It's a babby!"

'I can't describe to you how I felt at that moment. These disgusting creatures in their filthy moleskin trousers and belts with vicious-looking buckles, going up close to you. Inside I was screaming at them, don't touch my baby!'

Grace laid her hand over her heart. 'My baby – oh, when I uttered those words to myself . . . One of them bent down and picked you up. Actually lifted you, cradling you in a mocking sort of way, and took you down the steps. "Ah," he said. "Don't cry there." The others were jeering in a horrible manner. I thought they were going to make off with you . . .' She shuddered.

'They crowded round, making horrible comments – I can't remember . . . But then one said, "Look – his face's got blood on it!" They assumed you were a boy, I don't know why. They said, "Ugh – d'you think it's only just been born?" They all made jeering and retching noises, bending over. One of them dropped his hat. I remember him stooping to pick it up.

'The lad holding you said, "Who wants it, eh?" He started to circle with you, swinging you as if he was going to throw you and you were screaming louder and louder. "'Ere – catch!"

'I screamed then. As I ran down the steps—' – Mercy saw her face contort with disgust – 'there was blood running down my legs. I shouted and shouted, "Give me my baby!" I must have looked like something from Bedlam. I felt like a madwoman. I was snarling – it was pure instinct, like an animal. I would have done anything, scratched their eyes out – killed them if necessary.

'"Is it yours then?" he said, and I shouted, "Give me

my baby" again. He pretended he was going to throw you at me, looking round at the others. Then, carelessly, he handed you over.' Grace's arms made the motions of holding a child.

'"Shouldn't leave 'im lying around next time!" one of them shouted. They went off laughing, shouting back more crude remarks.

'You were still crying so wretchedly. You were hungry, and I was shaking. I couldn't stop my teeth chattering, like someone with a fever.' She glanced at Mercy. She was sitting bent over the table, her arms wrapped round herself as if now, too, she was frozen, but her eyes were fixed on Grace's face.

'My legs could scarcely hold me up. I took you back to those icy school steps and sat down, soiled and damp as I was. And then I . . .' She broke off, tears rushing from her again, her voice high, cracking so that for a time she struggled to speak. 'I did the one thing I'd avoided doing up until then, the thing I knew would entangle my heart with you for ever. I unfastened my clothes and let you suckle. You had all those instincts ready and you sucked strongly while I cradled your head . . . And I cried. I don't know how long we sat there exactly. I must have slept a little, keeping you warm. When I woke my head was leaning against the wall and it was getting light. I was filled with panic. Someone might see us!

'I had to hurry and put you down. But still then I couldn't leave. I watched until I saw a lady carry you in. And then I knew you'd gone from me.' Her voice sank to a distraught whisper. 'For ever.'

A sound came from Mercy. A high, unstoppable whimper. Her head was in her hands, the backs of them resting on the table, for she was bent right over as if felled by grief, curled like a cowed little child.

'Mercy!' Grace stood up in alarm. 'Oh, my dear – my dear child!' Trembling, she went to stand behind her. The girl's shoulders were heaving, but some time passed before the sound of her weeping broke into the room, so far did it have to travel from the very depths of her.

'Oh . . .' Mercy gasped and broke into desperate sobbing.

For a long time Grace hesitated behind her, racked herself by the heartbreaking sound. Very cautiously she reached out her hand and laid it on her daughter's shoulder.

Later, when they were a little calmer, Grace offered to leave. 'You may want me out of here . . .'

But the thought of this woman – mother, her mother – leaving now with so much still to say was suddenly appalling to Mercy. She could feel her resistance falling away.

Grace gently requested tea, thinking the activity might steady her, and, in a daze, Mercy went out to the tap in the yard to fill the kettle. Hungrily, Grace watched her slim figure for echoes, resemblances, and they were only too easy to find.

'It'll be a few minutes,' Mercy said awkwardly, as she put it on to boil.

'Of course,' Grace smiled.

Mercy felt very strange. Exhausted and churned up. She had done her best to keep a barrier up between her own howling loneliness and this woman who had given her away. And she had failed, broken down completely. The story she had told of that filthy, leaking attic room she had inhabited, when all her life she had been used to the comforts of greater wealth, the anguish of the night of her birth as well as Grace's undeniable grief had made her begin to understand. Both had been helpless, the mother as much as the child. They had drawn a step closer. But now the moment of most acute emotion had passed, it was hard for them to know how to talk to each other again. They were silent, looking at each other awkwardly, and then away. Both began speaking at once, then faltered.

'No – you, please,' Grace said.

'It's just – your father. Dorothy said he was very strict.'

Grace sighed. She stood holding on to the back of a chair. Mercy saw how smooth and well kept her hands were.

'All my young life my father ruled everything. I suppose I let him. My mother did the same. Both of them are dead now. They were religious people in the worst sense – rigid, afraid . . . After – after I'd had you, I mean, because everything was different from then on – he made me marry Neville, my husband. He thought Neville shared his views . . .' She gave a harsh laugh. 'Well, there was a mistake. The one and only thing they had in common was that they were both bullies. But those were my alternatives at the time: destitution or Neville. Father said he'd cast me out if I didn't marry him. I'd disgraced myself; now I had to do precisely as I was told. D'you know, at the time it didn't seem to matter. I felt as if my life was over in any case.' She sighed. 'My agony was in having given you up. Perhaps when I had you I could have found some home for fallen women like myself. Even kept you. But the only choice I could see then was to get back into the safety of home or perish, alone and starving.'

She stopped talking. Mercy looked guardedly at her.

'It's all right, dear – but I've been talking so much that I've barely even heard your voice.'

'But you know about me.' Her tone was still accusing. 'You've been watching me all my life. What I want to know is: who is my father? If your life was so sheltered, how did it happen?'

She blushed at her own bluntness and saw the colour flame in Grace's cheeks as well. The kettle murmured loudly in the background.

'Oh—' She sank down at the table again with a long sigh. 'Of course you want to know. I was such a foolish, ignorant girl. Romantic, but with not the first idea . . .' She broke off for a moment and without looking directly at Mercy said, 'Was James Adair – forceful with you?'

The burning in Mercy's cheeks heightened until she thought she might catch fire.

'Dorothy told you that as well. Of course – Dorothy tells you everything. Like what sort of clothes I should wear so you could go out and decide for me. Buy me the clothes I should have.'

'Oh no – I didn't buy them! How could I have done? I have no money of my own. No, they were passed on – from friends who had girls. I made up charitable causes and so on that I was giving them to. I didn't choose them.'

Mercy digested this. Grace seemed to have had as little choice in her life as she had had herself.

'No,' she said eventually. 'He wasn't exactly – didn't knock me about. Not the first time. But he forced me all the same. I was afraid of what he'd do if I didn't . . . I didn't know what he'd do, or what I should do. Then he came back another night and he was rough, pushed me down, made me . . .' Once more she started to cry. She no longer seemed to have a guard on her emotions. The kettle gushed out steam behind her and she turned, hiding her face as she brewed the tea.

Grace had been drinking in her words, the sound of her soft voice. She was conscious of the gulf between their experiences, yet in this one, very fundamental one, they were the same: each being alone in the world with a child.

'I'm so, so sorry Mercy. If I'd had any idea he might behave so appallingly I wouldn't have dreamed of suggesting you go there. It astonishes me that he's of such weak character. He seems so . . . upright.'

'I know,' Mercy said, turning. 'That's why I couldn't believe it, even while it was happening.' She brought Grace her tea. 'Please – tell me about my father.'

'Oh dear.' Grace sighed again. 'I was in love with your father. I was young – well, not so young, of course – and very naive and innocent. I have only one younger sister, Ruth, so there was no one to show me the way. Our mother was a true Victorian. Never breathed a word about the physical aspects of life. Your father wasn't of our – of my – class . . .' She fiddled with the spoon in her saucer, abashed. What was Mercy's class, after all?

'He came to our house as a gardener and handyman. His name was Daniel. Danny. He was so beautiful. Dark brown, curly hair, brown eyes, a smile which just lit up his face. And he was ambitious. He wanted to move on – didn't want to stay in service and I used to encourage him. He liked to talk to me – we were much of an age. I fell in love with him.' She gave a sharp, ironic laugh. Mercy watched her with absolute attention. 'Helpless with it. I'd have done anything for him. Anything he asked. After some time we became lovers. You might ask how, since I was so ignorant of the meaning of it. But it was such a gradual thing. He had a little room at the back of the house. It wasn't difficult to be alone. He led me, little by little, not forcing, so that when we were – united – for the first time I hardly knew how I'd reached this point, but I knew it was something I couldn't undo. That it was wrong, morally. Yet I felt so safe with him. We learned together and the pleasure of it grew. It was exciting, illicit.' Mercy heard her tone soften as she spoke of it. 'We were like children really. I didn't even know that was how babies came.'

Her tone grew desolate and she looked across at Mercy. 'Of course in the end I fell pregnant and it all came out. My father dismissed him at once. I hoped he'd wait for me, that I could escape – we'd marry and have our child. He left Birmingham soon after. He wrote, before I'd even given birth to you, telling me he was going to America. To start afresh.'

Mercy thought how many people connected with her had crossed that ocean.

'He did go. He succeeded in that. Two years after he arrived he was killed. An accident on the railway. We never heard exactly what. Another man he'd teamed up with wrote and told us. Just a note, no more.'

Mercy looked perplexed. 'Told your father?'

Grace was about to say something, but checked herself, seemed to be looking at Mercy with a new kind of dread. She spoke very carefully, watching Mercy's face.

'No, not my father, Mercy. When Danny came to work in our house he came to join his sister. His name was Daniel Finch.'

Mercy seemed to stop breathing for a moment.

'Yes, my dear. Dorothy is your aunt.'

She leant across the table and dared to take Mercy's spare hand in her own. Mercy didn't resist.

'You have hands like his.' She looked searchingly into Mercy's eyes. 'He was a good man, your father. He didn't love me as I loved him, but he had a lot of love in him.

He and Dorothy came from a terribly unhappy family and they looked after each other.'

For a second she raised Mercy's hand and brushed it against her lips before releasing her.

'Dorothy – my aunt . . .?' Mercy was still dazed. 'So that's why – that's what kept her with you.'

'Dorothy would have stayed with me anyway. She came to us when she was fourteen. She loves me and I her,' Grace said matter of factly. 'But we shared these extra bonds – Danny, and you. We had you, from a distance. She was absolutely distraught when that Mabel Gaskin took you. She'd been ill, you see – you remember, perhaps? We were at our wits' end and Dorothy felt it was her fault. We'd hoped to get you adopted by a good family so you could have had a proper life and been better cared for.

'When Dorothy found you at Mabel's and we saw how it was, your attachment to Susan, we thought the only thing to do was wait until you were old enough to go to work and then we could help find you something worthwhile and safe. Oh, those years were terrible. Seeing you suffering with that woman, so poor and ill-treated! You have no idea how much time we spent talking about how we could change things and help you without Neville suspecting. By then I had the boys to consider . . . Your brothers.'

She stopped, seeing again how deep in shock Mercy was. The trembling had started again and she was very pale.

Mercy felt as if a landslide was happening inside her, everything tumbling, splintering, tilting, the person she had always thought herself to be torn apart. And yet, she knew a sudden, slow-awakening joy.

'My brothers,' she whispered. 'My mother . . . my aunt . . . Oh my God!' Her eyes were stretched wide. 'Oh, I can't take it all in.'

Suddenly she found Grace was kneeling close in front of her on the hard floor, her head bowed.

'Mercy – all I ask is that you'll let me see you sometimes and get to know you as I should. And one day – one day – I hope you'll be able to understand a little and begin to forgive me.'

Mercy couldn't speak. Very slowly she stood up. Grace looked up at her and Mercy held out her hand to help her to her feet. They stood facing each other, close in height, their hair precisely the same bright gold, both trembling. There was a second's hesitation, then Mercy held out her arms, sobbing as Grace embraced her tightly, her face washed with tears of love and relief.

'I've got a mom!' Mercy cried over and over. Her voice was broken, childlike. 'Oh, I've got a mom!'

'You have, my darling one.' Grace stroked her hair, held her close, trying to soothe her. 'You've always had a mother, and she's always loved you.'

This made Mercy sob even harder.

They stood for a few moments, the mother comforting her daughter, the daughter the mother. They could start, very gradually, to weave together the threads of all their lost years. It was a beginning.

Chapter Forty-Three

For someone who'd been married before and was now in any case living in sin, Mabel was surprisingly girlish and mithered the morning of the wedding.

She went down to the public baths on the Moseley Road and treated herself to a good soak before Mercy and Mary helped her into her wedding garb: a calf-length skirt and flared jacket which she belted tightly at the waist, all in navy pinstripe. Under the jacket she wore a cream blouse and rounded it off with navy shoes with straps, and a straw boater to which Mary pinned a posy of yellow roses.

'Look at me,' she said, holding out her arms as Mary tightened the belt round her. 'I'm all of a quiver! I'll never get through this blooming service, I'm a bag of nerves!'

'You look very nice,' Mary told her. 'Doesn't she, Mercy?'

'Yes,' Mercy agreed generously. 'You really do, Mabel. You should stop fretting.'

Mabel did in fact look splendid. The suit flattered her broad, curvaceous figure and the deep blue set off her dark colouring. Her hair was coiled low on her neck, and she looked a handsome, mature woman, despite sounding much more like a sixteen-year-old.

Mary was also spruce in a pale blue frock. She had lost her gauntness now her children were older and her face had taken on a rounder, almost sweet look.

'You look lovely too, Mercy,' she said wistfully. 'But then you always do.'

Mercy was wearing her white dress with the sailor-suit collar. It was mid-calf length and loose at the front. She'd plaited her hair and twisted it into a simple knot at the back, leaving a few soft, wispy curls round her face, which had more colour back in it now she was over her morning sickness. She helped Rosalie into her pink bridesmaid's dress.

'It's lovely!' Rosalie twirled round. 'Oh, thank you, Mabel! It's the prettiest frock I've ever had!'

'You deserve it,' Mabel said indulgently. 'You've been a real good kid, what with yer mother and all that's happened.'

Everyone made noises of agreement.

Food was laid out under a muslin cloth on the table and Alf emerged from the pantry where he had been getting himself scrubbed up over the sink. His best suit was a tight fit on him now.

'It'll have to do, though,' he said, patting his stomach. 'One thing about you, wench, you can at least cook.'

'Cheeky bleeder!' she retorted. 'I've got a bit more know-how than that, I should 'ope!' and she gave him a suggestive wink.

Mercy wrapped a bit of sacking over her dress to keep it clean and heated the kettle. She watched Alf combing his hair in his shirtsleeves, intently turning his head this way and that in front of the little mirror, looking like an anxious young lad on his first date. Mercy smiled wistfully at the sight of him. He and Mabel would be happy enough together. At least something good could come out of all the tragedy of the past years.

The women were to leave in half an hour, Alf going on a bit earlier.

'Here – a cuppa to keep you going,' she said when it was ready.

'Oh, ta,' he said as if she'd offered him a large slug of whisky. 'I could do with that, I can tell yer.'

She sat sipping her tea, hoping the little fruit cake she'd baked would be all right and the bread wouldn't curl and wanting everything to go well for them. The baby was kicking now, more and more. She could feel its insistent flutter. But she was still a very tidy size. In the loose dress no one who didn't know could have guessed.

She looked round at the others' faces, all quiet and solemn as the moment approached. The thing to do now, she thought, is to go on. Try and put away the past. I've got a future and it starts today. With a surge of excitement she reminded herself for the umpteenth time that she had family coming to the wedding. Real family. Grace had asked humbly whether she might be at the service.

'I shan't impose any more on your hospitality,' she'd said to Mabel on Sunday before she left. 'I'd just like to be there with Mercy – well, and you.' Grace had tried to swallow all rancour she felt towards Mabel. 'You brought her up, after all.'

Mabel appeared a bit bemused, before remembering to look self-righteous and aggressive. 'Well, if that's what Mercy wants,' she said, in the tone of someone who'd never had anything but Mercy's best interests at heart.

Mercy found both of them looking at her. She gave a tense smile, and nodded.

'Thank you,' Grace said. To both of them. 'Thank you so much.'

They made quite a procession down Catherine Street and along the Moseley Road. Neighbours from Angel Street turned out to wave and wish them well, and there were a few well-meaning whistles as Mabel strode majestically along, smiling her gap-toothed smile. She looked a happy woman.

Behind her walked Mary and family, the Ripleys and McGonegalls and some others who tagged along to see her wed.

Mercy heard Josie Ripley say to Mary, 'Ain't she got a husband already somewhere?'

Mary looked round indignantly at her. 'It's all regular. She told the vicar like – I mean 'e deserted 'er nearly ten year ago!'

The square tower of St Paul's loomed with impressive solidity in the sunlight, though its stones were blackened with soot. Mercy could hear small birds twittering in the trees round the church. Taking in a long, nervous breath, she leant her head back and felt warm sunlight on her face.

Mabel, Rosalie and Mary waited outside while the rest of them went in. None of the neighbours were church-goers. The McGonegalls occasionally went to St Anne's to Mass in a fit of guilt, but they all seemed to feel muted and out of place in the gloom of the church. As Mercy's eyes got used to it she saw how stately and beautiful it was inside, how you could see leaves rippling through the coloured glass. For a second she was back in the hall of the Hanley Home, dreaming her way through the long window.

Mercy soon heard the clip-clip of well-made heels, and felt her heart leap with shy expectation. That's the sound of my mother, she thought. Mother. She'd saved a third row pew. She turned, and in astonishment, saw not only Grace, but Dorothy and Robert, and another smaller boy with almost white-blonde hair. In a haze she stood up, feeling everyone's eyes on them.

Grace smiled at her, adoringly, defiantly. This was her daughter. She wanted everyone to know. Mercy moved to the far end, Grace and the boys following her, and Dorothy sat by the middle aisle. She leant foward and gave Mercy a long, meaningful look which said, I know you know everything. But there'll be time afterwards. Plenty of time.

Grace took her hand and squeezed it and Mercy smiled. She thought she might explode with the amazement and wonder of the past few days. None of it had fully sunk in yet. But she kept saying to herself, I'm not alone any more. I'm not alone in the world.

'This is Edward,' Grace whispered, as the organ began to play softly in the background. 'You're very alike.' Edward stared at her with naked curiosity and Mercy found herself doing much the same in return.

'Dorothy says you looked very like that – he's ten.'

'I suppose,' Mercy mused, her eyes not leaving the boy's face. 'But I don't remember any mirrors.' She reached out her hand nervously, not knowing what to do, and smiled.

'Hello – I'm Mercy.'

'Edward,' he said with grown-up solemnity. 'Pleased to meet you.'

Mercy laughed softly. 'I'm pleased to meet you, too.'

'She's coming!' someone hissed, and they all stood up as the wedding march struck up and Mabel appeared at the back of the church. Alf peered round at her from the front.

Mabel, having no living relatives to accompany her, had rather unusually asked Mary to walk her down the aisle. Mary was all smiles, Mabel more nervous and solemn, and Rosalie behind, with her little posy of pink and white carnations.

The church was only a quarter full, but everyone there wished them well. Mabel joined Alf at the front, the door closed at the back.

They all stood up and sang 'Praise My Soul the King of Heaven'. At the words, 'ransomed, healed, restored, forgiven,' Mercy felt Grace looking at her and their eyes met for a moment. Mercy was struck with admiration for her, coming here, laying herself bare to everyone. It had taken some guts, that had.

The service began. The heavy door at the back opened and closed a couple of times to let in latecomers. Mabel and Alf said their words with dignity. They looked small and humble standing side by side under that immensely high ceiling in their plain clothes, the only sort they could afford.

Mercy felt a great sadness rush through her as they finished their vows. However much she tried to forget, to count her blessings, it all surfaced unexpectedly. She was to have been married. She and Paul had made their promises to each other and she had rejected him. Missing him gnawed away at her inside. She looked down at her hands folded in her lap, tears in her eyes. The feeling had to go away sooner or later, this ache for him. The door must close, she thought. It just wasn't meant to be. And this was no time to be dismal. Hiding behind the pretence of wiping her nose, she surreptitiously dabbed the corners of her eyes. Grace kept looking round at her. Couldn't seem to stop looking at her. She tried to smile.

The ceremony was almost over and Alf, hat in hand, and Mabel were soon exchanging their first kiss as a married couple. Everyone was smiling. Mary Jones's eyes were wet.

They stood to sing 'Now Thank We All Our God.'

As soon as the first, rather ragged verse was underway, Mercy felt a tap on her shoulder and turned. One of the churchwardens had crept along the side aisle and whispered discreetly in her ear.

'Sorry miss – but there's someone outside requires your assistance.'

Who on earth? They'd asked for some ale to be delivered at the house, but surely to goodness he hadn't come here to see her about it? She put her hymn book down and with a baffled shrug said to Grace, 'I'll see you outside.' She followed the warden, very much on his dignity, to the back of the church.

'Didn't want to disturb you but it seemed urgent like,' he said stiffly, pulling the door open. 'There you go . . .'

There was no one in the porch, so she went out, bewildered and rather irritated. What was so urgent that it couldn't wait until they'd finished? She looked from side to side.

'Mercy.'

He stepped out from under the trees. His face was sallow, exhausted-looking, the suffering in it plain to see.

'Paul,' she said, at a loss. 'Oh heavens – Paul.'

They stood looking at each other, the hymn sounding thinly from inside the church.

'How did you get here?' she asked him, somehow calmer than he was. His agitation was obvious, his hands gripping the edges of his open jacket. His face was even thinner than she remembered, fatigued. The sight of it wrung her heart.

'You told me the name of the street. So I asked – in a

shop. They said you'd gone to a wedding, and I thought at first . . .' He shrugged helplessly.

'No – oh, no! It's Mabel – and Alf. My . . . my . . . the people I live with.'

He turned away a fraction. 'My father died last week. So I—'

'Oh Paul.'

'Mercy, why did you write that letter? What on earth happened? I haven't been able to sleep, to think straight. I had to ask myself, were you just playing with me – all the time? Is my judgement completely wrong? Was everything that happened just a . . . a . . .' He put his hand to his forehead. 'I knew you, or thought I did. You were so straight, so true. I can't make sense of anything. I thought you'd just write back and say everything was all right, that it was just a mistake, joke even . . .' He raked his hand through his hair.

She looked anxiously over her shoulder. 'They'll be out in a minute, come round here.'

They crept round the side of the church under the shade of the trees. A blackbird rose from one of them, chirruping in alarm. Mercy felt weak, trembling, but she still had a small pool of calm inside her. She longed to put her arms round him, to comfort, spread her love round him, but that would be wrong. She would tell him the worst, the truth, and then he could forget her as she had tried to forget him. He deserved to know. She would tell him straight, bluntly, the thing a man would least want to hear.

Standing apart from him she looked into his eyes. He watched her, arms folded as if to protect his heart, yet his eyes were so full of tenderness she was forced to look away again. Her own expression was brave, but infinitely sad.

'I'm expecting a babby.'

He was silent for a moment, then his hands hung loose at his sides. His tone was flat, defeated.

'Oh – I see.' He was struggling to take it in. 'So you're already married then.'

'No, Paul, I'm not.' She told him with a truthfulness that was almost brutal, about James Adair.

'It happened twice. I didn't know how I could stop him and I didn't want it. If you can believe anything I say, please believe that. I'd never have thought it of him then – and I was so frightened . . . didn't know. I just didn't know what to do.'

Her distress began to seep through, despite her efforts to remain calm. She put her hands over her burning face. This was the most horrible, the dirtiest moment of her life, facing all this again, having to tell him of all people.

When she looked up, he too had his face in his hands. It's over now, she thought. He knows the very worst of me.

After a moment he said brokenly, 'I came wanting to be angry with you . . .' He looked up at her. 'Did you love him?'

'Love him?' She was aghast. 'How can you ask me that? Paul, I was spending every waking moment I could with you. It was like a nightmare – every time I went back to that room. I couldn't tell you what was happening. I felt so ashamed, so used and dirty. I'd try and put it out of my mind in the day, almost as if it were happening to someone else. And with you – you were the one I loved with all my heart. I still . . .' Her control was slipping away from her. 'Oh Paul, I've wanted you so bad I can't even tell you. I was so scared and sick and ashamed when I got home – when I found out there was a babby and it wasn't all going to go away. I didn't want you to know because . . . How could I tell you something so disgusting about me so that you'd despise me? I had to run away from the Adairs in the middle of the night and I wrote to you, and I thought, better just to . . . to cut it off. Finish it.' She wiped her eyes and looked up, overcome to see tears in his.

'Mercy.' He stepped closer to her, cautiously. 'Do the Adairs know about this child?'

'No! They must never know! It would make her so unhappy and even more, I don't want him to know. I can survive without him. He lied to me,' she finished furiously. 'He used me like a dirty handkerchief and he said it wouldn't happen. I wouldn't have a babby – as if he knew! No – I may be alone, but I don't want him anywhere near.'

The door of the church opened and they heard whoops of laughter as Alf and Mabel came out to be showered with rice.

Paul grasped her hand and pulled her even closer to the wall, out of sight.

'Tell me something.' He spoke with immense intensity, his face close to hers, eyes still wet with tears. 'Tell me truthfully whether you could . . . whether you still feel anything for me.'

She saw the anguish with which he waited for her answer. 'Oh Paul, of course I do,' she said gently. 'There's only one man I love with all my heart and that's you. I've never stopped loving you and I've missed you so much sometimes, I felt like coming to find you. Except I knew it was all impossible. That it's hopeless now. Sometimes I think I'm fated always to be on my own.'

'Why?'

'Why what?'

'Why should you be alone?'

'Paul,' she reminded him gently. 'I'm carrying another man's child. How could I expect you to forgive that, however much I didn't want it?'

Paul suddenly pressed his hands to her face, lifting her chin a little. His palms were hot on her cheeks.

'Say again that you love me.'

Tears ran down her face. 'I do. I love you.'

'And I love you. YOU. I told you before, whatever the past, whatever we are and what we've done, or what's been done to us, I want to spend the rest of my life with you. I can't live without you. Not properly.'

'But this isn't the past, Paul, it's now.'

He released her, but stayed close. 'Do you think, in the great scheme of things, that my bringing up a child that isn't mine is so very terrible? Mercy, I'm not looking to you for purity or perfection or any of that mumbo-jumbo. I'm so sorry for all you've suffered believing I was, but you were wrong. I've learned that surviving is about more than just staying alive. It's about holding on to the few worthwhile things there are, the things that make sense, that you can love.'

They stared into each other's eyes, both their faces wet with tears. He reached for her hand. 'Now, once more, my dearest love – please will you be my wife and share your life with me?'

'Yes,' she whispered, weeping. Then finding her voice, 'Yes. Yes!'

As if in response to their promises a cheer broke from the front of the church as their arms reached for each other, cheeks, then lips meeting, each clinging to the most precious thing in life.

*

Grace was standing rather at a loss with Dorothy at the front of the church while the rest of the party talked and celebrated in the sunshine. Mabel and Alf posed for a couple of photographs, solemnly side by side. There was food waiting at home, but no one was in a rush. It was a lovely day and a celebration, so what was the hurry?

Holding Paul's hand, Mercy led him shyly round to the jubilant little crowd. Grace looked relieved, then puzzled on seeing her.

Mercy stopped him for a moment. 'Paul, I've got summat else to tell you. This has been the strangest, most wonderful week of my life.' Her eyes radiated joy and excitement, but Grace could also see that Mercy's face was flushed from recent tears and her heart filled with anxiety for her.

'I want you to meet Grace Weston,' Mercy said, leading Paul over.

Each of them shook hands, smiling politely, a little baffled.

'Paul – Grace is my mother. My real mother. And mother – Mom,' she giggled, still unused to saying it, 'this is Paul Louth, the man I dearly love and am going to marry.'

Paul and Grace both dealt with these surprises with perfect courtesy and gladness. Mercy took huge delight in introducing him to the boys – 'my half-brothers' – and to Dorothy.

'Dorothy Finch is—'

'I remember you talking about Dorothy,' Paul said.

Dorothy's eyes were welling with emotion.

'Yes, but Dorothy is my auntie – oh Dorothy, come here!' Both very tearful they hugged and hugged each other.

'You don't know how often I've wanted to tell you,' Dorothy sobbed, 'only I couldn't.'

Mercy took Paul's arm. She felt she wanted to hold and hug everyone around her all day long. 'If you're all confused we'll explain on the way back,' she said. She looked round anxiously. 'You will come back, won't you?'

'Well,' Grace was uncertain. 'If Mabel doesn't mind.'

'She won't,' Mercy said firmly. Suddenly she broke away from Paul, and for the first time in her life, went to Mabel and kissed her cheek.

'You be happy now,' she said. 'You just make sure.'

Mabel looked startled, then grinned. 'I'll do me best.' She patted Mercy on the arm.

The wedding party made its unhurried, celebratory way back along the Moseley Road, Mercy, in the middle of it, arm and arm with her mother and her husband-to-be.

Grace looked round at her beautiful, indomitable daughter, who had in the last hour transformed into someone lit up by great happiness. Grace, too, was full of a calmness and joy she had not experienced for many, many years. A sense of rightness and completion. She was not anxious about her husband. She had kept Mercy from him for twenty years and she would continue to do so. The rest of them would not let her down. Neville was an irrelevance.

But there was one anxiety. Her eyes met Mercy's and then she glanced at Paul.

Does he know? her eyes queried. Does he know the truth?

Mercy's eyes shone back at her full of deep, unclouded joy.

He knows, hers responded. He knows. And he forgives.

Grace smiled and squeezed her arm. Bless you, that loving pressure said. Bless you, my darling. Be happy.

Epilogue

Margaret Adair picked up the letter from the table in the hall and frowned at the rather childish hand.

'What's that?' Stevie said, full of questions as ever.

Margaret patted his head rather absently. 'A letter. I don't know who from. You go on upstairs now, darling, and see how Nanny's getting on with the twins' breakfast. Then she'll take you all out.'

She took the letter into the sitting room and sat by the window, slitting open the envelope.

The address at the top provided no enlightenment. It was simply 'Birmingham, May 1923.'

Dear Mrs Adair,

I've been meaning to write to you for such a long time to apologize for leaving you and Stevie the sudden way I did. I was sorry to do it, especially with you having the baby on the way. There were some bad problems in my family and I had to go. I hope you can forgive me. I did miss you.

I expect Stevie is a big boy by now and has forgotten me long ago. But please give him a big kiss and cuddle from me.

You might like to know that I'm married. My husband is an engineer working at the Austin, and we have two children and another on the way. Our two little girls are called Susannah and Elizabeth and they are very healthy and full of energy.

We had a very special surprise last year. I had met, after many years, a Mr Joseph Hanley who founded the home where I started life and we had become friends. I'm sad to say he died last year, but he left me a tidy little sum of money which has been a great blessing for our family life.

We are all in good health and hope you are too. My warmest regards to you and your family. Perhaps one day we shall meet again.

Yours,

Mercy (née Hanley)

Margaret read the letter twice, with a mixture of emotions. She had been hurt and saddened by Mercy's mysterious flight from their house, had worried about her, and was delighted with news of her happiness. Yet something about the letter troubled her. Mercy's reasons for leaving them that way didn't seem quite right. Surely she had been on bad terms with her family such as it was? And why could she not have have talked her troubles over, not dashed off like that as if she were eloping?

'Who's that from?' James popped his head round the door before setting off for work.

Margaret looked up. 'It's the strangest thing. It's from Mercy – little Mercy Hanley – you remember?'

The immense pang which passed through James Adair's heart at the mention of her name did not register in his face. He stepped into the room, hands in trouser pockets.

'Our little fly-by-night? Ah yes – what news of her?'

'She sounds very well. She's married, two little girls already. But she doesn't say who to.' She turned the paper this way and that. 'No address or anything.'

'Hmm. Curious. Still, there we are. And you say she's well and happy?'

'Seems to be, yes. I'm glad for her. Odd business that, altogether.'

'Odd, yes . . .' James said dismissively. 'Anyway, must go. Give Stevie and the girls a kiss for me will you? I'm in a bit of a hurry.'

'All right, dear. Have a good day.'

James left, then on second thoughts came back and unexpectedly kissed her cheek, caressed her shoulder.

'Goodbye, my darling.'

She smiled up at him in happy surprise.

Some days later, the postman pushed a thin, cheap envelope through the letter box of a terraced house in Bournbrook which had a climbing honeysuckle lazing, sweetly scented, up its front wall.

Mercy picked it up in the hall as Paul came downstairs with the two girls. Susannah, determined to walk down by herself had a mass of blonde curly hair like a corona with the light from the landing window behind her, and striking dark brown eyes. The little one, Elizabeth, in Paul's arms, was unmistakably going to have his long, sensitive face and brown hair.

Paul sat Elizabeth down on the hall floor. 'There now, miss, you can crawl about – and keep off the stairs.'

He crept up behind Mercy and caught her by the waist, stroking her swollen stomach. The baby was due in four months.

'Your family coming round in droves today?'

Mercy laughed. Paul loved teasing her about her family, Grace's and Dorothy's eagerness to share her children, and the house was hardly ever quiet. Even after nearly three years of marriage she was still in a state of wonder at the richness of her life. The love of her family, and this house, their house, to which she could welcome them, with space and running water and a generous strip of garden for the girls out at the back. Paul had just built Susannah a swing from the pear tree.

'Oh, I dare say someone will be round!' she said.

Paul rested his head against the back of hers for a moment. Her hair was hanging loose and he lifted a hank of it to kiss the back of her neck.

'Look,' she said, squirming with pleasure. 'From America.'

They read it together, he over her shoulder.

'Yola and Tomek!' Mercy said. 'Oh – they've moved again, look – the address is new. Maybe now they'll have a bit more space for all these babbies of theirs.'

Yola already had three and was due with the fourth.

The letter was very short. Slowly, gradually they were learning to write English as well as speak it.

'*WE ARE ALL GOOD*,' Tomek had written carefully in capital letters. '*NEW PLACE IS GOOD. YOLA HAS A BABY BOY.*'

'Oh, lovely!' Mercy exclaimed.

'*EVERYTHING FINE. WE HAVE FOOD AND GOODS. WE ARE ALL FINE AND HOPE YOU TOO FINE. LIFE IS GOOD. TOMEK PETROWSKI.*'

'Life is good.' Mercy turned in Paul's arms, still holding the fragile letter. She felt her embrace returned with equal passion and gratitude.

'It is, isn't it?' she said. 'Very, very good.'